"I want the truth," Sal

She set her tote bag d
Todd. "Who was Laur
affair with, right? He was fooling around with a woman
named Laura. You were his best friend. You must have
known."

"Laura?" He frowned. "Laura who?"

"She wrote him letters." She started rummaging through
her bag. Hearing things clink and rattle, he tried to guess
what she'd packed in it. A key chain, for sure. A tire chain.
A pair of cymbals. Some plumbing hardware. Enough
spare change to keep a Las Vegas slot machine fed for a
year. Chopsticks. A lot of crinkly paper.

Her hand emerged from the hidden depths of the tote,
clutching some of that paper—a bulging manila envelope.
"Letters," she said, hurling the envelope on his desk. "Icky
love letters…. Purple-prose letters. Nauseatingly poetic….
Read them."

"Reading them would be a betrayal," he said, cringing
inwardly at how pompous he sounded.

"Bringing them into my house was a betrayal," she
argued. She hoisted her cacophonous tote bag off the
chair and slung the straps over her shoulder. "Call me
when you're ready to tell me the truth," she said, and left.

He stared after her as she marched through the newsroom.
Then he swiveled back to his desk, shook out the manila
envelope and unfolded the letter on top. It was a love
letter. No question about it. It was a love letter to Paul,
and it was signed, "Love, Laura."

Who was Laura?

And how could Paul have kept this a secret from his best
friend? How could he have kept this from Todd?

Watch for the newest romantic comedy from
MIRA Books and
JUDITH ARNOLD

LOVE IN BLOOM'S

Coming May 2002

JUDITH ARNOLD

LOOKING FOR LAURA

MIRA®

ISBN 1-55166-828-9

LOOKING FOR LAURA

Copyright © 2001 by Barbara Keiler.

MIRA and the Star Colophon are trademarks used under license and registered
in Australia, New Zealand, Philippines, United States Patent and Trademark
Office and in other countries.

Visit us at www.mirabooks.com

Printed in U.S.A.

Mom and Dad, this one's for you.

I could not have written this book without the
unwavering support and encouragement of
Charles Schlessiger, my agent and dear friend.
Thanks, also, to the editors at MIRA,
for having faith in me; to Anne Stuart,
for inspiring me, holding my hand
and giving me a kick in the pants as needed;
and to my husband, Ted, and sons Fred and Greg,
for filling my life with love and laughter.

One

Three months after the funeral, Sally decided it was time to start going through Paul's things.

She had survived the blur of days following his death, sometimes weepy, sometimes giddy, sometimes clinging to Rosie or leaning on her own friends and sometimes shutting everyone out, hiding in the bathroom, where she found that chiseling dried toothpaste from the sink gave her spirits a boost. She'd survived the dozens of casseroles people had brought her, pots and platters heaped with enough food to feed a high-school football team, as if Sally's neighbors thought bereavement meant a person couldn't throw together a nutritious meal. Some of those casseroles had been pretty bad, too. Candace Latimer from across the street had presented Sally with a concoction that included baked beans, cocktail wieners, yellow onions, croutons and a bay leaf. It had looked kind of like the fake vomit they sold in novelty shops.

Sally had graciously thanked Candace and put the casserole in the freezer, where it sat for a few weeks. Then she'd emptied the glop into the garbage, scrubbed the Pyrex dish spotless and sent Rosie across the street to return it with Sally's thanks.

She had vanquished the last of the donated food and reclaimed her freezer several days ago. She'd opened a special savings account for Rosie with the life insurance check—Paul had named Rosie the sole beneficiary. And if Sally invested the money wisely for her daughter, it would easily cover all of Rosie's college costs in thirteen years so Rosie wouldn't have to make extra money by taking an off-campus job serving coffee and cinnamon buns in a café, where she might strike up a flirtation with a customer and wind up in trouble the way Sally had.

She wasn't sure exactly how the insurance money was going to work out. Paul had written his will so that the money would go to Rosie but she wouldn't be able to touch it until she turned twenty-one. If the money was supposed to see Rosie through college, why did Rosie have to wait until she was nearly done with college to gain access to it? Sally would need to confer with a lawyer about that. Or she'd have to discuss it with Todd Sloane. She would rather not talk to him—in fact, she'd rather have nothing to do with him at all—but she had no choice. Paul had named him the executor of his will.

As if he hadn't trusted Sally.

Well, he hadn't. Not when it came to practical matters. Sally considered herself enormously practical, but Paul's idea of practicality had never jibed with hers. She'd thought economizing on the food budget by eating an occasional vegetarian dinner was practical. He'd thought eating an occasional vegetarian meal was offensive. She'd thought hanging a dream catcher above Rosie's bed so Rosie would have a rich and imaginative dream life and would remember her best dreams in the morning was extremely practical. Paul had thought Sally was a superstitious twit.

On the other hand, Sally had thought that driving an Alfa Romeo convertible coupé in the winter, when the back roads were slick with black ice, was absurdly impractical, and Paul had told her she didn't know what she was talking about. And now look. He was dead.

His will had been entered into probate. She'd never thought she would have to familiarize herself with such legalistic terms, even though she'd been married to a lawyer. Paul used to say things like, "I spent the morning over at the courthouse, entering Richard Salazar's will into probate," and Sally would nod and pretend she knew what he was talking about. He'd loved talking about his work, so she'd done her best to listen, to insert comments that made her sound as if she understood what he was saying. "Poor Richard," she might say. "I know he was in his eighties, but he seemed so much younger. He always came into the New Day Café at ten-thirty sharp for a hazelnut decaf, one cream, two sugars. It's hard to believe he's dead and you're doing that probate thingie with his will."

It was hard to believe Paul was dead, too, but less hard than it had been three months ago, when Officer Bronowski had walked into the café in the early afternoon—not his usual time—and removed his hat and said, "Mrs. Driver," with such a somber expression she'd felt a chilly pinch at her nape. "Your husband's been in an accident."

She'd had time to get used to it. Time to heal. There would be a scar, but she'd go on. She had to, for Rosie's sake even more than her own. Rosie needed a mother, and Sally needed a life.

On this mid-April Sunday, black ice did not exist. The sky was so clear Sally could see deep into it, as if nothing stood between her and outer space. The afternoon air was warm and dry, baked by a sun that had nothing better to do than remind people that even in Winfield,

Massachusetts, ninety miles west of Boston in the foothills of the Berkshires, winter didn't last forever.

Sally's yard needed work. The beds were matted with rotting leaves and dead twigs. The lawn needed thatching, and the accumulated sand where the grass met the street had to be swept. The porch could use a fresh coat of paint, and if she chose to paint it the same bright orange she'd painted the front door, Paul wouldn't be able to complain.

She could hang wind chimes if she wanted, and he wouldn't be able to complain about that, either. She could design a mural for the garage door and plant a pink flamingo in the front yard. She wondered if pink-flamingo statues were available in New England, or would she have to travel to Florida to get one? Maybe she and Rosie could take a vacation: Walt Disney World and pink-flamingo shopping. Rosie would probably love the flamingo more than the Magic Kingdom.

But before she busied herself with outdoor tasks, she was going to tackle the more pressing chore of dealing with Paul's things. They'd been lying around the house for three months, nibbling at her consciousness, but today she was going to face the task of going through everything, sorting it out, packing up what her husband had left behind. She'd pulled her hair back from her face with a star-shaped clip, and dressed for hard labor in a pair of blue denim overalls and a long-sleeve red-and-white striped shirt. All red white and blue, she looked patriotic and brave.

Some of Paul's stuff she'd appropriated, even though his will hadn't stipulated she could. He'd explicitly left her the house, and she felt that bequest ought to include everything of his inside it. His cuff links, for example. He'd been the only man she knew in all of Winfield who wore cuff links, and she'd always considered them pretentious, but now that they were hers, she might be able to fashion them into a brooch. Or earrings, if she looped wires through them. She was sure she had some spare earring loops.

His pens were pretentious, too. He preferred fountain pens. Whenever she used a fountain pen, she wound up with more ink on her fingers than on the paper.

She'd already discarded most of his toiletries. She could use his razor—in fact, she often did, which used to annoy the hell out of him—but she had no use for his soap mug and badger-bristle brush. If she had a son, she'd have saved those manly items for him. But Rosie was never going to use them. Sally had discarded his whitening toothpaste because she secretly believed that whatever ingredient bleached the teeth caused cancer or maybe gallstones. She'd added his antifungal cream to the garbage pail, and the little clipper he'd used to trim his nostril hairs.

His suits she would give away. Someone could make use of them. Some needy street person would look quite dapper in the double-breasted blue suit with its fitted jacket and cuffed trousers, the charcoal-gray cashmere, the pearl-gray summer wool. Some recent college graduate preparing for his first job interview would look magnificently professional in one of the suits, purchased from Goodwill for a price he could afford.

Paul's wardrobe nearly filled the entire bedroom closet. She'd never minded ceding the closet to him. She preferred to keep her dresses in the antique armoire in the hallway. Paul had never believed it was a real antique. He'd called it a piece of junk, and given that Sally had picked it up at a garage sale for only thirty bucks, he was probably right. But she adored the way the mirrored doors were losing their silvering, looking almost rheumy, and the nicks and scratches on the sides had intrigued her. It had a history, of that she was certain. And if it had a history, it was an antique, as far as she was concerned.

So she'd let him take over most of the closet for his expensive suits, his monogrammed shirts and tailored trousers. She'd let him fill the closet floor with neatly boxed shoes: cordovan loafers, black loafers, brown loafers, regular sneakers for tennis, high-tops for basketball, deck shoes for hanging out, moose-hide slippers for cold winter nights. She'd let him take over the top shelf with his belts, all coiled like snakes—black, brown, smooth or textured leather, brass buckles, silver. She'd used her sliver of the closet for her bathrobe and a few blouses, but her dresses hung happily in the armoire.

She stared at the closet, trying to figure out the best way to start. From behind her, Rosie's voice floated into the room through the open window. She and Trevor Finneran from next door were playing in the backyard, their five-year-old voices as shrill as air-raid sirens. "Let's pretend we're pirates," Rosie instructed Trevor, who was wimpy enough to agree with everything she suggested. "We have a parrot and a big ship and we're on the Bounding Main."

"The what?" Trevor asked.

"The Bounding Main. It's this big street in the middle of Bounding."

"Okay."

Sally smiled. Hearing them made her want to abandon the closet, race downstairs and out the kitchen door and sail the Bounding Main with them, even if it was just a big street. She wanted to do anything but deal with Paul's clothing.

Maybe she wasn't ready for this, after all.

No, she was. She really was.

But when she opened the closet door, the suits hanging from the rod made her think of the way Paul had looked in them. The sleeves of his jackets dropped from the shoulders, as if his arms were in them. The lapels lay flat, as if against his chest.

All right. She would attack his dresser first, and move on to the closet later.

She crossed the room, feeling greatly cheered that she didn't have to handle all those heavy closet garments, the wool, the leather. He probably had heavy items in his dresser, too, but the dresser was next to the window so it had a lighter aura.

She tugged open the top drawer, pushed aside the velvet boxes holding his cuff links and lifted out his linen handkerchiefs. Eight of them, all neatly laundered and folded. She'd known how he liked them done, and she'd considered him rather prissy about it—they were just going to get shoved into a pocket of his trousers, after all—but she'd wanted him happy, and it had made him happy to have his handkerchiefs washed and folded with a certain military precision.

She would save the handkerchiefs. Rosie could use them. Maybe she'd inherited her father's prissy-handkerchief gene.

After replacing them in the drawer, Sally closed it and opened the second drawer, which was full of undershirts and boxers. Closing her eyes, she conjured an image of Paul in just a pair of beige silk boxers. He might have been fastidious and conservative, but he'd looked damn good in underwear. He'd had a lean, compact body, economical and masculine. It was no wonder she'd enjoyed his flirting the first time she'd noticed him at the

New Day Café. No wonder she'd flirted back. No wonder when he'd asked her if someday she would actually have a cup of coffee with him instead of simply serving him a cup and then rushing away to take care of other customers, she'd said yes. No wonder she'd agreed to move on from coffee to a glass of wine with him, even though she was a year shy of the legal drinking age, and from a glass of wine to a kiss, and from a kiss to a night in his bed.

It was no wonder that when she'd found herself pregnant, she had asked him to marry her.

He'd wanted her to get an abortion, she recalled a little less sentimentally. But when she'd refused, he'd come around. He'd done the right thing and married her, and once Rosie arrived he'd doted on her. It had all worked out. Sally had loved him, and she'd folded his handkerchiefs correctly, and he'd been happy. She'd gotten him to laugh when he was exhausted from work, and she'd compensated for the vegetarian dinners by grilling T-bone steaks every now and then, and roasting tarragon chicken stuffed with wild rice. And when she'd caught him in just his boxers as he was getting undressed for bed, she'd gleefully thrown herself at him, reminding him of why he'd wanted her to join him for a cup of coffee in the first place, why it had led to what it led to, why they belonged together.

Maybe she wasn't ready to deal with his underwear, either.

The third drawer held assorted short-sleeve shirts— polo shirts, T-shirts with logos on them, his gray Columbia University shirt that he never wore. The fourth drawer held long-sleeve shirts—rugby shirts, Henley shirts, all those British-sounding shirts.

In the bottom drawer he kept sweaters. She had to

struggle a bit to open that drawer because the sweaters bulked against the frame, but she wedged her hand in and pressed them flat until the drawer slid free. The sweaters were, like all his clothing, of the highest quality—Shetland and cashmere, imported from cold northern countries like Scotland, Ireland and Norway. The sweaters were too big on her, but she was going to keep them, anyway. Being engulfed by an oversize sweater made her feel safe. For the first week after Paul had died, she'd slept in one of his sweaters.

She pulled that sweater out and held it up in front of her. Then she crossed to the mirror and studied herself. The smoky-gray wool made her skin appear pale and pink, her eyes icy blue. She no longer resembled the haggard, miserable woman she'd been three months ago when she'd worn it to bed. She looked like someone in control, someone who knew what she was doing.

"Ha," she said out loud. She never knew what she was doing until she did it, and even then she often wasn't sure.

She tossed the sweater on the bed and pulled out another sweater, and another. The fisherman's sweater came out, the burgundy V-neck, the brown crew neck. As she pulled that one out, it fell loose, releasing a manila envelope that had been tucked into its folds.

Puzzled, she tossed the sweater onto the bed and lifted the envelope from the floor where it had fallen. She flipped it over—no writing on either side, but its contents made it thick enough to strain the wire clip that held the flap shut. She unbent the tabs and lifted the flap. Inside was a stack of folded papers.

She sank onto the bed, not caring that she was sitting on Paul's favorite Nordic sweater, the one with little deer knit into a white-on-black pattern. Carefully, she shook out the papers. They were stationery, she realized. Letters. A secret piece of him. She felt almost as if she were trespassing, as if she should stuff them back into the envelope and toss them back into the drawer out of respect for his past.

But Paul's entire life was past. All he was was his past.

Besides, she was too curious not to read them.

She lifted the top letter from the pile, smoothed it out and read:

Dearest Paul,
We are starting a new year and my yearning for you is stronger than ever. Every word you said to me today is etched on my heart. Every touch, every sigh is permanently embedded in my memory.

A love letter. Paul had saved love letters from an old flame. As his most recent and final flame, Sally knew she didn't have any grounds for jealousy, but still, the fact that he'd saved the letter, saved *all* these letters, irked her.

Just a little, she assured herself. Just because she was his wife, and wives deserved to be irked by saved letters from old flames.

She reread the new year's greeting, with its etches and touches. "Isn't she the poet," she muttered, finding the prose cloying. Paul had never been one for sweet talk.

She tried to remember the last time he'd worn the brown sweater. Certainly not during the past winter, or the winter before. He'd been protesting the color brown, she'd recalled. Too many people were wearing brown, and he'd been determined to stick to grays and blues,

just to spite the fashion trend. She wondered if he'd forgotten the letters were even there.

She read on:

I understand how hard it is for you to get away.
But please, please try. For both of us. We are soul
mates, and our souls will shrivel if we can't be together. We nourish each other; apart, we grow
parched. Life is short. If there's no love for you at
home—

A sharp chill skimmed down Sally's spine, causing her
to shiver so violently the letter dropped from her hands.
It sat in her lap, something so toxic she didn't want to
touch it, yet she had to remove it, had to remove the entire
pile of letters from her knees before they ate through the
denim of her overalls and started in on her flesh.

She stared down at the letter. She didn't want to keep
reading, but she couldn't stop.

If there's no love for you at home, leave home.
Come to me, where you will find all the love you
could possibly want. I miss you. I want you.

                                        Laura.

"Go ahead, Trevor—use your cutlass!" Rosie
shrieked outside in the yard. "That's that stick in your
hand, it's a cutlass. Run it through! Ahoy!"

I miss you. I want you. Laura.

Sally clutched the letter. Her stomach clenched. Her
throat burned. Her lungs ached. *If there's no love for
you at home, leave home.*

But there had been plenty of love for him at home.
And he hadn't left home, Sally realized. He'd never left,

except to take his stupid little sports car for a drive on a January morning when the roads were icy.

What was she getting so keyed up about? This woman had to have been writing to him more than six years ago, before he and Sally had made a life together.

Before he'd met Sally, though, he'd lived alone. So he really didn't have a home, with or without love.

Her heart picked up a jogging rhythm, loud, regular thumps. She felt the pulse in her brain, echoing through her skull. If she read the other letters, she was going to wind up in a bad place emotionally. She ought to just stick the whole mess in the trash and forget about it. Whoever she was, this Laura person had written to Paul before he'd met Sally, and he'd saved her letters because Sally was so pathetically unliterary, and that was all there was to it. She didn't want to think he'd saved them because he still carried a torch for Laura all these years later. Sentimentality, that was all it was. Nostalgia. A little macho pride.

Reassured, she unfolded the next letter:

Dearest Paul,
Your wisdom resonates within me hours after you have left. What a fine mind you have…

"Jesus," Sally muttered. He'd been a small-town lawyer, not Einstein. His mind had been better than average, but "resonating wisdom" was overstating it by a bit.

…That we could share our thoughts on Sartre the way we share the pleasures of our bodies…

"Christ," Sally elaborated. Who was this woman? And why couldn't she have dated her letters with the

year as well as the month and day? This one was dated
October 4. A great day for sharing thoughts on Sartre,
apparently.

In the six years Sally had known Paul, he had never
once mentioned Sartre, not even in his sleep. These
letters had to predate his marriage to her. Laura had
probably been a college sweetheart, one of those earnest New York City types, flat chested and partial to
Peruvian woven vests, the kind of woman who smoked
imported cigarettes and took herself very seriously.
Paul had saved her correspondence to remind him of
his foolish youth, before he'd moved to Winfield and
discovered the far healthier romance of life in a small
city with a college and a couple of mills for ambience,
and clean air and friendly folks and coffee shops like
the New Day Café.

The heat of your hands on my body renders me
nothing but sensation. When you make love to me
I am "being and nothingness"...

Sally laughed, then felt guilty. Laughing made more
sense than taking the letters seriously. Or maybe it didn't
make more sense. Maybe it just offered a degree of pro-
tection, like whistling past a graveyard. Something awful
was in these letters, something profoundly threatening.
But she was allowed to laugh, because what little she
recalled of Sartre from her interrupted schooling was so
unerotic she couldn't imagine associating his philosophy
with sex.

Sex. With Paul. This woman was writing about sex
with Sally's husband. Sally had never felt like being and
nothingness after she and Paul had gone at it. She'd usu-

ally felt like eating. Sex with Paul used to make her
hungry.

Okay. So it was a college fling, from his days at Columbia, where hormonally hyped scholars rationalized
their lust by overlaying it with a shimmer of intellectu-
alism. Sally began to feel better about the whole thing.

Smiling, she picked up the third letter:

Dear Paul,
Once again I must thank you for your sweet gift.
Its very vulgarity makes it more precious to me.

Vulgarity? *Very* vulgarity? What had he given her?

Someday, perhaps, you will tell me where this knife
came from—Hawaii, I assume?—what it means,
what its significance might be. For now, its significance is that it comes from you.

The only vulgar knife Sally had ever seen was the
pocketknife that had belonged to her father, with the
topless hula dancer painted onto the faux-pearl handle.
Paul had given her a beautiful gold band when they'd
gotten married, but she'd lacked the funds to buy a wedding band for him. So she'd given him the most precious
thing she'd owned—the hula knife.

"Very vulgarity" would certainly describe it. And the
hula dancer would imply Hawaii.

Where had that knife gone? After he'd died, the police
had given her a packet containing what they'd called his
effects—his watch, his wallet, his nail clipper, his keys,
the fountain pen he'd had clipped to his shirt pocket. No
pocketknife. She didn't think he'd carried it with him—
if someone at his stuffy law firm had ever seen him

slitting open an envelope with it, they might have taken his partnership away.

She was pretty sure he'd kept the knife in his top drawer with his handkerchiefs and cuff links. Setting aside the letters, she stood and crossed back to the dresser. The top drawer contained exactly what it had contained a few minutes ago: Cuff links. Hankies. His Columbia school ring. A cigar trimmer from that pretentious period when he'd thought cigars were cool.

No hula knife.

Where could it be? Why hadn't she seen it since his death? A knife like that didn't just disappear.

Apprehension gnawed at her. She slammed the drawer shut and returned to the bed. The letters had gotten scattered, but she had no idea if they'd been in any sort of order, and she didn't care. She plucked the top one from the pile and lifted it to read:

Dearest Paul,
I am still reeling from what you told me today. I wish I'd known sooner. I am in shock. The dishonesty troubles me, and yet. Yet. Yet I still want you. What does that make me, Paul? What does that make us?

"What did he tell you?" Sally asked the letter.

Sin is a meaningless concept. Trust is the most meaningful concept there is. You betrayed my trust, and hers. And yet...and yet...

"Stop with the yets already," Sally snapped. "And yet *what?*"

Your wife doesn't have to come between us.

Sally suddenly had trouble making out the words. They jumped all over the page—and then she realized that the page itself was jumping, because her hands were trembling as they held it. Her heart stopped its loping beat—in fact, it seemed to have stopped altogether. Maybe she was dead, even though she could still see the page, feel the lump of Paul's Norwegian sweater under her thigh, hear the giddy children's voices wafting in through the window. Maybe she was alive and dead at the same time. Maybe this was being and nothingness.

"Trevor!" Rosie scolded. "*We're* the pirates. We get to pillage. *Pillage.* That's a little town in Bounding. Don't you know anything?"

Maybe Paul was a pirate, Sally thought, letting the letter slip from her fingers and drift to the floor. Maybe the best way to pillage was armed with a vulgar hula-dancer knife. Maybe Sally was the one who didn't know anything.

Or maybe she just wished she didn't know anything. She knew very little, but it already seemed like way too much.

Two

Todd Sloane's mother was calling him. Not by phone, the way normal people communicated with each other, but by holler. Her voice trumpeted across the newsroom that separated their offices, a booming honk: "Todd! Where's that editorial you ran last Friday about the sewer expansion?"

Todd took a deep breath and let it out slowly. If he were still a smoker, he would have exhaled jets of smoke from his nostrils, but he'd given up the nasty habit four years ago, not long after Denise had left him. Somehow, once she was gone he'd no longer felt a craving for nicotine. The divorce had forced him to acknowledge that he wasn't cut out for self-destruction after all.

So he exhaled only air, no smoke. The exercise of his lungs soothed him.

He picked up his phone, punched Helen Sloane's extension and listened to her phone ring through her open door and his. "What?" she bellowed into his ear.

His office was walled in glass to provide a view into the newsroom. His mother's office was also walled in glass. He could see her standing beside her desk, all five foot two robust inches of her, with her hair shaped like a helmet and dyed a peculiar shade of red. There was an undertone of purple to it, although he doubted she was aware of the way it looked when light hit it from above.

She was a good woman. She also happened to be a pain in the ass, and Todd didn't want to deal with her or her obsession over the bonds the city of Winfield wanted to issue to cover the cost of the sewer expansion.

"Mom," he said calmly into the phone. "I taught you how to use the computer to call up previous issues of the paper. Everything's online, so you can log on and type www-dot-valleynews-dot-com."

"I hate that Internet stuff," she complained. "I don't see why you can't just bring me over a copy of the editorial. A real copy. On paper."

"I don't have one handy," he said gently. "If you don't want to read the editorial online, you can call up the file. You type 'editorials' and then last Friday's date—"

"You know what? You know what it is, Todd? It's this computer. I hate it. I really hate it."

It was the computer—and it was much, much more. His mother wanted the *Valley News* to be run the way she and his father had run it when they'd taken it over from Todd's grandfather forty years ago. All the reporters had worked on manual typewriters then. They'd smoked heavily and drunk even more heavily, and they'd run on brains and balls. His mother had run harder than anyone else, because she'd had more balls than the rest of the staff combined.

But that was then and this was now. Todd's father had had the good sense to retire as copublisher, but his mother was hanging on, insisting that she was essential to the functioning of the newspaper, when all she did was interfere, meddle, disagree with him and holler across the newsroom like Heidi calling for the straying sheep to return to her Alp.

"Listen, Mom—why don't you take the rest of the day off," Todd suggested. "You can catch up with Dad. He's probably at the fifth or sixth hole by now. You can golf the rest of the course with him. It's a beautiful day. You shouldn't be stuck in the office."

"I don't want to golf. I hate golf. The only reason your father is golfing instead of working is that he's losing his marbles. I know you're in denial about this, Todd, but it's true. The man has Alzheimer's."

"He doesn't."

"See what I mean? You're in denial. This morning he forgot what to call a doorknob."

"He never knew what to call a doorknob," Todd argued. It was true. His father had always been noun challenged. "His doctor doesn't think there's anything wrong with him."

"His doctor doesn't live with him. Neither do you. I'm telling you, he's losing his marbles. He's lost at least three marbles so far, and given that he only started with maybe a dozen, that's a lot of marbles."

"Mom—"

"I heard that you came out in favor of the bonds. Todd, I hate when you run editorials without checking with me first. I'm the publisher, don't forget."

Emeritus, he thought, but didn't say so. When he'd taken over the paper as publisher and editor in chief, he'd given his parents the grand-sounding title of co-publishers emeritus, which he figured would be enough to send them merrily on their way into happy retirement. His father loved to golf. His mother loved to travel. He had envisioned them traveling from golf resort to golf resort for at least nine months of the year, leaving him to yank the *Valley News* into the twenty-first century without any flak from them.

"Winfield's growing," he said patiently. "We need more sewer capacity."

"Winfield has gotten big enough. It ought to stop growing. That's the editorial stand you need to take."

Todd might have pointed out that she considered Winfield's growth just swell when it contributed to the increased circulation of the daily paper. More readers meant more sewers, though. People read the newspaper and went to the bathroom, frequently at the same time. Todd sensed a direct connection between ingesting news and egesting waste, and he would have been glad to explain that to her.

But he had long ago stopped explaining anything to his mother. She believed what she chose to believe, and she believed it with all her heart. She believed his father had Alzheimer's disease; she believed computers were evil; she believed Winfield had enough sewers.

He didn't want to deal with her. If Paul had been available, Todd would have phoned him and said, "Meet me at Grover's after work and help me plot the murder of my mother." Paul would have understood.

Damn. He missed Paul. The stupid bastard. Why had he gone and wrapped his car around a tree? Who was Todd going to fantasize about murdering his mother with now?

Eddie Lesher, maybe? The kid loomed in Todd's office, blocking Todd's view of his mother—a definite plus. But he was barely twenty four, skinny and whiny—three minuses. The last thing Todd needed when he felt the urge to whine was someone even whinier than he was.

Eddie had joined the staff of the *Valley News* as a

general reporter last fall, after the *Boston Globe* had "restructured," as he'd euphemistically phrased it. Todd knew the kid had been fired, and he'd had little trouble finding out why: Eddie had spent a full week developing a human-interest piece about a woman who ran a body-piercing establishment, and the only reason was that he'd had a crush on the woman. There had been no story there, his editor had told him to drop it, but Eddie hadn't dropped it. So the *Globe* had dropped him. They weren't going to miss him. They had dozens of dewy-eyed twenty-somethings spilling out of journalism schools, begging for a chance to work for peanuts at a reputable paper.

The *Valley News* was reputable, but it didn't have dozens of budding journalism school graduates begging to join its staff, so it sometimes wound up hiring people like Eddie. Under Todd's management, it had increased daily circulation above forty thousand, and he was exploring the possibility of issuing a Sunday edition, an idea that gave his mother apoplexy—which added to its appeal. The paper supplied news not just to Winfield but to the surrounding hamlets and farming communities. It had a staff of twenty reporters. Sure, it was respectable. It wasn't the *Globe,* but it didn't have to be.

"Hey, Todd, I was thinking?" Eddie began in his nasal voice. "There's this homeless guy living under the railroad bridge on the east end of town. He just suddenly appeared, maybe because the weather got warmer. I was thinking I could do a story about him."

"What kind of story?" Todd asked. He believed the idea had possibilities, but it was up to Eddie to figure out what they might be.

"Well, like, about where he came from." Eddie

slouched in the doorway, looking in dire need of food. His physique reminded Todd of a wire coat hanger.

"Give it one day," Todd warned. "Not two. Show me what you've got by tomorrow at noon, and if it's any good, we'll see."

"It'll be good," Eddie insisted, running a hand through hair that was already thinning. "I see this is as a really important story, Todd. A story about the people society left behind."

Spare me, Todd thought. Earnest sentiment was not an asset in the news business. "You know what his story is going to be?" he asked, softening his tone so Eddie wouldn't be too demoralized by the truth. "The guy's a drug addict. He got kicked out of his apartment for spending all his rent money on crack. He lived in a shelter until the temperature rose above freezing, then decided he'd rather be outdoors. Okay? We're not talking about a noble savage, Eddie. We're talking about a loser. Every city's got a million of them."

"Winfield isn't a city," Eddie pointed out.

"Which is why we've only got a few." Through the panes of glass he could see his mother hunched over her computer, her lips moving and her hand convulsively squeezing the mouse. If forgetting the name of a doorknob was a symptom of Alzheimer's, then surely talking to yourself because the three-click process of calling up a file, which had been explained to you a hundred times, was too challenging was also a sign of Alzheimer's. Both his parents were loony. Maybe he could get a two-for-one discount when it came time to lodge them at the local nursing home.

"I really think I can tug some heartstrings with this story," Eddie persisted.

"Don't get carried away," Todd warned him. "We're

not exactly venturing into Pulitzer territory here. You have until tomorrow. Make it count.''

Eddie lingered in the doorway, giving Todd a hopeful gaze. Big mistake. Todd could stare down anyone, especially when he was pissed off. And through no fault of Eddie's, Todd was seriously pissed off.

After a moment, Eddie conceded, turning and slinking out the door. His trousers were too big. On a high-school kid they might look stylish, but on a cub reporter they looked like poorly sized hand-me-downs.

At least he was gone. But that meant Todd once again had an unobstructed view of his mother. Her lips were still moving as she squinted at her computer monitor, her brow furrowed, her shoulders bunched. She seemed to be trying to twirl a strand of her hair, but it was lacquered into place and her fingers kept slipping behind her ear.

She was a good woman, he reminded himself again. His parents were good people. He came from a good family.

And right now, he felt like shit. Before Paul died, he used to find his parents tolerable, even amusing. But since the accident, everything rubbed him wrong. A guy needed a best friend to vent to. Paul had always been so calm, so steady. He used to listen to Todd, commiserate, offer good advice. He never made mistakes.

Correction: he'd made one mistake. It was a whopper, and in rectifying that mistake and doing the right thing, he'd put his future on a leash. Had he known that his future would last only six more years?

Of course not. He'd just been the most decent man in the universe, that was all. A scrupulous attorney, a solid husband, a stylish dresser, a stalwart friend. Someone who could talk Todd down when the trivial irritations of daily living threatened to beat him to a bloody pulp.

And now Paul was dead, leaving Todd to cope with his parents, his newspaper, his staff and the sewers of Winfield all by himself.

"Todd?" his mother howled. "This computer doesn't work! Everything I tell it to do, it ignores me!"

Smart computer. He swiveled his chair so he wouldn't have to see her. Gazing out at the newsroom, he saw a few reporters tapping away at their computers, which apparently worked well enough. Several desks were empty; those reporters were out chasing exciting stories about the mayor's weakness for bad puns, the zoning board's weakness for kickbacks, the police chief's weakness for driving way above the speed limit and insisting he was doing so only to keep his reflexes sharp in case he ever had to engage in a high-speed chase. Winfield was a city with enough weak souls to fill eighty pages a day, augmented by national and international news lifted off the wires and lots of advertising. God bless those weaknesses for keeping the *Valley News* in the black.

The door at the opposite end of the newsroom swung open, and the irritation quotient of Todd's day doubled. In walked Sally Driver. The dizzy waitress. The queen of flake. The grieving widow.

He would have considered Sally in more kindly terms if he'd believed for a minute that she and Paul had been made for each other. They hadn't been. She'd trapped the guy using the oldest trick known to womankind, and being the moral man that he was, Paul had done what he'd had to do. But she hadn't trapped Todd, and he was under no obligation to be nice to her.

Everything about her annoyed him, from her long

frizzy hair to her innocent smile to her too-big body. She wasn't fat, but she was bulky, broad shouldered and round hipped, and she emphasized her fleshiness by wearing swirling, gauzy dresses that looked like castoffs from a third-rate summer-stock production of *A Midsummer Night's Dream.* Whatever the opposite of delicate was, that was Sally.

She'd been utterly wrong for Paul. He'd been neat and contained, as organized in his demeanor as he was in every other aspect of his life. He'd never had a hair out of place; she never had a hair *in* place. He'd been logical; she was manic. He'd never gone anywhere without condoms, yet she had somehow managed to get herself knocked up. The immaculate conception, Todd used to call their daughter, who looked enough like Paul that Todd suggested he consider suing the condom company.

He wasn't in the mood to talk to Sally today. He wasn't in the mood to talk to her *any* day, but especially not today, after having endured his mother's ineptitude with a computer and her insinuations about his father's mental health, and the discouraging prospect of Eddie Lesher in search of a socially relevant story.

Ignoring Margaret, the office manager, who tried to stop her, Sally stalked through the newsroom, her stride ominously resolute. A large tote bag woven out of pastel-dyed straw hung on a strap over her shoulder, and her hair flailed around her face in ripples of reddish-brown.

Todd braced himself. He hadn't seen her since the meeting in the office of one of Paul's law partners for the reading of Paul's will, three months ago. Todd had been both honored and dismayed that Paul had named him the executor. The job would be tedious and time-consuming, and it would mean continuing contact with

Sally, but he respected Paul's desire not to give her the opportunity to mismanage his estate.

He hoped she hadn't come to argue with him over the will. Paul had left her comfortable, and the rest was going to Rosie. If Sally had any intention of messing with that, Todd would set her straight.

She swung into his office and he realized, somewhat belatedly, that she was furious. Her eyes were usually a gentle blue, but now they seemed diamond-hard and cold. Her hands were clenched into fists and her bosom rose and fell with each determined breath. Something strange was dangling from her ears. Gold dice, maybe.

Paul's cuff links. She'd looped them through gold wires, and now they hung from her ears, looking ridiculous.

"What do you want?" he asked none too graciously. He knew Sally didn't expect courtesy from him. They'd never bothered to pretend a fondness for each other when Paul was alive. They certainly weren't going to pretend now.

"I want the truth," she retorted.

He was distracted by the rhythm of her breathing. Her breasts were plump beneath the bodice of her floral-print dress. Paul had always claimed to prefer petite women— yet one glance at Sally's voluptuous figure and he'd succumbed like a drooling adolescent.

Fortunately, Todd was immune to her endowments. "What truth?" he asked, refusing to smile or offer her a seat. If he did either, she might mistakenly believe she was welcome.

She set her tote bag down on one of the visitor's chairs with a clunk and glowered at him. "Who was Laura?"

"Laura?" He frowned. "Laura who?"

"You tell me."

He sighed with forced tolerance. "Look, Sally—some of us have important jobs to do. If you want to play Twenty Questions, we'll have to do it some other time. I've got a newspaper to publish."

"I'm not playing Twenty Questions. I want to know who Laura was. Some woman Paul was having an affair with, right?"

Todd was shocked into silence. Paul having an affair? He didn't believe it. He couldn't. Todd had known Paul for fifteen years, and he just wasn't the sort to do that. Affairs were too messy.

He tried to imagine it. Tried to visualize Paul sneaking around, making coded telephone calls, contorting himself for a little fun and games in the Alfa Romeo's bucket seats. No, Paul wasn't that limber.

And beyond that, *no,* he wouldn't have an affair. He was too decent. Decent to a fault, in Todd's opinion.

"He was fooling around with a woman named Laura. You were his best friend. You must have known."

"You're crazy," he told her. If she was suffering from delusions, he wished she would take her delusions and suffer somewhere else.

"She wrote him letters. He saved them." She started rummaging through her tote bag. Hearing things clink and rattle in there, he tried to guess what she'd packed in it. A key chain, for sure. A tire chain. A pair of cymbals. Some plumbing hardware. Enough spare change to keep a Las Vegas slot machine fed for a year. Something scratchy—a currying brush, perhaps. Chopsticks. A great deal of crinkly paper.

Her hand emerged from the hidden depths of the tote, clutching some of that paper—a bulging manila envelope. "Letters," she said, hurling the packet onto his desk. "Icky love letters."

He glanced warily at the envelope. "Icky?"

"Purple-prose letters. Nauseatingly poetic. Who is this woman? I think she's got my knife."

"Your knife?"

"Well, technically, Paul's knife—but only because I gave it to him. It was a family heirloom, and she's got it. Who is she?"

"I have no idea," he insisted.

Sally scrutinized him through fierce eyes. "You don't have to cover for your buddy anymore, Todd. He's dead."

That was it. He was done indulging the lunatics in his life. "I'm not covering for him," he snapped. "I don't know what you're talking about. He wasn't having an affair. Why would he, when he had such a wonderful wife?"

Ignoring his sarcasm, she poked a finger at the envelope on his desk. "Those letters were written to Paul by a woman named Laura. She dated them by month and day but not year. But they must have been written within the past five years because they acknowledge that he's married, and that he lied about it to her for a while. And he gave her the knife I gave him. She must have mailed these letters to his office, because if she'd mailed them to our house I would have seen them. But I've got no envelopes, no return address."

"You read his mail?" Todd wished he could sound more indignant than he felt. Paul *was* dead, as she'd pointed out. If he'd found a stash of mysterious letters after the death of a loved one, he'd probably have a peek at them, too.

"I found them in a drawer of his dresser. Which

means they were mailed to his office and he brought them home and hid them inside his brown crew-neck sweater.''

"Inside his sweater?" That was weird. Not very Paul-like at all.

"Why would he bring them into our house?" Sally started pacing around the small glassed-in cubicle, not waiting for an answer. "Maybe he liked to take them out and reread them when I was out. Maybe that was how he started his day. I usually left for work by six-fifteen. He'd get up, get Rosie ready for school, eat breakfast...and maybe he'd grab one of his letters from Laura and reread it to fire himself up. Or after I went to bed—maybe he'd pull out one of the letters, sneak into the bathroom and jerk off."

"That's uncalled for."

"Is it?" She halted in her minicircuit around the room and glared at him. "The man was having an affair, and I'm supposed to talk about him like he was a saint?"

"He wasn't having an affair," Todd said with certainty.

"How do you know that?"

"If he had been, he would have told me."

"He would have told you, and he would have sworn you to secrecy. He would have said, 'Whatever you do, don't let Sally know.'"

True enough. But the fact was, Paul *hadn't* told Todd, so Todd didn't believe any of it. Sally was a wildly imaginative woman. In the throes of her grief, she'd concocted this sordid myth based on a packet of letters that Todd couldn't imagine Paul stashing inside a brown crew-neck sweater.

Still, the packet sat before him, daring him to examine its contents.

She must have sensed his curiosity. She stormed back to his desk, jabbed her finger at the envelope and said, "Read those letters, Todd. Read them and tell me why your very best friend would have given my knife to a woman who writes such icky stuff."

"Reading them would be a betrayal," he said, cringing inwardly at how pompous he sounded.

"Bringing them into my house was a betrayal," she argued. "Knowing her was a betrayal. Telling her there was no love in our home…" Sally's voice cracked, and Todd noticed a flash of tears in her eyes. "That was a betrayal." She drew in a deep, steadying breath and squared her shoulders. "And pretending you don't know anything about her, Todd—that's a betrayal, too."

It would have been, if he'd been pretending. But he wasn't. He honestly had no idea what Sally was talking about.

The conviction in her voice unnerved him. He stared at the envelope, suddenly uneasy. If it contained what she claimed, if someone named Laura had sent love letters to Paul, if he'd had an affair… Damn it! To have an affair and not tell Todd was the worst betrayal of all.

"I'll read them," he promised, unable to look at Sally. He was embarrassed to think he viewed keeping one's adultery a secret from one's best friend a worse betrayal than committing the adultery itself. Of course it wasn't, but still… Paul had known Todd longer and better than he'd known Sally. They'd met as freshmen at Columbia. Todd's closeknit family and small-town pragmatism had appealed to Paul, and Paul's coolheadedness and class had helped Todd keep things in perspective. They hadn't been quite opposites, but they'd complemented each other in pleasant ways. Paul had weaned Todd from cheap beer to microbrewery beverages, and Todd had

introduced Paul to cross-country skiing and burned lasagna—which tasted better when washed down with microbrewery beverages. Todd had suggested that Paul
move to Winfield after law school, to practice in Todd's
hometown, and Paul had enjoyed the town's slower
pace, its backdrop of rolling hills and the fact that it
enabled him to be a very big fish in a small pond.

He and Todd had double-dated. They'd compared
notes. Paul had told Todd that Denise was too self-
centered, and after the divorce Paul had exercised great
restraint by saying "I told you so" less than a hundred
times. Paul had known about the women Todd dated,
he'd known about the women he slept with—not because Todd talked a lot but because they'd been best
friends.

So wouldn't Paul have told Todd about Laura if she
was at all significant?

"I'll read them," he repeated, lifting his gaze to Sally
and praying with all his heart that she would go away.

"Call me when you're ready to tell me the truth," she
said, an undeniable threat underlining her words. Then
she hoisted her cacophonous tote bag off the chair, slung
the straps over her shoulder and left his office.

He stared after her as she marched through the newsroom and out the door. Then he swiveled back to his
desk. The envelope sat on his blotter, beckoning, taunting. There was something foul about the entire situation,
something sleazy about the act of reading a dead man's
private correspondence, something dishonorable about
letting a suspicious widow tarnish the memory of a good
man.

But the only way Todd could prove Paul had been a
good man was to refute the contents of the envelope. If
he read the letters, he might discover that Sally was as

nutty as he'd always assumed. Or he might recognize the letter writer as an old acquaintance of his and Paul's from their college days, or perhaps a client of Paul's who had expressed herself ambiguously in her correspondence. Perhaps Paul had saved the letters because he thought they were funny or absurd.

Reading the letters might be tantamount to dancing on Paul's grave—but it might also be tantamount to planting flowers on his grave, salvaging his reputation. Todd owed it to his best friend to redeem him.

He opened the flap of the envelope and shook out the letters, all of them neatly folded in thirds, handwritten on unlined parchment, fancier paper than he was used to handling. The creamy weight of it seemed overindulgent, almost fetishistic.

"Shit," he muttered, wondering if Sally had screwed with his head. Since when did he pass judgment on paper quality?

He unfolded the letter on the top of the pile and started to read. His gaze inched along the florid handwriting, the even more florid phrasing, and he found himself swallowing hard, several times. Partly because the writing was sweet and thick enough to choke on, and partly because...

Shit. This was a love letter. No question about it. It was a love letter to Paul, and it was signed, "Love, Laura."

Who the hell was Laura?

And how could Paul have kept this a secret from his best friend?

Three

At eight-fifteen, Sally stomped into the New Day Café, still fuming. Todd had had nearly an entire day to get back to her. He'd had plenty of time to read the revolting letters, recognize that there was nothing he could tell Sally that she hadn't already figured out and telephone her to say, "All right, so you caught him. He was screwing around with a bimbo with literary pretensions. But he didn't mean to. He couldn't help himself. He really, really loved you."

Did she actually want to hear that? If she did, would she believe it? Could Todd say anything that would make her feel better?

Probably not. But she wanted to hear from him anyway. As Paul's best friend and confidant, he had to have known about Laura. And since Paul wasn't around to apologize, Todd could apologize for him.

She didn't like arriving at the café after eight. Before the accident, she used to be at the café in time for its six-thirty opening. Greta would have been there for two hours by then, baking the first round of pastries and preparing the trays for later rounds that Sally and the others could slide into the industrial ovens and cook fresh as inventory demanded. Greta would receive a daily delivery from a bakery that specialized in bagels, and a delivery of coffee beans, which she would grind on the premises so they'd be optimally fresh for brewing. Then Sally would come in, unlock the cash register and set up the tables, and Greta would leave.

Greta was a fabulous baker, and as shy as Sally was gregarious. She'd been operating the New Day Café for fifteen years before she'd hired Sally as a waitress, and Sally had turned the place from a sleepy little nook where early-shift workers stopped by for a quick cup of coffee and a warm apple turnover into a prime meeting spot that stayed open until midnight, serving coffee and pastries during the morning hours, light sandwiches at lunch and cappuccino, espresso and slices of cake in the evening to the college kids who were too young to get served at the bars in town.

Sally had loved being an early-morning shift worker, and she'd been able to keep that schedule when Paul was alive. Her routine had been to wake up at five forty-five, give Paul a kiss and slip out of bed, leaving him to sleep for another hour or so. She'd dress out in the hall by the armoire, then creep into Rosie's room and kiss her, too. Rosie could be a handful when she was awake, but asleep she was one hundred percent angel, a plump little mound of girl under her downy yellow blanket, her hair a mess of auburn curls and her thumb conveniently positioned near her mouth in case she needed an emergency suck. In the predawn twilight she smelled of baby shampoo and powder, and her eyelashes were long against her cheeks. She was truly the most marvelous creature in the world.

Later, when Sally was busy serving the morning customers at the New Day Café, Paul would wake up, get Rosie dressed, fix them both breakfast and take Rosie to school. It was their special time together, that morning hour, and Sally used to be so glad they could have it.

Now, though, she couldn't rid herself of the suspicion that Paul might have been tossing a granola bar in Rosie's direction every morning and then abandoning her to drool over his poetic missives from Laura. Or maybe he'd been calling Laura during his Rosie time, planning a tryst, whispering erotic secrets to her, swearing to her that there was no love in his house. If he used his cell phone, Sally would never find out, since the cell phone was billed to his office.

Or maybe—even worse—Laura would sneak into the house after Sally was gone. Maybe Paul would only be pretending to sleep through the alarm. He'd lie motionless in bed, listening for the sound of Sally locking the door behind her, opening the garage door, revving the engine of her dilapidated Subaru and driving away. Then he'd bolt out of bed, dial Laura's number, let it ring twice and hang up. That would be their secret signal: *Sally's gone! The coast is clear!* Laura would hurry over, slip inside—had Paul given her her own key? Sally would have to change the locks—and race upstairs to the bedroom, where Paul would "render her nothing but sensation" while Rosie slumbered innocently in her bedroom at the other end of the hall.

The whole thing was so sordid, so tawdry, so... clichéd.

Trying to tamp down her indignation, Sally scanned the café's dining area to make sure Tina, one of the other waitresses, had business under control. A few of the regulars were there: Officer Bronowski in his crisp blue uniform, drinking a large morning blend, cream-no-sugar, and polishing off an eclair. The two suburban ladies—Sally didn't know their names, but they always ordered flavored decaf, bemoaned the fact that they were on diets and then succumbed to Greta's sticky buns and raspberry Danish—at a table near the window. And the mysterious guy in black who sat in the corner, sipping a cup of espresso and scribbling on the pages of a spiral notebook—writing a novel, Sally guessed. A brooding, angst-ridden tale of existential loss and ennui, being and nothingness.

Everything seemed to be under control. Tina stood behind the counter, sponging the polished marble surface. Sally had insisted on marble counters when the place was renovated a few years ago, even though they'd cost more than Greta had wanted to spend. "Stainless steel looks too institutional," Sally had explained. "And polished wood doesn't last as long. It gets nicked and gummy. Marble is indestructible, and it looks classy. New Day Café is a classy place."

"It is?" Greta had asked, apparently bewildered. She herself wasn't particularly classy. The offspring of German immigrants, she was a sixty-three-year-old widow who knew how to bake and not much else. She dressed in pilled cardigans and refused to read the newspaper because it had too much nastiness in it, and Sally imagined she would be baking her pastries at the New Day Café until the day she curled up and died, which probably wouldn't happen for another forty years. Greta struck Sally as being as indestructible as marble.

The café hadn't been classy when Greta had created it, but it was now, thanks to Sally. The windows were framed in cheerful blue-and-white striped curtains, and colorful abstract paintings hung on the walls—Sally had created them in her basement in one afternoon, then had them professionally framed so they would look like genuine art. Muted lighting draped the tables. The chairs, purchased during the renovation, featured cushions so a person could sit comfortably for a long time. "Why do we want them to be that comfortable?" Greta had questioned her. "They'll buy one cup of coffee and then occupy the table for hours because they're so comfortable. Better they should buy, drink and leave."

"We want the New Day Café to be a destination," Sally had explained. "We want people to think about lingering. Once we've got them in the door, we don't want them to leave. They'll buy another cup of coffee. Or a big chocolate chip cookie to munch on. This isn't a take-out joint. It's a cozy hangout."

"So, you got a business degree when I wasn't looking?" Greta had asked.

"No. I've just got a lot of common sense," Sally had assured her. It wasn't necessarily true, but she did seem to have good instincts when it came to the café. Every improvement she'd pushed through increased profits.

Greta had given her the title of manager three years ago, and she'd drawn up a contract that entitled Sally to a share of the profits. The job didn't pay as much as being a partner in a law firm did, but Sally and Paul hadn't really needed the money she earned. However, working at the café was essential to Sally. It taxed her brain in interesting ways. It gave her a chance to schmooze with customers. It got her out of the house so Paul and Rosie could bond in the morning.

Assuming Paul hadn't been spending his mornings bonding with Laura, the mistress of overheated prose.

Tina tossed her sponge into the small sink behind the counter. She had a vague look about her, her eyes unfocused, her smile enigmatic. Tina was a sophomore at the college, as Sally had been when she'd started working at the New Day. Like Sally, Tina needed money; like her, she was energetic and willing to work hard.

Unlike Sally, however, Tina was not going to get accidentally pregnant. Sally was not going to let her.

It seemed odd that Sally could feel so maternal toward Tina when she was only six years older. But six years filled with marriage, a baby, home ownership, a job, widowhood and betrayal could age a person fast. Sally was feeling quite old at the moment.

"What's wrong?" she asked.

Tina turned her glazed eyes to Sally. She wore her hair in a spiky short style, the better to display the assortment of studs, hoops and dangly earrings adorning her lobes. That was another thing that made Sally feel old: not just Tina's array of earrings but her hairdo. Sally sometimes felt she'd been born in the wrong decade. She should have been a flower child. She would have loved the original Woodstock. She would have loved living on a commune somewhere, kneading bread and adding freshly harvested herbs to her vegetarian dishes, which she would serve to hearty, sturdy, unbearably sexy young men with long hair and beards, who would adore her because she was smart and gentle and nurturing.

Instead, she'd wound up with a clean-shaven lawyer, and she sold food someone else had baked.

She wore her hair long, though—usually loose down her back, but braided for work. She was pretty sure she was smart, and she tried to be gentle and nurturing, at least with people who deserved it, like Rosie and Tina.

Tina's smile expanded slightly, the corners of her mouth edging outward. "Wanna see something?"

Sally wasn't sure she did. But her sense of responsibility toward Tina compelled her to nod.

Tina scanned the room. Officer Bronowski was just finishing up, crumpling his napkin into a wad and pushing his chair away from the table. He was the only cop who ever came into the New Day Café after eight in the morning. The early-shift cops stopped by at opening time, and they slurped their coffee standing at the counter or took it with them in lidded paper cups. But Bronowski always arrived a little later, and he always ordered one of Greta's prissier pastries—a wedge of carrot cake, perhaps, or a blueberry tart, or biscotti with slivers of blanched almonds adorning the top.

Paul used to say about Bronowski, "I think he's a little light in the trousers." Sally would defend the cop, arguing that enjoying an elegant pastry was no more an indication of homosexual tendencies than eating greasy doughnuts was an indication of heterosexual tendencies. Paul didn't eat greasy doughnuts, did he?

Only because he didn't want to gain weight, he'd explained. He was definitely heterosexual.

He was also dead, and since Bronowski had been the policeman who'd very sweetly, gently broken the news to her that her beloved husband—that lying, cheating son of a bitch—had left this world for the next, Sally would defend the officer's sexuality, whatever it might be, until the end of time. She was happy to welcome him with a smile each morning and serve him whatever delicacy he wanted.

She and Tina waited until he'd donned his cap, nodded his farewell and left the café. The suburban ladies were still going strong, gossiping in high gear, and the dreary artiste in black was scribbling fervently in his notebook. No one needed their attention right now.

"Come here," Tina whispered, motioning with her head that they should go into the kitchen.

With a parting look toward the customers, Sally reluctantly trailed Tina into the narrow room where Greta performed miracles with flour, sugar, butter and eggs.

Huge canisters of ground coffee stood along one counter, and trays of unbaked pastries covered the long table that occupied the center of the room. Sally glanced over her shoulder; no one in the café seemed aware that she and Tina had ducked out for a minute.

When she turned back, Tina was untucking her Winfield College T-shirt from the waistband of her baggy khakis. She hoisted the shirt up under her armpits, peeled down the stretchy fabric of her bra and exhibited her left breast to Sally. Tattooed above the nipple were the letters H-O-W-A-R-D.

"Howard?"

"Isn't it cool?" Tina's smile reached full strength. "I just had it done this past weekend."

"Why on earth did you name your breast Howard?"

"That's not my breast's name. It's my boyfriend's name." Tina let out a giddy little sigh.

Sally gripped the edge of the counter to keep from clamping her hands on Tina's shoulders and shaking her until centrifugal force tore the ink letters from her skin. "You tattooed your boyfriend's name on your breast?" she asked, trying not to sound hysterical.

Tina nodded and offered another fizzy sigh. "Friday night. What do you think?"

I think you're an idiot. I think you must have gotten into college via some special affirmative action program for dimwits. "What are you going to do if you break up with him?" she asked.

"Oh, that won't happen," Tina vowed with all the certainty of a young, naive imbecile. "I love Howard."

"You love Howard." It occurred to Sally that perhaps there were worse things than accidentally getting pregnant at the age of twenty, marrying for the sake of the child and blindly convincing yourself that you loved your husband so the marriage would seem acceptable. Etching six ugly blue-black letters permanently into your breast was definitely worse. "I don't suppose Howard loves you enough to get 'Tina' tattooed on his penis?"

Tina giggled and her cheeks grew rosy. "Well, of course not. You can't get tattooed *there*."

"Why not?"

"Well, like, it's so...wrinkly. I don't know. And anyway, that would look so weird. Like, if you misread it, you might think it said 'Tiny' instead of 'Tina.' I don't think any guy would want to go around with the word *tiny* tattooed on his...well, you know."

"Penis," Sally said, because uttering the word appeared to have the same effect as shaking Tina by the shoulders would have had. The girl blushed, she flinched, she looked flustered. "If he loved you as much as you think he does," Sally observed, "he ought to be willing to put up with that humiliation."

"Well, and anyway, I just don't think you can do it there. Like, the needle would hurt too much."

"This—" Sally gestured toward Tina's breast, which she'd tucked back into her bra "—didn't hurt at all, I take it."

"Well, I don't really remember. I mean, once it's done, you sort of forget about it."

"How can you forget about something like that? Every time you get undressed, you'll be reminded of it." Sally clicked her tongue and shook her head, feeling unbearably old.

"We better go back out," Tina muttered, her smile fading. Evidently, Sally's reaction to her tattoo was not what she'd hoped for.

But how could she have expected anything different? She and Sally got along well, but Sally was a mother.

A widowed woman with a checking account, insurance and a car. Someone who might have believed in ever-lasting true love when she'd been Tina's age, which seemed terribly long ago, but who'd stopped believing in it the instant she'd found those letters stashed inside Paul's brown crew neck.

The suburban ladies were gone when she and Tina returned to the dining room, but the grim young man in black was still at his table, scribbling away. Tina glanced at the clock behind the counter and cringed. "I gotta go. I've got Social Ethics at ten."

Sally remembered Social Ethics from her brief sojourn at Winfield College. It was a guaranteed A, and always solidly enrolled. She hadn't been able to squeeze into the class because upperclassmen had had priority. If her life had taken a different turn, if she'd been able to stay in college, she would have taken it, even though she had no idea what "Social Ethics" meant. As far as students were concerned, it meant an A.

"Go ahead. It's dead here," Sally urged, although Tina still had twenty minutes before the class would begin. She would probably need those twenty minutes to recover from her disappointment that Sally hadn't flung her arms around her and said, "What a fine, wise decision, to tattoo 'HOWARD' onto your bosom! I'm so proud of you."

Nodding, Tina lifted her backpack from the floor under the counter. As she straightened, the door swung open and Todd Sloane walked in.

Sally grimaced. Todd was not a regular at the New Day Café. In fact, he wasn't even an irregular. She couldn't recall his ever having come into the café before.

He headed directly for the counter, aiming his eyes at Sally. "Friend of yours?" Tina whispered.

"No."

"He's cute."

"No, he's not." He most definitely wasn't cute. He was too tall, too rawboned, his hair too dark, his eyes even darker. His features might have been handsome if they'd had any sort of grace to them, but they were too harsh, too angular. His nose was big, which helped offset the sheer force of his gaze. His hands and feet were large. So were his shoulders. In fact, everything about him seemed large. She doubted he was deserving of a tattoo reading "tiny" on his penis.

What an odd thought. She'd never even thought of him in terms of sex.

And she wasn't thinking of him in terms of sex now, she reminded himself. She was thinking of him in terms of his anatomy. Merely glimpsing him made her think, *What a prick.*

He moved directly to the counter, his gaze sharp and hard. Tina peered up at him, looking even more lovesick than she'd seemed when talking about Howard. More than ever, Sally wanted to shake her. If there was anything worse than tattooing "HOWARD" on your breast, it was looking as if you were thinking about tattooing "Todd" on your other breast.

She gave him a smile so chilly she felt the cold twinge in her fillings. "Would you like a cup of coffee?" she asked.

"No." He stared past her at the blackboard on the wall, which listed that morning's available coffees. "Cinnamon hazelnut?" he read from the sign. "Kona?"

"The Kona is imported from Hawaii," Sally informed him.

His frown could curdle the cream in the insulated silver pitcher on the counter. "No kidding."

Maybe the prospect of admitting the truth put him in a lousy mood. Maybe the notion of coming clean to his best friend's widow befouled his spirits.

Tina was still studying him, rapt and misty eyed. "Would you like a cookie?" she asked in a whispery voice.

He eyed her with mild curiosity, his frown softening. It hardened again as he turned back to Sally. "I don't know," he muttered.

"You don't know if you'd like a cookie?" Tina asked hopefully.

"Go to Social Ethics, Tina," Sally ordered her.

Slumping, Tina trudged out from behind the counter, adjusted the strap of her backpack on her shoulder and waved. "See ya," she said, heading for the door. The legs of her pants sagged around her shoes and brushed the floor with each step.

Todd stared after her for a minute, then frowned. "Social Ethics?"

"Something you wouldn't know anything about," Sally retorted. If not for the letters, Todd would have been nothing more than her late husband's pal. But with the letters he'd become Paul's accomplice, his partner in crime. He'd become the living embodiment of Paul's deceit, which meant she could be as nasty with him as she wanted.

"Look, Sally." He bent close to her over the counter, so he could keep his voice down—as if the black-clad chronicler had any interest in their conversation. "I read those letters and I'm stumped. I don't know who Laura is."

"Liar."

"I swear. Paul never told me he was cheating on you."

"He told you everything."

"Not this."

"Then you agree that those letters prove he *was* cheating on me?"

Todd considered his answer, his face softening again, becoming less angry, more reflective. "I don't know."

"What else would they be? A correspondence with his grandma? Come on, Todd—don't defend the indefensible. Your very best friend in the whole wide world was an adulterer. Maybe you covered for him when he was alive—"

"I didn't!"

"—but it's a little late to be covering for him now."

Todd drummed his fingers on the counter. They were broad and blunt tipped and clean. She lifted her gaze to his face. Cute? Tina was obviously a woman of weird taste—anyone who could fall so deeply in love with a man named Howard that she'd tattoo his name above her heart was by definition weird—but Sally would never call Todd cute. He was gruff. Seething. Haunted. His hair was mussed and wavy, his apparel expensive yet somehow dowdy, the blazer a dull gray tweed, the trousers not quite baggy enough to be fashionable but not tight enough to look tailored, the charcoal-gray shirt wrinkled. *Cute* was for puppies and candy canes, blue jeans and dimples. Todd didn't have dimples.

"You want a cup of coffee?" she asked again, because he seemed tense. Nothing like a shot of high-octane caffeine to soothe the nerves, she thought sarcastically. But he seemed as if he needed something, and coffee was the strongest drug she could offer him.

"No. I've got to go to work. I just wanted to tell you I don't know anything about Laura."

If he was lying, he was good at it. He looked earnest

and bewildered, even upset. He wasn't entitled to be upset—it wasn't as if Paul had done *him* wrong—but he certainly seemed bothered by the whole thing.

"Where are the letters?" she asked.

"They're at my house."

"I want them back."

"Why?"

She had to think about that. Why did she want to possess the miserable evidence that her marriage had been a fraud? She wouldn't be using the fireplace until next winter, so she wasn't going to have occasion to burn them in the next eight or nine months. What did she need them for?

An excuse to hate Paul. An excuse not to miss him, not to mourn him, not to want to wrap herself up in his sweaters and think about what a wonderful husband he'd been.

"I was thinking," Todd said, "that I'd like to investigate this further."

"Investigate what?"

"Laura."

Oh, great. Todd was probably figuring that Laura had to be someone special. A hot prospect, gorgeous and sexy, someone Paul could love and Todd could approve of. She'd likely be the antithesis of Sally—rich, well bred, endowed with a *Hahvahd* accent. Maybe she'd gone to finishing school and was a member of the Junior League. Maybe she was thin and blond and wore miniskirts and laughed at Paul's jokes. Maybe she was kinky in bed.

Todd probably wanted to track Laura down so he could console the poor woman. She'd lost her lover, hadn't she? Todd could find her and ease her loneliness.

He could try his luck with her and learn whether she'd been worth Paul's breaking his wedding vows over.

Of course she'd been worth it. Paul wouldn't have broken his vows otherwise. He hadn't been the kind of man who did things just for fun. He'd always been intent, focused, organized. Laura must have fit into his life in just the right way. She'd thought the knife Paul had given her was vulgar, just as Paul had thought it was vulgar when Sally had given it to him. They'd probably laughed about it behind Sally's back, never acknowledging that Sally had given it to Paul because it had been the most precious object she owned.

If Todd had seen the knife, he probably would have laughed at it, too. He'd never done anything to hide his loathing of her. His best friend had married her under pressure, out of obligation. Todd obviously believed this was her fault.

"The letters belong to me," she said, mostly to spite him.

"I wasn't thinking of keeping them. I just wanted to hang on to them for a while, to see if I could figure out just who the hell she was."

"Why should you care?"

He ruminated for a moment. "I can't believe he'd do something like this behind my back," he finally admitted. "I was his best friend. I can't believe he kept Laura a secret from me."

"He kept her a secret from me," Sally pointed out.

"Of course he did. You were his wife."

She nearly reached over the counter and slapped him. But she sensed that he hadn't meant to wound her with his words. He looked too confused. He'd just fired into the air, and the bullet had wound up hitting her.

"You can keep the letters on one condition," she stipulated, grabbing the sponge and wiping the counter. She felt a surge of nervous energy. Offering to cooperate with Todd was an alien idea; it made her edgy.

"What's that?"

"Anything you find, you've got to tell me."

"No," he said quickly.

She did reach across the counter this time, not to slap him but to grab him. Unfortunately, she still had the sponge in her hand, and she wound up squeezing water from it onto his sleeve. Dropping the sponge, she clung to the soggy wool to prevent him from backing away. "You're not going to keep me in the dark, Todd. That's the deal. I've been lied to enough. Bad enough your buddy lied to me. I won't have you lying to me, too."

He stared at the wet spot on his sleeve, at her hand arched around it. Her fingers were stubby, her nails short and unpolished because she never had time to take care of them. Sally bet Laura had gorgeous hands, the sort of hands that could model in commercials for moisturizers and Swiss watches.

Todd didn't try to shake free of her, though. He simply stared at her hand on his forearm. After a moment, he sighed. "The thing is, anything I find out is probably going to hurt you. There's no need for you to go through that kind of hurt."

Did Todd want to spare her? Did he actually care enough to want to protect her from pain? He'd never expressed any concern for her before. Why did he suddenly want to be nice to her?

He didn't *want* to. He was only pretending to be nice so he wouldn't have to share with her whatever he might learn about Laura. "I've already been hurt by this," Sally argued. "Nothing you find out is going to hurt worse."

"I'm not so sure of that."

She released his arm, picked up the sponge and surprised herself by smiling. "In case you haven't noticed, I'm pretty tough. Go ahead and find out what you can, but if you don't tell me, you're dead."

"You're going to kill me?"

She shrugged. "It's too late to kill Paul, so I guess you'll have to do."

He pulled a face. "Okay, then. Open yourself up for more heartache. That's what it's going to be."

"I can hardly wait," she muttered, then turned from him. There was nothing more to say. Todd would find things out, he would tell her, and he would probably be annoyed when she wasn't as crushed as he'd expected her to be. Or else she would be devastated, and he'd be annoyed because she'd forced him to tell her this devastating information. Either way he'd be annoyed, which was fine with her.

He hesitated for a few seconds, then headed for the doors. She turned around. He looked rumpled from behind, like a basketball player who'd crammed his street clothes into his gym bag and now was forced to wear them wrinkled. She'd never noticed how long his legs were. On those unfortunate occasions when she'd been unable to avoid him, she'd generally had Paul to focus on, and she'd paid Todd as little attention as possible.

Cute? Not by any stretch.

Damn. She didn't want to have to depend on him for information. But she refused to remain in ignorance. Anything he found out, she wanted to know. She wasn't going to allow him to smirk behind her back. She was going to stay on top of this, get to the bottom of this, pull it inside out and expose it to the light, and if she got hurt along the way, big deal.

Four

The scent of coffee lingered in Todd's nostrils as he strolled east down Main Street, away from the retail enterprises that catered to the college kids—the boutiques, the convenience stores, the shops that sold perfumed candles and chunky pottery and T-shirts that said Perfect GPA: Gross Party Animal—and toward what he'd always considered the *real* Winfield. He passed Town Hall, an oppressive gothic edifice of dark granite and leaded glass. It was the sort of building inside which you could imagine people arguing endlessly about the capacity of Winfield's sewers. He passed the bank, the post office and the stubbornly untrendy Gould's Department Store, where his parents purchased all their clothes, just as their parents had before them. He passed squat two-story brick and brownstone buildings containing the offices of dentists, accountants, surveyors, chiropractors, insurance brokers and Madame Constanza, tarot card reader.

Downtown ended at the railroad tracks, an overpass above Main Street that descended to street level at the station a few blocks south. The building that housed the *Valley News* was just steps from the station; the newspaper used to receive its rolls of blank newsprint via the rails, so proximity to the station had been necessary. Now trucks brought in the newsprint, which was stored in a warehouse on the outskirts of town, and buses were the primary mode of public transportation. The train stopped only once a day in each direction. Every few months, Todd would write a staunch editorial urging Amtrak to increase passenger service to Winfield for the sake of the environment.

He wasn't in the mood to write any staunch editorials today. He'd already stopped in at his office, heard his mother fulminating about her modem through her open door and ducked out before she could catch up with him. With time on his hands and an office to avoid, he'd strolled up Main Street to the New Day Café to tell Sally he'd read the letters.

He'd never been inside the New Day Café before, partly because the coffeemaker in the lounge at the *Valley News* produced perfectly adequate coffee, partly because he was reluctant to patronize any establishment that had a rhyme in its name, but mostly because he didn't feel like having to be pleasant with the woman who'd hoodwinked his best friend into a marriage five and a half years ago. In fact, if he hadn't been looking to waste a few minutes that morning, he wouldn't have entered the place today. He could as easily have telephoned Sally that evening to tell her he'd read the letters and he had no idea who Laura was. But he was restless, disturbed enough by the letters not to care if the New Day Café's name rhymed or if discussing the letters with Sally in person might not be the smartest thing to do.

He'd exerted himself to resist the café's charming decor, the lush java fragrance permeating the air, the spiky young waitress with the glut of earrings and Sally herself, big and flouncy in a denim jumper and hoop earrings so large they could double as tire rims. He'd ignored his sudden thirst for a tall, steaming cup of black coffee and the pang of nostalgia for his carefree youth, when spending hours arguing with friends over coffee about whether Shakespeare actually wrote Shakespeare's plays had seemed like a worthwhile way to kill an afternoon. He'd refused to acknowledge that Sally's hair looked almost fiery in the sunlight streaming through the window, brown with licks of hot red whipped through it. He'd shut his mind to the possibility that maybe the reason Paul had slept with Sally in the first place was that her hair was remarkable when the sun struck it.

Sally's hair didn't matter. What mattered was that her life and Todd's now intersected in two places: they'd both been close to Paul, and they'd both been duped by Paul.

Todd didn't want to give the letters back to her—not because he wished to spare her more pain, as he'd said in the café, but because he didn't want to have to deal with her as he continued his investigation into Laura's identity. Todd wasn't through with the letters yet. He wouldn't be through with them until he'd found Laura and compelled her to explain what the hell Paul had been up to, having an affair and not telling his best friend about it.

Paul had betrayed Sally, but even worse, he'd betrayed Todd. They'd known each other so long, so well. Todd had shared with Paul his mortification about having been cut from his high school's basketball team because he hadn't run fast enough, and Paul had confessed his resentment over the way his superrich parents used to jet-set around the world, leaving him to the care of nannies and boarding schools. Paul and Todd had talked about everything that mattered: football, sex, cars and work...yet Paul hadn't talked to Todd about Laura. If Sally was hurt, Todd was even more hurt. Sally had been just some woman Paul had knocked up and married. Todd had been Paul's *best friend,* damn it.

He veered north, deciding to pay a call on Wittig, Mott, Driver and Associates, Attorneys-at-Law. The firm where Paul used to be a partner was located in an angular fieldstone-and-glass building planted on the corner of Main and Clancy streets like a souvenir the Jetsons might have left behind. Back in the sixties it had probably looked daring, streamlined and modern. Now it looked like an architect's worst mistake.

"Driver" had not yet been expunged from the glass front door. Then again, neither had "and Associates," although from the day Paul had been named a partner, the firm had had no associates. It had two secretaries and in the summers a clerk, usually a law student on his school break, some poor sucker who'd been unable to land an internship at one of the prestigious firms in Boston or New York. But it sounded grander to call the firm Wittig, Mott, Driver and Associates than Wittig, Mott, Driver and Some Poor Sucker.

They did decent legal work at Wittig, Mott. When Paul had been there, they'd done superb work. But the firm was doomed to be a small-town, small-time operation: real estate, wills, minor torts and misdemeanor defenses. *Court TV* was never going to find anything worth filming in Winfield. Case law was not made in this town nestled into a valley surrounded by farms, vacation meccas and mediocre ski slopes. The Constitution had never been challenged in Winfield—and if it ever was, someone would be sure to hire counsel from Boston or New York to handle the matter.

Patty Pleckart was stationed at the receptionist's desk when Todd entered. He'd gone to school with her, and during his junior year had had biblical knowledge of her on the sofa bed in the guest room of Dan Kajema's house during a party when a lot of bad wine had been circulating. Todd and Patty had had trouble looking at each other for the rest of that year, but then they'd both gotten over it. Now Patty was married and fat, and whenever they ran into each other, Todd chivalrously acted as if he'd never seen her without her panties on.

"What brings you here?" she asked. No need for professional formality between them.

"I was wondering if I could have a peek inside Paul's office," he said.

She eyed him suspiciously. She always eyed him suspiciously, as if the mere sight of him forced her to relive that embarrassing night at Dan's in her mind.

"What do you want in Paul's office?"

"He was my best friend," Todd said, managing not to choke on the words. Best friend? The schmuck hadn't even told him he was having an affair with some lady named Laura! Best friends didn't hide that kind of information from each other. But he kept a straight face and said, "I just...miss him."

Patty didn't look moved.

"I miss him a *lot*," Todd emphasized, trying to put a tremor in his voice.

"What does that have to do with his office?"

"If I could stand in it for a few minutes, maybe I'd feel closer to him."

Patty's expression changed from merely suspicious to affronted, as if she viewed his request as perverted. Who cared what she thought, though? She hadn't considered him perverted twenty years ago.

She still didn't seem prepared to admit him into Paul's office. "I really, *really* miss him," Paul lamented.

Pursing her lips, she pulled a key from the center

drawer of her desk, unwedged her broad hips from her chair and waddled over to Paul's office. The lock gave with a quiet click, and the door swung inward.

"Thanks," Todd said, slipping inside and closing the door behind him.

Paul had always been tidy, and even in death his anal neatness hovered like a ghost in the room. Three months he'd been gone, and everything was just as he'd left it: the blotter clear, the computer protected by a dustcover, the chair positioned squarely against the desk. The file cabinets shut, the slats of the blinds all adjusted to the same angle, the framed photo of Rosie in a peculiar felt hat—one of Sally's whimsies, no doubt—positioned on the credenza so Paul would be able to see it from his desk.

Todd didn't have time to lapse into awe over Paul's fastidiousness. He was supposed to be grieving in here. He had to work fast.

He moved behind the desk and tugged on the drawers. All of them were locked. Damn. If there was a clue in his desk to Laura's identity, Todd wouldn't be able to unearth it.

He crossed the thick carpet to the credenza and opened the cabinets below the shelves. He found stacks of folders, legal pads and other office supplies, including a box of computer diskettes. The disks looked unused. He doubted he'd find anything on them.

If Laura had been a client of his, Paul would have her records not just on file but on disk. Where would he keep his active disks? Besides locked in his desk.

Todd searched the room frantically. Any minute now, Patty could return, and she'd expect to find him in deep grief over the tragic loss of his dear friend. He couldn't let her catch him scouring the room like a two-bit detective.

Visible from the credenza side of the room, a wall of shelves stood behind Paul's desk. The shelves held books, a humidor from Paul's cigar period, a polished brass clock and a carved wooden box.

Todd hurried across the room, lifted the hinged lid of the box and found—yes!—a few computer diskettes. He grabbed them, shoved them into the pocket of his jacket and spun around as George Wittig swept into the office. The firm's senior partner, George was a doughy-faced man of indeterminate age, although Todd guessed him to be at least sixty. He'd been Todd's parents' lawyer since before Todd had been born. Dressed in a brown suit from Gould's—Todd recognized the cut; his father had at least three identically tailored suits—George shook his head until his jowls trembled. "You shouldn't be in here, Toddy," he said.

Todd gritted his teeth. Few things irritated him more than his parents' friends calling him Toddy. "I just wanted to be surrounded by Paul's aura," he said solemnly, sliding his hand discreetly into his jacket pocket to disguise the shape of the diskettes he'd taken. "His death has been very emotional for me." He was pleased by the catch in his voice. It made him sound tormented. Circling the desk, he sniffed dramatically and hoped he wasn't overdoing the bereaved act. "I still miss the guy, you know?"

"We all miss him," George said dryly. "But that doesn't give you the right to go nosing around in his office."

"I wasn't nosing around. I was—"

"Feeling his aura. Jesus Christ, Toddy. Since when do you subscribe to that fuzzy-wuzzy New Age crap?"

"I don't know." Todd sighed heavily. "The death of a dear friend can put things in a whole new perspective." For instance, the perspective of someone who'd just found out the dear friend in question had been a lying bastard.

"You know, I only took him into the firm because of you," George said. His complexion looked wan. The man didn't get enough sun. Maybe Todd's father ought to drag him out to the golf course for a little fresh air.

"Are you thanking me or blaming me?" Todd asked.

"Thanking you. He put us all to shame. A fine, fine lawyer." George observed a moment of silence. "But that doesn't mean I want to hang around in his office feeling his aura."

"It looks as if no one has touched a thing here," Todd pointed out. "That seems pretty New Age to me."

"Patty won't allow it. She's the sentimental one in the firm. Clings to memories the way lint clings to a good wool jacket."

Great, Todd thought. She probably clung to her memory of that time at Dan Kajema's, too.

"I think you should leave," George said. "Too much sentiment will turn you into a sissy."

Todd had gotten all he was going to get out of this visit. "You're right," he said with credible conviction. "I'd hate to turn into a sissy." He preceded George into the reception area and heard the lock slide into place as George closed the door behind them.

George wrapped a paternal arm around Todd's shoulders—he had to reach up; Todd denied him the kindness of stooping—and walked him past Patty's desk to the front door. "Perhaps you'd be better off mourning Paul by making a donation in his name at the hospital," he suggested.

"Perhaps I would," Todd agreed, feeling Patty's distrustful gaze following him even after he'd exited. The sun slapped him hard in the face and he blinked a few times. He felt suddenly overloaded by his morning, first an encounter with Sally and then an encounter with Paul's aura.

But he had computer disks. Five of them—his index finger traced five edges in his pocket. Maybe Laura was on one of those disks. Maybe when Todd loaded them onto his computer, he would find out exactly what kind of man he'd once considered his best friend.

"Why are we going here?" Rosie asked.

Sally handed her an animal cracker. Animal crackers were easier to digest than most answers to the questions Rosie asked. They also kept her mouth occupied long enough to shut down her questioning mechanism for a few minutes.

Sally needed more than a few minutes to figure out why she'd driven over to the condominium complex where Todd lived. Evening was sinking down into the valley, compressing the light and forcing the trees and faux-facade town houses to release lavender shadows across the landscaped grounds. The development was shamelessly ticky-tacky, the rows of units staggered and shingled in such a way an observer might overlook the fact that they were all basically identical. It was the sort of place that seemed to shout, "Divorced people live here."

Sally hadn't known Todd's ex-wife too well. The woman had accompanied Todd to Sally and Paul's on-the-fly wedding—a few words from a judge, followed by a cocktail party at the Olde Colonial Tavern—and a few weeks later Paul had informed Sally that Todd and

Denise were separating. "They were a terrible couple," Paul had told her. "They were too much alike."

She'd seen that as proof that Paul believed he and Sally were a perfect couple, because they were nothing alike.

"Look," Rosie exclaimed, scampering to keep up with Sally as she stalked down the winding path through the complex. "I ate its head. It's the headless-horseman monster!" She galloped her decapitated horse cracker through the air, then popped it into her mouth. "I killed it," she declared proudly. "So why are we going here?"

Sally glanced at the scrap of paper on which she'd noted Todd's address: unit 27, in the row of four town houses to her left. Taking Rosie's hand, she slowed her pace slightly. "We're going here because this is an old friend of your daddy's."

"My daddy's dead," Rosie reminded her. "How can he still have friends?"

How, indeed? The philandering creep didn't deserve friends. And if Todd maintained that he was still Paul's friend, then he was a creep, too.

Lacking an answer, she dug another animal cracker from the box in her tote and handed it to Rosie. She took a cracker for herself, too.

Rosie chomped onto the cracker and grinned. She was wearing her purple cloche with the floppy pink silk flower on it—she adored it, and Sally didn't mind her wearing it even when it didn't match the occasion or the rest of Rosie's outfit, which today consisted of blue overalls, a chestnut-brown turtleneck and her lime-green sneakers with sparkly laces. Sally always let Rosie choose her outfits, and Rosie possessed a bizarre sense of color and style. Paul used to hate her getups: "Damn it, Sally—it's Easter Sunday! She can't wear pink jeans and a yellow polo shirt to church!''

That was last year's Easter. This year, Sally had taken Rosie to the Unitarian church, which she preferred to the staid Methodist church Paul used to insist they attend on the two holidays a year they felt obliged to honor organized religion. Sally liked the Unitarian church because the minister's husband was both black and Jewish, which seemed to sum up what God was all about to Sally.

Ironically, this year, Rosie had chosen to wear a dress for Easter—along with her purple hat.

''Here's his building,'' Sally said, leading Rosie up the porch steps to the door labeled 27. She rang the bell and waited.

''Why are we going here?'' Rosie asked again, peering up at her.

If Sally put her off with another animal cracker, she was going to get suspicious. She was no fool. She knew when her mother was trying to silence her. ''I need to talk to this man.''

''About Daddy?''

''About something he has that belonged to Daddy and now belongs to me,'' Sally said, pressing the doorbell button again.

This time, the door swung inward, offering Sally an eyeful of Todd Sloane's chest. He filled the doorway, tall and lanky in a pair of old jeans and a shirt that was untucked and hanging open.

He had quite a chest. Sally could see only a narrow swath of it, framed by the edges of his shirt, but that swath was sleek with muscle. The skin was golden, and a dusting of dark hair spread across the upper portion.

The lower portion, she noticed, was punctuated by an innie belly button.

She forced her gaze up from that belly button, past the contours of his rib cage to his throat, his chin, shadowed by a day's growth of beard, his hair damp and curling, and finally his mouth, which curved markedly downward. He was not happy to see her.

"I'd like the letters back," she said, figuring the sooner she got them, the sooner she and Rosie could flee from Mondo Condo and go back to her house with its bright orange door. Imagine what would happen if someone tried to paint *his* front door orange. The Conformity Police would storm the place, slap on the cuffs and charge the resident with the high crime of imagination.

"No," Todd said.

"Mommy says you're my daddy's friend," Rosie declared, peering up at him.

He stared down at her, his expression filled with pity. Sally wanted to slap him. How dared he pity her daughter? Rosie didn't deserve anything remotely like pity. She was a goddess. A noisy, lively, rambunctious goddess, and if she missed her father, it was only because he hadn't betrayed her the way he'd betrayed Sally.

"I was your father's friend," Todd confirmed. "You've met me before. Don't you remember?"

"Nope. How come your shirt isn't buttoned?"

He shot Sally a quick look that said, *Your kid needs manners.* Sally only smiled.

Grudgingly, he stepped back and waved them inside. Once they were crowded in the tiny foyer, he shut the door and crossed his hands over his chest. He glared at Sally, waiting for her to speak.

"How come your shirt isn't buttoned?" she asked.

"Look." He sighed but made no move to close his

shirt. "I'm on my time, okay? This is my house. I just took a shower. I don't have to button my shirt if I don't want to."

"That sounds like your kind of logic," Sally told Rosie, who nodded and wriggled her hand free from Sally's. She wandered into the living room, Todd right behind her as if to protect his treasures from a dangerous threat. But there were no fragile treasures in the living room, as far as Sally could tell. Big, overstuffed furniture, a mess of newspapers—including the *New York Times* and dailies from Springfield and Boston—scattered across the coffee table, books shoved willy-nilly into built-in bookcases along one wall, a pair of athletic socks on a footstool near one of the easy chairs and an array of model cars displayed on a sideboard. Rosie raced directly to the cars, reaching for the most flamboyant, a five-inch-long dune buggy painted metallic turquoise.

"Don't touch that," Todd snapped. Two long strides carried him across the room, enabling him to beat her to the cars by less than a second. He barred her from the display, and she poked her lower lip out in a sulky pout.

"She lost her father," Sally reproached. "Can't she even look at your toy cars?"

"They aren't toys," Todd explained, blocking the sideboard with his body as he buttoned his shirt. "I built them myself. It's a hobby."

A hobby? What a quaint idea, Sally thought, studying Todd in a new light. She would never have taken him for a hobbyist. He was too important, too busy, too worldly. Paul had never had a hobby—unless getting some action on the side was considered a hobby—and Paul had been Todd's best friend.

"They could break very easily," he explained to Rosie, who glowered up at him.

"Do you have anything else she could play with?" Sally suggested.

Todd scowled. "I don't have kids, and I didn't know you were coming. So no, I don't have anything else she could play with."

"Here, Rosie." Sally rummaged through her tote until she located a pencil and a spiral-bound pad of lined paper. "Why don't you draw a picture while Mr. Sloane and I talk."

"Are you gonna talk about Daddy?"

"Possibly." She handed the pad and pencil to Rosie.

"Do you have any cookies?" she asked Todd, clutching the pencil in one hand and the pad in the other.

"No."

"He wasn't expecting us," Sally reminded her. "I'll give you another animal cracker and you can draw a picture, okay?"

"I want two animal crackers," Rosie said.

"Fine." Sally fished two crackers from the box and extended them toward Rosie, who spent a good minute shifting the pencil to the same hand that held the pad. She took the crackers and glared at Todd. Obviously, she didn't like him. He had no cookies and he wouldn't let her touch his precious little toy cars.

"Come into the kitchen if you're going to eat those." Todd stalked past a dining alcove and into a small, dark kitchen that smelled of roasted chicken.

"Are we interrupting your dinner?" Sally asked, following Rosie, who followed him. She honestly didn't care if they *were* interrupting, but it seemed only polite to ask. Especially since the kitchen smelled so home-cooked-mealish. Was Todd a good cook? Did he go to a lot of trouble preparing meals for himself?

Paul had hated cooking, and he'd been compulsively neat. Maybe opposites attracted in best friends as well as lovers. Or maybe he'd been cheating on Todd with another best friend, the way he'd been cheating on Sally with another woman.

"It can wait," he said, adjusting a dial on the wall oven and flicking on a fluorescent overhead light. The kitchen had no windows in it, Sally noted. She would die if she had to work in a kitchen with no windows.

Rosie climbed up into a chair at the small butcher block table in one corner. Kneeling on the seat, she stuffed one cracker into her mouth and flipped through the notebook, searching for the perfect page to draw on. Once she found it, Sally turned to Todd.

He was tucking his now-buttoned shirt into the waistband of his jeans. She watched his flattened hand slide in and out of the denim, shoving the shirt in.

Just as she'd never thought of Todd as building model cars, she'd never thought of him as having a real chest. She felt slightly disoriented, even though he was now covered. He angled his head in the direction of the living room, and Sally nodded and led him out of the tiny kitchen.

"I want the letters back," she said in a low voice once Todd had joined her.

"I'm not done with them yet."

"I don't care. I've been thinking about this all day, and I decided I want them back."

He shook his head. "Sorry."

"They're mine. They were Paul's, and Paul died, and that makes them mine."

He shook his head again. "You seem to forget that

I'm the executor of his will. I know exactly what he left to you. I don't recall the letters being part of his estate.''

"They were part of his personal effects," she argued. "I found them in a drawer in my room. That makes them mine."

"He didn't leave them to you."

"He didn't leave them to you, either," she retorted.

He shrugged. "I'll give them back to you when I'm through with them. For now, I need them."

"Why? Are you going to have a handwriting analysis done on them?"

He gazed thoughtfully at her. "That's not a bad idea," he murmured.

It was a ridiculous idea. She'd said it just because she wasn't as good an arguer as he was.

"I'm trying to figure out who Laura is," he explained. "Once I do that, you can have the damn letters back."

"Why are you trying to figure it out?"

"Because…" He faltered, then glanced toward the window overlooking the front lawn and let out a weary breath. "It's not like you were the only one he lied to. I was his best friend, Sally. And he never breathed a word of this to me. Not even a hint. It pisses me off."

"Oh. It pisses you off." As the aggrieved wife, she was pretty pissed off, too. Yet the hurt she sensed in Todd's voice was genuine. The anger in his eyes was real. He felt cheated on as much as she did. Even if she didn't like him, she could sympathize, and out of sympathy she could avoid sarcasm. "What do you think will happen if you figure out who Laura is?"

"I don't know." He shrugged. "Maybe I'll figure out who Paul was."

He was my husband, Sally wanted to say. *He was the*

father of my daughter. He was a two-timing jackass.
"How are you going to find her?"

Todd studied Sally's upturned face in the filtered light
from the window. Annoyance still resonated in his
frown, but she saw more in it—acquiescence, a reluctant
kinship. No pity, thank God. "I sneaked into his office
today," he said in a near whisper, as though he thought
Rosie might hand him over to the authorities if she over-
heard his confession. "I stole some of his diskettes."

"Why?"

"I thought, maybe this Laura was a client of his.
Someone he met through work."

"So you brought his diskettes home?"

"Yeah. I was going to have a look at them after dinner."

Sally had to admit she was impressed by his enter-
prise. She couldn't have gotten into his office. She'd
never gotten along with anyone at the firm. This hadn't
bothered her; lawyers had never been her favorite people. Years after she'd married Paul, she was still astonished to think of herself as the wife of an attorney.

But her failure to become friends with Paul's colleagues had never been an issue. He'd kept his professional life separate from his home life. She'd never gone
to the firm's Christmas parties, and she'd never regretted
missing them. If one of his associates had telephoned
him at home, she hadn't had to knock herself out making
small talk, asking how the kids were doing and whether
that stubborn crabgrass situation had been licked. She'd
simply said, "Hang on a minute—I'll get Paul."

So it would never have occurred to her to snoop
around in Paul's office. If she'd showed up there, that
surly receptionist, Patty Pleckart, would have become
suspicious, whereas most of the people who worked at

the firm had known Todd since his diaper-rash days and wouldn't question his reasons for stopping by.

If she'd stolen Paul's work diskettes, though, she wouldn't have waited until she'd finished dinner before loading them onto her computer to see what nuggets of information they contained. She would have tossed Rosie a fistful of animal crackers and then started plowing through the data.

To men, food was undoubtedly more important than the truth.

"Let's go look at them now," she suggested, searching for a computer.

He raked his hand through the thick, damp waves of his hair and contemplated her. "I don't think so," he said.

"Why not?"

"I don't think you should be here while I go through them."

Indignation flared inside her. She pulled herself straighter, stretching enough that she would have been standing eye to eye with Paul. Todd was a good six inches taller than Paul had been, and he towered above her, staring down at her. "What if you find out who Laura is and fall apart?"

"If I was going to fall apart over all of this, I would have fallen apart when I found the letters."

"I don't want you snapping in my house," he explained. "I don't want you blubbering and wailing and acting like a ninny."

"Oh, is that all?" So kind of him to care about her emotional well-being. "I promise I won't act like a ninny."

He opened his mouth and then shut it. He was tactful enough not to say what he was thinking.

At least he hadn't ordered her to leave. She crossed to the kitchen. "Rosie, honey, Daddy's friend and I are going to go look at something on his computer. We'll be—" She glanced questioningly at Todd.

Resigned, he turned toward the kitchen. "Upstairs, first door on the right," he called in to Rosie, then headed for the stairs without waiting for Sally.

She easily caught up to him on the narrow stairway. At the top was a hall with several doors opening off it. One must lead to his bedroom, she guessed, and another to a bathroom. The first door on the right opened into a study that could double as an extra bedroom. It contained a boring beige futon, another wall unit of shelves filled with disheveled rows of books and an L-shaped desk with computer equipment set up on its bland white surface. A small stack of black squares rested next to the computer. The monitor featured a screen saver that depicted a cartoon dog gnawing on the corner of the screen, swinging its head and growling ferociously while the screen image seemed to peel away from itself and into his teeth.

Rosie would have loved it.

Not bothering to offer Sally a seat, Todd dropped onto the wheeled swivel chair in front of the desk. He loaded the first diskette from the pile into the machine and booted up its contents.

A director's chair stood in one corner of the room, and Sally dragged it over to the desk and sat beside Todd. In the bright light of his desk lamp, she could see the fatigue that creased the skin around his eyes, the stubble of beard that darkened his jaw, the twitch at the corner of his mouth, a sign of annoyance or tension or both.

"What is it?" she asked, angling her head to view the screen. A column of names and numbers appeared.

"Looks like phone numbers," Todd said, scrolling down the monitor as he scanned the names. "No one named Laura on the list."

"Maybe Laura was her nickname. Or the pet name he used for her."

Todd snorted. "Did Paul ever use pet names?"

"Never." He even called Rosie Rose most of the time. He'd complained more than once that Sally sounded more like a nickname than a real name. He'd asked why her mother couldn't have named her Sarah, and Sally had suggested that he ask her mother himself. She knew he never would. He considered her mother several castes below him—which she was, but he hadn't had to be so snooty about it. He'd spoken a few words to her at their wedding, but otherwise he'd pretended the woman didn't exist.

At least her mother wasn't a hypocrite. At least she didn't collect florid letters from a lover and hide them inside a brown sweater.

Todd opened another file on the disk. More phone numbers. "Who are all these people?" he wondered aloud.

"Clients?"

"Doubtful. He would have kept his clients' phone numbers with their files, not in a separate list."

Sally skimmed the list. "There aren't any female names on there at all," she observed. "I'll bet that's his alumni list from his old prep school. He was class something-or-other."

"Something-or-other?" Todd twisted in his chair to look at her.

"Vice president or secretary. I know he wasn't president. It really steamed him that he wasn't."

"All right." Todd pulled the diskette out of the computer and inserted another. When he loaded it, the screen filled with a blaze of color, and thumping music—drums followed by a noodly melody—emerged tinnily from the speakers flanking the monitor. "What the hell—?"

"It's a game," Sally guessed. "Arch-Enemies."

"You're kidding." Todd gaped at the monitor as the colors exploded with kaleidoscopic effect. "What was he doing with a computer game at work?"

Sally shrugged.

Through the speakers came the sound of a man howling in the final throes of some fatal agony. Todd removed that disk and inserted another. More pounding drums and a squeaky, whiny melody.

"Mommy?" Rosie hollered up the stairs. Her footsteps merged with the drumbeats. "Mommy, are you playing DragonKeeper?"

"Is that what this is?" Todd muttered.

Sally nodded and turned in time to see Rosie enter the room. "We're not playing it, Rosie. Daddy's friend just wanted to see what was on this diskette."

"I know how to play DragonKeeper." She darted to the desk, her eyes round and glowing rapturously as an animated dragon filled the screen, exhaling flames through its nostrils. "Press control and an arrow key," she instructed Todd. "It'll get you to the setup."

"I don't want to get to the setup," he told her.

"But it's a cool game. Set it up, Daddy's Friend. I'll show you." She didn't wait for Todd to follow her orders, but instead scrambled onto his lap and hit the control and arrow keys herself. The dragon disappeared, replaced by a screen of writing.

Todd peered helplessly at Sally. "Get her off my lap," he mouthed.

"She wants to play," Sally whispered.

"*I* don't want to play."

Sighing, she reached around Rosie's taut little tummy and hauled her onto her own lap. "No playing Drag-onKeeper. Daddy's friend needs to look at some more disks."

"But that's a great game," Rosie insisted. "It really is, Daddy's Friend."

"My name isn't Daddy's Friend," Todd growled at her. "It's Todd. Mr. Sloane."

"Todd Mr. Sloane? That's a silly name. You should just get rid of the mister part." Rosie arranged herself more comfortably on Sally's lap. Sally remembered when the little girl weighed only twenty pounds, or thirty. She weighed forty knee-crushing pounds now, but Sally still loved holding her on her lap.

Rosie handed Todd another diskette. "Try this one. I bet it's Dark Thunder."

He looked quizzically at her, then inserted the disk into the drive. Within three seconds, the title "Dark Thunder" filled the monitor. "How did you know that?" Todd asked, awe tempering his obvious irritation.

"These are Daddy's games," Rosie said. "He kept them in a little wooden box at work."

"He did?" Sally asked.

"How did you know that?" Todd asked simultaneously.

"He tol' me," Rosie answered with forced patience, as if she believed she was addressing two morons. "He tol' me he kept them hidden there. If you're not gonna play, I'll go back downstairs and draw some more. But it's really not fun without colors, Mommy. You didn't bring any crayons with you, did you?''

"I'm afraid not." She let Rosie slide down her legs to the floor.

Todd stared after her as she scampered out of the room, then turned back to Sally. "Maybe she knows about Laura."

"No," Sally said sharply. She'd already imagined that possibility, and it made bile rise in her throat. As venal as Paul had been, she refused to think he would have risked letting Rosie find out about Laura. "She knows about computer games because they're designed for immature children. Like Paul," she added spitefully.

"I think we should ask her about Laura."

"Absolutely not." Sally shook her head. "I don't want her being questioned about this disgusting situation."

"What makes you think it's disgusting? Maybe Laura was a classy lady."

"Sneaking around with another woman's husband? Real classy."

He leaned back, and his chair went with him, hinging backward until he was nearly reclining. "Maybe I can sneak back into his office and look around some more," he said.

"Why the hell should you care?" Sally asked, still fuming. "It's my problem. It's my pocketknife he gave her. It was my marriage that was a sham."

"Maybe my friendship with him was a sham, too," Todd said, seeming to struggle with the words. "Paul was like a brother to me, you know? We told each other everything. And he never told me this." He swiveled in the chair and straightened. The chair back straightened with him. "He had a good reason not to tell you about Laura. He had no reason not to tell me."

"Perhaps he didn't trust you," she said, knowing it was a mean thing to say but not caring. "Perhaps he thought it was none of your business."

"Well, you found those letters, and that made it my business."

"*Mine,*" she asserted. "*My* business. *I* found the letters."

"And I'll figure this thing out." He pondered for a minute, then frowned. "It bugs me. I think maybe there's a mistake, or—or maybe it was some fantasy thing. Maybe Laura doesn't even exist."

"The letters exist. And my knife is gone."

"You're sure about that?"

"I've searched everywhere it could be—and some places it never would be. It's nowhere."

"Maybe he gave it to Rosie."

"He gave a knife to his five-year-old daughter? Uh-huh."

Todd conceded with a nod. "Okay. Maybe he lost it."

"And maybe I'm the reincarnation of Catherine the Great." She snorted. "It was in a letter. She wrote about the knife. She described its *very vulgarity.* That's got to be the same knife I gave him. It's got to be."

"Okay." His eyes met Sally's, and for a flickering instant she thought, *Tina's right—he* is *cute.* That notion evaporated as soon as it formed. He was just a guy, as selfish as his supposed best friend, believing he'd been wronged more than she had. There was nothing cute about him, nothing at all.

"I want the letters back," she said.

"You'll get them back," he promised, pushing himself to stand. "As soon as I'm done with them, they're all yours."

"Whatever you find out I want to know. Because they *are* mine, even now. I want to know who Laura is. I want to know why Paul jeopardized our little girl's happiness because of her."

Again Todd opened his mouth and then shut it. He had thin, wide lips, she noticed. The kind of lips designed for slow, lazy smiles.

"Whatever you find out, I promise I won't blame you," she swore.

He looked dubious. "All right. Stay out of my way, though, okay? Let me handle this."

"Of course." Not a chance, she thought. No way was she going to stand idly by while Todd prowled through Paul's office, discovering information already well known to Sally's five-year-old daughter. No way was she going to let Todd steal her anguish, her quest for the truth...or her letters.

This was *her* disaster, not his.

Five

Officer Bronowski entered the New Day Café at his usual time, gaunt and towering in his crisp uniform. Sally shot a glance toward Tina, who was listlessly rinsing one of the stainless-steel coffee decanters. Circles rimmed her eyes, and her hair strayed from her barrettes and stuck out in weird tufts around her face. She must not have slept much last night. Either she'd been studying into the wee hours, or she'd been doing the horizontal two-step all night with Howard.

She made no move to get Officer Bronowski his daily coffee and pastry, so Sally sidled past her and faced the cop above the counter. Smiling, she said, "Good morning. What can I get you today?" as if this day were different from every other day and she had no idea what he might want.

"A cup of coffee, Mrs. Driver," Bronowski said in his dull, guttural voice. "And I think I'll try—is that an apple turnover?"

"Peach," Sally told him. "They're wonderful."

"All right. A peach turnover."

Still smiling, she plucked a tissue of wax paper from the box and lifted a turnover onto a plate for him. Then she filled a cup with the breakfast blend and poured in exactly the amount of cream Bronowski liked. He paid and nodded, and she nodded back, her smile refusing to quit as he crossed the room to a table near the window.

Paul had been wrong about him. He wasn't light in the trousers. He was reserved and maybe a little awkward, but she bet he had more horsepower in his engine than anyone named Howard.

Why was she thinking about men and horsepower? she wondered.

During the first weeks after Paul's death, she'd thought about sex constantly, about how she wasn't getting any, how she might not get any ever again—or at least for a while—because mourning came with its own set of rules, and one of them, she was reasonably sure, was that the bereaved widow wasn't supposed to think about sex, let alone pursue it in a productive way. But by the time a month had passed, her craving for sex had faded, and she'd recognized that it had been based more on having lost Paul than on being horny. Gradually, she'd grown accustomed to sleeping alone, waking alone, sharing her days with Rosie and then retiring to the bedroom she shared with no one.

She'd assumed that eventually, sex might seem like a reasonable option for her. Not right now, but in time, when the pain faded. Once she'd found the letters from Laura, however, she'd decided she hated men so much that doing without sex for the rest of her life seemed like a good idea.

So why was she thinking about it now? Why was she thinking about it in the context of Officer Bronowski, of all people? He was tall and gawky, with buzz-cut hair and a glum smile. Not her type.

Of course, Paul hadn't been her type, either. Before she'd met him, her taste had run to big, sloppy, teddy bear fellows who lacked the patience to make sure they were tidy and impeccable, men who believed that expertly tailored apparel and expensive hairstyles were a waste of money. She'd liked guys who weren't polished to a high gloss, who might be less than a hundred percent tactful, who said what they were thinking and backed up their words with actions.

Men with sexy chests.

Paul had had a sexy chest, she reminded herself—but when she closed her eyes and tried to picture it, she couldn't. All she could see was Todd with his shirt untucked and gaping. Todd, the tall, gruff jerk who thought he and he alone could track down his best friend's favorite pen pal.

"Tina?" Sally moved close behind her so she could speak softly. "Can you watch things for a few minutes? I want to make a phone call."

Tina sighed melodramatically and tossed down the damp cloth she'd been using on the decanter. "I suppose."

"What's wrong with you? You look like you didn't get enough sleep."

"I didn't." Her voice quivered with what sounded like sublime self-pity.

"Why not?"

She sighed again, a great, gusty puff of air that seemed to originate in the soles of her feet. "Howard told me he's planning to transfer to Dartmouth."

"Oh." Dartmouth was only a couple of hours away by car. Surely this wouldn't doom their relationship. "Any chance he'll get in?"

"I don't know. He's so smart. I don't know what I'll do if he goes to Dartmouth."

"You could date him long distance."

"But there are *girls* there. He's going to meet them and forget all about me."

"How can you say that? He loves you."

"If he loved me, he wouldn't want to transfer to Dartmouth." Tina fingered the cloth she'd been using to wipe the decanter. Her voice was still quivery, shimmering with wretchedness. "He says his father went to Dartmouth and always wanted him to go. But he rebelled against his father and wound up at Winfield College, instead. But now he says he's tired of being rebellious and he thinks he ought to honor his father's wishes."

It sounded as if Howard was a wimp, knuckling under to his father when he ought to be knuckling under to Tina. Sally's impulse was to tell Tina to forget about him, but forgetting him would be impossible. Every time she undressed, she'd have his name staring at her from her left boob.

"I'm sure you'll work it out," Sally said, although she was sure of no such thing. She would love to solve all Tina's problems for her, but right now she had her own problems to deal with. "Could you watch things for just a couple of minutes?"

"Yeah, sure. Bronowski's gonna want his refill in exactly 12.3 minutes. I'll be ready."

"I'll be back by then," Sally promised. "I'm just going to make a phone call." She patted Tina's shoulder, then hurried down the counter to the kitchen and through it to the closet-size office near the back door. Greta kept two file cabinets and a desk in there, everything clean to the point of sterility. Sally had been working at the café for three years before she learned that only one file cabinet contained business documents—billing records, tax records and the like. The other file cabinet contained nothing but recipes.

She entered the tiny office and bumped into the desk, which took up so much of the available space that it was nearly impossible not to bump into it. Hoisting herself up to sit on it, she reached around the computer for the phone and dialed the number of Paul's old office. On the second ring, Patty Pleckart answered. "Patty," she said, "this is Sally Driver."

"Oh. Hello," Patty said with all the enthusiasm of a corpse.

"I have a question for you."

"Uh-huh."

"Did Paul have any clients named Laura?" Sally might not be able to snoop around in Paul's office, but she thought Todd's hunch that Paul had met Laura through work seemed plausible.

"Why do you ask?" Patty said, suspicion oiling her tone.

Sally had worked out a story last night, lying wide-eyed in her bed and trying to figure out how to get information Todd had been unable to dig up. Now she answered Patty's question with well-rehearsed composure. "I just received a condolence card from someone named Laura. In her note she implied she'd known Paul in a professional capacity, and I wanted to send her a response. But the envelope got wet and her return address and last name were blurry so I can't read them." Did that sound as good to Patty as it had sounded to Sally at two in the morning?

"Oh. Well. Let me look."

Yes, it sounded good. Of course it did. Todd, the intrepid reporter, the muckraker, the only man in Winfield willing to take on city hall in the matter of sewer improvements, had failed in his mission. Sally might not be a newspaper editor with a degree from Columbia University and a shitload of connections in town, but she was obviously a lot smarter than Todd.

Patty put her on hold. She shifted on the desk, smoothing her paisley skirt under her. Sitting on the hard surface, she felt pressure on the bones in her bottom. She'd lost a few pounds in the past couple of months. All those flavorless, well-intentioned casseroles had suppressed her appetite.

Patty returned to the line with a click. "He had two clients named Laura," she reported. "Laura DelVecchio you probably know. She lives right here in town. She was at the funeral."

"Of course," Sally said, thinking, *Laura who?* She didn't remember half the people who'd clasped her hand and recited clichés about brilliance-struck-down-in-its-prime and how Paul was in a better place now—which, when Sally had thought about it, seemed kind of insulting, as if being dead was better than being married to her. If Laura DelVecchio had been among those mealymouthed mourners, Sally doubted she was the same Laura who had written Paul the letters. A woman having an affair with a married man wouldn't have been likely to shake Sally's hand and murmur platitudes in the funeral parlor. She'd have stayed away, or at least not introduced herself to the grief-stricken wife of her lover.

Nonetheless, Sally scribbled Laura DelVecchio's name on the message pad Greta left beside the phone. "I think it must be the other Laura," she lied smoothly, "because in her note she said she'd only just heard that Paul had passed away."

"Well, that would be Laura Hawkes, from Boston."

"Yes, that's it," Sally said with conviction.

Patty read off her address and Sally wrote it down. After abundantly thanking the secretary, she hung up and whooped a laugh. Take *that,* Todd, she thought. All his sleuthing had come up empty. But Sally's sleuthing had paid off. He could keep the damn letters as long as he wanted. She didn't need them to figure out who and where Laura was.

One simple phone call, and she was hot on the woman's trail.

He was standing on her front porch when she arrived home with Rosie a little after four o'clock.

As Sally steered her car up the street, Rosie spotted him and said, "Look, there's Daddy's Friend with the computer games. See, Mommy? On the porch."

Sally saw. Muttering a few juicy words, she jammed a little too hard on the brakes. But Rosie's safety seat held her securely in place.

"Did you use a swear, Mommy?" she asked.

"Of course not."

"It sounded like you said fuck."

"I didn't. And don't you say that word, either."

"What does it mean?" Rosie asked.

"It means, this is a word I should not say." Sally coasted to the house and into the driveway.

At least his shirt was buttoned and his hair was dry. It looked as if he had combed it several hours ago and then spent much of the intervening time standing in a wind tunnel. Dark waves tumbled over themselves in a wild mess that needed someone to tame it.

Actually, Sally preferred wild to tame. But not when it came to Todd or his hair. She didn't prefer anything about him.

She stopped the car and reminded herself to be courteous. He'd been courteous to her when she'd dropped by his home uninvited and interrupted his supper. And anyway, she had nothing to lose by being courteous. She was way ahead of him in the Laura race. She could be generous in victory.

She unfastened the buckle on Rosie's car seat and helped her out of the cushioned shell. Then she hauled her tote bag from the back seat and smiled politely at Todd. "Hi."

"Hi," he said. No sharp edge to his voice, no accusation in his gaze. No hostility in his loose-limbed posture.

He must have come to return the letters. He must have realized that Paul's betrayal of her was much greater than his betrayal of Todd, and he was going to do the gentlemanly thing and let her be the more aggrieved party.

"I was wondering if I could talk to you for a few minutes," he said, sounding almost friendly, even a little apologetic.

She liked this. She liked Todd minus his arrogance, Todd kissing up, Todd being obsequious. Not that asking her for a few minutes of her time was the same thing as throwing himself prostrate at her feet, but she liked it.

"Sure. Do you want to come in?"

"Thank you."

Todd being obsequious would likely grow nauseating after a while, she realized as she unlocked the door and led him inside. He didn't care for her. Never had, never would. If he was acting nice, it had to be because he wanted something from her.

"Did you win Dark Thunder?" Rosie asked as they gathered in the entry hall.

He peered down at her, obviously bemused. "What?"

"Dark Thunder. The computer game. Did you win it?"

"No." He must have sensed that Rosie needed a more elaborate answer than that, because he added, "I don't enjoy computer games."

"But you have them. That's stupid, to have things you don't even enjoy."

"Those were your father's games," Todd explained.

"Did you bring them here? I could teach you how to play them and then you'd enjoy them. I could teach you even if you're stupid. Lots of stupid people play them. Do you want an animal cracker? That's one of my favorite snacks, except for scones."

"Scones?" He shot an even more bemused look at Sally.

"I bring leftovers home from the café. Blueberry scones are her favorite." She headed down the hall to the kitchen to get Rosie some animal crackers. She supposed she should offer Todd a drink or something, too. He hadn't offered her anything at his home yesterday, but she could be more hospitable than he was. "Would you like a beer?"

The question seemed to stun him. He halted in the kitchen doorway, staring at her as if he wasn't sure who she was. She hoped he'd say no to the beer, because there were limits to how sociable she wanted to be—especially while he had the Laura letters in his possession. But she didn't regret having offered the drink, because it threw him off balance.

"No, thanks," he said. "I just wanted to ask you something."

She tossed her bag onto the table and pulled a box of animal crackers from the cabinet for Rosie. "Go ahead and ask," she said, setting the box on the table before Rosie.

His gaze circled the room, taking in the stained-glass

ornaments that hung on hooks suctioned to the window, the sun filtering through the tinted glass to spray multicolored light on the opposite wall. He continued his survey of the room, which was larger than his kitchen but furnished with older appliances. Several of Rosie's drawings were fastened to the refrigerator with magnets. A wicker basket filled with coupons, pencil stubs and scraps of string stood on the counter. The braided rug on the floor was slightly off center. Rosie had probably kicked it out of position when she'd scampered into the room.

"Do you wanna learn how to play DragonKeeper?" she asked before taking a lusty bite of one of the crackers. "I'm real good at that game, too. I'm prob'ly the best computer-game player I know, now that Daddy is dead."

"I can't believe your father was much of a computer-game player," Todd remarked. "He had too much important work to do."

Oh, yes. Important work, Sally thought, suppressing a snort. Important work like plugging people's names into boilerplate wills and proofreading real-estate sales contracts. And scheduling rendezvous with his paramour. Very, very important work.

Todd let his gaze settle on the doorway. Sally guessed that he wanted to leave the kitchen. To get away from Rosie, no doubt. If Sally had been feeling vindictive, she would have ignored his hint and made herself comfortable in the kitchen, forcing him to remain there, as well. But he'd been exerting himself to be nice, so she decided to exert herself, too. Kissing the crown of Rosie's head, she said, "Daddy's friend and I will be in the living room."

Todd gestured for her to precede him from the kitchen, and he followed her into the living room. Unlike his, it wasn't teeming with books and model cars. It was occupied by a collection of stuffed beasts—Rosie's menagerie—and enough potted plants to reforest large swaths of Brazil. Teeming with life and color, it was a much prettier living room than Todd's.

Sally settled on the sofa, and he perched on the ottoman in front of what had once been Paul's easy chair. Paul used to growl whenever anyone else sat in it, and for the first few months after he died, Sally hadn't been able to bring herself to use it. Once she'd found the letters, however, she'd happily slouched in it, desecrating it by propping sweating glasses of iced tea on the upholstered arms of the chair and resting her feet on the ottoman without removing her shoes first. Who cared? Her husband had defiled their marriage. She could defile his chair.

She watched Todd fold and unfold his thick fingers, tap his foot, scrub a hand through his hair. Then he offered a patently strained smile. "I was going through that list I found on one of the disks from Paul's office," he said.

"The list of his classmates from prep school?"

"I don't think they're from prep school," Todd told her. "I called a few of the numbers. I went oh-for-five. None of them prepped with Paul."

She tried not to look as curious as she felt. She was grateful to Todd for sharing this information with her, and it made her want to know more. "Who were they?"

"Other lawyers, mostly."

"Really? All those names?" Just a bit more proof that there were too many lawyers in the world. "Why was he storing their phone numbers on a disk?"

"I thought you might know."

She pondered the possibilities. "He wasn't serving on any American Bar Association committees," she said. "Maybe he was planning to run for office in the ABA."

"One of them said something..." He eyed her, as if trying to decide whether to share his information with her.

She gave him what she hoped was an ingratiating smile.

"He implied that Paul wasn't satisfied with his current position."

"You mean, he was thinking of leaving Wittig, Mott, Driver?" Sally fell back against the sofa cushions. A strange lump dug into the small of her back. Reaching behind her, she pulled Mr. Pinko, Rosie's stuffed baby pig, from where he'd been wedged into the upholstery and tossed him onto the floor with the other animals. "No," she said. "He would have told me if he'd been planning to leave the firm. He had no reason to want to leave. His home was here in Winfield. His family. His roots." But not his mistress. Laura Hawkes was in Boston.

Oh, God. Had he been planning to abandon her and Rosie? To move to Boston, join another firm and start a new life with Laura?

That Sally could have been living with him, sleeping with him, building her life with him while he'd been plotting under her nose to run off and join a new practice sent a ripple of horror through her. She already knew she'd been blind when it came to her husband; now she was learning she'd also been deaf and extremely dumb.

"Maybe he wasn't looking for another firm to join," Todd suggested. "There were at least fifty names on that list. Why would he be looking into fifty different partnerships? I think maybe the list was for something else."

She tapped her fingers together to burn off nervous energy. "Maybe it was a list of experts," she suggested. "Lawyers who'd tried certain kinds of cases. He might have wanted to have a list so if he ever faced a similar case he could call someone for help." As if he ever faced a case in Winfield that would have taxed his knowledge of the law. Oh, those wills and real-estate transactions! Bring on the courtroom powerhouses!

"Well, here's what I was wondering," Todd said, leaning forward and resting his elbows on his knees. "Maybe Laura is one of those names. I know, they were all men's names, and the few I called were men. But they could have been covering for Laura, or Laura could have been the partner of one of them. And she *could* have been on the list. Some of the names had just initials."

"Was there an 'L'?"

"No, but... Look, if he was having an affair that he didn't want anyone to know about, he'd disguise her name, wouldn't he?"

"By hiding it in a list of fifty other names? Or do you think he was having affairs with all fifty people on the list?" It was an outrageous charge. Paul didn't have enough energy to have that many affairs. Even as fit as he was, he'd never have been able to juggle fifty tootsies. He'd still been making love to Sally, after all. Sally plus Laura plus fifty more? No way.

"Or maybe Laura was the wife of one of them. Maybe they were lawyers he'd met at parties, and Laura was at one of the parties."

"If he went to parties, he didn't take me along," Sally told him. As happy as she'd been not to have to socialize with his business associates, now she wondered whether he'd been even happier. Without her by his side, he'd been free to hit on other women.

If he went to parties. Which, Sally was reasonably sure, he didn't. Not very often. Not in Winfield.

"I was really hoping you might be able to help me out here," he said. She didn't like the way Todd was looking at her. His eyes were too dark, too beseeching. She could imagine him asking for a bank loan, or wheedling information for a newspaper article out of the mayor, or inquiring if a sweet young thing might consider spending the night with him. With his dark, dangerously beautiful eyes, he probably had an easy time of enticing people into doing his bidding.

She wasn't a mayor or a loan officer, and she definitely wasn't a sweet young thing. Yet simply looking at him made her regret that she couldn't help him out.

She could. She could tell him about Laura Hawkes in Boston. She'd found out about Laura Hawkes herself, outinvestigating the investigative reporter with a fancy degree from an Ivy League school of journalism, the fellow with a million connections in town, the man who knew about everything and everyone, from the mayor to Joey the Crazy Guy, who stood on the corner of Main and East streets, playing a steel drum and improvising calypso songs about the pedestrians strolling past him, from the president of Winfield College to the locals who played pool all night in the neon-lit bars on the south side of town.

But he didn't know about Laura Hawkes.

Sally did.

He'd come to her hoping she could help him. If she wanted to, she could. If she thought about the fact that they'd both been deceived by Paul, and he did have that list and it might hold some vital piece of information that she might eventually need...

She could help him. If she felt like it. If she forgot how annoying it was to have him staring at her with those deep-set eyes, using them to seduce her into not hating him.

Or she could help him for the extremely selfish reason that joining forces with him might enable her to find Laura Hawkes more quickly and efficiently.

"All right," she said. She'd probably regret mentioning this once she thought about it, but she didn't feel like thinking about it anymore. She didn't feel like acknowledging that Todd had somehow gotten to her. She was tired—it had been a long day—and for some reason, she didn't have the strength to despise him right now. "I'm going to Boston this weekend to find a woman," she said. "Her name is Laura Hawkes, and Paul knew her, and maybe she's the one. If you want, you can come, too."

Six

Sally stood on her front porch, hands planted on hips, and glowered at his car. "You drive a Snob?"

"It's a *Saab*," he said, clamping a lid on his temper, "and I'm doing the driving today." He had to remember that she'd been extraordinarily generous in sharing her information with him—and letting him accompany her to Boston. But he'd be damned if he'd travel to Boston in her car. She drove a soup can on wheels, and if he was going to embark on a two-hour drive, particularly with her in the seat next to him, he wanted to make sure his transportation wouldn't conk out en route.

Her little girl pushed past her and scampered down the porch steps. "What a cool car!" she screeched.

Take that, Sally, he thought smugly. *Your daughter has better taste in cars than you.* And why shouldn't she? She carried Paul's DNA in every cell of her stumpy little body.

Sally descended from the porch at a plodding pace, disapproval emanating from her in nearly palpable waves. Todd stood resolutely beside his silver 900S. Three years old, it took as good care of him as he did of it. Its five-speed manual gave him the power he needed, and its leather seats gave him the comfort he deserved.

She frowned as she circled the car, scrutinizing its

slanting hatchback as if it were the devil's personal ski slope. "Well, if you insist on doing the driving, I'm going to have to get Rosie's car seat."

"Her what?" He spun around, searching for the little girl he'd fleetingly liked because she'd said nice things about his wheels.

"Her car seat." Sally yanked up the garage door and vanished inside.

"She's not coming with us, is she?" he shouted into the garage's shadows.

Sally emerged holding an object of molded plastic layered with padding in strategic places. "Of course she's coming with us. What did you think, I'd leave her home alone?"

"No. I thought you'd leave her home with a baby-sitter." *Like a normal person,* he added silently.

"She's coming with us," Sally said with finality. "Does that car of yours—" her nose twitched in disapproval when she uttered the word *car* "—have a tape deck or a CD player?"

"A CD player."

"Fine." Sally ducked back into the garage for a moment, then returned, still carrying the car seat. Her voluminous straw tote bag dangled by its straps from her forearm, and her broad-brimmed straw hat was going to block his side vision if she insisted on wearing it in the car. She also had on one of her billowy dresses, a soft blue shade that seemed to mirror the cloudless spring sky, white anklets and leather sandals.

He watched with increasing apprehension as she swung open the back door of his car, arranged Rosie's seat and set her straw hat on the leather upholstery next to it. "Okay, Rosie—hop in!" she hollered to the kid, who seemed to have vanished. "Rosie? Rosie!"

The girl darted into view from the side of the house. "I was just saying goodbye to Trevor," she explained as she climbed into the seat. Sally belted her into place and straightened up.

Todd felt trapped. Sure, she'd been generous, but that didn't give her the right to subject him to her child for a long drive. Especially when the child had on a stupid purple hat. What was it with these Driver women and their hats?

He was not a hat person. His hair was too thick. It felt clumpy under a hat—and when the hat was removed, his hair looked even clumpier. Sally's straw hat seemed to have had a negligible effect on her hair, which flowed down her back in long, undisciplined ripples of red-tinged brown.

She made herself ominously at home in the passenger seat, arranging her skirt, propping her tote on the floor beneath the glove compartment, smoothing the shoulder belt between her breasts and folding her hands in her lap. Shoving his misgivings to a vacant corner of his brain, he got in behind the wheel, revved the engine aggressively—just in case Sally had any questions about how powerful his beloved car was—and backed out of her driveway.

She's doing you a favor, he reminded himself. *She's cutting you in on her deal.* That fact only added to his irritation, however. It pissed the hell out of him that she'd gotten information from Patty Pleckart, information he'd failed to get. For God's sake, he'd been Patty Pleckart's lover in high school, more or less. Why had Patty given the answer to Sally and not him?

Either because he hadn't posed the right questions and Sally had, or else because his performance with Patty in high school had been so excruciatingly bad she was still punishing him for it all these years later.

"Where exactly in Boston are we going?" he asked.

"Just drive into town. We'll figure it out from there," Sally said.

Her vagueness stoked his dread. "I like to know where I'm going."

"I bet you never ask for directions, either." She twisted in her seat to check out the kid. "Are you okay, Rosie?"

"I'm bored," Rosie replied.

Terrific. They hadn't even reached the town limits, and Rosie was already bored. In another ten minutes, she'd probably be screaming at the top of her lungs. In fifteen, she'd be trying to climb out the window. Where was the child-lock button for the back-seat windows? He knew there was a switch somewhere that would prevent Rosie from opening them, but he had no idea where it was. Before today, the button had been irrelevant to his life.

Sally turned forward, dug through her bag and pulled out a compact disc. She scrutinized his dashboard and pressed the radio power button. "Good Vibrations" blasted through the rear speakers, causing Rosie to shriek.

He twisted the volume dial to a quieter setting. Obviously, the child's delicate eardrums couldn't withstand classic rock.

"You listen to The Beach Boys?" Sally asked incredulously.

"It's up to the deejay what I listen to," he said. He wasn't going to defend his choice in radio stations to her. She probably liked New Age stuff, gongs and bells and flute-voiced women chanting holistic gibberish. He loved rock. Any kind, old, new or in between. Every FM button on his car radio was set to a rock station.

If Sally's CD had gongs and bells and flute-voiced women on it, Todd was going to object, loudly and firmly.

She studied the radio's controls long enough to figure out how to make the CD tray slide out. "I hope you don't mind," she thought to mention before inserting the CD. He braced himself for gongs.

Instead he heard the strum of an acoustic guitar, and a chipper male voice embark on a cute, bouncy jingle: "I'm a porcupine and I'm okay, just as long as you stay away..."

"What the hell is that?"

"'Animal Sweet,'" she told him.

"What the hell is 'Animal Sweet'?"

"They sing songs about animals. Sweet is a pun—it's like the songs are a suite. S-U-I-T-E," she clarified, maybe for Rosie's sake. Todd was a newspaper editor; he knew how to spell.

They'd reached the Mass Pike. He had never in his life suffered from motion disturbance, but the prospect of driving east for the next hour and a half listening to songs about animals gave him an idea of what car sickness might feel like. "You'd rather listen to this than The Beach Boys?"

"It's Rosie's favorite CD."

"Rosie's taste in music sucks."

Sally glanced over her shoulder again, as if concerned that Rosie might have heard this unforgivable insult. She couldn't have heard it; she was singing along with the CD. "'I'm spiny and shiny and whiny sometimes, I'm sticky and tricky and prickly sometimes, and I'm a porcupine *all-l-l-l-l* the time!'" Her voice was lusty and painfully flat.

"She's only five," Sally whispered, turning back to him.

"You shouldn't have brought her along."

"She loves Boston."

"She's only five," he said, tossing Sally's words back at her. "How can she love Boston?"

Sally's fingers curled palmward and she pursed her lips. "The truth is, she's never been to downtown Boston before. It's important for children to visit cities. I never saw a city until I was fourteen—and the city was Albany, New York, so it hardly counted. I want my daughter to grow up exposed to different things."

So far, her daughter had been exposed to a flaky mother and a two-timing father. Compared with them, Boston was safe and dull. "You never saw a city until you were fourteen?"

"I never went anywhere."

"Why not?"

Sally sighed. "I wasn't..." Another sigh. He let his gaze stray from the highway long enough to catch a glimpse of her faint, wistful smile. "I wasn't raised the way you were. Or Paul. I grew up in a trailer behind my grandparents' house in a little podunk town forty miles from Albany. There was nothing to do there, nowhere to go. People watched television, they shopped at the local stores, and for excitement they tried to come up with ways to separate the tourists from their money."

"Tourists?"

"Trout fishermen. I grew up in trout country."

Trout country. He hadn't known such a thing existed.

"We had some of the finest trout rivers in the world running through our area. People would come from all over to fish. The local stores would overcharge them for everything. A ten-dollar hamburger. A five-dollar glass of beer.''

"It sounds like Boston," he commented. "Except for the trout."

"Anyway, I think Rosie should be raised with a broader perspective on things. She should know that a universe exists beyond Winfield, and it's hers to explore." Sally sighed yet again. "Besides," she said in a quieter voice, as if Rosie might hear over the cloying "Animal Sweet" music that filled the car, "I want this Laura person to see Paul's daughter. I want her to see what she was jeopardizing: the happiness of the sweetest, brightest, most vulnerable little girl in the world."

Sweet, bright and *vulnerable* were not words he would use to describe Rosie Driver. She struck him more as the kind of girl who believed the whole wide world existed for the sole purpose of giving her something to explore.

He sent another quick look Sally's way. A trailer dweller from trout country. Why hadn't he known this? Why hadn't Paul told him? Had Paul been afraid Todd would sneer?

He wasn't that narrow-minded, even if he did drive a Snob—a *Saab*. And he hadn't had to know about Sally's deprived background to sneer at her. He'd done ample sneering based on the assumption that she was a waitress who'd conned his best friend into marrying her. Which she was.

But never to have seen a city until she was fourteen? And then to lose her urban virginity to *Albany?* It was almost tragic.

They drove for a while in silence—or at least, as much

silence as could exist with "Animal Sweet" resonating from Todd's top-of-the-line Bose speakers. A new song began: "Why get a puppy when you can get a guppy?"

"This music is really bad," he muttered.

"I didn't have to tell you about Laura Hawkes," Sally reminded him just a touch defensively.

"If you'd gone into Boston alone, you would have botched it. You need me here with you to make sure the whole thing doesn't get fucked up."

"Number one, I don't need you here, there or anywhere. And number two, watch your language. Rosie's only five."

"I know how old she is," he retorted, though he silently pledged to avoid swearing around the kid. "And you do need me. Your car would have died somewhere west of Worcester. It's not fit for long-distance driving."

"How do you know that?"

"Paul told me."

"He told you my car wasn't fit for long-distance driving?"

"He told me it wasn't fit for a run to the supermarket."

"He never mentioned his concerns to me." She lapsed into thought for a moment. "Do you suppose he wanted my car to die on me?"

Good question. If Paul had been concerned enough about the condition of Sally's car to discuss it with Todd, why hadn't he discussed it with Sally? Why hadn't he suggested that she ditch the car and buy herself something more reliable? It wasn't as if they couldn't afford a new vehicle.

Had he wanted Sally to get stranded somewhere? Had he wanted her to wind up on the shoulder of a road, trying to flag down a passing motorist for help because her car had given up the ghost? What if she'd been picked up by a sicko, a demented road warrior looking for someone to rape and then slaughter? Was that what Paul had wanted for his wife?

Or had he simply been making snide jokes about her car—as Todd recalled, Paul had described it as something that might pass for a lawn ornament in certain less enlightened parts of Appalachia—as a substitute for making snide jokes about her?

Even without Laura added into the mix, Paul hadn't been a faithful, respectful husband to Sally. A faithful, respectful husband would have taken his wife to Kendrick Ford-Porsche-Toyota or Route-9 Buick-Audi-Mitsubishi and bought her a new car.

Todd suffered a twinge of sympathy for Sally—and disloyalty toward his friend. Fortunately, it passed before he could analyze it.

"Mommy, I'm hungry," Rosie shouted from the back seat, between verses about a cute newt in a camouflage suit.

"We're not stopping," he warned Sally.

"Of course not." Sally rummaged through her bag and removed a box of animal crackers. Amazing, he thought: the beasts Rosie didn't butcher with her ghastly singing she could butcher with her teeth. If she misbehaved during this outing, he'd report her to some fanatical animal-rights group. They'd know what to do with her.

"So what exactly is our plan once we get into the city?" he asked, trying to sift the emotion from his voice. He didn't want to be experiencing exasperation, pity or anything else in relation to the Driver women. Like the well-trained journalist he was, he preferred to remain dispassionate.

"Let's worry about getting there first."

"I'm not worried about getting there. I'm worried about what we'll do once we're there."

"Find a parking space, I suppose. The last time I was in Boston, that took over an hour."

"Why didn't you park in a garage?"

"I couldn't find any. We weren't in the downtown area. We were in a part of town called Brighton. Remember, Rosie?" she called over her shoulder.

Rosie was too busy singing along to hear her.

"Why were you in Brighton?" he asked Sally. He wasn't sure where Brighton was, except that it wasn't a neighborhood he'd ever bothered to visit while he was in Boston.

"I needed to buy some Chinese herbs. There's a fabulous shop in Brighton, Ying's Emporium."

Of course. Didn't everybody drive two hours to Boston so they could buy herbs at Ying's Emporium? "What were you going to do with those Chinese herbs?" he asked.

She opened her mouth and then shut it. From the corner of his eye he noticed a flush tinge her cheeks. "None of your business," she mumbled.

Curiosity rose like lava inside him, hot and thick. "Were you going to poison him?" he guessed, keeping his voice down in case the cute-newt ditty ended and Rosie heard them in the silence between songs.

"Of course not!" Sally whispered. "Why would I want to poison him?"

"Because he was seeing Laura behind your back."

"I didn't know about Laura until it was too late to poison him."

True. "So what did you need the herbs for?"

"A recipe."

"For what? Moo goo gai pan?"

Again her mouth flapped open and shut. Again her cheeks darkened. "A brew that was supposed to have...aphrodisiac qualities."

"Ah." He passed a sluggish eighteen-wheeler, then stole a look at her while he was checking his side mirror. She'd driven all the way to Boston to purchase ingredients for an aphrodisiac. She really must have wanted to turn Paul on. Maybe she'd sensed Paul withdrawing from her—saving his best stuff for Laura—and she'd hoped the aphrodisiac would help her win him back. Or maybe she'd wanted it for herself. Maybe her sex drive had evaporated, and that was why Paul had turned to another woman. Todd liked that explanation; it let Paul off the hook.

Only so much, though. It might justify Paul's having the affair, but not his refusal to tell his best friend about it. The guy was still a shit for locking Todd out of his life that way.

Besides, Todd wasn't a big fan of infidelity. He couldn't justify it, even if Sally had been frigid or aloof—which he couldn't imagine, given that she seemed to boast an overabundance of passion. Anger, indignation, aggressive self-certainty, maternal righteousness...passion.

He glanced at the slow truck he'd passed, now receding in his rearview mirror. He glanced at the buildup of traffic where the main feeder from Hartford and New York City merged with the Mass Pike, the blur of grass and trees lining the roadway, the signs warning of tolls, exits and rest stops—anywhere but at Sally. Surely she'd need more than a few Chinese herbs to turn herself into a love goddess. He tried to envision her in something slinky, but she wasn't a slinky woman. She had too many curves. A big bosom, a rounded ass, wide shoulders. All that voluptuous hair spilling down her back. He couldn't visualize her in a teddy, a garter belt, anything from the Victoria's Secret catalog. Maybe a satin robe, wine red, held shut by a sash around her waist. Nothing on underneath. Maybe first she'd take a hot, steamy bath in a tub full of scented oils—or Chinese herbs from Ying's Emporium. And then she'd sprawl out on a bed in that satin robe, and sip a cup of Chinese-herb tea, and shift her long legs...

She did have long legs. A less observant man might not have noticed, since she was always wearing shapeless below-the-knees dresses that did nothing to flaunt whatever assets she had. But judging by her stride and the sway of her hips, Todd could tell her legs were long. Long legs on a woman were his idea of an aphrodisiac.

Not that Sally had ever made him feel anything other than loathing. And pity, since she'd been shafted by her dead husband. And maybe a little kinship, since *he'd* been shafted by her dead husband, too.

And curiosity about the Chinese herbs. Okay. He'd cop to curiosity.

"How much longer till we get there?" Rosie asked. "I'm bored."

"You know, this music is really boring," he pointed out, aiming his comments at Rosie even though he couldn't look at her. "How about if we listen to some rock and roll? You like rock and roll?"

"I like Nirvana," she said.

There was hope for the kid. "Open the glove compartment," he ordered Sally. "There's a Nirvana CD in there."

"I don't like Nirvana," she muttered.

"You've been outvoted," Todd informed her, wondering if the music they'd been listening to had been her choice and not Rosie's all along.

By the time they passed the I-495 exit, Todd and Rosie were singing along to "Polly Want a Cracker." Rosie faked most of the words, which was probably just as well.

Sally excavated in her tote bag until she found a pair of sunglasses, and slid them on. They were elliptical and nearly opaque, and they lent her an unexpected glamour. The next song came on, and when he kept silent he could hear that Rosie was definitely faking the lyrics—but that was all right. Let her fake it while he contemplated the woman at his side, a woman who brewed X-rated potions and wore chichi sunglasses. A woman who refused to relinquish her dignity, such as it was, even after her husband had betrayed her.

A woman who didn't like Nirvana, he reminded himself.

They passed through the final tollgate. Boston's skyline loomed, a silhouette of dark gray towers that, from a distance, offered little to distinguish it from most other midsize cities. He knew once they got into downtown Boston that perception would change. The bland, boxy skyscrapers camouflaged a world of redbrick and brownstone, arching trees and street lights that resembled gas lamps, convoluted roadways designed three hundred fifty years ago as cow paths, mass-transit trains that borrowed the public streets and stopped at the red lights, then vanished into underground tunnels. Boston was a quirky city, and he appreciated its quirks.

He didn't like getting lost in it, however. "Where are we going?" he asked, hoping that now that they were breathing city air, Sally would clue him in on their destination.

She reached back into the maw of her tote bag, rattled some chains and hubcaps inside it, and produced a small notepad, which she flipped open. "Mount Vernon Street," she said.

"You wouldn't happen to know where that is, would you?"

"Boston," she told him. When he shot her an impatient look, she shrugged innocently. "Well, what could I do? Telephone the woman and ask for directions? She'd want to know why we were coming to see her."

"You could have concocted a lie."

"Paul was the liar in our family, not me," she muttered too softly for Rosie to hear.

"Of course," Todd scoffed. "You never lie, and 'Animal Sweet' is better than The Beach Boys. How did you get the scoop on this Laura person from Patty Pleckart, anyway?"

Sally pursed her lips and turned to stare out the windshield.

"Lied through your teeth," he guessed. She'd lied better than he had, too. His lie about wanting to surround himself with Paul's aura hadn't bought him more than a few computer games and that mysterious list of names and phone numbers. He wondered if Laura Hawkes's number was on the list, if her life intersected with Paul's computer diskettes in any way.

"There are lies, and there are tactics." Sally's voice was gritty. "Paul lived a lie. All I did was employ tactics to uncover the truth."

He knew the difference between Paul's lying to his wife—and lying by omission to his best buddy—and Sally's lying to Patty Pleckart. But he felt like giving Sally a hard time, if only to honor Paul's memory.

He'd been listening to Paul give Sally a hard time

from the day they wed—or, more accurately, from the morning Sally had confronted Paul with the news that she was pregnant. During their regular get-togethers at Grover's for drinks after work, Paul would tell Todd about Sally's rattletrap car, her lack of common sense, her sprout-and-tofu recipes, her inability to grasp intellectual concepts more complicated than the daily horoscope published in the *Valley News* and her insistence on hanging some sort of yarn contraption on the wall above Rosie's bed because she thought it would influence the kid's dreams. Todd had had trouble following Paul the evening he'd described the yarn thing, but then, Todd had consumed more than his usual quota of beer that night. He would have had trouble following a supermodel into a bedroom.

None of which mattered right now. More important than truth, more vital than tactics, he needed to know where Mount Vernon Street was. "Maybe you should have just called Laura and come clean with her," he said, thinking that would have been preferable to meandering aimlessly among the perversely twisting, weaving, shape-shifting streets of downtown Boston.

"If I'd come clean with her, she wouldn't have agreed to meet with me. I want to see her," Sally said.

The city was dead ahead, rising around the turnpike. "There's a map of Boston in the door pocket," he said, gesturing toward her door. "See if you can find Mount Vernon Street."

She removed her sunglasses and hooked them over the curved neckline of her dress. Then she wrestled with the map, unfolding and refolding it, shaking it smooth, propping it against the dashboard, smoothing a crease and squinting at the mesh of lines marking the streets of the city. "Use the key," he suggested.

"I know how to read a map." Her squint pleated her forehead. She tilted the map, angled it to catch the sunlight blasting through her window, flipped it over and found the key. "Mount Vernon Street," she murmured, running an unpolished fingernail down the column of teeny print. "Okay...Mount Vernon Street." She flipped the map over again, a production of rattling and flopping, the unwieldy folds drooping against her knees, hitting the glove compartment, blocking half the windshield until she smoothed the paper and got it to lie reasonably flat. "Okay. It's right here. Near—" she squinted and rotated the map, hitting his hand with it. He shoved it back at her and checked his knuckles to make sure he hadn't suffered a paper cut "—the State House."

"The State House." He sort of had an idea where that was. He'd been there a few times, most recently a year ago at the invitation of the state assemblyman who represented Winfield, a bombastic, overweight fellow whose chief qualifications for office, as far as Todd could tell, were that he knew all four verses of "The Star Spangled Banner" and was on a first-name basis with everyone in the Rotary Club and the Winfield Chamber of Commerce.

"There must be a parking garage somewhere near the State House," she said.

"There must be." If only he knew where. "What's the nearest exit?"

She squinted at the map some more. "I think you have to go north on this road here." She nudged the map toward him.

He wasn't going to read a map while navigating through the rapidly thickening traffic. "What road?"

"I-93."

"I'm starving," Rosie wailed from the back seat.

"We'll have some lunch as soon as we get there," Sally assured her.

"Get where?"

"Boston."

They were already there, in Boston, wedged into a tight mass of nearly motionless cars. The clogged traffic made Todd lose his appetite. But who cared whether he wanted lunch? This was Sally's show, Sally and Rosie's. He was just the chauffeur.

By choice, he reminded himself, nudging his car forward, feeling adrenaline singe his nerves as a fat black SUV dared to cut him off. He'd felt grateful when Sally had included him on this outing, and he'd volunteered to drive. If the ladies wanted to eat, eating was what they'd do.

He took the first exit he saw, only because the bumper-to-bumper stuff was making him itch. Someone honked at him. He honked back. The light ahead was red, and three cars ignored it, speeding through the intersection. By the time he reached the corner, the light had turned green. He wondered if he ought to stop.

"There's a garage sign." Sally extended an arm across the front of his face, missing his nose by a millimeter. "See?"

He saw. He also saw that the road he was on was one-way the wrong way. He searched for a turnaround and followed a car coasting through a red light. Someone honked at him as he coasted through the red light, too.

He didn't care. He and his Saab were going to reach that garage. They were going to get a spot, even if there was only one spot left in the entire six-story structure and he had to duel another driver to the death for it. He was going to triumph over the eternal damnation of Boston's roadways and *park*.

Actually, the garage contained a fair number of empty spaces—probably because the obscene parking fees scared away anyone lacking a six-figure income or a sizable trust fund. Before he could turn off the engine, Rosie had unstrapped herself from her booster seat and swung open the door, nearly banging it against the Mercedes parked in the adjacent space.

"Watch it!" he warned her—too late. She was already out of the car, scampering across the concrete, endangering herself even more than the metallic silver finish of his Saab's door.

Sally shot out of the car after her, moving with surprising swiftness. No doubt she'd had lots of practice snagging her runaway daughter—but he was still awed by the speed with which she ringed an arm around Rosie's waist and swooped her off her feet. Like a calf roper at a rodeo, she restrained her wild daughter. And she didn't even need a lasso.

Sighing, he climbed out, flexed his knees to uncrick them and rolled his head from side to side to loosen the muscles in his neck. Sally and Rosie trooped back to his car, laughing as if Rosie's having bolted out into the potential path of cars had been a game. He would have cursed, but he'd resolved to keep his language clean around the kid.

Sally reached into the car for her tote bag and her wide-brimmed hat. Straightening, she met Todd's gaze. She was smiling, a broad, breezy smile that he suspected was left over from her romp with Rosie. "Let's go get some lunch," she said brightly.

And then they would locate Laura Hawkes, and they would torture her until she confessed her affair with Paul and explained why Paul had neglected to tell Todd about the relationship. "He was afraid it would place you in a moral quandary, and he wanted to spare you that," she would say, or, "He'd intended to tell you, Todd, because you were his very best friend, but I begged him not to. I didn't want anyone to know. Please, blame me not him."

After which he and Sally would go home and live happily ever after. At least he would. Sally could decide for herself what state of mind she wanted to live ever after in.

They walked through the echoing garage to the door leading out to the street. "I know where we are!" Sally boasted. "That open-air place with the jugglers and musicians. What's it called?"

All Todd knew was that it wasn't called Mount Vernon Street.

Rosie seemed enraptured, not just by the noise and bustle of the city, the density of the traffic, the neck-craning heights of the buildings and the masses of pedestrians clogging the sidewalks, but by her mother's words. "Jugglers and musicians? I wanna see!" She nearly broke free of her mother and darted into the street, but Sally was apparently ready for this breakaway. She locked her hand around the girl's wrist and held her on the sidewalk.

"Quincy Market," she remembered. "When I was at Winfield College, I once spent a few days in Boston with a classmate. Her parents lived in Brookline, and we stayed at their house and took the T into the city every day. Spring break."

Todd recalled the spring break he and Paul had spent in the Bahamas. Paul's parents had rented a villa for the boys on Cable Beach. All Todd had had to pay for was his airfare.

Spending a week on Nassau was little different from

spending a couple of days in Boston. It was one thing to think of Sally as a hick from the sticks, and another to think of himself as a pampered member of the bourgeoisie. Oddly enough, she seemed to have more vivid memories of her big vacation in Beantown than he had of his in the Bahamas. He recalled getting a nice tan, visiting a casino, picking up some bikini-clad babes from Duke University on the beach and having a good time. But he didn't glow in reminiscence.

Sally was glowing. "I remember seeing a fabulous one-man band here," she told Rosie, who obediently clung to her mother's hand and gazed up at her as they waited for the light at the corner to change. "He played a banjo with his hands and wore a harmonica on a brace around his neck. And he created a contraption out of two guitars, with foot pedals that worked another pick so it strummed across the guitars. The pedals also controlled a bunch of percussion. You know what percussion is, Rosie, don't you?"

"Banging on stuff. Will he be there today?"

"I don't know, honey. It was a long time ago. But I bet there'll be musicians."

"What about the jugglers?"

"I hope so." Swept across the street in a throng of pedestrians, Sally and her daughter surged ahead of Todd. He hurried to catch up, wondering why he felt envious of Sally's enthusiasm over a street musician she'd heard years ago.

As they entered the sprawling outdoor plaza of Quincy Market, he recalled his own visits to this place. The last time had been about a year ago, when he'd been in town for a journalism conference and everyone had escaped the hotel for lunch in the open-air arcade. His memory was of cheap food at posh prices, pigeons grubbing for scraps around the outdoor tables, shoppers racing in and out of high-end boutiques and a bizarre life-size sculpture of an erstwhile Boston Celtics coach seated on a park bench.

"We'll get some food here," Sally was telling Rosie when Todd caught up to them. "There's a food court here somewhere. In that building, I think. This is all very historical, Rosie. All these buildings are very historical."

Todd didn't think the Warner Brothers boutique was especially historical, with its bronze castings of Daffy Duck and Bugs Bunny guarding the door. The Starbucks didn't look too historical, either. And he couldn't recall Crate and Barrel having much to do with the American Revolution—unless maybe they'd supplied the crates and barrels that had held the tea tossed overboard during the Boston Tea Party.

Sally and Rosie surfed a wavelike swarm of people into the building Sally had identified as the very historical food court. Todd was tempted to let them vanish from his sight. He didn't like the edgy emotion he was feeling in her presence—not just that inexplicable envy but something else, something beyond his usual irritation with her. Something about her silly hat and her exuberance. It pinched him, stung, made him want to turn around, head back to the overpriced garage and drive away.

But while he had access to the car, Sally had access to Laura Hawkes's address. And if he abandoned Sally and the kid in Quincy Market—even if he swore it wasn't his fault, they'd simply been pulled away from him by the crowd's undertow—Sally would never share information with him again.

Hell, she'd never even talk to him again. He weighed

the pluses and the minuses and decided to follow her into the food court.

Aromas of world cuisine clashed in the air as he worked his way through the crowds mobbing the food stands that lined the building's central walkway. Fried dough. Souvlaki. Pizza. Bagels. Dim sum and dough-nuts, chicken soup and chop suey. If the U.N. were crossed with a coronary victim's stomach contents, this food court would be the likely result.

"Rosie wants tempura!" Sally hollered to him above the din of reverberating voices. "I think there's a tem-pura place at the other end!"

"I want pizza," he said, mostly because the pizza place was at this end.

"Let's meet by the door!" she shouted, gesturing to-ward the door where they'd entered and then spinning away, her flamboyant hat all he could see of her.

He waited in line to buy two rubbery slices of pizza and a large Coke. There was a better pizza place in Win-field. There was probably a better pizza place in Cal-cutta—which this place filled with hungry, grasping hordes reminded him of. He grabbed a stack of napkins and a straw and retreated to the doorway, scanning the crowds for Sally's bobbing hat. If only Rosie had wanted pizza like a normal five-year-old, they could have been devouring their food by now and figuring out the quick-est route to Mount Vernon Street.

But no, she had to have tempura.

The door opened behind him. "Here we are," Sally announced from the steps outside. "It was easier to walk around the building than to try to plow through all those people. There's an empty bench here. It's so beautiful out. Let's enjoy the sun."

Todd didn't want to enjoy the sun. He wanted to hear

Laura Hawkes explain why Paul hadn't told him the truth, and then he wanted to go home.

Rosie clearly didn't want to go home. She scampered ahead of her mother, who was balancing a cardboard tray of goodies, and searched the plaza for a one-man band. "Where did he stand, Mommy? Was he over there?"

"He was sitting," Sally informed her, settling onto a bench, balancing the tray beside her and unslinging her tote from her arm. "Come eat your tempura, Rosie." She slid along the bench to make room for Todd. "What did you get?"

"Pizza." He slumped onto the bench, as far from her as he could sit, and scowled at the limp slices on his paper plate.

"How could you buy pizza? They had so many exotic foods." She carefully pried off the lid of a cylindrical container. "I got chowder. The guy who served me called it 'chowdah.' Chowdah," she repeated, obviously savoring the sound.

"Look!" Rosie shrieked, prancing in front of the bench and pointing across the plaza, where a crowd had formed. Above the crowd a woman in a clown's baggy, colorful satin costume perched on a towering unicycle, juggling a bowling pin. Actually, Todd wasn't sure it could be called juggling when only one bowling pin was involved. She threw it up, caught it, wiggled to and fro on the unicycle and tossed the bowling pin into the air again, watching it spin end over end and then drop into her hand.

"Eat your tempura," Sally urged her.

"I wanna watch the juggler!"

"Eat your tempura while you watch the juggler."

"I wanna go over there." She pointed at the crowd.

"Eat first."

"I'm not hungry," Rosie declared.

To her credit, Sally refused to indulge her. "Eat first," she repeated, handing Rosie a cardboard plate that held several deep-fried slabs of something and a small cup of black liquid.

Poking out her lower lip, Rosie accepted the plate. She took a reluctant bite of tempura.

"I can't believe how beautiful it is," Sally remarked, beaming at the cloudless sky above them, the pricey shops, the throngs of people who'd escaped the neighboring buildings for their lunch hour and were sucking on ice-cream cones, slurping gourmet coffee and wrapping themselves in the mild spring air. If Todd lived in Boston, he'd probably want to get outside during his lunch hour, too. Except that outside in Boston was about as refreshing as inside in Winfield.

Sally sipped her chowder, scooping the milky fluid with a plastic spoon. "I think we'll be able to walk to Mount Vernon Street from here," she predicted.

"How far is it?"

"Rosie, stop bouncing around while you eat." She turned to Todd. "On the map it was only a couple of inches."

He'd seen maps on which an inch represented ten miles. "I didn't plan on this trip being an all-day excursion," he reminded her. "I want to find this woman, talk to her and go home."

"We're here and we might as well make the most of it. Okay," she addressed Rosie with a nod. "You can watch the juggler now. But don't wander off."

Rosie dropped her plate onto the bench between Sally and Todd and raced across the plaza, her shoelaces glittering as the sun struck them. They must have had metallic threads in them.

Todd eyed Sally warily. Her hat threw a semicircular shadow over the upper half of her face, but he could see her eyes. She'd hung her sunglasses over the neckline of her dress again, and their weight tugged it down, revealing a swatch of honey-colored skin, smooth above the curve of her breasts.

She wasn't beautiful. Not even pretty. Not his type, anyway. But he could see why, in a moment of brainlessness, Paul might have been attracted to her.

"I don't want to walk ten miles to see this woman."

"I'm sure it isn't ten miles." She swallowed some more soup and smiled. "Mmm. This is so good. I've been talking to Greta about whether we ought to serve soup at the New Day Café during lunchtime. We sell sandwiches, but soup…I don't know. What do you think?"

Why was she asking his advice about her coffee shop? Before last week, he'd never even been inside the place. He had no idea who Greta was, let alone whether soup would sell well.

"Especially in the winter," she went on. "I don't think we could make chowder this good, but maybe a nice hearty vegetable soup. I'll have to think about it." Her smile waned. "I used to ask Paul stuff like that. He had good ideas sometimes."

"He also had bad ideas," Paul pointed out, because it made him uncomfortable to hear her say nice things about the son of a bitch.

"Screwing around with Laura was a bad idea," Sally agreed somberly. "Giving her my knife was an even worse idea. I want to get my knife back, Todd. That's one of the main reasons I want to see Laura—to get my knife back."

He grimaced. He hadn't counted on her confronting

The Other Woman and demanding her knife. God knew, it could turn into a fight. Weapons might be drawn—a tacky pocketknife, a sharp hairpin. Blood might be shed. *His* blood, if he wasn't careful.

Why had he wanted to come on this stupid trip? He was going to wind up trapped between Paul's two women, at least one of them armed with a cheap knife. He visualized his obit as it would appear in the *Valley News*. Front page, above the fold, given that he was the newspaper's head honcho: Brilliant Editor Cut Down in His Prime: Winfield's Favorite Son Mortally Wounded in Battle of Bitches.

"So what's the plan?" he asked. "We eat, we hike ten miles, you get your knife back and then we head back to Winfield?"

"It's not ten miles."

"We don't know how far Mount Vernon Street is from here."

"We can walk to the Public Garden. It'll be pretty. Don't they have those bird boats there?"

"The Swan Boats," he said. They were paddleboats with large carved swans decorating them. Tourists took rides in them. Bad enough he and the Drivers were wasting time at Quincy Market; he didn't want to waste time on the Swan Boats, too.

"Rosie would love a ride on one of those boats. Oh, let's do that, Todd."

"Sally, we're here on a mission—"

"And that mission will be accomplished, whether or not we take a boat ride. How often do any of us get to Boston? Rosie's never been on a Swan Boat. If her father had ever taken her to Boston, he would have made sure she took a boat ride. She doesn't have a father anymore, so it's my job to make sure she gets a boat ride."

Despite her smile, he saw a shimmer of tears in her eyes. Grief over her loss? A widow's despair? More likely the flash of sorrow was on her daughter's behalf.

Todd downed the last of his pizza crust and washed away the starchy flavor with a swig of Coke. ''If you're really serious about yachting around the Public Garden, let's get moving. We've got a long trek ahead of us.'' He sounded gentler than he'd expected, but he couldn't seem to force impatience into his voice.

''I'm sure it's not that long a trek. Maybe a mile at most. Probably less.'' She crumpled her napkin and stuffed it into the empty tub from her chowder. He glanced toward the crowd where the juggler on the unicycle was performing.

Rosie was gone.

Seven

"Todd, calm down," she said, moving in easy strides toward the mass of onlookers who stood in a tight circle around the clown. Rosie was inside that circle. She'd wormed her way to the front so she could see the clown better. Sally knew her daughter liked to be as close to the action as possible. She could easily see the bright purple of Rosie's hat in the throng.

But Todd was frantic. The instant he'd glanced toward the crowd and gasped, all the color seeping from his face as he vaulted to his feet, she'd realized that nothing she said would reassure him. He wouldn't stop panicking until she had Rosie in her arms.

"She just disappeared," he ranted. "Just like that! What if she...? What if someone...?"

"Don't worry. I can see her," Sally murmured, deftly threading a path through the crowd to where the pint-size girl in the purple hat was standing, her head tilted back and her eyes round with rapture as she watched the clown. "She's right there, Todd." He was worrying that Rosie had gotten lost or been snatched by a kidnapper; Sally was worrying only that Rosie would become so obsessed with juggling clowns on unicycles she'd want to become one herself. She would pester Sally relentlessly about getting a unicycle. When Sally refused to buy her one, she would sneak into the garage one weekend morning while Sally was sleeping late and break her old tricycle into pieces so she could convert it into a unicycle. She would cut up her pajamas in an attempt to fashion a clown costume. She would take to tossing apples in the air, trying to juggle them, and they'd drop to the floor and get bruised, and then she'd refuse to eat them.

Not that Sally had anything against her daughter's becoming a clown, or a juggler, or both. When she was a little older, though. Maybe after she had a year of first grade under her belt.

"Sally—Sally, she's..." Todd continued to babble, his voice somehow reaching her ears through the dense swirl of city sounds—traffic, chatter, footsteps against the patterned brick and cement expanse of the square. "What if she's gone? Boston is a huge city. She could be—"

She could be on Mars for all the attention she paid her mother or Todd or anyone else besides the clown. Just as Rosie filtered out everyone else, Sally filtered out everyone other than her daughter up ahead of her and Todd behind her, his anxious words reaching her as if he was connected to her on a private phone line.

At last she got close enough to snag Rosie's hand and tear her from her reverie. Rosie turned, her expression a mixture of awe at the performance and vexation that her mother was interrupting. "We have to go now," Sally said briskly, hauling her through the crowd and catching Todd's arm with her free hand as she met up with him. She pulled them both clear of the congregated spectators, then loosened her hold on Todd.

"See? She's fine," she said.

"I thought—" He let out a long breath. His eyes still had a wild fear in them, dark yet gleaming, like black patent leather. He swallowed a few times and his shoulders relaxed. Through his forest-green shirt and tweedy brown blazer she could see the shift in his body, the easing of his muscles as tension lost its grip on him.

She wanted to laugh at him for becoming so unnecessarily frightened. But more than amused, she was touched by his concern. She had a clear sense that he wasn't exactly infatuated with Rosie, yet he'd been as upset by her presumed disappearance as a doting relative might have been.

That he cared so deeply for her safety was really sweet. If Sally ever called him sweet, though, she suspected he would consider it an insult. So she kept her thoughts to herself.

Rosie seemed unaware that she'd caused alarm. "I'm hungry," she announced. "Can I get an ice cream?"

"Maybe later. You just ate all that tempura. And anyway—" Sally glimpsed Todd's tight mouth, his still-glinting eyes "—we've got to go someplace now."

"Where? I wanna see the one-man band."

"He's not here today," Sally said. "Let's take a walk."

"Can I eat ice cream while we walk?"

"No." Still gripping Rosie's hand, Sally nodded at Todd. "Shall we?"

A little more tension seemed to leave him, but his lips remained taut, his jaw set. He should have worn a hat; the sun was glaring bright and he didn't even have any sunglasses. What if he got a sunburn? She knew Mount Vernon Street wasn't ten miles away—ten miles would take them well out into Boston's suburbs—but even a mile's walk under such a bright sun could leave a person with a pink, peeling nose.

Sally wasn't his mother. She could make sure Rosie

wore sunblock and a hat, but Todd was responsible for his own health. If he burned, he burned.

Festive kiosks lined the plaza on one side. Rosie's head swiveled toward them and remained in that position, her eyes taking in all the offerings. One kiosk was devoted entirely to Red Sox paraphernalia, another to bonsai plants, another to stained-glass-window ornaments. Sally's attention skewed to that one. She had eight ornaments suctioned onto her kitchen windows. She couldn't really add more without making the room resemble a secular cathedral, but why limit the stained-glass ornaments to the kitchen? Paul was dead. Who was going to complain if she stuck a few ornaments on the living-room window?

Before she could stop to study the kiosk's offerings, Rosie gave her arm a yank and headed for another kiosk. "Look, Mommy! Look, Daddy's Friend!"

Sally looked. The kiosk was draped with beaded necklaces, each holding a small pendant of clear glass. Inside the glass was something small.

"Rice," Rosie said.

Sally lifted a necklace and scrutinized the glass bubble. Inside it was a grain of rice with writing on it. The curve of the glass container magnified the writing: "Betty."

"I want one!" Rosie demanded.

"You want a necklace that says Betty?"

"I want one that says Rosie."

The fellow manning the booth was short, and his snug T-shirt clung to muscles that would have looked more proportional on someone twice as tall. "I can make one that says Rosie," he said.

"Make one?"

"I write on rice. You want one that says Rosie?"

He wrote on rice. Sally was momentarily distracted by the understanding that this man had actually trained himself to master such a bizarre skill. What sort of intelligence would inspire a person to take up the craft? Had he once been looking for something to doodle on and a grain of rice had been lying in front of him, beckoning? Or had he consciously plotted a course that would lead to virtuosity in rice inscription? Had he started out on lima beans, and then moved on to kernels of corn, and then flakes of oatmeal?

"Sally," Todd murmured from behind her.

She peered over her shoulder. "I know. You want to get to Mount Vernon Street."

"It's not just that. It's..." He gestured toward the rows of beaded necklaces hanging from hooks beneath the kiosk's roof. "It's rice."

"He actually writes on the rice. Here, look." She handed him the necklace that said Betty.

"And some people see the Virgin Mary in a cheese Danish. Let's not waste time on this."

"Please, Mommy?" Rosie begged from Sally's other side. "He'll make me one that says Rosie."

"I might even have a Rosie one already made," the muscleman said helpfully, pawing through the strands of necklaces in search of a grain of rice with Rosie written on it.

"I want you to make one special for me," Rosie asked. "Okay? Okay, Mommy?"

She wasn't whining, wasn't wheedling. Rosie didn't whine or wheedle. When she wanted something, she asked for it directly, simply. Sally admired that about her. "How long will it take?" she asked the muscleman.

"A few minutes. I work fast." He used a pair of

tweezers to pluck a single grain of rice from a jar on the kiosk shelf.

Sally gave Todd an ingratiating smile. The sun was directly overhead, and he lowered his lids against the glare. The skin at the outer corners of his eyes folded into tiny creases. "A few minutes," she repeated the muscleman's promise. "He's going to write Rosie's name on a piece of rice."

Todd seemed at a loss for words. And truly, what could he say? What could anyone say about such a thing?

"Maybe he'll make one for you, Daddy's Friend," Rosie suggested, then recited to the muscleman, "Todd Mr. Sloane. Can you fit that all on a piece of rice?"

"Don't bother," Todd muttered, digging his hands into his pockets and turning to stare at the pedestrians strolling past, those fortunate souls making progress toward their destinations, unrestrained by a demanding child who wanted a novelty necklace.

He looked a little haggard to Sally, as if he hadn't quite recovered from his earlier scare. Sally wondered whether she should have been scared, as well, whether her failure to panic at Rosie's sudden disappearance meant she was a bad mother. But she knew Rosie. She would never voluntarily go off with a stranger, and if a stranger tried to snatch her, she'd scream bloody hell and probably bite the stranger, too. When it came to Rosie, Sally knew what to worry about, and what not to.

Even so... Todd's expression right now—impatient, exasperated, annoyed—reinforced her assumption that he wasn't overly fond of Rosie. Yet if he didn't like Rosie, he wouldn't have been so distraught when she'd momentarily slipped from their view.

"There, see? Just a few minutes." The muscleman

had been bowed over a magnifying glass with a light attachment, one of those stand-alone models that Sally had seen in doctors' offices to aid doctors in their examinations of splinters, infected cuts and toenail fungus. The man used his trusty tweezers to lift the rice grain he'd been working on, dropped it into a glass bulb and fastened the bulb to a beaded necklace. "There you go. That's twenty dollars."

"The sign says twelve dollars." Sally pointed to the price list above his cash register.

"This was custom-made."

"Custom-made? You said you had a Rosie rice already made. If we'd bought that one, it would have been twelve bucks."

"But you didn't buy that one."

"Because you couldn't find it."

"And your daughter said she wanted me to make one just for her. Right, Rosie?" he asked, dangling the necklace in front of her.

Rosie earned a few points by pressing her lips together and peering up at Sally, rather than confirming the muscleman's story and grabbing the necklace. "In other words," Sally persevered, "if you'd made this necklace ten minutes ago, it would have been twelve dollars. But because you made it while we stood here—promising you a guaranteed sale—it's going to cost twenty dollars."

"Because it's custom-made," he insisted.

Todd hauled his wallet from the hip pocket of his khakis and handed the guy a twenty-dollar bill. "Let's just go, all right? Rosie, take the damn necklace and let's go."

Sally wanted to protest. The man had ripped them off for eight dollars—and even if he hadn't, the necklace ought to have been her expense, not Todd's. Rosie was her daughter, after all.

But he was already striding away, Rosie trotting to keep up with him while simultaneously easing the necklace over her head. It got caught on her hat and Todd paused to help her lower the pendant around her neck.

He was doing this because he felt sorry for Rosie, Sally decided. He was being extra nice to Rosie because Rosie's father had been a two-timing piece of scum, and while a rice necklace was a poor substitute for an honorable father, it was the best Todd could do.

Sally hadn't expected to experience any warm feelings toward Todd. His patrician car, his musical preferences, his general testiness and resistance to enjoying a lovely afternoon in the big city ought to have filled her with her usual loathing toward him. But he'd bought Rosie a necklace—for which Sally would pay him back—and he'd helped Rosie to put it on. And now the two of them were resuming their walk, a few steps ahead of Sally as she collected her thoughts and tried to remember that she didn't like Todd.

Well, she didn't. He'd been Paul's best friend. Guilt by association.

She accelerated her pace to catch up to them. They'd reached a monstrous-looking concrete building that appeared to have been designed by an engineer on bad drugs. "City Hall," Todd told her as they passed it.

"It's ugly," Rosie commented, gazing at its cubistic facade of gray grids and narrow windows.

"Yeah," said Todd. "It is."

Well, Sally thought, there was something they all agreed on.

"I'm guessing we just keep on heading west and we'll reach Boston Common in a few blocks," Todd said.

"The State House is over there, so Mount Vernon Street should be in the area." He raked a hand through his hair, shoving it back from his forehead. "We should have brought the map along with us."

"We'll find the place," she said confidently.

"We could have stuffed the map into your tote bag. You've got room in that thing to stash an elephant."

She gave him what she hoped was a withering look.

"I guess if we put the map in there, it might have gotten lost." Todd glanced at her tote. "Have you ever put something in that bag and then never seen it again?"

She checked the urge to lash back at him. "A play-mate of Rosie's once disappeared in my bag," she dead panned. "Three days later she finally emerged. She'd survived by nibbling on the standing-rib roast I always carry with me."

Todd's gaze caught hers and he grinned. Two little creases framed his mouth, matching the creases around his eyes. When he smiled that way—not a snide smile, not a grudging smile but a genuine one—she could almost see why Tina had thought he was cute.

"Where are we going?" Rosie asked, distracting Sally from that foolish notion.

"Mount Vernon Street."

"Why?"

"We want…" She hesitated, then took a deep breath and answered, "We want to see a friend of Daddy's."

"Another friend?" Rosie digested this. "He sure has a lot of friends."

Let's hope not, Sally muttered, although more than once she'd considered the possibility that Laura hadn't been Paul's only infidelity. Perhaps he'd had dozens of affairs with dozens of women, all but one of them wise enough not to leave a trail of florid letters in their wake.

But then, Laura was the one Paul had given the pocketknife to. That alone made her more significant than any of Paul's other possible floozies, more deserving of this surprise visit.

"I miss my daddy sometimes," Rosie told Todd. She walked flanked by the two adults, a tiny slice of filler sandwiched between two slabs of grown-up. "Do you miss him?"

"Sure I do," Todd said, then caught Sally's eye again. He wasn't smiling this time. He was looking for help.

She had no help to offer. If Todd missed Paul, he missed him. Sometimes even she missed him, although she no longer missed him late at night when her bed seemed huge and her body empty, or on lazy Sunday mornings when they used to unfold the Sunday *Boston Globe* and grab different sections—he liked the front page, the Focus and the Business sections, while she preferred the Arts, the magazine and whichever section carried Ann Landers. They'd sit basking in the tinted sunlight streaming through her stained-glass ornaments, sipping coffee as strong and well brewed as anything she served at the New Day Café, and they'd flip the pages and munch on fresh fruit and leftover turnovers from the café, which she'd bring home and warm in the oven so they tasted just-baked.

She used to miss Paul on Sundays. But now she mostly missed him when it was time to drag the garbage pail down to the curb on trash-collection day, or when she didn't understand one of the insurance reports or documents she'd been sent since his death. Of course, if he hadn't died, she wouldn't have been getting all those reports and documents—but she sometimes wished he would come back from the dead and translate them into plain English for her.

That was about it. She no longer missed his smell, the sound of his voice, the growl of his stupid Alfa Romeo as he coasted up the driveway at the end of the day. She no longer missed his meticulousness, the order he brought to their bathroom, the critical inspections he gave to the backyard after Jimmy Stephens from down the street had mowed it. She no longer missed his pontificating about the relative quality of a wine he'd just opened. She no longer cared whether the wine had breathed or not before she drank it. Actually, she didn't like the idea of wine breathing at all. It made the wine sound alive, a beast in liquid form, still respiring while people consumed it.

But Rosie was allowed to miss her father. And for Rosie's sake, Sally sometimes pretended she missed him, too.

"Does this friend of Daddy's miss him?" Rosie asked Todd.

Sally sent him a sympathetic look. She didn't know why Rosie was questioning Todd, except that she had probably grown tired of Sally's answers.

Todd looked miffed by Sally's refusal to bail him out and take over the discussion. He shrugged and said, "I guess she might miss him. I don't know. Maybe we can ask her when we see her."

Oh, great. What a fun conversation that would be: "Hi. I'm the widow of your dead lover. He gave you my knife and I want it back. This is the daughter of your dead lover. If you happen to have a shred of morality lurking inside you somewhere, you might want to feel guilty about the fact that you were screwing around with the father of this adorable, innocent child. And this guy here is your lover's best friend, who is really ticked off that he was never informed of your illicit affair. By the way, your writing style stinks. And just one more thing—do you miss him?''

For the first time since she'd gotten into Todd's car three-plus hours ago, Sally wondered whether tracking Laura Hawkes down was such a good idea. She shot a look Todd's way, but he was staring ahead as if calculating the distance to the next streetlight.

Did Sally really want to say all those things to Laura when she saw the woman? Did she really want to look into Laura's eyes and think, *Paul sacrificed his wedding vows for her. He chose her over me....* Did she really want to meet a woman who could have sex with Paul and think of Sartre?

No. But she wanted her knife back. It was important to her. It had sentimental value. She'd given it to Paul with a heart full of love, and he'd squandered this precious gift, passing it along to a woman who'd ridiculed its very vulgarity. They'd probably both laughed at it—and at her.

She wanted the knife back, damn it.

"Trevor is my best friend," Rosie was informing Todd. "He's kind of a wuss, but that's okay. Maybe I should have gotten a necklace for him." She fingered her rice pendant thoughtfully. "Mommy, can we go back to that man and get a necklace for Trevor?"

"I don't think so." The odds of the guy having a Trevor necklace already made were slim, and Sally wasn't about to get ripped off for an additional eight bucks while another rice grain was customized.

"Anyway," Rosie continued blithely, turning back to Todd, "Trevor lives next door to me. He's a boy."

"I figured, with a name like Trevor." Todd didn't sound entirely comfortable with the conversation, but he was giving it his best. Sally appreciated his effort.

"What do you do?" Rosie asked him.

"Do? You mean, my job?"

"Yeah."

"I edit the *Valley News*. You know what that is?"

Rosie nodded. "Mrs. Varney tore it up for paper mashy. She's my teacher."

"Papier-mâché," Sally corrected her.

"We made piñatas in school. Do you know what they are?"

"Something made out of my newspaper," Todd guessed.

"Well, silly—first you tear the newspaper up and you dip the pieces in this slimy paste. Then you put the slimy pieces on the donkey."

"The donkey." Todd sounded a bit uncertain but mostly resigned.

"Because it's a piñata. That's a donkey made out of paper mashy. So you put these slimy pieces of newspaper on it until it looks like a donkey, and then you let it dry, and then you paint it, and then you hit it with a stick until it breaks."

"That sounds like a worthwhile activity," Todd said wryly. "You take my newspaper, tear it, dip it in slime, mold an ass out of it and then hit the ass until it breaks. What ever happened to Red Rover?"

"We play that, too," Rosie assured him. "But the piñata is filled with candy."

"Ah. That explains it. You put candy inside the slimy tatters of my newspaper."

"I don't know how the candy gets inside," Rosie told him. "*I* don't put it in there. It just gets in there somehow. And then, when we break it open with a stick, all the candy comes spilling out. It's cool."

"I bet it is." The look he sent Sally over Rosie's head had crossed the line from wry to downright sardonic.

"It's an old Mexican folk custom," Sally explained. As a newspaperman, he ought to be more enlightened about foreign cultures. Of course, she'd learned about piñatas through Rosie. Maybe you had to have a young child to know about them—or you had to be Mexican.

"I don't know about the candy," Todd commented. "But I like the part about breaking the thing apart with a stick. It sounds like a great way to let off steam."

"Do you enjoy hitting things with sticks?" Sally goaded him.

"Only when I'm looking for a cathartic experience. Is that the State House up ahead, or am I hallucinating?"

If he was hallucinating, she was, too. She saw the stretch of verdant open space that marked the eastern edge of Boston Common, and looming to her right the majestic dome of the State House. Her heart fluttered with excitement, and she pointed toward the dome. "Look, Rosie. Can you see it?"

"See what?" Short as she was, Rosie couldn't see past the buildings rising beside them along the sidewalk.

"Just up ahead. See the park?" Sally redirected her index finger straight ahead, to the looming expanse of green, an oasis in this urban environment. They could all have been nomads in the desert, stumbling upon grass and trees after their long trek.

Except it hadn't really been a long trek at all. Certainly not ten miles. Not even one mile.

At last they broke around the corner and into the open space. Rosie saw the State House now, massive and austere, lording over one corner of the Common. "Is that it?" she asked.

"That's it. That's where the governor works, and all

the state assemblymen and representatives. Do you know what they are?''

"Politicians, right?'' Rosie seemed almost as excited by the State House as she'd been by the juggling clown. Then again, Sally supposed there wasn't much difference between juggling clowns and politicians. "It looks like a castle.''

Sally didn't agree, but she wouldn't argue. She supposed the pillared building, with its lengthy flight of entry steps and massive doors, could pass for a colonial, democratic castle of sorts. It was far too public for that, though, not a place where lords and ladies might dance the minuet together, but rather a place where wealthy descendants of people who sailed to America on the *Mayflower* would gather to come up with ways to patronize the masses. It definitely had a Dead White Males aura about it.

"I wonder if we have time for a tour of the building,'' she said.

"No,'' Todd said almost instantly.

"Why not?''

His glare hinted that he lacked a good answer. "It's Saturday,'' he finally said. "They don't give tours on Saturdays.''

"How do you know that?''

"The government doesn't do business on Saturdays. The place is closed.''

"What if they're debating a bill? Maybe they're going to debate it all weekend long. Some vital bill about worker safety or protecting the pink-toed butterfly—''

"The pink-toed butterfly?'' Todd snorted. "Since when do butterflies have toes?''

"They do in one of my books,'' Rosie told him. "Mommy, are there pink-toed butterflies in that castle?''

"Try green-butted caterpillars," Todd muttered, but Sally heard him. Rosie probably did, too. For the next two weeks, Rosie was going to be questioning her about green-butted caterpillars.

Before Rosie could ask anything, Sally navigated them across the manicured lawn of the Common, passing the State House and emerging from the park a couple of blocks beyond. "Mount Vernon Street is in this direction," she told them.

"Does Daddy's Friend have toys?" Rosie wanted to know.

"I guess we'll find out," Sally answered.

"You had toys," Rosie reminded Todd. "Toy cars. You said they weren't toys, but they were. I could tell."

"Yeah?" He glanced down at her. "How could you tell?"

"They were little. And they had silly colors."

"Silly?" He looked indignant.

"Turquoise blue? That's a silly color for a car. And anyway, they were much too little to be real cars."

"They're called model cars," Todd told her. "I made them."

"You *made* them?" Yet another thing to impress Rosie today—the juggling clown, the rice writer and now this: Todd had made his toy cars. In another minute, she might start hyperventilating from all the excitement. "How did you make them?"

"There are kits. Model kits. You paint the pieces, fit them together and glue them."

"Why?"

"Because…" He frowned, as if hoping to squeeze an answer out of his forehead. "Because it's fun."

"It would be a lot more fun to play with them. I don't see why you bother to make them if you aren't going to play with them after. When I make things with my Legos, I always play with them after.''

"This is different.''

"Why?''

Again he frowned. ''Because I'm a grown-up,'' he finally said.

Fortunately for him, Sally was able to change the subject. ''Look—there's Mount Vernon Street.''

It was, like the rest of the Beacon Hill neighborhood, a charming road lined with redbrick town houses. Sally suspected each town house was a single dwelling, which would mean each resident was a gazillionaire. Had Paul fallen for Laura Hawkes because she was rich? That would hardly make sense. He had family wealth, and he'd earned a good living with Wittig, Mott, and really, what did anyone need all that money for? The cost of living in Winfield was not the same as on Beacon Hill in Boston.

Even more peculiar, Laura Hawkes had been a client of Paul's. Sally had gotten the woman's name and address from Patty Pleckart by asking about his clients named Laura. Why would a gazillionaire Bostonite hire a lawyer from Winfield?

If she was sleeping with him, hiring him might have made their assignations simpler. Maybe Laura Hawkes was married, too. Maybe she'd hired Paul so she would have an excuse to slip away from her husband and meet Paul somewhere. ''I've got to go see my lawyer,'' she would tell her husband. ''I'll be home tomorrow. Try not to be nothingness without me.''

"Swank territory,'' Todd murmured, his gaze sweeping over the freshly painted, paneled front doors, with their brass knockers and mail slots, the wrought-iron railings along the front steps, the neat, quaint shutters framing each window. If affluence had an odor, Sally would have keeled over from the stench.

"This is it," she said, halting in front of one of the houses and gazing up the stone steps to the front door.

"This is where Daddy's Friend lives?"

"That's right." She hesitated at the foot of the stairs, trying to gather the courage that suddenly seemed to have fled from her. She recalled the collection of letters she'd found, and all they had implied. She remembered her missing pocketknife. She thought about Paul, her husband, the father of her daughter, the man she'd vowed to love, honor and cherish till death did them part. She'd been wronged, conned, bamboozled, cheated...

But actually facing the woman who'd helped Paul to wrong, con, bamboozle and cheat was a whole different thing.

Yet she didn't hate Laura Hawkes. She'd never even met her.

Todd touched her shoulder and she turned to him, expecting to see sympathy in his face. What she saw was what she wanted to feel: hard anger. He'd touched her, not to comfort her but to nudge her aside so he could scale the steps, lift that shiny brass knocker and let it smack against the door. No hesitancy in him. No doubt. No worry about what to say.

He was bitter, he was righteous and he was prepared to take on Laura Hawkes.

Sally resented him for possessing all the boldness she lacked. But she was kind of glad he was there to be bold for the both of them.

Eight

After three unanswered knocks on the door, Todd discovered a doorbell, which was attached to the side of the vertical molding in such a way that it wasn't immediately visible. The only reason he could think of for someone to camouflage her doorbell was that she wanted people to use the fancy knocker.

All right. He'd used the fancy knocker. He'd admired its graceful curves and polished veneer, its oh-so-colonial attitude. But it wasn't getting the job done.

He pressed the doorbell, pressed it again, heard a series of variably pitched gongs each time he pressed it. It was as effective as the knocker had been. No response.

Turning, he gazed down the front steps at the two females who stood below, watching him. Two hatted females, one with eyes as round and penetrating as bullets and the other with eyes hidden behind her chichi sunglasses. The way the Driver women peered up at him gave him an elevated sense of himself. He was above, taking charge, taking care of business.

Or not, as it happened. Either Laura Hawkes wasn't home or she'd peeked out through an upstairs window, spotted a lady in a straw hat that resembled a flying saucer from a fifties sci-fi flick, accompanied by a kid in a purple hat the shape of which defied description altogether, and she'd decided not to answer her door.

Todd didn't care. Well, he did care—he was frustrated that he couldn't simply meet Paul's mystery lover and get the story he'd come for, like the trained journalist he was. But he was glad he'd been the one to scale the stairs, manipulate the knocker, locate the doorbell and hear the gongs resounding on the other side of the six-panel door.

So far, the day had gone all Sally's way. She'd played her god-awful CD during the drive, they'd eaten a hodgepodge picnic lunch at Quincy Market, Rosie had gotten her goofy rice necklace—but now it was his show. He was the one leading the charge. Sally had obtained Laura Hawkes's name and address, but Todd had rung the bell.

He realized Sally and Rosie were waiting to be debriefed. "No one's home," he told them, lingering for one more moment on the top step just because he liked the altitude.

They continued to peer up at him. He strode down the stairs like a modern-day Zeus descending from Mount Olympus. Once he reached the sidewalk, he was able to see Sally's face under the brim of her hat. He could even, if he stared really hard, see her eyes, ghostlike behind the dark lenses of her sunglasses. Her lips were pursed in a way that made her cheeks look hollow. "What are we going to do?" she asked.

He hadn't thought that far ahead—but when he did, he saw only one option. "I guess we'll have to go home." An excellent option it was, too. They could drive back to Winfield, and he could return to Boston on his own, perhaps tomorrow, and visit Laura Hawkes without Sally and her kid tagging along. He could cruise down the Mass Pike—listening to rock and roll the entire way—and skip the Quincy Market detour. Now that he knew the destination, he could park right in the neighborhood, knock on Laura Hawkes's knocker, ring her chime and find out why she and Paul had gone sneaking around behind Todd's back.

"We're not going home," Sally said definitively. "We can wait."

"Wait?" Like hell. He didn't want to spend another hour or two in downtown Boston, struggling through awkward chats with the kid, spending money on crap for her and having heart attacks whenever he lost sight of her. "What if Laura's out of town for the weekend?"

"What if she's on her way home right now?" Sally countered. "It would be such a waste if we drove back to Winfield without seeing her and then it turned out that if we'd waited ten minutes we would have seen her."

"What if it turned out we waited four hours and she never showed up?"

"Well, I wasn't thinking we'd just sit here on her steps and do nothing for four hours. We could take a walk and then come back in a while and try again."

"I don't want to take a walk. We already took a walk. We're going to have to take another walk to get back to my car. I don't even want to *think* about walking," he said, then realized how petulant he sounded.

"Or," Sally suggested, "we could take a ride on a Swan Boat."

"Swan Boat?" Rosie bleated. "What's that? I wanna go on a Swan Boat!"

Todd clamped his teeth together so the blasphemy rolling across his tongue wouldn't escape. He did not want to go on a Swan Boat. He especially didn't want to go on one with Sally and Rosie. Swan Boat rides were for tourists. They were pointless. They were corny.

"All right," Sally was saying. "Let's take a ride on

a Swan Boat, and then we can come back and see if she's returned home. That sounds like a great idea.''

It sounded like Todd's definition of the Third Circle of Hell. It also sounded like Todd's loss of his status as the commanding officer of this army. Sally was taking over once more. The next thing he knew, she was going to be singing songs about porcupines.

Or swans. Was there a song about swans on that stupid CD of hers? A swan song.

Shit.

Sally and Rosie were already bounding down the sidewalk in the direction of the Common. They were holding hands and skipping, like classmates in a schoolyard. After the Swan Boat ride, if Laura Hawkes still wasn't answering her door, the two of them would probably draw a hopscotch grid on the sidewalk and play that for a while. And when that got old, Sally probably had a set of jacks in her tote bag. Or a couple of jump ropes. Or a hula hoop.

Sally didn't look like a schoolgirl, of course. She was clearly a woman, her long hair swaying heavily under the brim of her hat, her hips shimmying with each step, the skirt of her dress swinging around her legs. She was skipping only because Rosie wanted to skip.

He realized that Rosie, not Sally, was running the show. Who was he kidding? He'd stupidly thought this trip was primarily for his benefit, secondarily for Sally's. He and Sally were the ones who wanted to eyeball Paul's mistress. Rosie had come along only because Sally had grown up in a trailer and wanted her daughter exposed to such exotica as street clowns and kitsch kiosks.

But somehow, Rosie had wound up in charge. She was the one who'd wanted to watch the damn clown and buy the damn necklace—and in both cases, she'd gotten

her way. She was the one who'd sung along with both
the animal CD and Nirvana. Now she wanted a Swan
Boat ride, and she was going to get that, too. Like a
eunuched slave, Todd followed silently behind her and
her loyal handmaiden, otherwise known as Mom. Queen
Rosie's wishes were their commands.

If Rosie weren't Paul's heir, the sole creature through
whom his DNA would survive into the future, Todd
wouldn't put up with this. It amazed him that Paul had
put up with it. But then, Paul had had Laura to help him
endure.

Maybe that was what Todd needed: a woman to help
him endure. He dated, he socialized, he had sex less
often than he'd like, but significantly more often than
most septuagenarians, high-school students and in all
probability his parents—but maybe he needed someone
special. A woman who would write passionate letters to
him, even if that passion was about as genuine as rhine-
stones. A woman who dreamed of his touch. A woman
who would care enough to be indignant if she learned
he was attached to someone else. The women he dated
in and around Winfield... Somehow, he doubted any of
them would throw a fit if they found out the relationship
wasn't exclusive.

The Public Garden loomed, lush with buds and early
blossoms. The trees looked as if a painter had dabbed
their slender branches with green, and spikes of tulip and
daffodil pierced the warming soil. In the distance Todd
saw the pond where the Swan Boats sailed. Rosie saw
it, too. She let out a triumphant yelp and started running
toward the pond. Why wasn't she tired? Didn't little girls
need naps?

Accept the inevitable, he advised himself. Rosie
wanted a boat ride, and she was going to get a boat ride.

He'd ride with her, just to make sure she didn't disappear again. It was one thing for a child to vanish amid a throng of fans admiring a clown, and another thing for a child to vanish while on a boat in a lake. Todd's nerves could take only so much.

Sally announced that she wanted to ride on the boat, too—and that she would pay. Todd didn't argue. Nor did he argue, though he desperately wanted to, when the boat operator pointed out an empty section on one of the bench seats and said to Rosie, "Now, you sit nice and still between your mommy and your daddy."

She didn't have a daddy, Todd reminded himself. She missed her father, even if her father had been an asshole. Todd could pretend to be her father for the duration of the boat ride.

Besides, if he told the boat man that he *wasn't* Rosie's father, the guy would assume Todd was Sally's boyfriend. He definitely didn't want anyone to make that assumption—even though when she removed her sunglasses, her eyes were as bright as Rosie's, sparkling with joy over a stupid paddleboat ride. Even though the afternoon sunlight got caught in her hair below the brim of her hat and made it shimmer the color of new pennies. Even though, as she adjusted herself on the seat, the neckline of her dress shifted, drawing his eyes to her generous bosom.

Which he didn't care about. He'd never been a breast man. Denise had been as slim as a supermodel, and he'd married her, hadn't he?

Also divorced her.

Why was he thinking about Sally's breasts? He was on a boat, with Rosie wedged between him and Sally and a park on the verge of exploding into spring all around them, hints of flowers everywhere, the scent of new grass and apple blossoms obliterating the stale odor of the city beyond the Public Garden's borders. Might as well make the best of it. Might as well pretend he was Rosie's daddy, the husband of a woman with substantial breasts.

After the boat ride, they stopped to admire a row of bronze sculptures depicting the mother duck and her babies from *Make Way For Ducklings,* a book Rosie had apparently memorized, given her involved explication of the plot. "We read it in school," she said.

"This is the same school where you hit donkeys with sticks?"

"Not real donkeys," she reminded him solemnly. "Real donkeys would kick you if you hit them."

"There seems to be an animal motif running through your life," he observed as Rosie hunkered down to scrutinize each bronze duckling. "*Make Way For Ducklings,* papier-mâché donkeys, animal crackers, those animal songs on the CD and now a Swan Boat ride. You know what you need?"

Rosie fingered her rice necklace and gazed at him. "A zoo?"

"A pet."

Sally sent him a warning look, which he blithely ignored. "A pet what?" Rosie asked.

"I don't know. Dogs are fun."

"Do you have a dog?" she asked.

"No. But I had one growing up, and it was great. Every child needs a dog."

Rosie turned to her mother. "I need a dog," she said.

Sally's expression, meeting Todd's above Rosie's head, turned from mild warning to dire threat. He knew if he pursued this discussion with Rosie, Sally would hate him forever. That seemed as good a reason as any.

"A big, sloppy Saint Bernard would be fun. Or a pit bull. They're supposed to have great personalities."

"Stop," Sally muttered, adding to Rosie, "He's teasing you. Pit bulls can be mean."

"Or you could get something exotic. An iguana, maybe. They're cute little lizards."

"They grow enormous," Sally interjected. "They're something like five feet long when they reach maturity."

"Five feet long?" Rosie was so excited she pranced in a circle around one of the ducklings. "I want a—what's it called, Daddy's Friend?"

"An iguana."

"An iguana. Can I have one, Mommy?"

"No." Sally's look evolved from merely threatening to outright lethal. "We can't deal with a pet right now, honey. You're in school and I'm at work. Who'd take care of the pet when no one was home?"

"He could take care of himself. We could train him. You know what I'd like?" She addressed Todd, who was clearly much more receptive to the idea. "A chimpanzee. We could train him to cook and clean, and then he could play with me and Trevor. And he could eat bananas."

"Chimpanzees love bananas," Todd confirmed.

"I think we're done with this conversation," Sally said.

"Or an ant farm," Todd suggested. "Ants make cool pets."

"I'll bet," Sally grunted.

"Do they farm? What do they farm?" Rosie wanted to know. "Corn? I have a book about farm animals, but it doesn't have anything about ants in it."

All the way from the duckling statues to Louisburg Square, Rosie questioned Todd about pets. They analyzed the pluses and minuses of gerbils, parakeets, tetras and tarantulas. And cats. Rosie finally decided the best solution would be for her friend Trevor to get a cat while she got a dog, and then when the cat and the dog grew up, they could fall in love and get married.

"A mixed marriage," Todd said. "Why not?"

"We're not getting a dog," Sally announced sternly. "What time is it? Maybe we should go back and see if Laura Hawkes came home."

"Does she have a pet?" Rosie asked, bobbing along between Sally and Todd, bouncing on the balls of her feet with each step. Todd decided the kid wasn't so bad after all. Given how effectively she was irritating her mother, Todd wouldn't begrudge her the boat trip or the necklace.

"We're not getting a dog," Sally repeated through clenched teeth.

Maybe that was why Paul had cheated on her—because she wouldn't get a dog.

She was so earthy and artsy, though, Todd would have expected her to be a dog person. Or a cat person. Or a menagerie person, lots of animals, a row of bowls by the back door, half of them filled with water and the other half filled with kibble. He would have expected her to live in a house filled with that musty kitty-litter scent, and a parrot would sit on a roost in her kitchen, commenting on what she was cooking for dinner. "Bwaak! More tarragon! Bwaak! Down with tofu!"

They reached the town house on Mount Vernon Street, and Todd's leadership juices once again began to flow. Rosie might rule the itinerary, but when it came time for action, Todd was the man.

He started up the front steps, but to his great annoyance Sally and Rosie accompanied him. No more adoring gazes from below. They crammed themselves onto the top step with him.

"I'll do the talking," he whispered as he rang the doorbell.

"Says who?" Sally whispered back.

"I don't want to intimidate the woman."

"I do."

He wished he could intimidate Sally. "I really think it'll be better if you let me do the talking."

"Can I talk?" Rosie asked.

"No," Sally and Todd said simultaneously.

The door opened as far as a safety chain would allow. The safety chain was brass, as shiny and yellow as the knocker on the door. The woman behind the chain was shadowy. Todd could see one suspicious eye; the door hid the rest of her face.

He rearranged his expression, losing the scowl he'd worn for Sally and attempting a benign smile. "Hi. I'm looking for Laura Hawkes." He paused, tension creeping along his nerve endings as he waited to see if Sally was going to keep her mouth shut.

She did.

"Who are you?" the woman behind the door asked.

"I'm Todd Sloane. I'm a friend of Paul Driver's. This is Paul Driver's daughter, Rosie—" he gestured toward her "—and his wife, Sally."

"His widow," Sally muttered.

"His widow," Todd corrected himself.

"Paul who?"

Surely the woman had to know the name. She'd sent a couple of dozen sentimental letters to him, after all. "Paul Driver," he enunciated.

"He was a lawyer with Wittig, Mott, Driver and Associates, in Winfield, Massachusetts,'' Sally supplied. ''He did legal work for you.''

''Winfield? Oh my God. Paul!'' The door slammed shut, then opened again, this time unfettered by the safety chain. The woman who filled the doorway was skinny, with streaked blond hair cut into an odd geometric shape. Her face was an assemblage of straight lines and sharp angles. She wore a tunic and gray stretch pants that emphasized her thinness. ''Is Paul dead? How awful!''

She seemed genuinely upset. But not distraught. Not wrenched, not wretched, not mangled by the gears of tragedy. Of course, if she was Todd's Laura, she would have known about Paul's death for months and gotten past that stage of acute grief. His soul-mate lover would have wondered why she hadn't heard from him, and she would have made some inquiries and learned her lover's fate.

He just wasn't...sure. He studied the woman standing in the marble-tiled foyer of her elegant town house, as slim and sleek as a model in a cigarette ad. Her breasts would barely fill a training bra, Todd noted. Why would Paul, a man who'd lost his mind over a buxom waitress, knocked her up and felt obliged to marry her, have an affair with a woman who had no bosom at all?

For contrast, maybe.

''You are Laura Hawkes, aren't you?'' he confirmed.

''Yes.''

''We were in town,'' Sally explained smoothly. ''We thought it would be a courtesy to meet personally with Paul's clients here in Boston to let them know.''

''That's so kind of you. Please—come in. I'm so sorry.'' She turned to Sally and clasped her hand. She wore several rings, including a textured silver band around her thumb, and her nails were polished the color of scabs. "What a terrible loss. He seemed so young."

"He was thirty-three," Sally told her, removing her sunglasses with her free hand and doing a creditable job of appearing sad. "He was in a car accident."

"I'm so sorry! Oh, I just—I'm shocked. Can I get you something to drink?"

Todd decided he was glad Sally had taken over the social obligations. It gave him a chance to size Laura up. Was she Paul's sweetheart? She could be. Or she could be the world's greatest actress, slicker than an oil spill. But if she was faking it, why would she have invited them in for a drink?

His ruminations were interrupted by the sound of scrabbling claws against marble, accompanied by a staccato yipping. A small furry creature bounded into the foyer and skidded across the polished floor. "A dog!" Rosie cheered.

Actually, it looked more like a large, hairy guinea pig. Laura Hawkes reached down and scooped the animal up. Its legs continued to churn for a minute, as if it thought it was still on the floor. "Calm down, Butch," she murmured, stroking the beast's scruff. It yipped some more.

"Mommy says I can't have a dog," Rosie complained.

Laura and Sally exchanged a look. Understanding? Hostility? Todd couldn't interpret it from either direction.

"Would you like some juice, or tea?" she offered, still stroking the furball. "Or something hard, maybe. Jesus. Paul's dead? We could all use something hard."

"I want something hard," Rosie remarked. Sally rummaged in her tote bag and produced a handful of animal crackers. Todd doubted that was what she'd had in mind.

She might be only five years old, but he suspected she knew exactly what a hard drink was.

Laura pivoted on the cube-shaped heel of a pair of dangerously fashionable black shoes and started down the hall, beckoning with a jerk of her razor-sharp chin that they should follow. Todd tried to catch Sally's eye, to see if she was as baffled as he was. She might have already figured Laura Hawkes out. She might have already deciphered the dimensions of the woman's relationship with Paul. If she had, she didn't share her insights with him. She didn't even share a glance with him.

Lacking a better choice, he followed Sally and Rosie as they followed Laura. The hall was short, decorated with abstract paintings that looked vaguely obscene, and it led to a sun-filled kitchen at the rear of the town house. Laura lowered her pet to the counter, where he hovered anxiously, as if afraid to jump down to the floor from such a towering height.

The kitchen was a gourmet chef's dream: granite counters, a six-burner gas range, a refrigerator as big as the closet in the spare bedroom of his condo. Laura Hawkes was most definitely rich.

So why had she hired a small-time attorney from western Massachusetts to handle her legal business? If she could live at one of the priciest addresses in Boston, if she could get her hair coiffed by someone who clearly used the most elite drugs, why would she have used Paul as her legal representative?

Not that he was a bad lawyer. But no downtown billionaire would travel all the way to Winfield to get her will written.

"Would you like some milk?" she was asking Rosie.

"No, thanks. I'd like something hard."

"She'll have milk," Sally interjected.

The poor dear, Laura mouthed, her eyes brimming with enough pity to fill an ocean. Sally pressed her lips together sternly, whether because she didn't trust Laura or because she didn't appreciate her condescending sympathy, Todd couldn't tell.

Laura filled a glass with milk for Rosie, who was distracted by the dog. She had to look up slightly to see it; it had to look down. They assessed each other. "He's so tiny," Rosie finally said. The dog was probably thinking the same thing about her.

"You can have a pastry too, if you'd like," Laura offered. "Do you know what a pastry is?"

"She knows what pastries are," Sally assured her. "She's actually an expert when it comes to pastries."

"I like blueberry scones best," Rosie added.

"So, you were a client of Paul's?" Todd was growing bored with the chatter about scones and dogs. Someone had to take charge of things, and once again, that someone was Todd.

"We bought a retreat up in Lenox," Laura explained, swinging open her oversize refrigerator. "Paul was recommended to us as someone who could handle the purchase."

"A retreat?" Sally asked at exactly the instant Todd asked, *"We?"*

"My husband and I." She pulled out a bakery box and shut the refrigerator door with her nonexistent hip. "My husband is Vigo Hawkes," she said, as if that was supposed to mean something.

It meant something to Sally. "Vigo Hawkes? *The* Vigo Hawkes?"

Who the hell was Vigo Hawkes? What the hell kind of name was Vigo, anyway?

"The," Laura confirmed, retrieving a plate from one

cabinet and three glasses from another. She plucked ice cubes out of a silver bucket with silver tongs and dropped them into the glasses, which tinkled in the frequency of fine crystal. "We found this nice little spread for sale in Lenox. Two hundred acres. Just what we needed. The architect has ideas you wouldn't believe. And of course, with Vigo overseeing things...well, I don't have to tell you."

You do have to tell me, Todd thought.

"So Paul handled the purchase?" Sally asked.

"Yes. He did an excellent job. No complaints. God. I can't believe he's dead."

She lifted a cut-crystal decanter filled with amber liquid and splashed a copious amount in each of the three glasses. Todd didn't know what it was, but he figured it was hard.

"He had that cute little office—I swear, the first time I saw it, I almost laughed out loud. That building was so prepostmodern. But you know, everything's kind of cute once you get west of the Connecticut River. Lenox is very cute. The Berkshires are incredibly cute for mountains."

"So, other than this land you purchased, did Paul do...anything else for you?" Todd asked, trying not to sound as impatient as he felt.

"Well, he walked us through the legal details. He was a very nice man. Very nice. I'll miss him. I'm sure Vigo will, too."

Todd wasn't sure Vigo would miss Paul, but he was pretty sure Laura wasn't the Laura who had written the schmaltzy love letters. The sooner they could take their leave of her, the sooner they could drive back to Winfield and put this entire pointless day behind them.

But Sally had helped herself to one of the other

glasses and was taking a sip. Shit. Now she and Laura Hawkes were going to get drunk together. "Ooh, this is good," Sally said. "Have some, Todd."

"I'm driving," Todd reminded her.

"It's apple juice."

"Not just apple juice," Laura corrected her. "It's fresh-pressed Granny Smith apple juice. I have my own press. The juice is quite tart," she warned Todd, handing him a glass.

He couldn't drink booze with a long drive ahead of him, but he really didn't want to drink apple juice. Even Rosie's milk would be preferable. Water would be fine. Water, and a nice cold beer once he got home. Two beers. Possibly three.

Laura lifted a cannoli from the bakery box and set it on the plate for Rosie. Then she and Sally dived into a discussion about juice presses and how they differed from cider presses, and whether a fruit press could be used to make carrot juice, which Sally had heard prevented cancer. "But supposedly, it turns your palms orange," she said, holding her hands palm up as if to demonstrate that her palms weren't orange.

"I hadn't heard that," Laura murmured. "The cancer part. I've heard about the orange-palms part...."

Listening to the two of them bond through conversation was almost hypnotic. Men didn't talk that way. If they had to talk to a stranger, they talked about basic stuff—the Celtics, the Red Sox, the Bruins—and they expressed themselves in single-syllable words interspersed with grunts. No long, mellifluous sentences about the nuances that differentiated Cortlands from Macouns and the intricacies of cutting-edge kitchen gadgets. In the same situation, two men would be saying, "So, how about the Celts?" *Grunt.*

Maybe Sally and Laura talked with an easy intimacy not because they were women but because they both knew who Vigo Hawkes was. Maybe that was the secret connection.

By the time Rosie had finished her cannoli, which left smears of cream and powdered sugar on her upper lip, the women had meandered through a discourse on Mixmasters, stock funds, stained-glass-window ornaments and architects who had obviously never cleaned a house, because if they had, they'd know not to make all those visually striking nooks and ledges that were impossible to dust. "Sally? We've really got to go," Todd finally broke in.

"Well...yes, I guess we do. Thanks for the apple juice. It really was wonderful. Rosie, what do you say?"

"Thanks for the pastry," Rosie recited, then added, "your dog is too small."

"Do you think so?" Laura gazed at the dog, still perched precariously on the counter as if he were another high-tech appliance. "You're right. Maybe he is too small. I should get a bigger dog."

"If you get another dog, I can take this one," Rosie offered. "Maybe he's small enough that my mom won't mind."

"We're not getting a dog," Sally said. "Not even a small one. Laura, it was really sweet of you to let us take so much of your time...."

And the two women were off again, launching themselves into another sisterhood dialogue, lots of take-care's and be-good-to-yourself's and don't-let-that-architect-steamroll-you's. Todd set down his half-full glass of glorified apple juice and trailed the chattering women to the foyer, letting their babble splash past him like sea spray. A few more take-care's and it-was-a-pleasure's and the front door was open. Escape was at hand, escape and an end to the incessant yakking.

Sally stepped outside, then hesitated and turned back. Todd clamped his mouth shut to keep from yelling at her that he was in no mood to stand around for another half hour while she and Laura rehashed the *Consumer Reports* rating on food processors one more time.

"I was just wondering, Laura—' she gave the woman a smile that was both shy and sly "—what you think of Sartre."

Nine

Laura Hawkes wasn't exactly sure who Sartre was. "Some philosopher guy, right?" she'd guessed.

Sally had already pretty well figured she wasn't the Laura they were looking for. For one thing, the woman was totally wrong for Paul: too cutting-edge, too urban, too expensive. Too nice. For another, she was married to Vigo Hawkes. Why would a woman married to Vigo Hawkes waste time with a small-town lawyer?

For a third thing, Paul would never have wasted his time with anyone who didn't know who Sartre was. He prided himself on his erudition. While he'd done the honorable thing by marrying Sally after she'd become pregnant, she had to wonder whether he would have been quite so honorable if she hadn't possessed at least a passing knowledge of the father of existentialism.

As they reached the City Hall Plaza, with its modern fortress of a building and its gray acres of concrete, Rosie announced that she had found Laura Hawkes's dog creepy. "He just sat up there on the counter," she said. "He should have come down and played with me. I liked the lady's pastry much better than I liked her dog."

"That pastry is called a cannoli," Sally reminded her. "It's Italian. Aren't we near Boston's Italian neighborhood?"

Todd glared at her. He'd been silent the entire walk

back to the garage, staring at the sidewalk three paces ahead of him and stewing. "I think it's time to go home," he said.

"But we're really close to the Italian neighborhood. What's it called, the North Side?"

"The North End. And we should be getting home." He made a big production of checking his watch. It wasn't yet five o'clock, and while the sun was fading westward, the sky still held plenty of easy golden light.

"We could just stop in at a bakery and pick up some cannolis. What's the big deal?"

"I want cannolis," Rosie chimed in. "I like them a lot."

Todd paused. He had his hands in the pockets of his trousers, his arms pinning back the flaps of his blazer. A light breeze toyed with his hair, fluffing the dense black waves. His nose was a touch pinker than it had been when they'd left Winfield that morning. The evening was mild, the air fresh and pleasant.

"In fact," Sally ventured, bracing herself for his resounding objection, "we could have dinner in the North End."

"Can we have cannolis for dinner?" Rosie asked.

"No, but you could get spaghetti, if you liked. Or ravioli, or lasagna—'

"With eggplant?"

"If you'd like."

"She eats eggplant?" Todd eyed Rosie skeptically.

"If we have dinner in the North End, you can see for yourself." What she really wanted to say was, *Stop being such a crab.* They'd enjoyed a lovely day. The Swan Boat ride had been dreamlike, the boat gliding silently around the pond, the trees in the park trembling with new life. They'd seen a street performer and met a fascinating woman who happened to be married to Vigo Hawkes, and now it was time to celebrate with an authentic urban–ethnic culinary experience.

Todd continued to scrutinize Rosie. It would seem that his entire decision hinged on whether he wanted to witness her consuming eggplant.

"What would you be doing tonight if we went home?" Sally asked. "Zapping a frozen entrée in the microwave?" Casting aspersions on his cooking ability wasn't really fair; the man knew how to roast a chicken. But she couldn't help goading him.

"Maybe I have plans for the evening."

A date? The thought had never occurred to her. She supposed he had a social life. There were no doubt a few women in Winfield who would want to date the eligible publisher of the region's largest newspaper. Tina thought he was cute, and given that she was on a tattoo basis with her boyfriend, she shouldn't even have noticed Todd. If Tina could think he was cute, other women must think so, too.

Then again, his plans for the evening might entail watching pro-wrestling on cable and drinking Jack Daniel's straight from the bottle.

"If you had plans, you wouldn't have invited yourself along on this trip," she said, emphasizing that it had been *his* idea to accompany her and Rosie to Boston, and therefore he wasn't in any position to dictate their departure time.

He lifted his gaze from Rosie to Sally. His eyes were opaque. She wished she knew whether something specific was bugging him or he was just a generic grouch, fed up with a day spent on a mission that hadn't produced the desired result. Or if he *did* have a hot date waiting for him back home. Or if he wanted to go home because Sally's presence offended him, and Rosie grated on him, and he couldn't bear an extra minute with either of them.

"All right," he said. "We'll eat in the North End."

Two and a half hours later, Todd paid an exorbitant fee to ransom his Saab from the garage, and they drove out into a velvet-soft evening. Rosie had gorged herself on eggplant parmigiana at a cozy trattoria. Sally had eaten calimari, the mere thought of which Todd evidently found grotesque, and he'd had some Italian preparation of steak. One thing he and Paul had in common, she concluded, was a deep and abiding affection for red meat.

After dinner, they'd strolled past the Old North Church, which Sally had explained to Rosie was where Paul Revere had received the two-lanterned signal that the British were coming by sea. Then they'd stopped at a bakery and bought half a dozen cannoli—two plain and one each chocolate, chocolate chip, amaretto and blueberry, because Rosie wanted to compare it with a blueberry scone. They'd traipsed back to the garage, settled Rosie in the back seat with the bakery box and Sally's sun hat, and rolled out into the jammed traffic surrounding Quincy Market.

"We're not listening to that animal CD on the way home," Todd announced, then hunched forward and squinted into the distance where the traffic had snarled around a complicated intersection.

"And I veto Nirvana."

"There are other CDs in there," he said, waving his hand toward the glove compartment.

She lowered the door and pulled out the small stack of CDs inside. He inched the car forward, braked and glanced at the pile. Before she could stop him, he slid one CD from her hands and popped open the case. "Cream," he told her.

She wasn't sure she liked Cream. It was a band that predated her birth, music her mother had listened to. Flower-power music, LSD music, music from the sixties, which survivors of the sixties seemed to think was vastly superior to anything written before or since—which would include Sarah McLachlan and Johann Sebastian Bach.

The CD came on, filling the car's interior with a twangy guitar, a catchy beat and a surprisingly sweet voice. "Eric Clapton's second band," Todd told her. "Or—I take it back—his third. He was in the Yardbirds, and then with John Mayall, then Cream."

So Todd was one of those rock-music-trivia buffs. He built model cars and knew Eric Clapton's résumé. For not the first time, Sally pondered the odd fact that he could have been Paul's best friend. They'd had so little in common—other than Columbia University and an attachment to red meat. And other guy stuff, she supposed. They'd enjoyed meeting at Grover's and whining over the vexations life tossed at them or basking in their professional achievements. They'd liked being big fish in the small pond that was Winfield. They'd understood each other on some level Sally would always be denied access to.

She listened to the music that filled the car, the fierce rhythm, the gliding melody. "This is good," she conceded. Evidently, some sixties bands were worthwhile.

"I thought you didn't like rock music."

"I never said that." She peeked over her shoulder at Rosie, who drummed her fingers against the padded

crossbar of her booster seat in time with the music. "I'm
not a big Nirvana fan. Their songs are so negative."

"You don't like negative music?"

"I don't like negative anything."

He sent her a quick look, then rolled the car forward
another inch. "Paul never told me that about you."

She felt a pinch between her shoulder blades at the
comprehension that another thing Paul and Todd had in
common was their willingness to talk about Sally behind
her back. Of course they'd talked about her—they'd
been best friends, at least until the Laura letters had
turned up. But contemplating specifically what Paul
might have told Todd about her—beyond the condition
of her car—made her uncomfortable. Had he listed all
the things he hated about her? All the things he resented?
Or maybe nice things, things that kept them together
even though theirs hadn't been a soul-deep love match?

What exactly did Todd know? What had he learned
about her through the filter of Paul's biases? She wanted
to ask, but she wasn't sure she'd like his answer.

"Whatever Paul told you about me you ought to take
with a grain of salt," she suggested.

"So far, everything he's told me about you was pretty
accurate." They were moving faster now, having gotten
past the bottleneck and reached the ramp onto the ex-
pressway—which was locked tight with traffic, cars
backed up waiting to merge onto the road—so their brief
flirtation with third gear came to a swift end.

"All right." She sighed. After another quick peek into
the back seat, where Rosie was bongoing away on her
car seat and ignoring the adult conversation, she fixed
her gaze on Todd. "I'll bite. What did he tell you?"

Todd slid his eyes sideways so he could look at her
without moving his head. "You can guess."

"No, I can't guess. Did he say I was a miserable shrew? A certified crackpot?" She lowered her voice slightly, just in case Rosie snapped out of her Cream-induced trance and decided to pay attention to their discussion.

"The second. Not the first."

"He thought I was a crackpot?" The bastard!

"Well, you are, kind of," Todd argued.

"He was the one screwing around with a woman whose letters are more effective than Ipecac."

"Ipecac?"

"It's a syrup that causes vomiting. You give it to kids if they drink Windex."

His upper lip twitched in distaste, then relaxed into a grin. "All right. He didn't choose his pen pals wisely. But you're still a crackpot, Sally."

"Give me three examples."

"Three?" The traffic began to move, slowly. "He told me you have this yarn thing hanging over Rosie's bed."

"A dream catcher. There's nothing crackpot about that. It's a beautiful wall decoration, and it's supposed to bring happy dreams and help you remember them."

"You never wear pants."

"That's not true!" What the hell had been wrong with Paul? Why would he have lied to his best friend about Sally's wardrobe? He'd never said anything to *her* about it. "I do wear pants sometimes. I just prefer the way skirts feel, the way they float around my thighs, all free and soft."

Todd swallowed and grimaced at the traffic.

"Three," she pressed him. "Three examples."

"You painted your front door orange."

"And it looks gorgeous. The color of a sunset. People are always commenting on our front door."

"I bet they are."

"Positive comments," she clarified. "Why should everyone's house look the same? Why not do something a little different?"

"See, that's the way crackpots think," he said, as if she'd proven his point.

"I don't think I'm a crackpot. I don't know why Paul would have said I was. I'd never call *him* a crackpot, even though he was very different from me. You're different from me. Do you think I should call you a crackpot?"

"No—because I'm not one. You *are* one."

"That's ridiculous. And Paul was a jerk to say so."

"You carry more stuff in your tote bag than most freighters carry in their cargo hold. Tell me that's not a crackpot thing to do."

"It's practical. When Paul was alive, half the stuff I carried around in my bag was for him. Guys love to ridicule women about how much they carry in their purses, but then, when they're done sneering, they always ask us to carry their wallet, or their eyeglass case, or snacks for the road, or toys for the kid. Men mock us, and then we get stuck lugging around all their junk." She thought about that for a moment, trying to savor her indignation, but it vanished in a small laugh. "You're right. Only a crackpot would carry around her husband's junk after he'd made fun of how much stuff she was carrying around."

A song came on, slow and easy. The singer crooned that it was sleepy time—actually, sleepy-time *time,* which, if they were going to bandy about the word *crackpot,* seemed like a crackpot lyric to Sally. But the song was teasing and drawling, soothing and subliminal. They'd reached the Mass Pike and the car was sailing along at a steady speed. When Sally turned to check on Rosie, she saw the child's eyes were closed, her head sagging against the upholstery.

"The power of suggestion," Sally murmured, smiling at how adorable Rosie looked when she slept. "This song knocked her out."

"It was a long day for her," he pointed out, surprising Sally with his empathy. "Don't kids her age usually take naps?"

"Some do, some don't. She doesn't nap too often anymore." Another peek at the dozing child filled Sally with maternal warmth, a sweet nostalgia for Rosie's napping years. Just months ago, she couldn't get through a day without a nap. Now she was so mature.

Turning forward, Sally smiled at Todd, who probably didn't notice because he was focused on the highway. "She had a great time today."

"Better than we did," Todd guessed.

"We didn't have a good time?"

"Well, we didn't accomplish what we set out to do."

"But other than that, it was good."

He risked a glance her way. "You think so?"

"Of course it was. We walked, we saw things—'

"We walked, and we walked..." A grin tugged the corners of his mouth. "Then we walked some more."

"We absorbed a little of Boston's history. We took a ride on a Swan Boat—'

"Which was about as exciting as sitting on a park bench."

"A moving park bench. In a beautiful park. All the flowers were budding, Todd. It was very pretty."

He seemed torn, as if he knew she was right but couldn't bear to agree with her.

"And we had a delicious dinner—'

"Your daughter ate eggplant and you ate squid."

"And it was delicious."

His grin grew wider. "You *are* a crackpot, Sally. A tolerable one, though."

She bristled, even though she sensed that calling her a tolerable crackpot was his idea of a compliment. A tiny part of her was touched that after so many years of antipathy he could compliment her. But she would have been a lot more touched if he'd said he thought she was a tolerable genius or a tolerable wit, or even a tolerable companion.

"So, what are we going to do about Laura?" he asked, pulling her thoughts back to practical matters.

"Laura Hawkes?"

"Well, we're not going to do anything about *her*. We've met her, and she's not the right Laura. Who the hell is Vigo Hawkes, by the way?"

"You've never heard of him?" When Todd shook his head, she said, "He's probably the best-known ceramist in America."

"Ceramist?"

"He makes pots."

"Pots."

"Clay pots. Beautiful ones. I wish I could afford one of his pieces, but I can't."

"He must charge a lot for them, given that fancy little town house where he hangs his hat—to say nothing of a couple hundred acres in Lenox. To say nothing of his wife. She looked like the sort of woman you'd need to take out a mortgage to afford."

"I thought she was charming," Sally argued.

"Her apple juice was disgusting."

"It was tart."

"It was vile. She struck me as the kind of woman who has whims that cost a fortune. An apple juicer? Come on. The woman needs a life."

"She seemed fond of Paul."

"Then she needs a life and a shit detector."

"He fooled me, Todd. I'm not going to put her down because she didn't realize he was a cheating creep. He didn't cheat her. In fact, he probably did an excellent job on her land purchase in Lenox."

"He was the best real estate lawyer in western Massachusetts," Todd conceded. "All the rich folks buying vacation places must have passed his name around." He drove for a minute, ruminating. "She thinks the Berkshires are cute."

"She's urban. She doesn't know better."

The CD ended, filling the car with a silence that felt warm and damp, like steam. "So, what are we going to do?" Todd asked, his voice soft but striking against the sudden stillness.

"About what?"

"About finding Laura."

"I don't know." She honestly didn't. After today, she was no longer sure she wanted to go chasing down other mysterious Lauras, barging into other people's houses, drinking their apple juice and becoming acquainted with their pets. She didn't know whether she wanted to spend other weekends traveling places with Todd. With Rosie, yes—Rosie could turn any outing into an adventure. But Todd?

"I could go back to the phone list on the disk from his office," he said.

"It's a long list."

"Maybe there's something in it."

"Or maybe we could give up."

Todd gave her a stare that lasted long enough for the car to drift across the broken line that marked their lane. He straightened the steering wheel and frowned. "What about your pocketknife?"

There was that. She wanted the knife back. "You're right. Let's not give up yet."

"What's so special about the knife, anyway?"

She sighed. It was truly an awful knife, chintzy and kitsch. If she explained why the knife meant something to her, she'd have to explain her life. She'd already given Todd enough ammunition when she'd told him she grew up in a trailer. If she told him about her father, all Todd's deepest prejudices about her would be reinforced.

So what? She was damn proud of who she was and how far she'd come, and if Todd gave her a hard time, she'd give him an even harder time right back.

"The knife belonged to my father," she told him.

"And?"

Sally sighed again. "And it was the only thing of my father's that I ever had."

"The only thing? What do you mean?"

She leaned back until her head touched the headrest, then observed the slope of his headlights as they struck the pavement. "I never even met him. Unlike Paul, he didn't choose to do the right thing. He might not have even known my mother was pregnant. They had a fling and he left town. He was a rambling man, as my mother used to say."

Todd glanced her way—not nearly as long a look as last time—but said nothing.

"All I ever had of him was that pocketknife. It was

a cheap thing, with a hula dancer painted on the handle. He'd left it behind when he took off.''

"You're kidding."

"No." She sat straighter, pressed her knees together and folded her hands in her lap, as if sitting primly would earn her a little respect.

"He knocked up your mother in the trailer, took a powder and left behind a knife with a hula dancer on it? Christ." A sardonic laugh escaped Todd. "It sounds like a country-western song."

"Oh, yes, that's me. Hillbilly through and through."

"You said it, not me."

"I am not a hillbilly. I grew up in upstate New York. We don't have hillbillies there." He laughed again, which fed her indignation. "I happen to have been accepted to Winfield College with a scholarship. I manage a prosperous business in town. I was married for nearly six years to a successful lawyer. So don't go turning me into some exemplar of poor white trash. *Exemplar,*" she repeated, enunciating each syllable. "See? I've got an impressive vocabulary, too."

His laughter faded. "Hey, don't get all defensive on me. I was just saying—'

"What were you saying?" she snapped.

"Nothing." He drove for a moment in silence, then asked, "Why did you give Paul the knife, if it was so important to you?"

"Because I—' No, not because she loved him. Even if that had been the reason, she wouldn't have admitted it. And it really wasn't the reason. Love hadn't been a part of it. "Because I thought he was a decent, dependable man," she finally answered, then nodded at the truth within those words. "My father wasn't decent or dependable, but Paul was—I *thought*—and giving him the knife was kind of closing the circle. My mother had given my father's knife to me, so it made sense for me to give it to the father of my daughter. I guess I thought maybe in time he'd give it to Rosie. I didn't know he was going to pass it along to some floozy mistress.'' The thought left a bitter taste on her tongue. Paul might have been more decent and dependable than her father, but not much. Bad enough that he'd cheated on her. Far worse that he'd given away an item she'd presented to him out of pure sentiment. The knife was her legacy, and he'd given it to some home wrecker with a penchant for gooey writing.

''You really want it back,'' he half asked.

''Yes.''

''Then we're going to have to find the right Laura.''

One word seemed to linger in the air: *we. We're* going to have to find the right Laura. Todd saw this pursuit as a joint effort.

Just days ago, she'd been wishing he would return the damn letters and let her go about tracking down their author without any input from him. She'd thought Laura was her problem, her crisis, and he didn't belong anywhere close to it. She'd been irritated that he wanted to include himself in the search, and she'd allowed him to come along today only out of some possibly misguided impulse.

But now that they'd survived the day, she wasn't as eager to continue the quest alone. For all his grumpiness, for all his prickly reactions, his scowling and eye rolling and obvious annoyance, Todd had made the trip to Boston more...well, interesting. Maybe even more fun, although she'd have to think long and hard before admitting that.

And he'd bought Rosie the rice necklace, which he hadn't had to do.

A minute passed. All she heard was the hum of the tires against the road, Rosie's faint snore, the purr of the engine. "You can pick another CD," he said. "There's a light in the glove compartment."

"Are you sure you don't want to listen to 'Animal Sweet'?" she asked.

He flashed a look at her, then realized she was joking and grinned. "Put on 'Animal Sweet' and you're walking the rest of the way home."

She removed the Cream CD from the stereo, opened the glove compartment and searched through Todd's collection. "Sting! I love Sting."

"You do?" He eyed her as she inserted the Sting CD into the tray in the dashboard.

"You sound surprised."

"I am. I like Sting, too."

"And I liked Cream. Hmm. If we both like the same two CDs, does that mean you're a crackpot?"

He laughed.

They drove deeper into the evening's darkness. Sting sang about lying in fields of gold with his lover, and beyond the car was a nearly empty road flanked by the silhouettes of trees and gentle hills against a deep blue sky. Todd leaned back in his seat, his right hand draped casually over the gear stick, his left hooked around the steering wheel. Sally wondered how tall he actually was. He barely had enough room to extend his legs beneath the steering column.

She didn't think they could be friends. Not really. Not knowing that he and Paul used to talk about her, that he'd been Paul's sympathetic confidant as Paul griped about her and poked fun at her, that he thought she was a hick, possibly psychologically impaired, the sort of woman his best friend would cheat on—maybe the sort who deserved to be cheated on.

No, she and Todd couldn't be friends.

But they could be colleagues. Comrades. Partners in a quest for the truth—and a knife.

Ten

Her house was dark and her kid was snoring. She obviously hadn't expected to arrive home so late; she would have left a porch light on if she had.

He hadn't expected to get back to Winfield so late, either. He'd thought they were going to drive into Boston, have it out with Laura and drive home, not turn the trip into a marathon of sight-seeing, shopping and dining.

He had to admit the meal he'd eaten in that cozy restaurant on a charming, narrow street in the North End had been pretty damn good. And even though he'd put more miles on the soles of his shoes in one day than he ordinarily did in a week, he felt invigorated, not tired.

The outing had been educational. He now knew that Sally Driver could use the word *exemplar* correctly in a sentence, and that Vigo Hawkes was famous in certain circles for making bowls. And that it was possible to write on rice.

He'd gained other knowledge, too. Knowledge of things he couldn't quite put a name to, things that zipped and zapped inside him like electrical currents, refusing to congeal into a solid, recognizable shape. Things that made him feel as if the day he'd spent in Boston had changed him somehow.

He braked to a stop in her driveway and turned off

the engine. She unclipped her seat belt and twisted to study her happily dozing daughter. "I hate to wake her up," she whispered.

"I can carry her in," he said, startling himself. What had made him blurt out such a suggestion? He wasn't even certain he liked the little girl who insisted on calling him "Daddy's Friend," as if "Daddy's" was his first name and "Friend" his last. She'd already taken him for that silly necklace. Did he really want to lug her dead weight into Sally's house?

Well, he'd offered. And Sally was looking so grateful, her eyes radiant even in the car's shadows.

She lifted her tote bag from the floor, then got out of the car and opened the back door. Rosie didn't stir, although her nose twitched slightly as the cooler outdoor air mingled with the car's warm interior. Sally released Rosie's seat belt and lifted the crossbar, then stepped back, leaving Todd to do the heavy lifting.

Actually, Rosie wasn't too heavy. Considering how much she'd packed away that day—cannoli, eggplant, tempura and intermittent animal crackers—she was a little creature. As he hoisted her into his arms, her arms dangled down his back, her chin dug into his shoulder, her feet poked his belt and her butt settled comfortably into the bend of his elbow. She shifted and sighed, her hat tumbling to the ground and her hair tickling his ear.

Sally gathered the fallen hat as well as her own straw hat, Rosie's car seat and the bakery box. She shut the car door, then sprinted up the walk to the porch ahead of him.

Maybe her front door wasn't that garish. If the orange had been as awful as he'd thought, it would have glowed in the dark. But at 9:00 p.m. on a half-moon night, it looked a rusty brown.

She wiggled the key in the lock and the door swung inward. She flicked on a hall light, then a light above the stairway. Todd followed her up, less aware of Rosie's limp body than Sally's animated one. Not for the first time, his thoughts wandered back to what she'd said about wearing skirts, how she liked to feel them flow freely around her thighs.

He'd never realized how arousing it was to hear a woman utter the word *thighs*. Especially when she was referring to her own thighs without criticizing them. Sally hadn't commented on the circumference of her thighs, their shape or their ratio of flab to muscle. She'd mentioned them in the context of freedom.

And he'd been thinking about that far too much during the drive home.

He felt more of those electrical pulses zooming around inside him. Something had become skewed today, something that should have remained stable and familiar. Something regarding the way he felt about Sally. She'd been her usual flaky self, dragging him all over the city, clunking around in a silly hat and toting a silly bag. And yet...

He couldn't seem to stop thinking about her thighs.

At the top of the stairs she turned on another light, which illuminated the second-floor hall. They moved past a freestanding wardrobe with a filmy mirror adorning the door, past a bathroom and into a bedroom at the end of the hall.

Todd would have known this was Rosie's room even without the assortment of toys cluttering the top surface of the dresser, the stuffed animals crammed onto the rocking chair in front of the window, the wallpaper featuring flocks of colorful balloons and the dirty socks piled on the floor in a corner. He would have known because on the wall above the bed hung a huge construction of colorful yarn strung between two sticks that had been lashed into an X.

The dream catcher.

The yarn was layered, some wrapped outside the sticks and some inside to give the object depth. When Sally turned on a night-light near the door, he could see some of the colors—turquoise, magenta and lime green accented with black and cream-colored strands. The ends of the sticks were trimmed with more yarn dangling in multicolored tassels.

It was an odd piece. Definitely not Paul's style. Not Todd's style, either—but he could sort of see why someone might want to hang such a decoration over a child's bed. Not *his* bed—it would give him nightmares, all that bright color looming just above his skull—but he could see it working for Rosie.

He lowered her carefully onto the mattress, centering her head on the pillow. She made a snorting sound, loud enough to wake herself up, but after blinking once or twice without focusing her eyes, she rolled onto her side and exhaled, as if expelling what little consciousness she'd had. Sally deftly pulled off the little girl's sneakers and worked the blanket out from under her, then spread it over her. She touched Rosie's hair, reminding Todd of the way it had felt against his neck, silky and fine.

What would Sally's hair feel like? It was much thicker than Rosie's, with all those hints of red. He bet it would feel heavier, denser, more womanly.

What the hell was wrong with him? Why was he thinking about her hair?

And her thighs.

She was Paul's wife, for God's sake. Paul's widow.

The woman Paul never should have married. Why should Todd give a damn about Sally's thighs?

She straightened up from the bed and smiled at him, and he found himself thinking about her thighs and her hair and her smile, too. Again he told himself that she really wasn't pretty. Her eyes were too far apart, her nose too broad, her chin too round. But when she smiled...

More electrons rocketed through him, glancing off his heart, ricocheting the length of his spine, detouring to his groin.

She nodded toward the door, then tiptoed around the bed and led him out into the hall. "Are you going to let her sleep in her clothes?" he asked in a muted voice as they started down the stairs.

"That's easier than trying to get her undressed while she's asleep. When she wakes up tomorrow and finds herself dressed, she'll think it's cool."

"Won't she worry about her missing hat?"

Sally grinned over her shoulder at him. "I'll tell her I took it off her so the dreams would be able to reach her head."

They arrived at the front hall. He spotted Rosie's purple hat, as well as Sally's straw sun hat, tossed onto a chair beside a small semicircular table, atop which sat the bakery box and Sally's tote bag. The car seat lay on the hardwood floor next to the chair.

"Can I get you—

"So what do we do?" he said simultaneously. They both stopped. Sally grinned again and he edged a step backward, trying to will away those tiny, prickly shocks that nipped at him from inside.

"I was going to offer you a drink or something. A cannoli, maybe?"

"Save those for Rosie. She likes them more than I do."

"A drink, then?"

"No, I'm..." *I'm much too tempted to say yes.* "It's late. I think I just want to get home." *Actually, I don't. But I should. I know I should.*

"I appreciate your doing all the driving today."

"Even though you hate my car?"

"Well, it's a bourgeois car. That's probably one of the reasons you bought it."

He shrugged. He wasn't going to admit how right she was. "You've got your CD, don't you? I don't want to find those sweet animals corrupting Nirvana in my glove compartment."

"I think I've got it." She turned away and poked around inside her tote. "Yes, I've got it. And you know what else I've got?" She poked around some more, causing the contents to clatter and clang. When she turned back to face him, she was armed with a small white tube. "Vitamin E cream."

He wasn't sure what to say to that. If she'd managed to lose a playmate of Rosie's in her tote bag for three days, why shouldn't she have a tube of vitamin E cream, whatever that was, in there?

"Let me put a little on your nose." She unscrewed the cap and touched a dab of ointment to her finger. "You got a sunburn today."

He wasn't going to let her smear that gunk on his nose. "I don't need—'

"It'll soothe the skin, keep it from getting dry and peeling."

"Really, Sally, I—'

She ran her finger gently over his nose. The ointment had no fragrance, and it didn't feel particularly greasy.

But having her rub her fingertips the length of his nose, across the bridge, over the slight bump where bone met cartilage and then down to the knob of skin between his nostrils…

It should have felt weird—and it did. But more than weird, it felt nice, her fingers moving on him, stroking his face, her hand so close to him, her whole body so close. Her freedom-loving thighs. Her breasts. Her hair. Her smile, a smile that transformed her features into something astonishingly sexy.

He'd blame that thought on the long day and the rich dinner he'd eaten, and Sting's seductive tenor serenading them during the last thirty miles of their trip. He'd blame it on the sheer exhaustion he felt, and the frustration of having gotten no closer to finding Paul's Laura, and the way Sally was gazing up at him. The way her fingers brushed his cheek, his upper lip, the whisper of her touch.

He snagged her wrist and eased her hand away from his face. Her arm was more slender than he'd thought, smoother. Did she rub vitamin E cream on her inner wrists? Was that what made the skin so soft?

He'd blame it on the night, on the moment, on the possibility that if a man spent enough time with a crackpot, he could go a little crazy, too.

Bowing, he touched his lips to hers.

She didn't pull back. Didn't wrench her hand from his grip and wallop him. Didn't gasp and jerk away and say, *What the hell is wrong with you?*

He could have handled any of those responses. But no. She did the one thing he couldn't handle. She angled her head, made a tiny moan and opened her mouth.

All right, then. He was crazy. For the next brief portion of his life, he was going to be an absolute lunatic.

He was going to grab Sally, haul her lush body against him, fill her mouth with his tongue and let those circuits fire wildly inside him.

Who cared that he didn't exactly like her? Who cared that he'd never in his entire life thought of her in sexual terms? Right now, *sexual* was exactly the term in which he was thinking of her.

She was a phenomenal kisser. Her tongue matched his, teased, taunted. She lifted the arm he was holding so she could cup her hand over his shoulder, and combed the fingers of her other hand through the hair at the back of his head. His pulse was thumping so forcefully in his skull she could probably feel the beat through his scalp.

God, he wanted her. He released her wrist so he could circle his arms around her waist and pull her even closer. He was as horny as a kid glimpsing his first centerfold, as out of control as a teenager his first time. The warmth of her breasts pressing into his chest made him nuts. The nearness of her hips made him want to shove up her freedom-permitting skirt and stroke her thighs, spread them apart, fit himself between them. He was dying for her. Sally. He wanted her, wanted her more than he'd ever wanted a woman before.

Sally.

Sally?

He drew back slowly, trying not to wrench out of her embrace. Withdrawing too abruptly would insult her. But his sanity was returning to him in a sudden, stunning rush, and as his brain took over the thinking from his gonads, he realized that kissing Sally Driver had to be one of the most bizarre acts he'd ever indulged in. Stranger than riding the New York City subway system for three days straight, which he'd done on a dare in college. Stranger than trying to teach his mother how to access the Internet. Far stranger than going all the way with Patty Pleckart at a high-school party.

As recently as a day ago, he couldn't stand Sally. Not standing her made sense to him. Nothing that had happened in the past two minutes made any sense at all.

He glanced down at her, almost afraid of what he'd see in her face. She appeared slightly dazed, deeply bewildered, as shocked as he felt. "Well," she said breathlessly, then stepped back, putting some more distance between them.

"Um, look—'

"It's just—the cream," she mumbled. "It'll keep your nose from peeling."

"Okay." The cream. Vitamin E. Maybe it contained some of those special aphrodisiac herbs from that emporium in Brighton. Maybe that was why they'd gone momentarily berserk.

"So, about Laura…"

"Yeah, I'll—uh—'

"Fine."

"Okay."

He inhaled, appalled at how shaky his breath was, and bolted for the door. Outside on her porch, he sucked in another deep double-lungful of air, hoping the cool night would yank his psyche back into alignment.

His psyche was all right. Unfortunately, a part of him located a bit below his psyche was still hot and hard and aching.

For Sally Driver. Jesus Christ.

He stormed down the steps and across the lawn to his car. Flung himself behind the wheel, revved the engine, ordered Todd Junior to chill out and backed down her driveway. He needed to get laid—by anyone other than Sally. He needed a cold shower. He needed perspective.

He needed…*something*. Anything. Anything other than Sally.

His best friend's wife. His best friend's weirdo widow.

That would explain it. She was a lonely widow. She'd gone without for a while, and he'd seemed convenient. She was only using him. Hey, he ought to be offended.

Except he could think of few things he'd enjoy more than being used by a busty, lusty woman with a keen sensitivity about the freedom of her thighs. Even if she was a flake. Even if she could be pushy and bossy and sanctimonious. Even if her five-year-old kid knew more about music than she did.

"Paul," he muttered, speeding down her street in a rage to get away from her. "Paul, you son of a bitch, this is your fault. This whole thing—the letters, the knife, the whole goddamn day and that kiss, that absurd, in-fucking-credible kiss… It's all your fault."

The woman who entered the New Day Café looked familiar to Sally. On the petite side of average and the far side of middle age, she had a compact body, a disproportionately long face and short, stiff hair, red with a faint undertone of violet. She wasn't a regular at the café, but Sally knew she'd seen her before.

She congratulated herself on knowing that much. Her mind had been as scrambled as a Spanish omelette since Saturday night. Thank God she hadn't had to work Sunday. If she had, she would have been useless. Worse than useless. She would have filled the sugar bowls with salt and burned the unbaked pastries Greta left. She would have burned the coffee. She might have burned the whole damn place down.

Instead, she'd stumbled through Sunday like someone

emerging from a fever-induced delirium. The morning sunlight had singed her eyes, but that was preferable to the alternative. Whenever she'd closed her eyes, she'd felt a deep, physical pull of memory—a memory of kissing Todd Sloane.

Ugh. Todd Sloane. The pompous boob. The driver of a Snob, the condescending twit, the defender and protector of Sally's cheating husband. Why on earth had she kissed him?

The worst part hadn't been kissing him. It had been stopping the kiss, ending it, watching him leave her house and wishing he would have stayed, wishing—God help her—he'd stayed all night, kissed her again, torn off his rumpled-journalist apparel and made savage love to her.

Paul had been good in bed, but he'd never been savage. It had never even occurred to Sally that she'd like savage. But one kiss from Todd, one unexpected, unrestrained, totally inappropriate kiss, and *savage* had become her new point of reference.

The entire incident left her profoundly disturbed. She'd sent Rosie next door to play with Trevor all day yesterday, and tried to lose herself in assorted sections of the Sunday *Boston Globe*. Thumbing through the so-called regional news section, she realized that the *Globe's* idea of regional didn't offer nearly enough coverage of Winfield, its neighboring hamlets and the orchards, granite quarries and ski slopes that occupied this part of Massachusetts. She'd reached for the phone, thinking she ought to call the publisher of the *Valley News* to recommend that they add a Sunday edition.

Then she'd remembered that the publisher of the *Valley News* was Todd Sloane. She wouldn't phone him even if her mouth had erupted in hives and she had to report that she was suffering from some deeply contagious infection that she'd likely passed on to him during those prolonged seconds of insanity in her front hall the previous night. She was not going to phone him, ever—other than to demand that he give her back the Laura letters and then stay far away from her.

She *had* enjoyed the Saturday they'd spent together, though. And when she'd kissed him, when they'd stood so close to each other during those few minutes in her entry hall, his eyes darker than the space between the stars in the night sky and his hair even darker than that, and his mouth had come down on hers…

Well, she hadn't regretted kissing him then. Only afterward, when she'd come to her senses, did she comprehend what a colossal mistake it had been.

"Has Officer Bronowski had his second cup yet?" Tina asked, directing a look at the tall, gaunt officer seated two tables to the left of the black-clad novelist and one table to the right of the trio of burly guys wearing Evergreen Landscaping T-shirts and devouring banana-nut muffins and jumbo lattes. Officer Bronowski was so predictable Tina and Sally would worry that something was wrong if he didn't order a refill precisely 12.3 minutes after he paid for his first cup.

Sally checked her watch. "It's only eleven minutes," she assured Tina. "How are you? How was your weekend? Has Howard made up his mind about Dartmouth yet?" She'd rather talk about Howard than think about the man in her own life—who wasn't in her life and who never would be, as long as she kept her wits about her.

Tina didn't answer. She was watching the woman who'd entered, the one with the hair so oddly colored and motionless it looked like the molded and painted plastic hair found on cheap dolls. The woman wore cream-colored linen slacks with crisp pleats running down the leg fronts, a tan linen blazer with brass buttons, a beige shell blouse and an artfully tied silk scarf featuring a paisley pattern. Gold marble-size balls adorned her earlobes, and a wide gold band and a matching gold ring with a hefty chunk of diamond embedded in it circled her ring finger. If not for her hair, she'd look like a well-groomed professional. A real-estate saleswoman, perhaps, or a deputy mayor in charge of the arts. As it was, she looked like a real-estate saleswoman or a deputy mayor whose hairstylist had been having a very bad day.

Where had Sally seen her before?

The woman stopped scrutinizing the pastries in the showcase below the counter and lifted her gaze to Sally. "My son said I had to come here," she announced. "But I don't know why."

Todd, Sally thought her mind still elsewhere, then silently berated herself for remaining fixated on him a full thirty-six hours after that stupid kiss. She faked a polite smile for the woman, and then it hit her. *Todd.* The woman was Todd's mother.

"He said I should come here and have some coffee and stay out of his hair," the woman continued. "Now, tell me, what kind of son would say that to his mother?"

Sally suffered a brief flashback to Saturday night, when she'd been in his hair, her fingers twining through the thick black waves, feeling the heat of his skin at his nape. She shook her head clear, forced another smile and said, "It's the kind of son who knows how good our coffee is. Today we've got our usual breakfast blend and a delicious Sumatra, and our flavored coffee is an almond-cinnamon."

"The almond-cinnamon is awesome," Tina interjected, reaching for the breakfast-blend decanter as Officer Bronowski pushed back his chair. In a perfectly timed choreography, she had the decanter poised and ready to pour the moment he slid his mug onto the counter. He smiled bashfully as she refilled the cup, nodded his thanks and moseyed back to his seat.

"It sounds appalling," Todd's mother said. "Almond and cinnamon? What's wrong with regular coffee?"

"We've got regular coffee," Sally said.

"Good old-fashioned coffee?" Todd's mother asked. "The kind of coffee that, when you ask someone for a cup of coffee, this is what they give you?"

"That would be our breakfast blend." Where had Sally met her? At her wedding, she recalled—Paul had wanted Todd's parents there because he'd developed a close relationship with them over the years. And at Paul's funeral. Mrs. Sloane had swooped down on Sally in the parlor of the funeral home, clamped both her hands around one of Sally's and said, "You don't know me, but—"

"Yes, I do," Sally had said.

"No, you don't," Mrs. Sloane had insisted. Then she'd introduced herself and babbled for a while about how she'd always admired Paul's height. "Todd is too tall," she'd said. "Paul was the right height. There wasn't too much of him. I never got a stiff neck with him."

Why had Todd told his mother to come to the New Day Café? Was Sally supposed to acknowledge that they'd met before? At a wedding and a funeral?

"You probably don't remember me—"

Sally cut her off. "You're Todd Sloane's mother," she said, smiling cordially.

"Helen Sloane. All right, I'll have some of that, what is it? Breakfast blend? Explain this, Sally—can I call you Sally?"

"Yes."

"Explain this, Sally—what exactly is blended in the breakfast blend?"

"Different roasts of beans," Sally told her. "Colombian regular roast, dark roast, a touch of mocha java. It's a nice combination. It tastes very…regular."

Helen Sloane gazed earnestly across the counter at her. "How are you doing, dear? You must miss Paul terribly. It's been awful for you, hasn't it."

"I'm doing okay, thank you."

"Just awful," Helen overruled her. "Tragic. Heart-rending. He was such a fine young man. I was so happy he was Todd's roommate in college. I thought, what a fine young man! He'll keep Todd in line."

"I don't think he did," Sally muttered.

"No, but he was a fine man. This is the breakfast blend, right?" she asked as Tina handed her a mug of coffee.

"Yes," Tina said. "You're gonna love it."

"What is wrong with the world that you can't just get a plain cup of coffee anymore?" Todd's mother issued a sigh deep enough to have originated somewhere in the vicinity of her kneecaps. "Just what is wrong with this world? I've had it up to here—" she karate-chopped the air next to her forehead "—with all this new stuff. The computer. You know? I've had it up to here with that blasted computer."

Tina sent Sally a hesitant smile, one that communicated, *Should I signal Officer Bronowski that we've got a problem, or do you think she's harmless?* Sally refused to smile back, afraid Helen would suspect they were laughing at her. "I'm sorry you're having computer problems. Would you like a pastry? We've got pear tarts today. They're wonderful. Also cheese Danish, banana-nut muffins, zucchini bread, bagels, croissants—"

"The thing is..." Todd's mother took a delicate sip of her coffee. "Mmm. This is good. What do I owe you?"

Tina turned and deliberately stared at the wall behind the counter, where a placard listed the café's prices. Then she turned back, a large, head-swiveling turn. "A dollar thirty."

"This is very good," Todd's mother murmured, un-snapping the flap of her purse and sliding two dollars from her wallet. "I'm not that old, but I remember a time when a person could put out a newspaper with nothing but a typewriter on her desk. None of this computer nonsense. A document was something you got from City Hall and wrote an editorial about. A file was a stack of papers in a manila folder. Enter was what you did through a door. Escape was what jailbirds tried to do. Am I making sense?"

"Absolutely," Sally said politely.

"Todd is trying to run an entire newspaper with these blasted computers. Fine, I understand, it's a new millennium. Computers are necessary. But they made type-writers obsolete. You see what I'm getting at? It's that feeling of obsolescence. My son tells me I'm in his hair."

Sally did see what she was getting at. Tina obviously didn't. She frowned, shrugged and wandered down the counter to the cash register to get Helen's change.

"Did Todd tell you he didn't want you to work at the paper anymore?" Sally asked. If the woman answered yes, Sally would add that to her already substantial list of reasons to hate the man.

"It's not as if I don't think he can run the paper. He grew up with it. He worked at every level, starting as a newspaper deliverer. We can't call them newsboys anymore, did you know that? Too many girls are delivering papers, so we have to call them newspaper deliverers. But Todd was the best deliverer we ever had. I'm not just saying that because I'm his mother. He really was the best. Never threw the paper on people's roofs, never missed a house, never missed a day—not even in a blizzard. Then, when he got older, he wrote copy, he sold ads, he did layout—the old-fashioned way, by hand. Now it's all done by computer. Everything's done by computer. It's a whole new world."

"We use a computer here," Sally said. "I'm sure you could learn how to use one."

"I don't *want* to learn," Todd's mother confessed. "I like doing things my own way."

"So Todd told you to leave the newspaper? He ought to be shot." Saying so cheered Sally.

Helen grinned, "Now, don't you go threatening my son with death." She sipped some more coffee. "So how is your little girl doing, Sally? Is she all right?"

"She's fine."

"She was the light of Paul's life, you know. I didn't see much of him after you two got married, but when I did, when he'd drop by the newspaper offices to visit Todd, he always told me Rosie was the light of his life."

"He was a wonderful father," Sally said, meaning it. As long as he wasn't having assignations with Laura when he was supposed to be taking care of Rosie, she'd give him bonus points for his paternal devotion.

"He'd always stop in at my office when he came to

see Todd. He was such a gentleman, your husband. Always had a friendly word for me. He never gave me a hard time about my struggles with the computer.''

"There's really nothing to working a computer," Tina pointed out as she handed Helen her change, then untied her apron and reached for her backpack. "If you can program a VCR, you can use a computer."

"I can't program a VCR," Helen admitted, then took another sip of coffee. "This is really good. I shouldn't be taking up all your time. I'll just go sit at that table over there."

"You aren't taking up our time," Sally said, but Helen held up her hands to silence her, then carried her coffee to the empty table near the black-clad scribe and settled into the chair.

"I gotta go," Tina said, slinging her backpack over one shoulder and heading for the door. "I've got my eugenics seminar."

Eugenics? They hadn't offered any seminars in eugenics when Sally had been a student at Winfield College. Perhaps Tina would learn from it that Howard wasn't worth breeding with. Or that he was. Perhaps his lack of a tattoo marked him as a higher order of human.

She waved Tina off, then braced herself as a throng of people spilled into the café: two businessmen toting leather briefcases and conferring solemnly as they eyed the pastries; two musty-looking professorial types, one male and one female, bickering about Joyce Carol Oates; three women in formfitting leggings, sweatshirts and headbands, apparently rewarding themselves after a vigorous workout. They ordered first: two zucchini breads with cream cheese, one cinnamon roll, three large cappuccinos. So much for all their efforts at the health club, Sally thought as she served up their high-calorie treats.

One of the businessmen answered a cell-phone call while Sally poured Sumatra coffee for them both. The professors transferred their argument from Joyce Carol Oates's philosophy of boxing to the relative merits of bran versus banana muffins—"Raisins are high in iron!" "Yes, but bananas are high in potassium!"

Sally sashayed the length of the counter in one direction and then the other, marveling at Tina's exquisite sense of timing in having left the café just seconds before this influx of customers. Nicholas, a rock star in waiting, would be arriving around eleven to help Sally with the lunchtime crush—serving coffee and light sandwiches paid him enough to keep him afloat until some record producer discovered him and landed him on the fast track to a Grammy. But eleven o'clock was more than two hours away, and by the time the professors finished arguing over who was going to pay for their croissants so they could resume arguing over Joyce Carol Oates, four more customers had entered, sidled up to the counter and ordered eight coffees, ten muffins and two large orange juices to go.

"You work too hard," Helen commented when the spate of customers finally trickled off. She had relinquished her table to the businessmen, both of whom were now on cell phones, talking with their callers while simultaneously communicating by hand signal with each other. Helen set her cup on the counter. "You ought to hire someone to help you out."

"This was unusual," Sally told her. "We always get an early crowd in, but then it typically quiets down until lunchtime. I don't know why it got so hectic in here." Not that she was complaining. Racing around and filling orders had kept her from thinking about Todd.

But now that his mother was hovering directly across

the counter from her, staring at her out of sharp, dark eyes that looked uncannily like Todd's, Sally started thinking about him again. About how he was a menace to her emotional stability, how he had really better give the damn letters back to her, how she could find Laura and get her knife without any help from him, how she owed him twenty bucks for the necklace he'd bought Rosie. How it was horribly unfair that the first man she'd kissed since her husband died had to have been Todd, and he had to have kissed like a virtuoso. A savage one.

"You need to hire more staff," Helen declared again. "I'm not an expert on the restaurant business, but I ran a newspaper with my husband for forty years, and I know when a business is understaffed."

"Good workers are hard to find," Sally said. "I get part-timers from the college, but they come and go, and their first priority is school. Most people who work here don't want to make a career of it."

"Who can blame them? I mean, what sort of twenty-year-old wants to spend the rest of her life pouring coffee in a diner? No offense meant," she added, evidently realizing that she had just come pretty close to describing Sally.

"If I could find older people, I'd be happy to hire them. It's not that I want to hire college kids. It's just that they're the ones available on a part-time basis."

"Oh, I'd bet there are lots of older people who'd enjoy working at a place like this. Not older, but *mature*. Mature people who feel obsolete in their other places of business. Someone who can serve coffee and snacks with a smile on her face will never be obsolete, am I right?"

Sally eyed Helen curiously. Was the woman angling for a job at the New Day? Now, that would be hilarious.

Todd's mother working with Sally. Working *for* Sally. Because her own son had evicted her from the newspaper she'd run for forty years. Because she'd had trouble learning how to use a computer.

Because her son was a coldhearted creep who could kiss like Casanova on his best day and then turn around and walk away without a backward glance. Because he could do that to the widow of his best friend, who'd turned out to be a faithless bastard.

Because the enemy of her enemy was her ally. Because if Todd had told his mother to get out of his hair, Sally wanted the woman on her side, so she could show Helen what loyalty and kindness were really all about.

Oh, the irony of it: Todd's mother working for Sally. Sally treating the woman with the respect and dignity she couldn't get from her own jackass son.

"If I could hire you," Sally said with a smile, "I'd do it in an instant."

Eleven

Todd was doing an AltaVista search of the word *thigh*, just for the hell of it, when he spotted a lanky man ambling through the newsroom. Walter Sloane was dressed for golf: hideous canary-yellow slacks, a plaid short-sleeve shirt, a woven white fabric belt and white shoes. Much could be said for golf, but its practitioners were rarely exemplars of good taste in fashion.

Exemplar. Loathsome word.

He hastily disconnected from the Internet before his father reached his office. Such luck, he thought sourly, that less than ten minutes after he'd gotten rid of his mother, his father would show up.

"Hey, there!" Walter bellowed as he swung through Todd's open door.

"Hi, Dad." He decided to be a good sport about his father's visit. His father wasn't his mother; Todd appreciated a little variety in his pests. "What's up?"

"I just thought I'd drop by. Where's your mother?"

"I sent her out for coffee." That sounded wrong; it wasn't as if he was treating her like a gofer, asking her to run trivial errands. "Coffee for herself," he clarified. "I thought she would enjoy a good cup of coffee instead of the industrial sludge we've got brewing here." And he'd thought she could spend a morning driving Sally crazy instead of driving him crazy. Sally deserved it, since she was the most driving-him-crazy woman in his life.

She would never drive him crazy again, he resolved. He was never even going to think about her again. Her exemplary thighs would never again preoccupy his thoughts.

His father's complexion was a rich chestnut hue, evenly darkened from the many days he indulged his passion for golf. Could spending hours in the spring sunshine cause senile dementia? Todd wondered, recalling his mother's frequent clucking about the old man's mental failings. Too many hours in the sun could cause wrinkles, he knew, and skin cancer. Perhaps his father ought to apply vitamin E cream to his face.

No. He wasn't going to think about what Sally carried in her bag. He wasn't going to think about what she'd rubbed on his nose. He wasn't going to think about the weird effect her touch had had on him, how it had made him infinitely more demented than his father would ever be. Todd was over that now. Completely cured. One hundred percent sane.

"What did you need Mom for?" he asked, leaning back in his chair and smiling at his father, acting as if he honestly believed his psyche had returned to full functionality.

"I wanted to talk to her about this great deal," his father said, arranging his long body in one of the chairs that faced Todd's desk. "My cousin Dale—you remember him, don't you?"

Todd nodded. Cousin Dale was the one who'd been married four times, or possibly five. Todd remembered him, but his wives were a blur.

"He owns a place down on Hilton Head Island. A

villa, I guess you'd call it. Villa. Fancy name for a condo, but you get the idea.''

"I get the idea," Todd said, hoping to speed things along.

"Anyway, his wife's daughter is getting married in San Diego in June, and Dale and his wife have to spend the entire month of June in San Diego. So Dale said that if we wanted, we could house-sit for him for the month. Villa-sit, I guess you'd call it.''

"Okay."

"It's right on a golf course. Overlooking the seventh hole, he tells me. Only drawback I can see, they've got a schnauzer.''

"So you'd be dog-sitting, too?''

"Dog- and villa-sitting. I'd have to take it for a walk twice a day. The dog, not the villa.''

"I figured."

"Not an onerous burden, am I right? Feed it, take it for a walk, scratch its belly. And we'd be overlooking the seventh hole. Sounds like a pretty sweet deal to me.''

"Mom doesn't want to go," Todd guessed.

"I mentioned it to her. She said she hates schnauzers. Do you remember her ever saying she hated schnauzers? I don't. But then, maybe my memory isn't as sharp as it used to be.''

"I've never heard her say anything one way or another about schnauzers.''

"So I'm not losing my mind?'' His father's face creased with a smile of relief. "I thought if she'd ever said anything about schnauzers, it's the sort of thing I'd remember. You don't forget when your wife says things about schnauzers, am I right?''

"I couldn't say, Dad. It's been a while since I had a wife.''

"I remember that," his father said, then chuckled. "A son's divorce you don't forget. I still regret that it didn't work out. What was her name again?"

"Denise." Todd wasn't alarmed. His father could never remember Denise's name even when Todd had been married to her.

"Denise. Right. You need a wife, Todd. A wife is a good thing." He reflected for a minute, his eyes fading. They brightened again. "Sometimes a wife can be a royal pain in the ass."

"I know."

"Your mother—she keeps going on and on about the schnauzer."

"It's not the dog she's objecting to, Dad," Todd pointed out. "She doesn't want to spend a month at a golf resort on Hilton Head Island. She's talking about the dog, but it's the golf she doesn't want."

"I'm telling you—a wife can be more trouble than she's worth. It's an incredible golf course. Mom and I visited Dale down there last year, remember? Great course. We had a wonderful time. Your mother says she hated the dog, but I don't remember her having any problem with it. We could spend an entire month there. It would be a vacation for us both."

"A romantic getaway," Todd said helpfully.

"A romantic golf getaway." His father shook his head. "Why won't she come to Hilton Head with me? And don't tell me it's because of the dog."

"She thinks the newspaper will fall apart if she leaves it." Todd leaned forward, seeing an ally in his father. "She's here all the time, pretending she's still running things. But she's not running anything. She slows me down, Dad. She wants to do things her way, but her way is about twenty years out of date."

"Here's an idea," Walter said, leaning forward as well, until their foreheads were only a few inches apart. He grinned conspiratorially. "Leave her to run the newspaper and *you* come to Hilton Head with me. We'll golf, we'll play with the schnauzer, and maybe you'll meet a new wife."

On a golf course on Hilton Head? Not likely. "I'd love to go golfing with you, Dad—" not true; golf bored him to tears "—but Mom can't run the newspaper by herself. She's still trying to figure out how to turn her computer on and off."

"She doesn't have any problems with our computer at home," Walter said, digging through his thick silver hair to scratch his head in a perfectly clichéd gesture of puzzlement. "I wonder why. Maybe it's because I do all the computer stuff at home."

If his father had mastered the minitower desktop Todd had bought for his parents last year, the guy couldn't be missing too many marbles. So what if he couldn't recall the term *doorknob?* He'd probably had to sacrifice a little memory to make space for all the computer skills he had uploaded into his brain.

"It's not that I don't love Mom," Todd said. "It's just that she needs to let go of the paper. If she had something else to fill her time, she'd be fine."

"Golf," his father suggested.

"Yeah, well, she's not as crazy about it as you are. Maybe you ought to compromise a little. One month at Cousin Dale's place, one month hiking around the ruins at Machu Picchu."

Walter wrinkled his nose in distaste. "I hate ruins."

"She hates golf."

"No, she doesn't."

"Dad, listen to her. It's not up to you to decide what

she likes." Todd didn't want to become his parents' marriage counselor, but he saw no good in their each separately reporting to him on the idiosyncrasies and obsessions of the other. They were both idiosyncratic, both obsessive. After forty years of marriage, they should have learned how to maneuver around each other's neuroses.

His peripheral vision snagged on a figure on the other side of the glass wall, striding toward his office. Sometimes Todd greeted Eddie Lesher's approach with dread. Not this time. He would rather deal with Eddie than give his father a tutorial on how to communicate with his wife.

"Look, Dad," he said a little too eagerly, grinning at Eddie as he neared the door. "I've got work to do. Eddie!" he greeted the young reporter who hovered on the threshold. Eddie was too skinny to fill the doorway. He sort of bisected it, though. "What's up?"

"Hi, Todd." Eddie nodded deferentially to Walter. "Hi, Mr. Sloane."

"Do I know you?" Walter asked, turning in his chair and giving Eddie a pleasantly befuddled appraisal.

Todd decided that not recognizing Eddie wasn't proof of incipient Alzheimer's disease. His father didn't work at the paper anymore. He came and went, and went more often than he came. "This is one of our staff reporters, Dad. Eddie Lesher. You'll have to excuse us—we've got work to do." There wasn't a single thing Todd would want to say to Eddie that couldn't be said in front of his father, but implying that they had important business to discuss seemed the most effective way to get his old man out of the chair and out of the office.

Walter was a little slow on the uptake, but he did finally hoist himself to his feet. "Listen, Todd, if your mother comes back here, convince her that she loves schnauzers.''

Todd smiled noncommittally and waved his father off. Wearing an eager grin, Eddie swooped down on Todd's desk. The phrase ''out of the frying pan, into the fire'' scrolled across Todd's mind.

''So,'' Eddie said. His smile put the *grate* in ingratiating. ''The piece I did on that homeless guy was good, huh?''

''It was very good.'' Not Pulitzer Prize material. Not even a contender for above-the-fold. But Todd gave credit where due. It had been a solid piece of reporting.

''So, I was thinking on doing a follow-up. There are three other guys living under the railroad tracks, and—''

''No.''

''You just said the first piece was good. I was thinking, maybe a series—''

''What could you say about Homeless Man Number Two that you haven't already said about Homeless Man Number One? He's poor. He's had some hard knocks. He wants to get his act together, but he's got a thing for cheap liquor and drugs. He wishes he didn't live in the shadow of the train trestle, but he can't seem to bring himself to walk the three blocks to City Hall, where they've got a really nice Social Services Department that could find him a bed in a shelter. Writing about this once is great, Eddie. Writing about it twice is overkill. Three times is a crusade.''

''Well, someone's got to help these men.'' Eddie slid his hands into the pockets of his jeans, which were so loose the fabric seemed to swallow his knuckles.

''And if you want to be the one to help them, you have my blessings. After work today, you can fix them a nice pot of stew and take it down to the overpass for them. But I'm not devoting any more inches to them right now. Where are you on the Reddi-Mart expansion story?"

"It's coming along," Eddie said, nudging the worn carpet with a sneakered toe. "The zoning board hasn't issued its approval yet."

"That's your story, Eddie. The expansion should be a no-brainer. Why don't you find out why the zoning board is dragging their feet over this?"

"They're just bureaucrats."

"Maybe they're just bureaucrats. Maybe they discovered that Reddi-Mart is dumping untreated sewage into the Connecticut River. Maybe they're looking for a payoff. Go find out."

"I'd really rather—"

"I don't want to know what you'd really rather," Todd warned him.

Eddie sighed forlornly, backed up toward the door, then hesitated. "I was wondering..."

Todd braced himself.

"Do you think there's room for another reporter to cover Winfield College? I really hate covering the zoning board."

"Winfield College doesn't generate enough news for two reporters. It barely generates enough for one, and that's Gloria's beat. Why?"

"I don't know. I just thought..." He gave Todd another beseeching smile. "All those cute female students up there... It seems like a waste, sending Gloria to cover them."

"There are cute male students up there, too," Todd pointed out.

"But they're younger than Gloria."

"Maybe she likes younger men. Or maybe—" he added a measure of steel to his voice "—she's a professional, doing her job with objectivity rather than using it as an excuse to flirt, which, I shouldn't have to tell you, is a good way to lose your job."

Eddie's smile grew sheepish. "Well, I thought it was worth a try," he said, backing up another step. "I'll go talk to someone on the zoning board."

"Good boy." Trying not to scowl, Todd swiveled back to his monitor, now filled with his favorite screen saver, which featured floating headlines. He'd programmed it to quote famous real headlines: Dewey Beats Truman. Japan Attacks Pearl Harbor. Ford to New York: Drop Dead.

He told himself he was better off reading the archaic headlines than doing an Internet search on thighs. He wasn't really interested in thighs, anyway. Just one woman's thighs—and he wasn't interested in them, either.

He needed a social life. He and Eddie both. Maybe he ought to climb out from behind his desk and do a little investigative work up the hill on the Winfield College campus. Why not? All those pretty undergraduate girls—

Who were more too young for him than the undergraduate boys were too young for Gloria.

Five or six years ago, the Winfield undergraduates wouldn't have been too young for him. Five or six years ago, Paul had married a Winfield undergrad—not by choice, but still. If he'd had his pick of the entire student body, he probably wouldn't have selected Sally, but at that age, Todd certainly couldn't have faulted his friend for checking out the campus action. A fresh, nubile young thing with a sparkle in her eyes and a touch of naiveté, glossy hair and a twinkly voice and plump, firm breasts, and free thighs....

He wondered how many undergraduates named Laura were enrolled at Winfield College.

He sat up so suddenly, the casters on the legs of his chair skidded on the smooth plastic that covered the carpet behind his desk. If Paul's Laura hadn't been a client, maybe she'd been a student. He'd screwed around with a student once. Why not twice?

Todd glanced through the glass wall at the newsroom. Gloria was at her desk, perusing a scholarly journal. Her oversize feet, shod in high-top canvas sneakers, were propped up on her desk beside her computer, and a wad of gum was receiving a violent working-over between her molars. Todd lifted the phone and punched in her extension. He watched Gloria glare at her ringing phone as if it were something evil. With a combination of reluctance and disgust, she reached across her desk and picked up the receiver.

"Gloria? Todd," he identified himself.

Her disgust ebbed slightly. Gloria was arrogant and prickly, but she was a damn good reporter, so he put up with her. And he paid her a substantial salary, so she put up with him. "Yeah?"

"Have you got a Winfield College directory from last year? Or maybe the year before."

"I've got them going back seventeen years," she told Todd. She hadn't been working for the *Valley News* for seventeen years—in fact, seventeen years ago the bulk of her writing would probably have been book reports for her eighth-grade English teacher—but her damn-good-reporter instincts made her hoard all sorts of useful references and resources.

"I don't need them from seventeen years ago," he said. "Just from last year and the year before."

"I got 'em."

In other words, if he wanted them, he could haul his butt out to her desk and fetch them himself. She wasn't going to bring them to him. He couldn't ask her to. If he did, she'd probably slap a sexism charge on him.

He needed to get away from his desk, anyway. Soviet Union Sends Cosmonaut Into Orbit was beaming across his monitor, and that reminded him of the way Sally Driver's kiss had sent him into orbit last Saturday evening. He was back on earth now—a bumpy landing, but he was safely on terra firma—and he was going to find out who Laura was so he could put his two-faced best friend and that best friend's aggravating widow, and her thighs, and her hair, and her steamy kiss, out of his mind forever.

Emerging from his office, he was blindsided by Stuart, the city editor, who yammered at him about the irate phone call he'd gotten from the school superintendent, responding to Todd's editorial on tenuring inept teachers. Todd nodded, sighed sympathetically, told Stuart he was not going to devote more than a single page to Letters to the Editor on the subject of tenure and continued through the newsroom until he reached Gloria's desk. She had resumed reading the scholarly journal; without looking up, she lifted her left hand, which held two Winfield College directories. He took them, thanked her, didn't wait around for her to say he was welcome—it would be a long wait—and returned to his office.

Aaronson, Laura. Adams, Laura. Ahern, Laura. Aikman, Laura. Albano, Laura. Anderson, Laura. Asturvian, Laura. Babcock, Laura...

Jesus Christ. The school had three thousand students, and half of them were named Laura.

All right. He could eliminate the freshmen. They would have arrived in Winfield last September, and Paul had died in January, so he wouldn't have had a chance to screw anyone in the freshman class long enough to present her with his wife's hula-girl pocketknife. Even sophomores might be a bit too young. He'd focus on juniors and seniors—

And faculty. Of course. Paul had been a sucker for a pair of plump, firm undergraduate breasts once, but surely he'd learned his lesson after a few years of marriage to Sally. If he were going to have an affair, it would be with someone wiser, someone more mature, more dignified. Someone, judging from the tone of the letters, who was a bit too well read. A Lord Byron scholar, maybe. A Byron scholar with a Sartre sideline.

Todd flipped to the front of the directory, which contained a list of all the professors and their campus offices and extensions, as well as the school's support staff. Laura Benson was on the physical education faculty.... No, Todd couldn't see Paul lusting after a sweaty, muscular jock. Laurie Cantaggio of the theater department, seemed like a possibility—but she was clearly a Laurie, not a Laura. Laura Ellroy was the assistant dean in the financial-aid office. Maybe. Laura Hahn held the Strumbacher Chair in Molecular Biology. Nope.

Laura Lovelace—security department. Maybe she had a sexy gun. Maybe she looked hot in a uniform. Maybe Paul liked to play with handcuffs. Would someone from the security department be so well versed in existentialism?

Laura O'Connor—botany assistant. If Paul had wanted to hang around with someone into gardening, he'd have hung around with his own wife. Sally was one of those earthy, organic types.

Laura Ruzeka—classics. Maybe. Laura Stratton—mathematics. Maybe. Laura Titwell—chemistry department lab manager. On the strength of her last name alone, she belonged on the maybe list.

Laura Walden—French. Promising. She could have read Sartre in the original. She could have lived for a few years in Paris, smoked too many strong black cigarettes, drunk too much overpriced wine in second-rate bistros and learned to take herself far too seriously. Laura Walden looked like a strong possibility.

In fact, she looked like the best possibility, given that the English and philosophy departments seemed to have a bias against hiring anyone with the name Laura.

Todd jotted down Laura Walden's name and office number on a memo pad. He added Laura Ellroy, Laura Lovelace, Laura Ruzeka and Laura Stratton—although he honestly couldn't see Paul getting it on with a math teacher—and Laura Titwell. He tore the sheet of paper off the pad, folded it and stuffed it into the breast pocket of his shirt.

Nearly noon, and his mother hadn't returned yet. Had she decided not to return because she'd discovered that life outside the *Valley News* was much more fun than life in her glass cage across the newsroom from him? Or had she and Sally sent each other into such extreme madness that they'd both wound up being strapped into straitjackets and trucked off to the nearest state hospital?

Either way, they weren't bothering him at the moment. He had a lunch meeting at noon with the deputy mayor, who was going to feed Todd and ply him with stories favorable to the current administration, and after that he had a meeting scheduled with his business vice president and his circulation and advertising managers to review preliminary data on whether to launch a Sunday edition of the *Valley News*. After that, he, Stuart and Gail—who was his wire services manager—would be getting together to do a front-page mock-up for tomorrow's paper.

But after all that, by around four o'clock, he could spare some time for a visit to the campus, where he could pay a friendly call on a couple of Lauras.

Maybe one of them would have an incriminating pocketknife lying on her desk. Maybe one of them would say, *Oh, you were Paul Driver's friend. You were the anchor in his storm-tossed life. You gave him a sense of family he never experienced growing up, a brotherly bond, the security of knowing who one is and where one belongs. Oh, yes, he talked about you all the time. He wanted to tell you about our relationship, and he was going to, if only he hadn't skidded his car into a tree.*

Maybe one of them would say, *If you were Paul's best friend, then you must know Paul's wife, Sally. And if you know Sally, I'm sure you understand why Paul turned to me for sex and affection.*

And Todd would nod and say, Of course I understand.

Even though he was no longer sure he did.

Twelve

Winfield College sat on a hill above downtown Winfield. A small hill, to be sure, and Sally ordinarily would have enjoyed a leisurely stroll up Main Street's gentle incline, observing how the shops lining the sidewalk evolved from practical to whimsical. The boutique specializing in candles and incense would have gone bust in a week if it had been located down near the railroad tracks. It was half a block from campus, though, and it was flourishing. The hardware store, on the other hand, was thriving where it was, a full block downhill from the New Day Café, which was located in the no-man's-land between town and gown.

She didn't have time to browse in the college-oriented boutiques today, however. She'd picked Rosie up at her school an hour ago, brought her home, and then Tina had phoned.

Fortunately, Trevor's mother, Marcia, had said Rosie could come to their house and play while Sally raced off to see Tina. Leaving Rosie and Trevor armed with make-believe bazookas and engaged in guerrilla warfare with a couple of imaginary giant squids in Trevor's backyard, Sally had driven as far as the café, where she'd abandoned her car in the employee lot behind the building. The college was only a short hike up the hill, and finding a parking place close to the campus was as difficult as getting e-mail from Mars, so it was easier to leave her car at the café and walk.

She couldn't help but think Tina was overreacting. Just because Howard had made up his mind to transfer to Dartmouth didn't mean Tina's life was at an end. She had lots of options. She could visit him at Dartmouth on weekends. Or she herself could arrange to transfer to Dartmouth. Or she could see a plastic surgeon about getting her tattoo removed. Or, if she broke up with Howard and didn't want to go the plastic surgery route, she could find another boyfriend named Howard. She could advertise in some singles chat room on the Web: "Attractive eugenics scholar, self-supporting, five-four, brown-brown, looking for brilliant, sexy, independently wealthy and kindhearted dude. Must be named Howard."

Sally wasn't sure why Tina had called on her. She had friends at the school, dorm mates, classmates she could turn to for comfort. It was probably the mommy–surrogate thing again, Sally brimming with wisdom, competent to guide her through this dreadful romantic crisis. Or perhaps she wanted to talk to someone whose romantic crisis half a dozen years ago had wrecked her own college career.

As Sally neared the baroque wrought-iron gates that marked the main entry to the campus, she thought about that wrecked college career. Coming to Winfield had been for her as transporting an experience as arriving over the rainbow had been for Dorothy Gale. She'd gone from being a smart-mouthed, earthy, ambitious straight-A student in her mediocre regional high school to a freshman at a genuine private college. She had figured she would attend a community college or a state university, but her English teacher had been a Winfield alumnus, and he'd known more about colleges than Sally or her mother. So when he'd urged Sally to apply to Winfield, Sally had applied. She'd been accepted and offered a scholarship, and that had seemed reason enough for her to go.

She'd liked Winfield, even though she'd felt out of place there. So many of the students had come from comfortable suburbs near cultural hubs—the bedroom communities of Boston, the ritzy villages along the commuter rail line in southern Connecticut, the pampered punks of northern New Jersey, a hefty handful of students from the towns surrounding Washington, D.C., a few exotic imports from Ohio and the Chicago area, even some long-distance immigrants from Texas and California. Sally hadn't been intimidated by her fellow students, but she hadn't exactly fit in with them, either. They'd all seemed savvier than her, cooler…richer.

Unlike her, most of them hadn't had to hold down real jobs. The scholarship students generally filled campus jobs—shelving books in the library, scraping and rinsing dishes in the dining-hall kitchen—but those were minimum-wage jobs, and the students who took them did so mostly because if they didn't, the college might reduce their financial-aid packages.

Sally had truly needed the money, not just to pay for the occasional pizza or movie but to cover the cost of her textbooks, bus trips home for the holidays, crew socks for gym class and towels for showering. "What do you mean, they don't have towels?" her mother had raged over the phone. "What kind of place is that? They always have towels hanging in the bathroom and spare towels piled up on a shelf somewhere."

"You're thinking of hotels, Mom. This is a dormitory. We're supposed to bring our own towels. Can you mail me some?"

"It would cost me more to mail you towels than it would cost you to buy them. Just get cheap ones, honey. Don't get bath sheets. When they call them bath sheets, they charge you twice as much."

Sally had needed towels, soap, a fluorescent lamp for her desk, highlighter pens and Post-its, a bulletin board and a radio. Once she'd landed the job at the New Day Café, earning a real wage supplemented by the loose change people tossed into the tip jar, she'd been able to buy all the gear she needed. She'd read the newspaper in the library's periodicals room so she wouldn't have to pay for it, and she'd hoarded single-portion boxes of cereal and extra fruit when she'd run her tray along the cafeteria counter, so she wouldn't have to buy late-night snacks. Monica Penn down the hall had given haircuts that weren't half bad for five dollars a pop, and the used clothes Sally had purchased at the Salvation Army store on the corner of East Street and Clancy had carried a kind of retro cachet, so she'd looked almost stylish in her recycled ensembles.

And in truth, she'd loved working at the New Day. She'd liked it more than she'd liked most of her classes. Greta was shy and terse, but Sally could relate to her more easily than she could relate to all those affluent, mollycoddled girls in her dorm, graduates of Miss Prissy's Prep, with adenoidal voices and perfectly streaked blond hair and an understanding of the nuances of field hockey. Sally had liked waking up before dawn and watching the sun rise as she ground and brewed coffee and bantered with the early-shift cops who started their day with a cuppa-joe and one of Greta's oversize muffins. She'd liked chatting with the laborers who stopped in, the shopkeepers who ran neighboring establishments, the city hall hacks and the UPS delivery guy and the handsome young lawyer who flirted with her.

She'd flirted back. Why not? Flirting with Paul Driver had come more naturally to her than writing a term paper on Sarah Orne Jewett's use of pine trees as a symbol of her characters' austere and leafless lives, or unlocking the secrets of ribonucleic acid, or explaining whatever the hell Sartre was talking about in *Being and Nothingness*.

Still, standing before the ivy-twined Winfield gates now, six years after she'd dropped out of school, Sally felt a twinge of regret. She'd completed two years. Only two more, and she would have become a college graduate.

When Rosie had been about three years old, Sally had mentioned to Paul that she'd like to go back to college part-time and finish her degree. He'd pointed out, with infuriating logic, that she had a job she enjoyed, a daughter she adored, and a house and a husband, both desiring a modicum of attention. "When are you going to find time to go to school?" he'd asked.

"I was thinking, maybe one class a semester. I can take classes that meet in the evenings—"

"So you wouldn't be eating dinner with us those evenings? You wouldn't be eating with Rosie?"

"Well, I just thought…"

"And when would you get your homework done? Weekends? Weekends are when you take Rosie out into the backyard and play with her, and work on your garden, or you bake, or you read. Do you really want to sacrifice that time to schoolwork?"

She really didn't.

But it would still be nice to get that degree. Maybe

now that Paul wasn't around to talk her out of it, she would investigate the possibility.

She passed through the gates and felt, once more, as if she'd landed over the rainbow. The air smelled greener and fresher on this side of the ornate wrought-iron portal—probably because the campus had expanses of lawn and lush plantings and no through streets clogged with cars spewing exhaust fumes into the atmosphere. Quaint paths cut across the lawns, weaving around mature maples and oaks, past budding rhododendrons and azaleas stirring awake in the new spring warmth. Majestic buildings of brick and brownstone rose up alongside the paths, gothic and imposing, their heavy glass windows whispering, "We are seats of knowledge. We are launch pads of privilege. Professors bore sophomores to tears in our rooms."

She strolled past the academic buildings, the administration buildings and the sprawling monstrosity of a library, its pillared Greco-Roman core annexed and expanded with wings dating from at least three different decades, designed by at least three different architects. She hiked past the language building, where she'd met her doom in a first-year Russian class with Gozbodin Markoff. All she remembered from that class was *Nye horosho,* which meant, "Not good."

Deeper into the campus stood the dorms, several quadrangles of bland brick buildings with smaller stand-alone residences surrounding them. Tina lived in Cabot House, one of the quad dorms. Entering the first quad under a brick archway that connected two of the dormitories, Sally had to veer around a game of Frisbee in which the three male participants were clearly showing off for a small gaggle of female onlookers. They jumped, they caught and tossed the disk in a single motion; they reached between their legs to snag it and flipped it behind their backs to launch it. The girls seemed impressed, but they were probably more impressed by the boys' dramatic hair and healthy young physiques than by their prowess with the plastic toy.

Rosie would have sniffed and turned away. Once you'd seen a clown juggling while perched atop a towering unicycle, a few boys playing Frisbee would seem pretty mundane.

Sally found the main entrance of Cabot Hall and pushed the door open. A student posted at the entry desk stopped and asked her to identify herself. "I'm here to see Tina Frye. I'm Sally Driver."

The boy ran his gaze from her hair to her sandaled feet and back up again. Although he had to be at least eighteen years old, he seemed much younger, his skin bearing lingering traces of acne, his hair shorn to the length of peach fuzz, his body swimming in an oversize T-shirt even though he was not a small person. If he looked that young to her, she probably looked that old to him. She was tempted to say, *Excuse me—I'm twenty-six. I am* not *old enough to be your mother.*

But she'd been summoned because Tina saw her as a mother figure of sorts. And she sure couldn't pass for a student, not in her corduroy jumper, dark tights and plaid shirt, not with her unfashionably long, wavy hair. Not with the tiny lines that edged her eyes, the little crease that folded the skin at one corner of her mouth. She didn't mind these souvenirs of her advancing age. She was actually kind of proud of them. But she knew they separated her from the students, whose greatest worries usually revolved around tomorrow's test or where to score an evening's worth of weed or whether some guy was going to ask them to the campus flick that Saturday, and if he did, whether that meant they were obligated to sleep with him afterward.

After assessing her, the boy lifted a desk phone, punched in three numbers and said, "There's some lady here to see Tina Frye. What's your name again?" he asked Sally.

Not the sharpest knife in the drawer. "Sally Driver," she said.

"Sally Driver," the boy repeated into the phone.

She turned to study the notices pinned to a bulletin board on the wall to her right. A pro-choice rally in front of the library Friday afternoon. A Celtic-music festival in the Higgins Auditorium on Sunday. A reading in the Boylston Reading Room by the poet-in-residence. Several pleas for rides to Boston, Long Island and Providence. Someone with a car offering regular rides to Hanover, New Hampshire.

Hanover, New Hampshire, was where Dartmouth was located. If Howard transferred to Dartmouth, Tina could catch a ride with whoever had posted that notice when she wanted to visit him.

The boy hung up the phone and cleared his throat, discreetly demanding her attention. "She's on the third floor," he said. "Room 314."

As it turned out, Sally didn't need to be told the room number. When she pushed open the third-floor fire door and emerged from the stairwell, she heard a stream of voices flowing out of one of the rooms. She followed the stream to its source: a closed door marked 314. The voices all sounded female, and they all seemed to be talking at once.

Sally knocked.

The door swung open to reveal a tear-stained, blotchy-faced Tina, her hair standing in odd tufts as if she'd been tugging at it. Her oversize Winfield College T-shirt drooped toward one shoulder, and her pants, as usual, were too baggy. "Oh, Sally, thanks for coming," she managed to mumble before collapsing in Sally's arms and sobbing inconsolably.

Sally half carried, half dragged her back into the room, a narrow rectangle not much larger than a walk-in closet, although six girls had somehow crammed themselves into it. Three sat on the unmade cot-size bed, one on the windowsill and one on the desk. The last one paced—two steps in one direction, two steps in the other. They all seemed deeply concerned with Tina's trauma. Indeed, they all seemed to share equally in it. Their facial expressions ran the gamut from distressed to distraught. They had shiny tear tracks striping their cheeks.

Sally was glad she hadn't arrived earlier. They might have all been blubbering then, and she would have had to mop the floor.

Although they were all uniformly weepy, Tina's friends came in a variety of sizes, shapes and colors. None of them had the streaked blond hair that had been so popular on campus just a few years ago. Their apparel ranged from gym shorts and sweatshirt to silk blouse and tailored flannel trousers.

They might have finished their communal bawling, but they were still sniffling. Like a Greek chorus, they echoed Tina's forlorn whimpers. Thank God they didn't all drape themselves over Sally the way Tina did. She could barely stand under Tina's floppy weight.

"The world hasn't ended," Sally said sharply—not because she wasn't sympathetic but because she wouldn't otherwise have been heard above the mournful chorus. "Get a grip."

"That's why I called you," Tina wailed, taking Sally's advice literally and gripping her shoulders.

"That's why she called you," a couple of the other girls confirmed in a resonant murmur.

"He's just a guy," Sally pointed out. "No guy is worth this much grief."

Tina peeled herself off Sally and sucked in a tremulous breath. "Everyone, this is Sally Driver, the coolest lady I know." Tina introduced her friends, a bevy of Caitlins and Amandas and Tanyas. Sally nodded and smiled at each of them, then promptly forgot their names.

"She'll tell you," the plump redhead predicted. "She'll tell you Howard is a piece of shit for doing this to you."

"She'll help you figure out how to hang on to Howard," the dark-skinned girl with the Rastafarian dreadlocks insisted.

"Listen, everyone, I've gotta talk to Sally alone." Tina gave her friends a brave smile and blinked furiously, no doubt fending off a fresh spate of tears. "We'll meet in Amanda's room later and drink Southern Comfort, okay?"

"Okay."

"Sure."

"Later."

The girls gathered around Tina, each offering a ritual hug before filing through the door.

The stillness in the room once they were gone was slightly disorienting. Sally gazed around, noticing for the first time the Brad Pitt poster on the wall above the bed—did Howard look like Brad Pitt? If he did, he might be worth all this drama—the textbooks piled on the desk next to a laptop; the bag of chocolate chip cookies; the empty beer bottles stacked along the top shelf of the bookcase; the stuffed teddy bear lounging on Tina's pillow, clad in a tiny version of her Winfield College shirt; and the four mismatched shoes mixing it up with the dust bunnies under the bed.

"Do you want a cookie?" Tina asked, shuffling across the room to the bag on her desk. She was barefoot, and the hems of her pants dragged with each step. "I know these aren't as good as what we sell in the New Day, but sometimes I, like, just want something kind of low quality, you know? Like, with preservatives and hydrogenated oil and stuff?" She unrolled the bag and popped a cookie into her mouth, then extended the bag to Sally.

"You make it sound so appetizing." Sally declined with a shake of her head. "Tina, can we talk about this? I left Rosie with a neighbor—" having a grand time killing squids, but Sally didn't say that "—so I'd like to find out what's going on with you."

"Nothing's going on with me," Tina said, then crumpled onto her bed and chewed. A few tears leaked from her eyes as she swept her tongue along her molars, causing one cheek and then the other to bulge as she scraped cookie mush from their surfaces. "It's going on with Howard. He told me he's definitely transferring to Dartmouth. He got accepted and he's transferring." Her voice dissolved in a sob. She reached for another cookie.

"I'm sure you're sad," Sally murmured, stating the obvious. She lowered herself to sit on the bed next to the teddy bear, leaving as much space as possible between Tina and herself. "But if it's true love, his being at Dartmouth won't have to come between you."

"There are *girls* at Dartmouth."

"There are girls here at Winfield."

"But *I'm* at Winfield. He doesn't need other girls if I'm around. I won't be around at Dartmouth."

"I thought you and he love each other."

"But he's a guy. You know how guys are. They think with their dicks. Ever hear the expression dickhead?"

Sally tried not to smile. "Not in reference to male thought processes. Tina, consider this. Dartmouth is, what? An hour away? Two hours? It's not such a big deal."

"It is if he goes up there and forgets about me. I *love* him, Sally. You know how much I love him."

Sally did indeed: so much she'd injected ink into her skin.

"We've got two more years of school. Two whole years when he's going to be up there and I'm going to be down here. It's like—like I don't think I can bear it."

"Of course you can bear it. You're smart and strong. You've got a good job, and you're a good student—"

Tina rolled her eyes at that.

"And you've got all those wonderful friends. They'll support you through this difficult time."

"They all think Howard deserves to be shot. Or castrated. Or disemboweled. That was Caitlin's idea."

"Well…so, you've got some violent friends."

"I don't want to disembowel him. I want to be with him." Tina licked the crumbs off her fingers and leaned toward Sally. "I thought, maybe you could give me some advice."

"I'm giving you advice."

"Not that advice. Different advice." A tiny smear of chocolate clung to Tina's lower lip. "Here was what I was thinking. Like, maybe, I could get pregnant, and then Howard would have to marry me."

Sally leaned away from Tina and scowled. The teddy bear's nose dug into her back.

"I mean, *you* did it, and it worked for you, right? I'm not saying—I mean, I know your husband died, and that really sucks and all. But for a while, you got to be together. He married you."

Sally swallowed. God, she felt old. She couldn't remember ever being as young as Tina. Even when she'd been Tina's age, she'd never been that young. "Tina, this is not a good plan."

"But *you* did it."

"Not on purpose."

"But you loved your husband, right? And then he married you. I mean, it worked."

Sally opened her mouth and then shut it, opened and shut it again. If she had a cookie, she'd be able to put her jaw motions to good use by chewing it. She knew she had to say something, but the only thought that hung tight in her mind was: *I didn't love my husband.*

Surely she'd loved him at the beginning. She'd loved him before she'd found the Laura letters. She'd loved him when he'd agreed to marry her, because his doing so was so honorable, so responsible. Given her own father's absence, she'd loved Paul for doing the right thing.

Hadn't she?

Hadn't she loved his body? And the way he'd kept his things so tidy, like some anal-retentive fanatic? And the way he'd manfully consumed the vegetarian meals she prepared, with only a few snide criticisms about how her tofu stew definitely had more flavor than foam rubber, and if he added a little salt it actually tasted like salt? And the way he used to dazzle her with his explanations of how the probate process worked?

His body. Yes, she'd loved his body—although he'd been kind of small. He'd stood only five feet nine and a half—he'd always made a point of mentioning that half—and he'd weighed less than she did during the last few months of her pregnancy. Not that she had anything against short men. Five feet nine and a half wasn't that short, and she was five-six herself, so it wasn't as if she'd towered over Paul, although even if she had, why would that have made a difference? She could be very politically correct when it came to size. The only reason she was even thinking about it was that it had been such a different experience to kiss Todd, who stood at least six feet in height. Probably more than six feet. Six one and a half, maybe.

And kissing him had been entirely different from kissing Paul because it had been impulsive, and she'd been tired and not thinking clearly, and he'd carried Rosie up the stairs so gently, and his nose had been pink. She certainly didn't love him.

"Sally?" Tina called to her as if from another county. Sally shook her head clear and returned her attention to Tina. "What I was thinking," Tina said, "was, I could just, like, not wear my diaphragm. Was that how you got pregnant?"

"I didn't have a diaphragm," Sally told her. In college, she'd figured that if she found herself in a long-term, solid relationship she would get one, but when she and Paul started seeing each other, it wasn't a long-term solid relationship. It went from a few dates to "I do" in a remarkably short interval. She hadn't gotten a diaphragm until after Rosie was born.

"So you just, like, did it without anything?"

"We had a condom failure," Sally said, feeling even older.

"Wow. That must have been hard to do—to make the condom fail so you could get pregnant."

"I didn't *make* the condom fail. I didn't want to get pregnant. Listen to me, Tina. Getting knocked up is not a good way to keep Howard. He might just run away if you tell him you're pregnant. Some men do that."

"He wouldn't. He loves me."

"If he loves you, you've got nothing to worry about with his going to Dartmouth, right?"

Tina eyed Sally dubiously. She'd obviously expected Sally to counsel her on the most effective way of trapping a guy.

"Trust me," Sally said. "You don't want to get pregnant."

"Why? Everything worked out so cool for you—except for that he died, but I mean, you love Rosie, don't you? You're glad you had your daughter, right?"

"Of course I love my daughter."

"So if you had it to do over again, you really wouldn't change anything, would you? I mean, except for his dying."

"I—" Once again Sally felt like a fish, her jaw pumping as she tried to wrap her mouth around the right words. "I don't regret for an instant having Rosie. But I wish I had finished college. And my husband was already done with his schooling. He could afford to support us. If you got pregnant, what would you expect Howard to do? Drop out of college and get a job to support you?"

"I could work, too. I could work more hours at the café."

"That's not a career."

"It is for you."

"Because I'm the manager. Because I worked there

for years, and I could afford to work there for years because my husband earned a good living from his legal practice. Listen to me, Tina—this scheme of yours is not the same thing at all.''

''So, you don't think I should get preggers?'' Tina looked crestfallen.

''I really don't.'' Sally slid along the bed until she was next to Tina, the rumpled blanket shaping a narrow blob between them. She wrapped an arm around Tina and gave her a squeeze. ''You have much better alternatives. While I was waiting to be allowed upstairs, I was studying the bulletin board by the front door, and you know what I saw? Someone offering a ride to Dartmouth.''

''Really?''

''You'll be able to get rides up there. You'll probably have to chip in toward gas, but it won't be expensive.''

''Really? There was someone looking for riders in Cabot House?''

''Sure. And I bet there are other people offering rides to Dartmouth in other dorms, too. Every dorm has a bulletin board like that, right? You'll be able to find rides.''

''Because I love him,'' Tina reiterated, as if she wanted to convince herself.

''I know you do.''

''And he really loves me. He says he does.''

''Then I'd suggest you skip the disembowelment.''

''Yeah.'' She hugged Sally back. ''Thanks for helping me work this out. I didn't want my friends to know I was thinking about getting pregnant because if I did it, I'd have to make it seem like an accident, you know? If I'd talked about it with them, they'd know it wasn't an accident, and it could have gotten back to Howard and then he'd never trust me.''

''So, you're okay?''

''Yeah. My friends and I are going to drink some Southern Comfort tonight. I think that'll be good.''

Sally tried not to wince. ''I've got to go,'' she said, shoving against the thin mattress and heaving herself to her feet. ''I'll see you tomorrow at the café, all right?''

''I don't work tomorrow,'' Tina reminded her. ''It's Tuesday.'' Tina slept late Tuesdays.

''Right. I'll see you Wednesday, then. And please, if you need to talk some more, give me a call. I don't want you doing anything stupid.'' That wasn't to say that Sally's life had been stupid, just that deliberately choosing that path would have been stupid.

She gave Tina one more hug, then left her munching on a cookie and headed down the hall to the stairs. Her mind was churning with thoughts she wasn't really pleased with, thoughts about whether her life had been stupid and whether she'd ever really loved Paul, and whether Paul's height hadn't bothered her until after she'd kissed Todd, which of course had been a complete aberration and, arguably, stupider than getting knocked up by Paul.

Emerging into the dorm's entry, she paused by the bulletin board. There it was, the index card advertising a ride to Dartmouth, surrounded by all those other notices—the pro-choice demonstration, the list of campus movies sponsored by the Winfield Student Organization, the poetry reading—which, Sally noticed, had taken place last week.

Which, she also noticed, had been given by Winfield College's visiting artist, Laura Ryershank.

Laura Ryershank.

Of course not. Paul had never taken an interest in poetry. And how would he have even met the school's visiting artist? The woman had visited last week, a good three months after Paul had skidded his car into a tree.

Shaking her head, Sally turned from the bulletin board.

And turned back.

Laura Ryershank.

Absolutely not.

With a nod at the fuzzy-scalped boy behind the desk, she shoved open the door and stepped outside the dormitory. The sky had lost a few degrees of light in the time it had taken her to talk sense to Tina, and the air had lost a few degrees of heat. She dug a cardigan out of her tote bag, slid her arms through the sleeves and started down the path that led out of the quad and back to the campus. Students swarmed through the door of the language building, milled near the main entrance to the library, bicycled past her, shouted to one another. Girls bowed their heads together and whispered. Boys engaged in shoving matches. Sally felt aeons older than all of them.

She wasn't the only older person strolling the walkways of the campus. A few professorial types wove among the students. She spotted a campus security officer on one of the paths, and a silver-haired woman smoking a pipe and wearing a tweed blazer stretched out at the elbows, and descending the steps of the main administration building a tall man with tousled black curls.

What the hell was Todd doing at Winfield College?

He must have spotted her, because he froze on the second step and stared straight at her. He was a little too far away for her to tell whether he was frowning, but it was a lot easier to imagine him frowning than smiling at the sight of her. She herself was frowning; she could feel the muscles contract in her forehead.

He stood between her and the college gate. There were other ways to exit the campus, but it would look pretty strange if she U-turned and hustled off in the direction she'd just come from. She wasn't afraid of him, after all. She didn't have to rearrange her life to avoid him. She could walk right past him, or even say hello to him if she had to. He still had the Laura letters in his possession, and he was the executor of her husband's will, so she was going to have to deal with him. If she'd managed to deal with him when she'd hated him, she supposed she could deal with him now.

But it had been easier to deal with him when she'd hated him—which she still did, she reminded herself, maybe hated him even more because he stirred up so many conflicting emotions inside her. She hated him because if he hadn't kissed her, she might have been able to go on hating him the way she used to. But now she had to hate him because kissing him had felt too good.

Trying to define the kind of hate she felt for him made her head ache. She relaxed her face into a bland smile and continued along the path she was on, knowing it was going to bring her right to the foot of the administration building steps.

He remained where he was, as if waiting for her, too arrogant to meet her halfway. Her forehead muscles cramped even more from resisting a frown than they had from frowning.

She told herself that in between hating Todd, she'd had some pleasant moments with him on Saturday. He'd been charming at dinner, telling Sally he'd learned to cook as a teenager because both his parents often worked at the newspaper until six or seven at night, and he'd

have been forced to live on peanut butter sandwiches if
he hadn't figured out how to roast a chicken or grill a
steak. He'd recited the first verse of Longfellow's poem
about Paul Revere for Rosie. He'd bought her that necklace, and he'd carried her up to bed so tenderly, careful
not to wake her.

She could picture the way he'd looked settling Rosie
on her bed, stepping back and smiling shyly. He wasn't
a father, used to lugging sleeping children around. Carrying Rosie had been so sweet, so manly...

And then he'd kissed Sally, and *manly* had developed
an entirely new definition for her.

As she drew near, his dark eyes narrowed on her and
he pressed his lips into a grim line.

"Hi," she said, her smile expanding. If her friendli-
ness bothered him, so much the better. "What brings
you to campus?"

"I had to see some people."

"What people?"

He didn't speak for a minute. A light breeze danced
past the building, shaking the baby leaves that budded
along the branches of a nearby oak and ruffling his hair.
"People named Laura," he finally said.

Thirteen

He didn't want to include her in this latest phase of the Laura search. But how could he keep her out of it? Whether or not he liked it, they seemed to be in it together.

Besides, he had some questions for her. For instance, what had she done to his mother? Helen hadn't returned to the newsroom until well past noon, and her ebullient spirits couldn't be attributed to caffeine consumption alone. She'd been chipper, she'd thanked him for recommending the New Day Café and she'd made a cryptic remark about how sometimes the road not taken was the road a person had to take. Then she'd shut herself inside her office and Todd heard not another word from her. At one point, when he'd left his own office to return Gloria's college directories, he'd glanced through the glass wall of his mother's office and caught her playing solitaire on her computer, her mouse in her right hand and a placid smile curving her lips.

He wanted to ask Sally about the miracle she'd wrought. He also wanted to ask her why she'd worn that silly straw hat on Saturday, because she looked so much better today without it. The sun played through her hair, stirring up all the red highlights. He wanted to ask her whether he was just imagining a spark of silver in her blue eyes. He wanted to ask her whether she'd lost weight, because he'd always thought of her as bulky, chubby even, but he didn't think of her that way anymore.

He had a question for himself, too: What the hell was wrong with him? He'd recovered from their kiss. He'd regained his mental equilibrium. Seeing her shouldn't put him into brain melt again.

She didn't laugh when he told her he'd just spent the past ten minutes tracking down Laura Ellroy, the assistant dean of financial aid. "She's married," he reported.

"So what? Paul was married, too."

Todd shook his head. "This wasn't the right Laura. She wasn't his type."

"Oh? What's Paul's type?"

Todd was no longer sure. There was a time he would have sworn Sally wasn't Paul's type. There was a time he would have sworn she wasn't *his* type—and that time included right now, he adamantly assured himself. "All I'm saying is, Laura Ellroy gave off happily-married vibes. I also checked out Laura Titwell from the chemistry department. She was my height and had me by a good sixty pounds."

"Maybe Paul found her heft attractive," Sally suggested.

"She would have crushed him," Todd said, then cringed. Offering her a graphic picture of what her late husband had been doing with Laura wasn't particularly tactful. He quickly continued, "And I dropped in on Laura Stratton in the math department. She reminded me of you a little. Young, flaky—"

"I'm not flaky!"

"You know what I mean."

"No, I don't." She pursed her lips and glowered at him. "Does she have children?"

"I didn't ask. Five minutes with her and I knew she couldn't have written all that purple prose in the letters. And anyway…"

"Anyway, what?"

"Why would he have an affair with a woman like you when he had you?"

"I was his wife," Sally answered. "It's not the same thing."

She had a point. Maybe Sally *was* Paul's type, and when he wanted an illicit thrill he found the same type, only in an adulterous version.

"Well, it doesn't matter. I don't think his Laura is on campus."

"What about Laura Ryershank?"

"Who?"

Gripping his forearm, she led him toward a pillar papered with campus notices. She studied the announcements and he studied her hand on the sleeve of his jacket. A casual touch, utterly meaningless, yet…it distracted him. The way the sun in her hair distracted him. The way his unraveling certainty about her distracted him.

"No, it isn't here. It's posted in other places, though," she said. Her hand tightened on him, her fingers surprising him with their strength as she pulled him down the path, past the library to another pillar covered with flyers. "Laura Ryershank was a visiting artist. She did a poetry reading on campus last week."

"What would that have to do with Paul? Last week he was dead."

"But she was a visiting artist. Which means she might have visited before. Here!" She found the flyer she was looking for and tore it free. The tape that had fastened the sheet to the pole took a bite out of the top edge.

He studied the announcement. Laura Ryershank, visiting artist, had indeed given a poetry reading in the library's Boylston Room last week.

"She's a poet. Think about those letters, Todd. The writing is poetic, right? The letters reek with poetry."

"Yeah, but... How would Paul ever have hooked up with her?"

"Visiting artist," Sally explained. "The way they used to do that when I was a student here was, someone would be the visiting artist for the year. She'd come and visit the campus once a month, give a couple of master classes or senior seminars, do some public thing—like a poetry reading, or a screening of a short film, or an exhibit at the campus museum—and then go off to be creative again. Laura Ryershank could have been visiting all year."

He shook his head. "Okay, so she was the visiting artist this year. That means the earliest Paul would have met her would have been when she started visiting Winfield College, in, what? September? I can't believe their affair lasted all of four months before he died. Nobody could have written that many letters in four months, right?"

"Why not? If she loved him she could have."

"Even if he wasn't writing back? You know Paul. He wouldn't have written that many letters in four months."

"She could have written anyway."

"He would have thought she was a pest."

"Not if he loved her." A shadow flickered across her face. The idea obviously hurt her, despite her belief that her husband was an ass.

He suffered a fresh flare of anger at Paul for having cheated on her—but it vanished almost as quickly as it struck. He wasn't under any obligation to feel Sally's pain. He'd gotten into this thing because he'd been feeling his own pain. That was enough pain for him.

She seemed to shrug off her momentary sorrow. Looking more resolute than before, she said, "It's possible they met somewhere else and started their affair. And then, to make things easier, she decided to apply for the visiting artist position at Winfield College so she'd have an excuse to come to town every month."

A little contrived, but not very. "Okay. For the sake of argument, let's say you're right. How do we find out more about Laura Ryershank?"

Sally thought for a moment. "I could ask Tina. You know, the young woman who works mornings at the New Day Café with me? She's a student here."

"I remember her." She'd had a bunch of earrings and a dopey-eyed gaze. She hadn't impressed him as being an exemplar of genius.

Exemplar? Stupid word.

The girl didn't have to be a genius to tell him and Sally whether this year's visiting artist had paramour potential. All she had to do was describe Laura Ryershank and let them know when Laura had first become connected to the college and how often she visited Winfield.

If Todd had gotten cozier with Laura Ellroy or any of the other Lauras he'd sought out that afternoon, he wouldn't even need to be pumping Sally's buddy for information. But he hadn't forged lasting friendships with the Lauras he'd met. He'd merely introduced himself and asked if they'd been acquainted with an attorney named Paul Driver.

Sally released his arm, which immediately felt lighter, as if a weight had been unstrapped from it. He wanted to swing it over his head, to celebrate its freedom—

except that it also felt cold, curiously bloodless. "Let me see if I can find a campus phone," she said. "I just came from Tina's room, so she's probably still there. Unless she's off chugging Southern Comfort."

"Why would she be doing that?" Todd asked.

Sally gave him a withering look. "Because she's in college," she said, as if stating the obvious.

Todd shrugged. No one he'd been acquainted with during his years at Columbia would have chugged Southern Comfort. Beer had been the chug of choice among his pals, although he'd known a couple of guys who preferred vodka—guys who'd never come within a mile of making the dean's list. Todd assumed the two issues were related.

Sally was heading for the front entry to the library. She maneuvered her way through the stagnant clusters of students at the main entrance, a gaggle of people in baggy jeans, Teva sandals and brightly colored warm-up jackets, backpacks slung over their shoulders and hair scrupulously unkempt. The students didn't make way for him as they did for Sally. He tried not to resent this.

A turnstile gate stood just inside the glass front doors. Sally tried swiping a card through the slot, but the gate refused to let them through. "Damn," she grumbled.

The foyer of the library smelled mossy, like damp socks or disintegrating books. Two female students swung through the turnstile coming out. They were both slim and blond and perky.

"Stop drooling," Sally snapped, nudging past him and exiting the building behind the bouncy blondes. Todd hadn't been aware of drooling. He'd only been objectively appreciating them. "We'll have to find a campus phone somewhere else," she continued as he followed her out. "My student ID doesn't work anymore."

"Why would it work? You're not a student."

"It worked the last time I used this library."

"Which was when? Six years ago?"

"Six months ago," she told him. "Maybe the magnetic strip went kablooey. I let Rosie play with the card sometimes. She likes to pretend she's a college student."

"She could sure pass for one," he muttered, accompanying Sally down the steps and along the path toward the administration building. "Why did you use the campus library six months ago?"

"It's much better than the town library," she said, sliding the handles of her tote up to her shoulder and shoving her hands into the pockets of her sweater. He felt safer with them there, away from him, posing no threat to his arm. "If you ever stopped writing editorials about the sewer system, you might consider writing an editorial about the lousy condition of the town library."

"Is it lousy?" He rarely used the place. When he wanted a book, he bought it. It was easier than going to the library—especially since he could order most books on the Internet—and the expense was worth the convenience to him. Books he didn't want to keep he gave away, and those he did want to keep found space on the bookcases in his house. He no longer had to argue with Denise about what to put on their shelves.

She used to like to display figurines. Figurines that had cost a hell of a lot more than books, as he recalled. She'd developed an obsession with Lladros, anemic porcelain renderings of happy peasants, milkmaids and rustics. Once, when he'd been whining about the Lladros to Paul over drinks after work, Paul had pointed out that things could have been worse; she could have been obsessed with those obnoxious little Hummel characters, chubby and maliciously gleeful in their pinafores and lederhosen.

In any case, he and Denise had been in total agreement over the disposition of the Lladro figurines during the divorce negotiations. She got them all, to his great relief, and he got miles of shelf space for his books and model cars.

"Don't you use the town library?" Sally asked. "You should. You're an editor. A man of letters." A scornful laugh escaped her.

"I *am* a man of letters."

"Then write an editorial about the library."

"If I feel like it," he grumbled. He didn't let his mother dictate the contents of his editorials. He sure as hell wasn't going to let Sally.

Inside the administration building—which, inexplicably, also smelled like damp socks—she located a campus phone and dialed a few digits. She listened for a minute, then hung up. "Tina isn't answering. I'll try her later." She swept past him down the hall to the door, her sandals clicking quietly against the linoleum floor.

He paused to gauge his mood. He felt irritated, and this should have pleased him. Irritated was what he was used to feeling around Sally. Not intrigued. Not amused. Not enticed by the voluptuous waves of her hair, the voluptuous curves of her body.

He had always considered her a pain in the ass, and right now his butt was twinging. But the twinge had a definite sexual component to it, which only irritated him more.

She strode out of the building, letting the massive door swing shut behind her instead of holding it for him. He caught it in midswing and heaved it open again. She was already at the bottom of the steps by the time he was outside. He noted the way her skirt flowed around her hips and down her legs. Her thighs were inside that floral fabric. Sleek, strong thighs.

He sprinted down the steps, not bothering to wonder why he wanted to catch up to her. She continued to march at a brisk gait, but his legs were longer than hers and he easily closed the distance between them. "So, what are we going to do about this poet?" he asked, the torn flyer still clutched in his hand.

"I don't know what *you're* going to do about it."

"What are *you* going to do about it?"

She shot him a quick, dubious look but didn't break her stride. "I'm going to investigate."

"Nancy Drew, huh."

"No, not Nancy Drew. Nancy Drew wasn't a cuck-olded wife."

"I don't think wives can be cuckolded," he remarked. "Only husbands. It's a gender-specific word." She might be an expert when it came to *exemplar,* but she **was** definitely on shaky ground with *cuckold.*

"Fine. Then what's the wife equivalent?"

"I don't know."

"Oh. And here I thought you knew everything," she said, her voice so drenched in sarcasm he was surprised she wasn't leaving an oily trail of it behind her. "Any-way, how I investigate this is no concern of yours."

"Of course it's a concern of mine."

"Because you're a cuckolded friend?"

That didn't sound right, either.

"Why don't you keep working on the names on that computer disk?" she suggested. "I'll deal with the poet."

"Divide and conquer, huh."

"Maximize our resources."

"Cover more ground."

"Avoid duplication." She glanced up at him and he was delighted—and then dismayed—to see that she was grinning. Somehow, they'd wound up in agreement, in sync. That old, comfortable hostility was dissipating, leaving him on unfamiliar ground with Sally once more, a strange place where affection filled the air and thoughts about thighs filled his mind. Thoughts about bosoms. About auburn hair and strong fingers, and blue eyes flecked with silver.

"I like you better when I don't like you," he admitted, surprising himself with his candor.

Her smile widened. "Does it help if I assure you I don't like you?"

He laughed. "It helps a lot."

"Good." She touched his arm again, her deceptively graceful fingers brushing against his wrist, and then turned and sauntered down the path to the gate. He remained where he was, watching her, trying to figure out why, if he didn't like her, he liked smiling and laughing with her. And why, long after she'd walked through the gates and out of sight, he still felt the warmth of her fingertips against his wrist.

Rosie arrived at the New Day Café at eight-thirty, accompanied by Trevor. Their school was having teacher workshops all day, which meant all the classes were canceled. Rosie had slept over at Trevor's house last night so Sally wouldn't have to worry about having her at the café before dawn, when Greta was still baking, Sally was doing setups and the first of the early-shift cops started moseying in. But Trevor's mother, Marcia, had appointments from nine through twelve, so Sally had offered to keep an eye on the kids until Marcia could pick them up again.

By nine-thirty, she was doubting the wisdom of this arrangement.

She'd given them wads of dough to play with. That had occupied them for a few minutes. Then she'd supplied them with crayons and paper. She'd kept them busy sweeping the kitchen, even though the floor was spotless, thanks to Greta's compulsive Teutonic fastidiousness.

Sally had given them more dough, which they'd cheerfully rolled into pea-size balls and thrown at each other. She'd fed them a treat—croissants with melted chocolate drizzled over them. Then she'd scrubbed the chocolate from their fingers and faces and combed the flakes of croissant out of their hair. How crumbs had gotten into their hair she didn't want to know.

The café was bustling. It always bustled. Her own fault, she supposed. If she hadn't goosed Greta into jazzing up the joint years ago, if she hadn't hung the curtains and the paintings and turned the place into a warm, welcoming bistro, it would still be the sleepy little coffee shop it had been when she'd first started working there, quiet and underperforming, barely profitable.

Instead, it was busy and noisy and earning tons of money. The scribe in black was at his usual table, sipping from a mug of French roast and writing feverishly in his notebook. The exercise ladies were unbuffing their buff bodies with blueberry tarts and jumbo mocha lattes. One of the salesclerks from the Batik Boutique up near the campus had just ordered six cappuccinos to go. Officer Bronowski would be showing up in about ten minutes.

Sally could have used Tina that morning. She could

have used anyone. Regrettably, she had Rosie and Trevor, who were no use at all.

"Pretend these are bullets," Rosie instructed Trevor as she rolled bits of dough into tiny pellets. She and Trevor occupied the floor in the doorway to the kitchen, at the far end of the counter. "If you get hit by one, you're dead."

"I don't wanna be dead," Trevor complained. He was a sweet, pale child, with wheat-colored hair, freckles and a wavering voice. One reason he and Rosie got along so well was that he usually deferred to her.

He wasn't deferring today. Sally devoted a good chunk of her attention to their conversation, even as she counted out change for the clerk from the Batik Boutique. She silently rooted for Trevor. Turning dough into bullets seemed gory.

"Well, what do you want them to be?" Rosie challenged him. She sat cross-legged, the knees of her denim overalls nearly white from wear and her purple cloche perched on her head. "They could be ice. Like sleet. Then when they fall, they make the road all slippery and you could slip and crash and die."

"I don't wanna die," Trevor insisted tremulously. "Can't we make them snow? Then we can build a snowman out of them."

"But if we made them ice, it could be like when my daddy died."

"But it isn't ice," Trevor insisted. "It's too warm, anyway. It's spring. There's no ice in the spring."

"They're magic pills," Rosie decided, fluidly switching to a new scenario. "When you eat them, you can go anywhere you want. So I can see my daddy if I eat one."

"Yuck!" Trevor giggled. "Are you going to eat one?"

"Sure. Are you?"

Sally pushed back the thoughts about Paul that Rosie's make-believe had inspired and tried to remember what was in the dough: flour, water, salt, butter. No raw egg. If Rosie ate it, it wouldn't taste good, but it wouldn't make her sick, either.

Assured that Rosie couldn't poison herself with the dough, Sally let the thoughts about Paul return—specifically, the understanding that Rosie wanted to see her daddy.

Sometimes she talked about Paul as if she expected him to walk through the front door at the end of the day and scoop her into his arms for a big hug. Sometimes she talked about him with anger—he was a poophead for driving his stupid car too fast, and she still remembered the time he wouldn't take her to the circus in Springfield, and the time he yelled at her during her own birthday party, which really hadn't been fair because it *was* her party and the birthday girl ought to get to do whatever she wanted, even if it was encouraging her guests to climb onto the garage roof and jump off.

Other times she didn't mention him at all.

Lately, she'd been talking about Daddy's Friend. All last night over dinner, she'd asked Sally about Daddy's Friend as if she'd smelled him on Sally's clothes or sensed him on Sally's mind. Sally hadn't mentioned that she'd run into him during her errand yesterday afternoon, but Rosie seemed to know. "I like Daddy's Friend's music," she'd remarked. "I think we should get some Nirvana CDs. I like Nirvana. They scream a lot."

Maybe Rosie needed a man in her life.

Fortunately, Sally didn't need one in hers. Unless, of course, he joined her behind the counter and helped her fill the order of the construction worker who'd traipsed in, his hard hat shaping a bright yellow shell over his skull and his paunch swelling above an impressive tool belt.

Behind him stood Jonelle from the hair salon across the street. Behind her stood an elderly man with tufts of white hair sprouting above his ears and a galaxy of age spots decorating his bald scalp. The door opened with a tinkle of the bell, and the next person to join the line was Helen Sloane.

Sally acknowledged Todd's mother with a smile and a wave. She was once again dressed like a real-estate broker, or maybe a high-school principal. Or an executive secretary. The woman exuded midlevel professionalism, in slate-gray trousers and a stylish pink sweater set that clashed with her hair. "The place sure is hopping today, isn't it?" she commented to the white-haired gentleman.

"Eh?" he bellowed.

Helen smiled at him, then edged past him and approached the counter. "Do you need help?" she asked Sally.

Sally recalled joking with her yesterday about her taking a job at the New Day. They *had* been joking, Sally was sure. A brief fantasy for a woman unappreciated by her son at her office, and an equally brief fantasy for an overworked coffee shop manager.

"It's *not* snow!" Rosie erupted from the far end of the counter. "It's *ice!*"

"No, it's not!" Trevor shouted back in a wobbly voice.

"What's with them?" Helen asked, rising on tiptoe to peer over the counter at the squabbling children. "You're baby-sitting?"

"I'm afraid so." Sally snapped a lid onto the cup she'd just poured and wedged it into a cardboard tray. "School's closed today."

"Let me lend you a hand. I'm not useless. I could pour coffee."

"Helen, I don't know—"

"Or I could watch those two. What are they throwing at each other?"

"Dough."

"Oh, for God's sake." Without waiting for permission, she hurried around the end of the counter, strode past Sally and planted herself in front of Rosie and Trevor, legs spread and arms akimbo. "Do not throw dough," she said, enunciating each word so precisely they stopped to gape at her.

"Who are you?" Rosie asked.

"I'm Helen Sloane. Do not throw dough."

"I didn't wanna throw it," Trevor defended himself. "She made me."

"Did not!"

"Did too! You said it had to be ice."

"I said it could be bullets."

"Don't throw it," Helen warned.

It occurred to Sally that Helen had matters under control at her end of the counter. She turned back to the construction worker and, with an apologetic smile, said, "Can I get you anything else?"

By the time the bell above the door had stopped tinkling and the traffic had dwindled, Helen and the children were seated under the center table in the kitchen, creating a village out of paper cups, paper plates and empty boxes from the plastic cutlery. No strains of bickering emerged from the room, no whimpering, no whining.

Half the tables in the dining area were occupied: the black-clad artiste scribbling, a pair of middle-aged women chattering over bran-apple muffins and herbal tea, a professional munching on a bagel while reviewing documents from a leather portfolio, and Officer Bronowski, who'd showed up an hour later than usual because he'd had to fill in for the DARE officer at the middle school. He was stoically nibbling on a sticky bun. In three minutes he'd be ready for his refill of coffee.

Aware of those three minutes ticking down, Sally spied on Helen and the children from the kitchen doorway. "You're a miracle worker," she praised Helen. "How did you get them to calm down?"

Helen gave them each a few plastic stirrers, then straightened up and dusted her hands. "I'm bigger than them. They had to listen to me."

"Mommy, guess what?" Rosie sent her a dimpled grin. "Helen is Daddy's Friend's mommy!"

"Yes, I know."

"I told her about the necklace Daddy's Friend brought me."

Bought you, Sally almost corrected, but she kept her mouth shut. She wondered whether Todd had told his mother about their outing to Boston, whether that was why she'd taken such an interest in the New Day Café. Maybe she'd wanted to eyeball the woman with whom her son had journeyed to the city, for whose daughter he'd invested in jewelry. Maybe Todd had implied things about their relationship....

A patently laughable idea. First of all, there was nothing to imply, and second of all, there was no relationship.

She measured Helen's expression, searching the woman's dark eyes and the creases weighing down the corners of her mouth for a sign of whether she knew or cared about her son's weekend activities. "A rice necklace," Helen said.

"That's right."

"It sounds ridiculous."

"It is."

"It's beautiful," Rosie insisted.

"How are things out there?" Helen gestured behind Sally. "Is there a line of customers?"

"Not at the moment." She checked her watch. "In ninety seconds Officer Bronowski will be wanting a coffee refill."

"Arthur Bronowski is a man of habit." Helen glanced at the children, satisfied herself that they were peacefully engaged, and joined Sally at the door. "I know all the cops on the force. You've got to when you're running a newspaper. They're sources, every single one."

"Really?" Sally couldn't imagine Officer Bronowski revealing anything worth printing in the *Valley News*.

"Not only are they sources, but they won't ticket your car if you're parked illegally while pursuing a story. Ask Todd. If he got a ticket for every time he parked illegally in pursuit of a story, he'd have to take a second mortgage."

"He doesn't write stories, does he?"

"Rarely now. But he used to. Believe it or not, *I* used to—before they put me on the shelf." She gazed out at the dining room. "So, you don't need me to pour coffee?"

"Do you really want to pour coffee? A woman who used to write stories for the *Valley News?*"

"I need to do something." She sighed and patted her hair, as if she thought a strand might have broken free of its lacquer. "My husband has this ridiculous idea of taking me to Hilton Head Island for a month. Golfing. Can you imagine anything more boring? For a whole month.''

"Some people enjoy golfing," Sally argued.

"The ball is too small. Why can't they use a bigger ball? And a nice paddle instead of those silly golf clubs. Whoever invented golf just wasn't using his head.'' She glanced over her shoulder at the children, hard at work under the broad aluminum table. ''That Rosie of yours is something. I can see why Paul always said she was the light of his life. She's a charmer. She reminds me of me.''

Sally refrained from grinning. "She isn't always charming,'' she said modestly, even though as far as she was concerned Rosie was close to perfect. ''You really worked wonders with them, though. I didn't know you were so good with children.''

"I'm not so good with them. I just don't put up with crap from anyone smaller than me—which isn't too many people, but such is life when you're short. Anyway, I've had experience with my grandchildren.''

"Grandchildren?" Did Todd have children? Paul had never mentioned any. Todd himself had never mentioned any. Did his ex-wife have custody of them? Did he ignore them, spending his weekends searching for a mysterious Laura in Boston instead of taking his kids to the roller rink and McDonald's?

"My daughter's children. Aged seven and four. Cassandra and Henry. I keep them in line.''

So Todd had a niece and nephew. So he had a sister. The influx of information stunned Sally, even though there was nothing particularly astonishing about any of it. ''Do they live around here?''

Helen shook her head. ''Outside New Haven. I don't

see them often enough. Walter and Todd always say that
if I retired I could see more of them. But Walter's retired
and he doesn't see more of them. He just sees more of
the golf course.''

Sally wasn't sure what to say. She couldn't solve
Helen's problems for her. She wasn't even quite sure
what Helen's problems were, other than that her husband
and son wanted her to retire and she was resistant to the
idea.

''So, yes, I was serious,'' Helen said. ''If you want
to hire me to pour coffee, I'm interested.''

''But…you're a journalist.''

''Journalists get lots of experience pouring coffee, believe me.'' She edged past Sally and strolled the length
of the counter. ''I could figure this out pretty quickly.
What's this—real cream? Not that chemical stuff, right?
And these? They look like honey buns.''

''We call them sticky buns.''

''Honey buns, sticky buns—what's the difference?
This place has to be more interesting than sitting in my
office trying to figure out the damn computer. It's like
an oxbow, my office. The river flows right past me, and
I'm this stagnant pool of water, drying up. Golf is making my husband lose his marbles. I don't want to lose
my marbles.''

''Working here could make you a little crazy,'' Sally
warned.

''A little crazy isn't such a big deal. A lot crazy I'd
worry about, but not a little crazy. So, what do you
say?''

''Well, I could use an assistant Tuesdays. Actually,
every morning from nine-thirty to eleven or so.''

''Mornings are fine.''

''I really think you ought to try it for a day to see if

you like it. It's not exactly the most exciting job in the world.''

''Who needs exciting? I did exciting. Forty years at the newspaper, I raked muck. I uncovered graft on the zoning board. Did you know that? Twenty-two years ago, I wrote a series of exposés that blew this town wide-open. Three members of the zoning board went to jail, thanks to me.''

''You must be very proud,'' Sally said.

''When Walter and I were running this paper, we helped push through the sewers. Way back, they didn't have city sewers. We ran articles, editorials—we even invested part of the newspaper's pension fund in the sewer bonds—and got an excellent return on the investment, I might add. Now Todd writes editorials about improving the sewer system, making it cleaner or something. I don't know. It's not like what we did.''

Sally suffered a pang of sympathy for Todd. Did he have to listen to his mother gripe all day about how under his management the *Valley News* wasn't as wonderful as it had been when she'd been at the helm, when a journalist could make her career on sewage and graft?

''Now my husband wanders from golf course to golf course while, cell by cell, his brain disintegrates. And me, I'm bypassed. I'm obsolete.''

If Todd made his mother feel obsolete, he deserved to listen to her gripe. ''If you want to work here, I'd love to have you,'' Sally said.

''Really?''

''Really.''

''Good. Because I know a great way to brew coffee. You crunch an eggshell into the grounds. That's how my mother taught me. I don't know what purpose the eggshell serves, but if you put it in, it makes a great pot of coffee. An excellent pot.''

And off she headed to the kitchen, whether to check on the children or to find an eggshell Sally couldn't say.

Fourteen

Todd stormed into the New Day Café, nearly knocking over the woman at the counter. She had long black hair of differing textures, as if someone had woven yarn and spiderwebs into it, and when she moved her hands the silver bangles circling both forearms jangled like the contents of Sally's tote bag.

If he hadn't been the editor and publisher of the region's preeminent newspaper, he might have been embarrassed by the fact that he recognized Madame Constanza, tarot card reader. But he knew her not from patronizing her downtown salon in search of spiritual guidance, but from writing a profile of her for the *Valley News* a few years ago, before he'd ascended to the editor-in-chief desk.

Madame Constanza wore a long red dress with an odd, crepe-paperish look to it. It was the sort of dress Sally might wear, except that Sally preferred more muted colors and she lacked Madame Constanza's heft. Madame Constanza was built like someone who did the carbo loading but skipped the marathon.

She stared at him for a long moment, then turned her heavily mascaraed eyes back to Sally, who stood behind the counter, and said, "Didn't I tell you there was a tall, dark man in your future?"

"You say that to all the girls," Sally reminded her

with a smile. Her hair was pinned back from her face in a style that emphasized the contours of her cheeks, the gentle curve of her jawline and her soft pink lips.

No. Her hairstyle didn't emphasize her lips. He didn't even notice her lips. As far as he was concerned, her lips didn't exist.

"Actually—" Madame Constanza sent him another assessing look "—I said there was a tall, dark, *handsome* man in your future. What do you think?"

"I think he's cute," came a voice from the far end of the counter. Todd glanced that way and spotted Sally's college-student assistant emerging from the kitchen carrying a tray laden with muffins. Their cinnamon aroma blended with Madame Constanza's patchouli perfume in an unfortunate way. Todd prayed for Winfield's resident prophet to leave so he could enjoy the scent of the fresh-baked muffins.

"Hear that, Todd?" Sally teased. "She doesn't think you're handsome."

He frowned—not because he took her words as an insult, but because her voice lacked an edge and her eyes were dancing. Could Sally Driver be flirting with him?

Was he actually pleased by the possibility?

Damn, but he missed the good old days when he loathed Sally and knew the loathing was mutual. He missed the days when he could snicker at her peculiar earrings—the pair she had on today appeared to be small silver-toned replicas of the space shuttle—and her orange front door and her ridiculous hair, which wasn't anywhere near as ridiculous as Madame Constanza's, of course, just as her space shuttle earrings weren't as ridiculous as the glut of hoops and beads adorning her assistant's lobes.

He missed the days when Paul was still alive, keeping

Todd anchored, keeping his mind focused on the simple, irrefutable fact that Sally was a fruitcake.

But Paul was dead, and he'd been posthumously exposed as a duplicitous bastard. And right now, as Todd viewed Sally and tried to interpret her playful smile, the pastry that came to mind was not a fruitcake but a warm, spicy muffin, round and moist, slightly crusty on the outside but soft and buttery on the inside.

The college girl reached Sally's side and busied herself transferring the muffins from the tray to a shelf behind the glass display case. Every now and then she cast a flickering look Todd's way. Her smile was much more openly coquettish than Sally's.

She thought he was cute. Not handsome but cute—which was probably a higher designation among women younger than twenty-one. Was she flirting with him, too?

If she was, it was undoubtedly just for practice. He was no Adonis, no exemplar of studly appeal. He was no exemplar at all.

In fact, he never wanted to think about the word *exemplar* again.

Sally wasn't flirting with him, either, he decided. She was simply taunting him, trying to undermine him, trying to keep him off balance—and very nearly succeeding.

"I need to talk to you," he said, determined not to let these three dizzy ladies—one a professional fortune-teller, one a student with earlobes as porous as a colander and one Sally—detour him from his mission.

"You'll have to wait your turn," Sally said calmly. She resumed waiting on Madame Constanza, who was apparently quite particular about her biscotti. She wanted one plain and one chocolate dipped—no, one chocolate dipped and one amaretto—no, make that two amaretto, but without all those blanched almonds on the top. Although now that she thought about it, all the amaretto biscotti had a generous sprinkling of blanched almonds on them, and she really wasn't in a blanched-almond mood, so perhaps it would be best to skip the amaretto biscotti and go with two chocolate dipped. And a plain one, just for the hell of it.

Todd stood at the counter beside Madame Constanza, twitching from the effort to remain patient. He'd like to tell Madame Constanza her fortune: someday in the not too distant future, someone was going to punch her in the nose for being so picky about her biscotti.

As irked as he was by Madame Constanza's dithering, he was even more irked by Sally. She looked so relaxed, so serene, as if she actually enjoyed plucking biscotti from their bin, pinching the long, crescent-shaped crackers in a square of rattling tissue paper, then setting them back down and sifting through the assortment in search of specimens lacking in almonds. She seemed to take enormous pleasure in serving her customer.

Well, good for her. But his mother was a whole different thing.

"I need to talk to you," he said again, once Madame Constanza had finally settled on three biscotti she could live with, paid for them and toted her little paper bag out the door in a cacophony of clinking bracelets and rustling skirts.

"If it's about Laura Ryershank—"

"No, it's not," he interrupted, then hesitated and tossed a quick look at her assistant, who ducked her head and blushed at having been caught staring at him. He turned back to Sally. "What about Laura Ryershank?"

"I asked Tina about her."

Tina promptly spun away from him and emptied a

sack of coffee beans into a grinder. The beans clattered down the metal funnel. The clatter was replaced by a rumbling buzz once she turned on the machine.

Todd tried to ignore the noise. "And?"

Sally glanced over her shoulder, then shrugged. "She says Laura Ryershank is beautiful and charismatic."

"Okay."

"She gave two poetry readings on campus last year that were such a big hit, she was hired to be the visiting artist this year."

"So she was in Winfield last year."

"Indeed she was."

He leaned toward Sally, resting his elbows on the countertop and murmuring, as if anyone could have heard him above the pulverizing drone of the grinder. "This could be the right Laura, Sally. This could be our lady."

Sally didn't back away. She held her position, her nose just inches from his, her lips—the lips he had absolutely no interest in—so close he could almost feel the air between their faces vibrate as she spoke. "It could be."

"We need to find her."

"I was going to make some calls this afternoon after I left here."

"I'll make calls."

"That's all right. I'm sure I can handle it."

"I've got resources you don't have."

Her eyebrows quirked upward. "Resources?"

"I'm a newspaper publisher."

"Oh." She smiled wryly. "And all I've got is a telephone directory. I can't hope to compete."

Her sarcasm reminded him of why he'd left his office and stormed up Main Street to the New Day Café that morning like Sherman marching into Atlanta. He was on the warpath, raring to burn and pillage. "You hired my mother."

The abrupt change of subject seemed to bewilder her. "What?"

"You hired my mother to work here. You gave her a job."

"Oh—well, it's just a few hours a week, to see if she likes it."

"Sally! My mother ran a newspaper! She's overseen staff. She's managed production, finances, union negotiations—she isn't a waitress!"

Sally leaned back a bit, her smile growing canny. "I'm glad to hear that, Todd, because we don't have waitresses here. So you don't have to worry about her being a waitress."

"Then what did you hire her to do? Grind coffee beans?" The coffee grinder shut off just as he spoke the last three words, which resounded starkly in the small dining room. He glanced behind himself and noticed that skinny cop Bronowski glaring at him over the rim of his coffee cup, his right hand hovering near his service revolver as if he expected Todd to erupt in violence. Evidently, shouting "grind coffee beans" in a coffee shop marked one as having criminal tendencies.

Todd held up his hands and smiled at the cop, demonstrating his harmlessness. Then he spun back to Sally. "What did you hire her to do?"

"Whatever needs doing. It'll be one full morning a week plus a few extra hours, just to see if she likes it."

"Sally." He took a deep breath and tried to recover his composure, which dangled just out of reach, like the string of a helium balloon floating up into the clouds.

"Sally," he said again, envying her her equanimity. "My mother can't work for you."

"Why not?"

The question brought him up short. All he knew was that yesterday afternoon, when his mother had shouted across the newsroom from her office to his, and he'd picked up his phone and dialed her office so they could talk to each other without screaming through glass walls, she'd surprised him with the news that she was going to be serving coffee at the New Day Café a few mornings a week. She'd added a garbled quote from a Robert Frost poem, recited a few clichés about turning over new leaves and rolling with the punches and told him she'd be starting tomorrow.

Todd had been fuming ever since. But now, standing eye to eye with Sally, he wasn't sure what about the situation upset him the most. Was it the notion of his mother engaged in what amounted to menial labor, a job that required no education or experience? Was it the subtle message she might be giving him, that because he'd made her feel unwelcome at the newspaper, she'd been forced to demean herself by accepting a waitressing position? Or was he infuriated by the fact that she'd be working for Sally?

He couldn't mention the servile nature of the job without insulting Sally or her assistant. Nor could he complain about the absurdity of his mother, a certified power broker in Winfield, a friend of the mayor and the college president and a member of the board of directors of at least three major philanthropic organizations in town, being employed by Sally.

"She's supposed to go to Hilton Head Island with my father," he said.

Sally picked up a dishcloth and wiped the counter. "No problem. She can start when they get back."

"They'll be getting back at the end of June."

Sally flashed him a puzzled look. "Two months? She's going to be gone for two whole months?"

"They aren't leaving until the beginning of June," he explained, then sighed. "If they go at all. My father really wants to."

"Ah." Sally's gaze narrowed slightly. She was studying him critically. Judging him. Condemning him.

"Ah? What's that supposed to mean?"

"It means, you don't want your mother to make any commitments that might interfere with what your father wants."

He couldn't miss the scorn weighing down her voice. "The trip is my father's idea, not mine," he said defensively.

"I don't suppose your father asked your mother for her input, did he?"

"Sure he did. It's a great opportunity. They have the use of his cousin's villa down there, gratis, for a month."

"Well, it's up to her whether she'd rather go there or stay here and work."

"Stay in Winfield and pour coffee for minimum wage, or golf and lie on the beach on Hilton Head Island for a month. You tell me which choice she ought to make."

"I *won't* tell you. It's her choice to make."

He shook his head and snorted. "And she thinks my father's going senile."

"Maybe he is," Sally said with a cheerful wink. "Maybe both your parents are nuts. You're genetically compromised on both sides."

"I am not." He took several slow, even breaths, cleansing his lungs and settling his nerves. He resented everything about Sally: her certitude, her martini-dry irony, her inexplicable alliance with his mother, the way her dress draped over her body. "I am not genetically compromised," he insisted. "I am worried that my mother took this job of yours only because she wants to make a point."

"Well, if it doesn't work out, she can always quit. It won't be the first time someone's quit on me."

"Why do they quit? Because you're a lousy boss?"

"No. They graduate from college and leave town."

"So my mother's going to be working the sort of job that usually goes to Winfield College students."

"She's young at heart. She'll fit right in."

"How did this happen?" His voice cracked slightly and his shoulders slumped. He gave up trying to be reasonable, trying to stay poised. "How did you and she hook up?"

"You were the one who sent her here," Sally reminded him.

"For a fucking cup of coffee!"

Sally glanced past him. Turning, he saw Bronowski rising, his hand once again hovering near his gun. Todd hadn't realized using the f word was a capital offense in Winfield.

But then Bronowski picked up his mug and approached the counter for a refill. Tina had the pot in her hands by the time the cop was within range. Bronowski looked much taller than Todd because he was so skinny, but Todd would bet that if they removed their shoes, no more than an inch in height would separate them. They exchanged glowers, and then Bronowski addressed Sally while Tina poured his coffee. "Everything all right here, Mrs. Driver?"

"Everything is fine, thank you. How was that apple tart?"

"Good," he said, taking his refilled mug from Tina, directing one final quelling scowl at Todd and returning to his table.

"What exactly do you have a bug up your ass about?" Sally asked. "Your mother wants to work here. I want her to work here. You don't want her to work at the paper. You ought to be thrilled by the way things fell into place."

He opened his mouth and then shut it. He *should* be thrilled. For a few mornings a week he was not going to have to worry about being summoned by transoffice hollering from her. He was not going to have to talk her through the intricacies of Windows 2000. He was not going to have to listen with filial respect to long-winded lectures on why he should or should not support the mayor's new sewer initiative.

• He should be ecstatic.

But *Sally*... Sally was going to be his mother's boss.

"You'll see," she said, her smile losing its acerbic edge. "It's going to work out perfectly. I like your mother. She's great with kids, too."

"Kids? What, are you opening a child care center on the side?"

Sally shook her head. "I had Rosie and a friend in here yesterday and your mother was terrific with them. She must have been a fantastic mother. It makes me wonder why you turned out the way you did."

Fresh indignation welled within him. "What's that supposed to mean?"

"It's supposed to mean—" her smile softened "—that you left your sense of humor behind when you left home this morning. Would you like a cup of coffee? It might help.''

He longed to say no, just because he didn't want her to be right. But it was Wednesday morning, he'd been in her company for all of ten minutes, and she'd been right about everything else, so she might as well be right about this, too. "Yeah," he grunted. "I'd like a cup of coffee."

"The Irish crème is very good," Tina remarked.

It sounded alcoholic—which might be exactly what he needed, but not this early in the morning. "I'll take the most normal coffee you've got. And one of those muffins," he added, remembering how enticing they'd smelled when Tina had brought them in from the kitchen. Remembering how they'd made him think of Sally, warm and soft inside and spicy.

Sally pulled a waxed tissue from a box and used it to grip a muffin. She started to place it on a plate, but he halted her. "To go," he said. He couldn't bear to spend any more time here, seated at one of those charming round tables beneath an incoherent painting, with Bronowski on one side and on the other some crazed guy dressed for a funeral, penning a manifesto in a spiral-bound notebook. He couldn't bear to spend another minute in Sally's presence, when she'd soundly defeated him on every level and yet lacked the arrogance to look smug about it.

Instead, he took his bag and his lidded cardboard cup, handed Sally a five-dollar bill, pocketed his change and headed for the door, resisting the urge to drop the coins into the tip jar near the cash register. Just the thought of his mother pocketing coins from that jar, an extra few nickels and quarters to supplement her wages, made him queasy.

Had everything fallen into place? It had fallen, all right, but he wasn't sure where or how far. All he knew was that he wasn't the least bit pleased.

She hadn't expected him to show up at her front door at six o'clock that evening, but she wasn't really surprised to see him standing on the porch when she answered the doorbell. At the café that morning he'd been fueled by a righteous anger that was totally unjustified. Now he looked weary and haggard, his fuel-gauge needle aiming at empty. The jacket he'd had on at the New Day was gone, and he stood before her in wrinkled khakis and an even more wrinkled white shirt, the collar open and the sleeves rolled up to his elbows. His hair was a tangle of black waves, and his expression was contrite.

"I'm an asshole," he said.

She grinned. "Now, there's something we agree on."

"Can I come in?"

Her Crock-Pot was going to buzz in a couple of minutes. She'd abandoned Rosie in the kitchen, assigning her the task of adding olives to the salad. If she remained on the porch with Todd, Rosie was going to add twenty olives to the salad and eat another dozen while she worked. Sally ought to start buying the kind with pits in them, so she could keep track of Rosie's olive consumption.

Even if she didn't have to check on her daughter and the stew, she would have invited him in. He'd apologized, after all, sort of. "Sure," she said, gesturing him into the hall. "Would you like something to drink?"

"As long as it isn't coffee."

She beckoned him to follow her down the hall to the kitchen, where she caught Rosie flagrantly stuffing a fistful of olives into her mouth. "That's enough," she said, pulling the jar away from her. "How many did you eat?"

"Hi, Daddy's Friend!" Rosie greeted Todd before justifying her gluttony. "I was starving."

"We're eating in—" she glanced at the Crock-Pot "—two minutes."

"Good, 'cuz I'm starving. Are you gonna have dinner with us, Daddy's Friend?"

"Could you call me Todd, please?" he asked, then lifted his gaze to Sally, as if searching for approval.

"Are you gonna have dinner with us?" she echoed Rosie.

"Um...sure. I guess. Actually, I was thinking about that drink you offered."

"There's beer in the fridge."

The Crock-Pot buzzed. Todd opened the refrigerator, pulled a bottle of beer from the door shelf and twisted off the cap. Sally emptied the stew into a serving dish and carried it to the table. Rosie brought over the salad, which appeared to be three parts olives to two parts everything else. Sally got the bread, a crusty, floury loaf she'd picked up at the bakery on her way home from the café, and Rosie got the butter. Todd sipped his beer, then took the chair Sally pointed out to him.

He peered through the glass lid of the serving dish. "What is it?" he asked delicately.

"Lentil stew."

"Lentil stew," he echoed, his upper lip flexing as if it wanted to curl in disgust.

"It's good," Rosie assured him, kneeling on her chair and passing her plate to Sally for a portion. "It tastes like glue."

"It does not," Sally refuted her. "And how would you happen to know what glue tastes like?"

"Well, it's gloppy like glue," Rosie explained. "It tastes like beans."

Sally could live with that. She spooned a portion onto Rosie's plate, helped herself and then passed the spoon to Todd, who dabbed a modest amount on his plate and stared at it dubiously.

"So," Sally said. She liked having Todd in an apologetic mood. She liked having him greet the food she'd served—food she knew damn well was delicious—with apprehension.

Mostly, though, she just liked having him in her house. The realization shaved a layer off her cheerfulness.

"So?"

"So, why did you call yourself that thing on my porch?"

"What did he call himself, Mommy?"

"A thing."

"An ass," Todd told her, editing lightly.

"Eeew. Yuck!" Rosie erupted in laughter. "Trevor says an ass is a donkey, but I know it's really a butt."

"That'll do it for the anatomy lesson," Sally cut her off. "So, Todd—I guess my real question is, what brings you here? Surely it can't be my wonderful lentil stew."

"It's not bad," he said manfully after taking a tentative bite of the concoction. He helped himself to several thick slabs of bread, sipped his beer and said, "If my mother wants to work at your café, who am I to say no? If you make her happy, Sally, I'll be happy."

"I can't promise I'll make her happy. But I think she'll enjoy the job."

"I don't know what my dad's going to do about Hilton Head, though."

"Perhaps you ought to let your parents figure that out."

He gave her a long look, as if she'd just delivered Solomonic wisdom. "You're right. I love them both, but I don't like them dragging me into their situations."

"Then don't let them."

He nodded. "I also...used my resources today."

In other words, he'd learned something about Laura Ryershank. She rolled her eyes toward Rosie, who was mining olives from the salad bowl, and rolled them back to him.

He nodded again, obviously comprehending her silent message. "So, Rosie, how was your day?" he asked.

"It was stupid," she said, then launched into a detailed description. A boy in her class had taught several of the other boys how to suck a straw half-full of milk, then aim it and exhale through the straw, squirting the milk at a chosen target. Milk had spewed back and forth long enough to cause a significant mess, and the school's head teacher had come to lecture Rosie's whole class even though the girls hadn't done anything wrong because they weren't stupid like the boys. Instead of recess, everyone had to stay indoors and clean the milk. It was utterly stupid.

And that wasn't all. Her teacher was also stupid, because she'd tried to teach the class the lyrics to a song she didn't know, and so she'd made up new words for the second verse, but her words didn't rhyme and they made the song sound stupid.

But wait—there was more. Ashleigh Cortez was stupid because she was wearing gold nail polish and bragging about it, like it was real gold, fourteen karat, she'd said, but it was just nail polish, not jewelry, and Ashleigh Cortez was stuck-up because her father was the chairman of the biology department at Winfield College and if it wasn't for him, no one from Winfield would ever get into medical school. At least that was what Ashleigh said.

Amazingly, Rosie was able to eat while she recited this soliloquy. She even chewed with her mouth closed most of the time.

Sally was grateful—and not just that Rosie chewed with her mouth closed. With her daughter monopolizing the conversation, she could sort her thoughts while she ate.

Todd *had* been an asshole that morning. But a man who could apologize was a rarity. Paul never used to apologize. When he'd made a mistake, he would rationalize it, explain why it really hadn't been his fault, or, if necessary, shift the blame onto Sally. If he came home late from work to an overcooked dinner, he would never say he was sorry; he'd say he had told Sally he was going to be home late, and her forgetfulness had led to the overcooked meal. If he broke a stained-glass ornament, responsibility lay not with him but with her, for having so damn many ornaments stuck to the window that a man couldn't make a sweeping gesture without knocking one off its suction cup hook. If he acted like an asshole—and as she reminisced about it, she realized that he did quite often—he always had a rationale for his behavior.

But Todd had acknowledged his own assholeness, which paradoxically made him seem like the exact opposite of an asshole to her.

And he was eating her lentil stew, eating it without complaining about how much he loved red meat. And he was listening to Rosie without yawning or glancing at his watch.

And he'd come to share the information he'd gathered about Laura Ryershank.

And his hands were...big. Large and manly as he wielded a fork, as he lifted a chunk of bread to his lips, as he took a swig of beer from the bottle. Sally hadn't had a man eating at her table since the day Paul had died.

She liked this. She liked feeding Todd.

"I'm done," Rosie announced, apparently referring both to her saga of school stupidity and her dinner. "Can I be excused?"

"I've got something for you, Rosie," Todd said, rising to his feet as she did.

Sally opened her mouth to protest that he shouldn't have brought Rosie anything. She still owed him for the rice necklace; she didn't want to be even more deeply indebted to him. And just because he'd behaved foolishly at the café that morning didn't mean he could exonerate himself by showering gifts upon her daughter.

But he was already on his way through the kitchen door. "It's in my car. I'll be right back."

"What did you get me?" Rosie singsonged, chasing him out of the room. "Is it a toy?"

Swallowing her misgivings, Sally cleared the dishes from the table. Todd had cleaned his plate and drained the beer bottle. As troubled as she was by her pleasure in feeding him, she was even more troubled by how naturally he'd fit into their kitchen, their evening meal, how easily he'd made himself at home. Just that morning she'd have been the first to label him with the word he'd used to describe himself.

But now she could almost convince herself she liked him. Which was…well, troubling.

Hearing his voice and Rosie's, she abandoned the sink and crossed to the doorway. They stood in the hall, Todd handing Rosie a stack of computer diskettes. "These are your dad's games, remember? DragonKeeper and Dark Thunder, and I don't know, some other games."

"Cool!" Rosie's eyes widened.

"I thought you'd enjoy them more than me. And they were your dad's, so…"

"Cool!" Rosie took them from Todd's outstretched hand. "Can I play them now, Mommy? Can I?"

"Um…I don't—"

Rosie swung back to Todd. "Thank you!" she said, then peered up at her mother hopefully. "Can I play them, Mommy?"

Sally caught Todd's eye. He nodded slightly. He wanted Rosie to play the games. Sally couldn't say no. "Sure. But turn the sound down. I don't want to hear all that booming and banging."

"Okay! Thanks! Thanks, Daddy's—I mean, Todd!" Rosie scampered off to the den, the laces in her sneakers glittering in the light from the ceiling fixture.

Todd gazed after Rosie until she was out of sight, then turned to Sally with a smile. "If you offered me another beer, I'd say yes."

"Help yourself. I've got dishes to do."

He trailed her into the kitchen. "I thought it would be better to talk about Laura Ryershank if Rosie wasn't around," he explained, swinging open the refrigerator and pulling another bottle from the door shelf. Wrenching off the cap, he planted himself right by the sink so he could confer with Sally while she filled the basin with soapy water.

She squirted a little extra soap, inhaled the lemon-scented steam rising from the water and shut off the faucet. "What did your resources come up with?" she asked.

He slouched against the counter, beer in hand, hair mussed. A faint shadow of beard darkened his jaw. He had extraordinarily dark, thick eyelashes. She'd never noticed that before. "This Laura has published three books of poetry, and they're all for sale at the college bookstore. None of them had her photo on the inside of the cover, so I didn't bother to buy them."

"Of course not," Sally said with a chuckle. "Why buy them for the poetry?"

"I don't like poetry, okay? If my mother quotes 'The Road Not Taken' one more time I'm going to muzzle her."

"That's a nice poem. 'Two roads diverged in a wood…'"

"I'll muzzle you, too," he threatened.

"Okay." She smiled sweetly at him. "Is your mother a Robert Frost fan?"

"No. She's just quoting the poem because she likes watching me destroying four years' worth of expensive orthodonture by gnashing my teeth." He put down his bottle, pushed away from the counter and unhooked the dish towel from the cabinet doorknob on which it hung. "How come you don't have a dishwasher?" he asked, taking the plate she'd just finished rinsing and wiping it with the towel.

"It's an old house. There was no dishwasher in it when we bought it."

"You could put a dishwasher in."

"I suppose." She scrubbed the tines of a fork until

they glinted. "I don't mind washing dishes. I've always found it kind of soothing."

He took the fork from her and spent more time than warranted drying it off. "So, this Ryershank woman lives in Great Barrington, which would put her less than an hour away from Winfield. Easy for Paul to see her, but far enough away that she might choose to write him letters."

"I wonder how he would have met her," Sally said.

"Maybe he attended one of her poetry readings."

She shot him a telling look. "You knew Paul longer than I did. Do you think he'd ever attend a poetry reading?"

"If he knew the poet was beautiful and charismatic?" He arched one eyebrow.

Sally felt the dishcloth slip from her fingers. "Are you saying he went out of his way to find beautiful, charismatic women?"

"Well..." He realized he'd divulged more than he should have. Then he shrugged. "Every healthy male does."

"Do you? Do you go to poetry readings just to ogle the poet?"

"If I heard she was beautiful and charismatic?" He shrugged again. "Nah. I prefer to ogle beautiful, charismatic women at the Chelsea." The Chelsea was a pool hall and bar a few blocks south of the *Valley News* headquarters, near the train tracks. "All heterosexual men go out of their way to ogle beautiful, charismatic women. If they don't, nine times out of ten it's because they're dead."

"And the tenth time?"

"They're with their wives." He held out his hand as if waiting for her to pass him something to dry.

She rinsed a bowl and delivered it into his towel-draped hands. ''All right. Maybe he attended a poetry reading and went berserk over Laura Ryershank. So berserk he had an affair with her—the only affair of his that you know about,'' she added, testing him. If he thought Paul had been within the realm of normal male behavior in sitting through a poetry reading, he might know of other instances when Paul had ogled women.

He didn't take her bait but simply dried the bowl.

''And he went berserk enough to give her my pocketknife.''

''*His* pocketknife. You gave it to him.''

''Whatever. Do you know exactly where in Great Barrington she lives? We could drive out there—''

''She's not there now. She's on the board of directors of a writers' colony in upstate New York. It's closed during the winter, but she helps to open it up in the spring.''

''Where in upstate New York?'' Sally didn't remember ever hearing about any writers' colonies when she'd been growing up—but then, she didn't hear about lots of things when she'd been growing up.

''In the Adirondacks. Somewhere west of Lake George.''

''West of the town or west of the lake?''

He looked stumped. ''I didn't know there was more than one Lake George. I've got the name of the town written down, though. We could figure it out.''

We. We could figure it out, he'd said. He was standing in her kitchen, drying her dishes and referring to her and himself as *we*.

''Are we going to make a trip there?'' she asked cautiously.

His gaze narrowed on her, and she was once more

distracted by his lush black eyelashes. They made the whites of his eyes look whiter, the irises darker. She felt a pulse flutter in her throat and had to swallow several times to keep from coughing.

"I was thinking, we could go this weekend. It's a bit of a trek, though. I don't think we could do it in one day."

"All right." She could probably tolerate two days in a car with him. They'd stay overnight in a motel. It would be an adventure. Maybe they could even spend a little time at the town of Lake George, playing miniature golf and eating cotton candy. They could take a boat ride on the lake, too. It would be a whole lot different from the Swan Boat ride they'd taken in Boston....

"But you're not dragging Rosie along," he warned.

The flutter disappeared, and resentment slashed through her, stiffening her spine. He'd been so nice to Rosie, listening to her boring monologue over dinner and then rewarding her with those computer-game disks. How dare he exclude her from their outing? "Of course I'm dragging her along."

"No."

"What do you mean, no?"

"It's a long trip, Sally. I'm not going to spend all that time in a car listening to 'Animal Sweet.'"

"You could listen to Nirvana," she said coldly. "I'm sure Rosie would be thrilled." She yanked the stopper out of the drain, and the bubbly water made obscene gurgling and sucking noises as it seeped out of the basin. She wished her anger would drain away, too, but it wouldn't. She was doubly exasperated—not just because he didn't want Rosie to accompany him, but also because she'd been feeling...affectionate toward him.

Fond. She'd been responding to his bedroom eyes, his sweet self-deprecation, his use of the word *we*.

Damn it. She'd started to like him, and now he was handing down orders like a control freak.

"Either Rosie comes with us," she threatened, "or…"

"Or you won't come? I can live with that." He took a long drink of beer, and she wanted to tear the bottle out of his hands and smack him on the head with it. The nerve of him, enjoying her beer while he dictated the terms of their expedition.

Yet she didn't want him going off to see Laura Ryershank without her. This Laura could really be the right one.

No way was she going off to upstate New York without Rosie, though. Especially on an overnight trip. What did he think, she could leave her daughter with strangers? Hire a nanny? Sure, Rosie had spent the night at Trevor's house now and then, but that wasn't the same as spending the night somewhere while Sally was in another state.

She hated him for snubbing Rosie—and worse, for snubbing her, implying that whether or not she came made no difference to him, implying that he'd be just as happy if she didn't come at all. She hated him because his hair was so dark and his jaw so sharp, and his hands were so goddamn masculine.

Paul's best friend. Two peas in a pod. Two birds of a feather. Two of a kind.

Two assholes.

And Todd was the prime asshole because he was the live one, standing in her kitchen and drinking her beer.

Fifteen

"I'll watch Rosie," Helen said.

"No." Sally topped off the insulated silver pitcher with cream and returned the container to the refrigerator under the counter. "Really, it's sweet of you to offer, but no."

Helen fussed with the waist sash of her apron. She'd donned it over her blazer and it looked ridiculous, but Sally didn't have the heart to tell her to take the blazer off. It was part of a slate-gray pinstripe pantsuit, and she obviously felt her grooming was extremely professional. It was—for another profession. Sally didn't know Helen well enough to give her sartorial advice, though. If she got confectioner's sugar on her perfectly tailored lapel, or some coffee splattered on her crisp two-button sleeve, maybe she'd rethink her work attire.

"I don't know why Todd wants to go to Lake George," Helen said. She toyed with the stack of napkins, pretending to tidy what didn't need tidying. "All I know is, it's got something to do with your husband. His being the executor of Paul's will and all, he's got to take care of this thing in Lake George that I guess has to do with the estate." She concluded by presenting Sally with a questioning gaze.

"Right," Sally muttered. Helen was fishing for information, but Sally wasn't going to eat the worm. That her husband had cheated on her was humiliating. That she had made it her mission to find Paul's sweetheart so she could retrieve a cheesy pocketknife was laughable. Bad enough that Todd knew. Sally would just as soon no one else did.

After a long pause, Helen must have assumed that Sally wasn't going to explain the purpose of the trip. "Well, since it involves your husband, you've got to be there."

"It involves my daughter's father," Sally pointed out. "Why shouldn't *she* be there?"

"Because she's a little girl and it's a long trip."

"She can handle a long trip." Sally had taken Rosie to see her mother a couple of times—and to Boston last weekend. The child was a wonderful traveling companion.

"You want to make her sit in a car for, what, five or six hours? And then sit through some boring meeting concerning Paul's estate or what have you. And then get back into the car for another five-hour drive. No five-year-old girl should have to go through that."

When Helen described it that way, it did sound pretty grim.

"Rosie and I could have fun together," Helen persevered. "A lot more fun than she'd have traveling all the way to some godforsaken place to do something with Paul's estate. Of course he was her father—but do you really think dragging her along with you is going to bring her closer to him, or help her adjust to his death?"

No, Sally didn't really think that. What she really thought was that traveling all the way to some godforsaken place alone with Todd would be disastrous. They'd bicker. They'd fight. She'd resent him because, without any effort, he made her far too aware of the lack of a man in her life—a lack that caused her to think about him in inappropriate ways, ways he didn't think about her.

And then they'd be stuck somewhere overnight. She'd be forced to have dinner with him—or she'd have to refuse to have dinner with him, which would be awkward and would make her look like a ninny. She'd have to spend the night all by herself in a dreary motel room, instead of sharing the experience with Rosie. Rosie's presence could brighten up even the dreariest motel room. Rosie would sing badly and talk incessantly and demand food. She'd make the trip fun.

"What's with that guy?" Helen whispered, nudging Sally and pointing to the man in black, who was seated at his usual table, sipping an espresso and attacking his notebook with a pen. "Is he a spy?"

"I think he's writing a novel," Sally whispered back.

"Really? A novel?"

"He's a regular. He comes here for coffee every morning, and he writes in his notebook."

"He looks very angry."

"Intense more than angry," Sally suggested. "I think he's just caught up in the passion of his story."

"Good for him, then. Everyone should get caught up in a passion every now and then." Helen gave a loving pat to the stack of napkins and smiled at Sally. Her smile was strained, as if her lips were rubber bands stretched taut. "So, you'll let me stay with Rosie while you and Todd take care of this business."

"No!" Sally wanted to laugh, or maybe to pluck Helen's lips to hear if they twanged. "Why are you so eager to send me and Todd off alone? If I didn't know better, I'd think you were..." She faltered, unwilling to give voice to the possibility that Helen was playing matchmaker.

"You and Todd? Don't be silly," Helen insisted so emphatically, Sally didn't believe her. "Todd's not a romantic. And you're in mourning. Poor Paul. *I'm* still in mourning over him, and I wasn't even married to him. Such a sweet boy. God, I miss him. You must miss him even more."

Sally figured that mentioning what a jerk Paul had been would be about as tactful as telling Helen her apron looked wrong with her outfit. Instead, she murmured, "You learn to keep going."

"Yes, well, you've done a fine job of that. I mean it, Sally. You've got more backbone than I'd ever realized when all I knew of you was you were Paul's wife. A lot of backbone. He'd be proud of you."

He'd be pissed at her—if not for the fact that she was surviving just fine without him, then for the fact that her opinion of him was currently off the scale at the low end. He'd be furious because she no longer thought he was Mr. Wonderful. He'd be defensive because she would never let him forget that he'd given away her knife.

"Then it's decided," Helen announced brightly. "You'll go with Todd. I can either bring Rosie home to stay with Walter and me, or I could stay at your house with her. Whichever you think would be easier on her."

"Are you sure you really want to baby-sit for her? She can be a handful."

Helen gave Sally a steady gaze. "You want to know why?"

"Yes."

"I like her."

Sally tried not to gape. "You like her?"

"She's spunky and mouthy. She's got more backbone than you and me combined."

Sally wasn't sure how to respond. Of course Helen liked Rosie—anyone with half a brain or half a heart couldn't help loving the child—but that didn't seem like enough of a reason for Helen to be forcing her baby-sitting services on Sally.

It had to be that Helen was trying to match her up with Todd. The idea was preposterous. They weren't the least bit right for each other. Sally and Paul hadn't been the least bit right for each other, either, but that was no reason for her to get into a relationship with another not-the-least-bit-right-for-her man.

Maybe Helen thought that if Todd and Sally hooked up, he'd be distracted enough to let her resume running the newspaper. Or maybe she thought that if he found a new lady, he'd give her some more grandchildren, who would live close by, unlike her other grandchildren in New Haven.

Maybe she knew the real purpose for Todd's trip, and she wanted Sally to be with him when he confronted Laura Ryershank. Maybe all her blather about what a fine young man Paul had been was so much bull. Maybe she wanted Sally present for the big showdown.

Of course, it was always possible that she liked Rosie that much.

"I'll think about it," Sally muttered, then headed for the kitchen, determined not to think about it at all.

Sally insisted on phoning home from Albany. Todd offered her his cell phone, but she said she'd prefer to use a pay phone—which Todd understood to mean she'd prefer to call Rosie from someplace he wouldn't be able to listen in on the conversation, the way he would have if she'd called from the car.

Stopping wasn't a bad idea, anyway. He could use the break to take a leak and buy a soda. He found an all-purpose pit stop on the highway, watched her vanish into an alcove where the pay phones were located, then made use of the men's room, emptying his bladder so he could get to work filling it again.

She was still on the phone when he emerged from the rest room and headed for the snack area. He pulled a chilled Coke from the refrigerator case and carried it over to the alcove, using sign and body language to ask whether she wanted him to buy one for her. She shook her head and turned her back to him.

She sure was chatting up a storm with Rosie. Todd wondered what they could be talking about for such a long time. It wasn't as if they'd been separated for months.

Maybe Sally just wanted to talk, period. She'd been uncharacteristically quiet during the first stretch of the drive. He felt bad about that. He'd thought maybe they could become friends on this trip.

The notion was so bizarre it made him smile. He and Sally had nothing in common other than Paul, whom they both used to love and now loathed. Yet Todd had tried, really tried, to make this excursion something more than an ordeal.

He hadn't said a word when she'd trudged out of her house lugging a suitcase that looked like a cross between Mary Poppins's carpetbag and a marine duffel. Todd knew Paul had owned a neatly matched set of leather luggage, but apparently Sally didn't care to make use of it. Perhaps Paul had brainwashed her into thinking she must never touch it. He could be very territorial about his things, a trait Todd had learned about firsthand during their freshman year of college, when he'd borrowed volume one of Paul's *Oxford English Dictionary* without asking. Paul had made it quite clear, in a lecture that had lasted a good twenty minutes, that the OED was *his,* not *theirs,* and that if Todd wanted to share something, he ought to ask first, and if he asked, Paul reserved the right to say no. Todd had thought he'd been doing Paul a favor by not asking, because Paul had had his nose buried in Alexis de Tocqueville's *Democracy in America* and he'd hated being interrupted when he was reading de Tocqueville. But he'd learned that Paul could be very prickly about other people using his things.

So Sally wasn't using Paul's luggage. In the interest of forging a friendship with her, Todd had suppressed the urge to make a snide remark about her moth-eaten valise. He'd stocked his glove compartment with CDs he thought she might like—no Nirvana, no Led Zeppelin, but instead the softer-edged stuff: Bonnie Raitt, the Gin Blossoms, that Eric Clapton disc with all the sappy songs on it.

He'd done a lot of thinking, and he'd realized that while antagonizing Sally came as naturally to him as singing in the shower, there was no point in encouraging hostility between them. He and Sally could do better. They could get along, and if they did, the trip would be a hell of a lot more pleasant.

Actually, he'd thought about more than that. As he pocketed his change and twisted off the cap of his soda bottle, he spotted Sally emerging from the telephone alcove, her denim jumper floating down past her knees and her hair a spill of curls. The sight of her reminded him that there were other reasons he didn't want to stay her enemy.

And the most important reason wasn't *that*. His sexual response to her was an interesting and totally unexpected phenomenon, but it wasn't why he'd wanted to achieve a détente with her.

The most important reason was Paul. Everything Todd had known about Sally he'd learned through the filter of Paul's perspective. Everything he'd ever thought of her he'd thought of in terms set by Paul. When he and Paul used to meet for drinks after work—never at the Chelsea, which Paul had considered too downscale for Winfield's most able lawyer to patronize, but instead at Grover's, with its pretentious wood paneling and Tiffany lamps and its proximity to the college campus—Paul would tell Todd things about Sally that Todd had believed. She was a slob. She was flakier than dandruff. She was dizzy, daffy and dim. Paul would regale Todd with Sally stories—about how she talked to the flowers in her garden, going so far as to christen some of them with names, how she thought she was safer driving an old car than a new one because anything that was going to go wrong with an old car had already gone wrong with it, how she fervently believed that the best way to potty-train Rosie was to let her run around the house bare assed so if she had to go pee-pee she wouldn't have to waste time dropping her drawers, how she thought tofu would prevent cancer and if you saw a rainbow you were supposed to close your eyes, spin in a circle on one foot and chant, "Light and color, color and light, now my wish is burning bright."

Paul would relate tale after tale, and Todd would roar with laughter at Sally's goofy antics and half-baked theories, never questioning whether Paul was being fair in talking about her that way.

Or loyal.

Paul hadn't been loyal, and that bothered Todd. He felt guilty for having laughed, guilty and a little ashamed. Especially now that he understood how deeply Paul's disloyalty ran.

He didn't speak until they were back in the car, the gas needle pointing at full and Bonnie Raitt crooning from the speakers. "How's everything with Rosie?" he asked as he cruised up the ramp and onto the highway.

"Fine." The phone call hadn't thawed Sally much. She was still chilly and terse, her hands folded in her lap, her gaze straight ahead, her eyes hidden by sunglasses.

He was determined to get a genuine conversation going. "Just fine? What were they doing?"

"Baking brownies."

He frowned. "I hope Rosie knows how to bake brownies. My mom sure doesn't."

"They were using a mix," Sally told him.

"You were on the phone a long time, considering."

"I made a second call."

He gave her a swift, questioning look. He wanted to ask whom she'd called, but that might sound too nosy. "How come?" he asked, instead.

She cut him a break and answered the question he hadn't asked. "I called the café. Tina offered to work this morning, which was good because Nicholas, who usually takes the Saturday-morning shift, was coming in late. I wanted to make sure everything was all right there."

"Was it?" At her silence, he added, "All right?"

"Yes." She leaned back in the seat, her hair bunching in the hollow at the base of her skull. Her flying-saucer hat sat on the seat behind her, and he hoped it would stay there until they got back to Winfield. It looked better on the seat than on Sally.

"Good." He'd had easier conversations with convicted murderers at the state prison.

She loosened up a bit more. "Tina said several people from the *Valley News* staff came in for coffee. Apparently, your mother has been talking the place up."

"I don't know why. The coffee we make in-house is terrific." He grinned to let her know he was joking.

Sally arranged her dress over her knees. "You have someone working for you named Eddie, right?"

"Eddie Lesher. Why?"

"Tina told me she thought he was cute."

"Eddie? Cute?" Tina had thought *he* was cute. He was much better looking than Eddie. "Eddie's a skinny twerp with Pulitzer dreams. He's earnest and whiny, and he's got the physique of a pipe cleaner."

"I swear, sometimes I don't know where her head is."

"Who?"

"Tina. Before she gets any ideas about this Eddie person, she really ought to deal with her breast."

Her breast?

"I don't know why I agreed to this trip," Sally remarked so casually he didn't immediately realize that she'd changed the subject.

He glanced at her to make sure she wasn't undergoing an emotional disintegration. She looked exactly as she had before, her eyes hidden, her head nestled against the headrest and her fingers woven together in her lap. "Look," he said soothingly. "I know you miss Rosie, but really, she would have been bouncing off the walls if she'd come with us. And we'll be home tomorrow. And meanwhile, she'll be pigging out on homemade brownies."

"It's not that. I mean, of course I miss Rosie. But I'm sure she'll be all right."

"So will you."

She scowled, as if she considered his comment painfully unnecessary. "It's a very long trip, just so I can have the pleasure of sticking my tongue out at Paul's girlfriend."

"You want to get your knife back," Todd reminded her.

"Yeah. My knife."

"You do want it back, don't you?" If she didn't... hell. Women. They were too unpredictable, too fickle. "I thought this knife was like your Holy Grail."

"It's a tacky knife with a hula dancer on it. And yes, I want it back, though I wouldn't put it in the same category as the Holy Grail."

"We want to find Laura, right? I've got a really strong feeling this poet is our Laura. We're going to see her, we're going to confront her and you're going to get your knife back. That's what you want, isn't it?"

"Yes." She sighed. "I just don't like this whole... overnight thing," she said.

He wished he could see her eyes—but even without seeing them, he had a pretty good idea what she was trying to communicate: she just didn't like this whole overnight thing. He kept sensing glimmers of a rapprochement between them, and then those glimmers would fade and they'd be enemies again.

He wanted to get rid of the enemies part. He wanted to spend a stretch of time with her in which they started out peacefully and ended up peacefully, and didn't endure a knock-down-drag-out in the middle. If he thought about it honestly, he'd admit he wanted more than that. The more time he spent with Sally, the more he understood what it was Paul had seen in her, since he clearly hadn't seen her wit and compassion and her earthy intelligence.

Todd saw those things, but he also saw the things Paul had seen. And truth to tell, he wanted a hell of a lot more than peace with her.

She'd seemed pretty relaxed with him that night he'd dropped by at her house and wound up staying to eat the weird lentil stuff she'd prepared. At least, she'd been relaxed until the end, when she'd undergone a one-eighty in mood and started radiating an anger so hot and glowing it reminded him of Chernobyl. But at first she'd been friendly. Probably because he'd apologized to her.

Maybe it was time to apologize again. "I'm sorry," he said.

"For what?" She didn't seem surprised. Rather, she sounded as if she was wondering which of his innumerable sins he was apologizing for.

He couldn't apologize for acting like an asshole, the way he had last time. So far today, his behavior had been unimpeachable. There were other things he could apologize to her for, though. He wasn't sure he wanted to, but if he hoped to salvage this trip, he might as well cleanse the stains from his soul. "I'm sorry that I used to listen to Paul when he talked about you."

She digested that. "What were you supposed to do, *not* listen to him?"

"Well—maybe I believed him a little too readily. And enjoyed it a little too much."

"Was he that nasty?" Her words were bitter, but he heard a quiver of vulnerability in them.

"He put you down, Sally. And I…" He exhaled. This apology business was truly unpleasant. He only hoped he'd feel better once he was done with it. "I didn't just agree with him. I encouraged him. If he had told me he was having an affair, I wouldn't have been surprised.''

"You would have felt he was justified," she said. Definitely more bitterness than vulnerability now.

"I—" Damn it, he would have. "I didn't know you then. All I knew of you was what Paul told me."

She huffed and folded her arms over her chest.

"It wasn't right. But he was my buddy and I listened without judging. That's what friends do—they listen and they don't judge."

"Even when their friend is doing something awful?"

"I didn't think he was doing anything awful. Along with the things I mentioned earlier, he told me you cooked tasteless vegetarian stews—and that concoction you made the other night wasn't bad at all, really. My point being, Paul wasn't honest with me. Not about Laura, and not about you."

"So why are you apologizing?" she asked loftily. "Paul was dishonest. He's the one who should apologize."

"I should apologize, too. I feel like an accomplice."

She studied him through the dark lenses of her sunglasses. "You don't think I'm all the nasty things Paul said I was?"

"Not at all," he said, meaning it. In another context, on another day, he might not have meant it quite so much. But right now, with a hazy sun seeping through the window and Sally next to him, strong and womanly, her arms golden and gracefully muscled as they extended from the short sleeves of her blouse, her nostrils quivering slightly as she breathed, her composure steady when she had to be hurting inside...

No. He couldn't think of a single nasty thing about her.

Her silence continued. He listened to Bonnie Raitt imploring some unnamed lover to have a heart, and his anger built. He'd *apologized,* damn it. He'd betrayed his Y gene and thirty-three years of conditioning to say he was sorry. If she didn't respond soon, maybe he wouldn't pull off the road. He'd just shove her through the window while the car was cruising at seventy.

"Do you know where we're going?" she asked.

They were heading toward a village called Mondaga Lake, a microscopic dot embedded in the Adirondacks. He'd pulled the directions off the Internet. He supposed he'd find it without too much reliance on luck.

But he wasn't sure she was asking him about whether he'd find Mondaga Lake. She might be asking him something profound and mystical, something about their destiny rather than their destination. Or she might be asking about whether they might actually make it to friendship.

"We're going north," he said, deciding he'd just as soon skip the destiny discussion. And the friendship discussion, too. That might just carry them right back to the land of hostility.

"Great," she said. Her lips curved into a shape that could pass for a smile. "North feels right to me."

Sixteen

If there was actually a lake in Mondaga Lake, Sally missed it—unless it was the large puddle of slushy water that flooded half the dirt parking lot outside Tubby's General Store.

When she'd been in high school, she'd worked at a place just like Tubby's—a back-road emporium that sold everything a person could possibly need in an outpost like Mondaga Lake or her hometown: bread, eggs, beer, tackle, bullets, beer, hunting and fishing licenses, thermal socks, ice, potato chips, tobacco and beer. And hard liquor. As a high schooler, she hadn't been allowed to touch the liquor at the store where she'd worked, of course. The state of New York had deemed her old enough to sell ammunition, but if a customer wanted beer or applejack, she had to step away from the cash register and let one of the older clerks ring up the sale.

What troubled her wasn't the rustic grunge of Tubby's but the slush rimming that huge puddle. Winter took its time leaving the mountains. Even in the waning days of April, traces of snow lingered. And there she was, wearing a short-sleeve shirt, a jumper and sandals.

She remained inside the car while Todd entered Tubby's to get directions to the writers' colony. She was warm enough where she was, but once she left the car she'd have to dig her sweater out of her bag, and maybe a pair of socks.

She watched the store's front door, which was plastered with advertisements for various brands of beer and cigarettes, and tried to imagine what the place's regulars must think of their poetic neighbors. Picturing someone as rhapsodic as Laura stopping at Tubby's for a quart of milk and pontificating on Sartre made Sally smile.

She'd started this journey with grave misgivings, but somewhere north of Albany they'd faded. It wasn't just that hearing Rosie's voice on the phone had reassured her. Her mood had lifted because of Todd.

He was being nice. Which should have compounded her misgivings, but she was tired of fighting with him, tired of viewing him as Paul's ally, his defender, his— what word had Todd used? Accomplice.

What he had said, in his own roundabout way, was maybe the nicest thing any man had ever said to her: that he'd been wrong about her, and he was sorry.

He emerged from the store, wrestling with a map that refused to fall back into its folds. The late-afternoon sunlight had a pink cast to it, giving his face a ruddiness that reminded her of the sunburn he'd gotten on his nose in Boston. She wouldn't have to worry about his getting a sunburn today. The trip had taken much longer than she'd expected, and the mountain road they'd been driving for the past half hour, a narrow, winding two-lane strip of pitted asphalt with a yellow stripe down the middle, was bordered by dense evergreen forests that blocked out the sun more effectively than the office towers of downtown Boston. When Todd opened his car door he let in a gust of cool mountain air that smelled sharply of pine.

"Is this like where you grew up?" he asked.

"Higher elevation, but the same basic idea." She took the map from him and deftly folded it. "Did he know where the writers' colony is?"

"I think so."

"What do you mean?"

"Well, he kept referring to a lunatic asylum, but I'm pretty sure we were talking about the same place." Todd turned on the engine and eased out of the parking lot. "It's about three miles down on the left. The entry is poorly marked—we must have driven right past it. Just a dirt driveway with a little brown sign next to it."

"Why does he think it's a lunatic asylum?"

"According to him, it was the site of a major skirmish a few years ago, when some hunters strayed onto the grounds. It's usually closed up by hunting season, so the hunters didn't think there would be a problem. But there was a literary conclave going on there, and these hunters suddenly appeared, and all the writers started throwing rocks at them. What kind of idiots would throw rocks at heavily armed deer hunters?"

"Literary idiots, I guess."

"Anyway, the incident became known as the Battle of Mondaga Lake."

"Was anyone hurt?"

"One of the hunters sprained his ankle. A writer fell and broke her wrist, and she sued the hunters for loss of income because she couldn't type for four months. Oh, and an all-season radial took a bullet through the tread and bit the dust."

Sally laughed. So did Todd. She must have heard him laugh before, but she couldn't remember ever really listening to the sound. It started as a rumble in his chest, then erupted into a bark of joy.

She couldn't believe she and Todd were convulsed in

laughter when they were just minutes away from meeting the home wrecker who had written all those gooey love letters to Paul. It would no doubt be an unpleasant encounter. Sally would demand her knife, and Laura might refuse to return it, and they'd glare at each other like two harpies picking over her husband's corpse. Not exactly the stuff of mirth.

Yet here she was, laughing with Todd, laughing at the silliness of the Battle of Mondaga Lake and laughing because his laughter sounded so wonderful.

"There it is!" she shouted between chuckles. "There's the little brown sign."

It stood next to a narrow dirt lane, a square of boards fastened to a short stake. Mondaga Colony was carved into the brown wood, deliberately rough-hewn, the letters constructed of only straight lines, the *O*s like squares and the slanting sides of the capital *A*s extended above the point so the letters resembled tepees. The sign looked like something a Boy Scout might construct in the hope of earning a merit badge.

Todd's laughter ebbed as he steered onto the lane. Orange pine needles carpeted the road, camouflaging ruts and roots that tested his Saab's shock absorbers. Sunshine drizzled thinly through the trees surrounding them, striking the windshield like raindrops of light.

He slowed the car as they bumped along the path, and slowed it even more as they neared a clearing, where the road opened into a circle in front of a massive lodge, two stories high, with wings extending on both sides. The roof sloped steeply and the log walls were interrupted by expanses of glass. Someone very rich must have built it. Sally hadn't realized poets could be that rich.

"Are you ready for this?" Todd asked.

She turned to him. All traces of his earlier humor were gone as he soberly scrutinized the lodge. He looked impressed, but not really daunted.

She wasn't daunted, either. She hadn't been daunted by Laura Hawkes's prestigious town house on Beacon Hill, and she wasn't going to be daunted by Laura Ryershank's literary retreat. No matter how awe-inspiring the place was, anyone who could write such nauseatingly gushing letters to a man who was someone else's husband didn't engender fear in Sally.

"I'm going to need my sweater," she said, then unbuckled her seat belt and pushed open the door.

The air outside was menthol crisp and bracing, not so cold that she instantly broke out in goose bumps but cool enough that she knew she'd be shivering within minutes. Todd hit the release button to unlatch the hatchback, allowing her access to her bag. She groped around in it until she found the thick blue cable-knit cardigan she'd brought with her. Her feet would survive without socks as long as she didn't stand outside for too long.

Once she'd wrapped herself in the warm knit wool, Todd locked up the car and walked with her to the front door, which was proportionately huge, constructed of dark, heavy wood, with wrought-iron handles instead of knobs. It took Todd and Sally several minutes of sleuthing to locate the doorbell, which was disguised by a decorative wrought-iron filigree. Todd pressed the button and they waited on the slate front step, Sally cuddling her sweater tightly around her.

No one answered.

She recalled their experience in Boston. Unlike that time, they weren't within walking distance of the Public Garden and its lovely Swan Boats today. They weren't even within walking distance of Tubby's General Store.

The miles they'd driven between that swampy parking lot and this place had been interspersed by a few mysterious driveways marked by roadside mailboxes, and nothing else but Mother Nature—trees, birds, moss-covered rocks, squirrels and chipmunks.

She peered at Todd. His chin set, his shoulders squared, he gripped one of the door handles and squeezed the lever with his thumb. The door opened.

He shot her a triumphant smile and pushed the door wider. Sally wasn't sure which satisfied her more—that they'd gained entrance or that she could get out of the chilly late-afternoon air.

They found themselves in a great room, cathedral ceilinged, with stone walls and exposed rafters, slate floors and oversize leather seating. It was someone's macho Adirondack fantasy, the sort of architecture New York power brokers might have chosen when they'd built their hunting lodges and family compounds a hundred years ago. Not a single warm or charming detail spoiled the room. No colorful pillows on the sofas, no bright curtains framing the windows, no whimsical knickknacks resting on the shelves. No stained-glass ornaments, no children's toys. The lighting, provided by wrought-iron chandeliers dangling from the cross beams, was dim, contributing to the overall gloom of the place.

She caught Todd's eye. His upper lip rose in a curl of distaste.

"Can you believe Paul would have screwed around with someone who hung out here?" she whispered. Her muted voice echoed against the room's hard surfaces.

"I don't know what I believe about Paul anymore," he whispered back.

"Hello!" a voice boomed across the room. Sally turned to see its owner, a tall, egg-shaped man in a yellow V-neck pullover, new jeans, moccasins and wispy gray-blond hair that floated around his skull like an ion cloud, approach them in long, bouncy strides. "Hello there!" he hailed them, his smile warming the room markedly. "What can I do for you? We're still getting set up. Were we expecting you?"

Sally wondered whether she should defer to Todd or speak up. She'd ad-libbed pretty well with Laura Hawkes, but this was different. This place was spooky.

Todd took over. "We're here to see Laura Ryershank."

"And you're…?"

"From Winfield College," Sally interjected.

"Winfield College! Wonderful!" The man clapped his hands, like a toddler presented with a balloon. "Is she expecting you?"

"No," Todd said. "It's a surprise."

"Even better. I love surprises." The man clapped again. He had a sweet, soft face, with pale blue eyes and a cushion of fat below his chin. "I'm Claude Macy. I suppose if you want to surprise Laura, I'd best not tell her you're here."

"We *would* like to see her," Todd said. "If you could just tell us where we could find her—"

"Oh, no," Claude said jovially. "She's working now, and you know what a bear she can be if she's bothered while she's working. We do have some other guests here, but they're all in their cabins writing, too. Our kitchen is up, though. If you stay for dinner, I'm sure Laura will emerge from her cabin for that. She'd never miss a meal."

Sally wondered if Laura was fat.

Todd checked his watch. "When is dinner?"

"At seven. Why don't I get you two settled in the meantime? I'm afraid I didn't catch your names...."

"Settled?" Todd asked.

Claude Macy's smile was so bright Sally wished she hadn't left her sunglasses in the car. "I assume if you're colleagues of Laura's from Winfield College, you'll be staying for the night. No problem. We have plenty of empty cabins. What were your names again?"

"Todd Sloane," Todd said, offering his hand.

Claude shook it, then extended his hand to Sally. "Sally," she said, opting not to mention her last name, in case Claude mentioned it to Laura. If she heard Driver, she'd know Sally was related to Paul, and she might lie low until they left.

"So, you'll stay the night, then. Do you have any bags?" Claude's expectant gaze shuttled from Todd to Sally and back again, as if he assumed it would take both of them to answer the question.

Sally wasn't sure what it would take. She smiled hopefully at Todd, who said, "We were planning to take a room at a motel."

"Oh, no. Absolutely not," Claude declared. "The nearest motel is over an hour away, and it has an infestation problem. It's run by locals, if you catch my meaning."

Sally caught his meaning: the poets of Mondaga Colony were still engaged in hostilities with the local residents. Maybe no bullets were being fired, but guerrilla warfare included casting aspersions on the local motel. Which, she acknowledged, wasn't exactly local if it was an hour away.

"Let me take you to a cabin," Claude insisted. "It'll be so much nicer than that old mildewy dive. We've just had all the cabins cleaned last week. The water's been turned on, they've got heat and electricity and they're ready to be used. Please—I insist. Winfield friends of Laura's are always welcome here.''

Sally glanced at Todd, who shrugged. "I'll get our things from the car."

"Why don't we all head out together, and we can go directly to the cabin. Ah, this is going to be so much fun," Claude went on, clapping his hands yet again. "Laura is going to be so surprised."

Indeed she would be. Sally followed Todd and Claude outside into the nippy air. "Are you a writer, too?" she asked him, partly to get an idea of how he might relate to Laura and partly because she was curious. He seemed much more bubbly than she'd expect of a poet. Of course, she'd never met a poet before, so she had no way of knowing how bubbly the average poet was. The closest she came to an acquaintance with any sort of writer was the fellow in black who spent every morning at the New Day Café, penning his master opus into a spiral notebook. He certainly wasn't bubbly.

"Playwright," Claude told her. "I work with the New York Poets Theater in Manhattan during the winter. I'm sure you've heard of them."

Sally smiled vaguely. She'd never heard of them.

"And I always come up here in April to help get the colony opened, along with Laura and the other usual suspects." He chortled at a joke she failed to get. Taking Sally's bag from Todd, he waited for Todd to haul out his own bag, a black rectangular suitcase with wheels and a telescoping handle that would have been easy to drag around on a smooth surface but was not at all suited for the uneven, needle-strewn ground. "The folks here now are all helping us to get the place whipped into shape. Hawley Dandrick is here." Claude spoke his name portentously, implying that Sally was supposed to know who Hawley Dandrick was. "And Tabitha Shula. She comes every year in July, but she's completing work on a book-length prose poem and needed a few weeks to finish it, so I told her to come on up and get some writing done between chores. It's going to be a masterpiece, I'm sure. Tabitha doesn't know how to write anything less than brilliant."

Sally could imagine.

"And the Ross twins came. They're brainstorming the third book in the Cargill series...."

She had no idea what he was talking about, but she let him ramble. He was carrying her bag, after all, leading the way around the mansion and down a trail that meandered through the dense woods. Glancing over her shoulder, Sally saw Todd lugging his wheeled suitcase by the handle, his gaze hard and assessing. Claude's daffodil-yellow sweater was the brightest thing in the forest.

As her eyes adjusted, she began to notice the buildings scattered through the woods, set on paths that branched off from the trail they were hiking. Small and rustic, the cabins reminded her of the Mondaga Colony sign at the entry to the compound. Except for the mansion, this place felt a lot like a Boy Scout camp.

"Here we go," Claude said grandly, leading them to one of the squat brown cabins. He heaved his shoulder against the door to open it, then flicked on a light switch and swept inside, gesturing for them to follow.

For a moment, all Sally saw was the bed. Singular. One wide bed piled with a patchwork quilt and four fluffy pillows. One bed.

She tore her gaze from it to take in the rest—the writing desk, the easy chair with its faded, inviting upholstery, the floor lamp beside it, the windows overlooking the woods. The two doors on the side wall, one opening onto a closet and the other onto a bathroom. The thick maple dresser. The knotty-pine walls. The matching night tables flanking the bed.

The bed.

"As I said, dinner will be around seven," Claude reminded them. "You'll see Laura then. And won't she be surprised!"

Won't she, indeed, Sally thought as Claude departed, shutting the door behind him. She turned from the door and her vision filled with the bed. "Todd?"

He dropped his suitcase with a thud. "Yeah?"

"There's only one bed."

He contemplated this, as if it were news to him. "I'll sleep on the floor," he offered.

She looked at the plank floor, covered in several places by thin braided rugs. "You can't do that."

"Okay. *You'll* sleep on the floor."

"Todd."

"We'll share the bed."

She opened her mouth, then puffed out a long breath and reconsidered what she was going to say. If she'd still hated Todd, sharing a bed with him would have been no problem. She could have rolled on one side, presenting him with her back and hovering near the edge of the bed. She could have pretended he wasn't there; she had a good imagination. As long as he didn't snore or hog the blanket, she could ignore him.

But she didn't hate him. He had apologized to her. He'd played mellow music instead of Nirvana during the drive. And he'd laughed. His laughter had changed everything.

"We could still go find that motel," she suggested.

"Sure. The one with the infestation problem." He

crossed the room to the floor lamp and clicked it on, then turned to Sally. "We're this close to meeting Laura," he said, holding his thumb and forefinger less than an inch apart. "Once we see her and have our say, we're probably going to get our asses kicked out of here. Claude isn't going to extend the hospitality of this wonderful writers' colony to two people who've come to flay his good buddy Laura. So don't worry about it."

He had a point. They'd probably wind up at the motel, where they'd be able to rent separate rooms, with separate beds and separate infestations. She'd have her knife back, and Paul's lover would be left with a sizable dose of guilt—Sally hoped—and the furnishings of this cabin would no longer be relevant to her life.

"All right," she said. "I won't worry about it."

It turned out that Laura Ryershank did miss meals sometimes. Claude relayed to the motley group of writers seated around one end of the long pine table in the main building that Laura was going great guns and couldn't be disturbed. "When the colony is in full swing," he explained to Sally and Todd, "some guests prefer to have their meals in their cabins. They don't want to break up the flow."

"The flow?" Todd asked.

"The flow of their writing."

Seated next to Todd, Sally could tell that his esteem of the Mondaga writers was not high. Every time Claude clapped his hands—which he did with alarming frequency—Todd winced. When the Ross twins—Sally couldn't tell Mickey from Marty; they both dressed in navy-blue crew-neck sweaters and khaki trousers, and their eyeglass frames were identical—talked, he pulled a face. Tabitha Shula, who stood as tall as Todd and had ebony skin and a buzz cut, spoke in epigrams, her voice hoarse from the cigarettes she repeatedly leaped from the table and raced outdoors to smoke. Hawley Dandrick was a burly fellow with a muscular beard and a Hemingway attitude.

Todd seemed to hold them all in equal contempt.

Unlike him, Sally found them fascinating. She pumped them with questions about their writing projects, and they obliged her with verbose answers. The Ross twins were involved in a multivolume series that involved fantasy elements and universe building. It sounded interesting to Sally, although she doubted she'd want to spend thousands of pages on fantasies that weren't her own. Tabitha had a tendency to declaim rather than speak; she would utter a majestic pronouncement about tribes of women, then bolt from the table to inhale a Marlboro Light on the slate patio visible through the French doors. Claude described his New York Poets Theater, which staged T. S. Eliot's *Murder in the Cathedral* annually. When asked, Hawley blithely reminisced about the Battle of Mondaga Lake. In his version, he single-handedly mowed down three hunters with chunks of granite and deflected a bullet with his steel-toed shoe.

Todd didn't say much as he downed his dinner, a vegetarian lasagna that Sally found so tasty she inquired about the recipe. For all his contrition about having misjudged her, he seemed to be sitting in judgment of their dinner companions—and finding them guilty on all charges, whatever those charges were. Unconventionality, perhaps. Flights of fancy. Overweening self-importance.

"We'd really like to see Laura," he murmured to

Claude. Sally detected a taut thread of impatience in his voice; she wondered if Claude noticed it.

"And I'm sure she'll be delighted once she sees you, too," Claude commented amiably. "She adores Winfield. She always speaks so highly of her special friends there."

Had Paul been one of her "special" friends? Sally wondered. Did she have other "special" friends? Had she been screwing half the town?

"But when the words are flowing," Claude continued, "you just can't interrupt them."

"It's bad karma," Tabitha interjected.

"And they must be flowing quite marvelously for Laura to have missed dinner. I'll have to bring her a tray so she doesn't starve."

"We could bring her the tray," Todd volunteered.

"Oh, no, we couldn't let you do that. Seeing you would interrupt the flow."

"Bad, bad karma," Tabitha intoned.

"But make yourselves at home. Sooner or later, the flow is going to dry up and our queen will emerge. In the meantime—"

"Queen?" Todd pounced on the word. "Is Laura your queen?"

"More like a goddess," one of the twins said.

"She's so beautiful," the other twin added.

"A goddess among poets," Claude confirmed.

Sally's spirits deflated. A beautiful goddess poet. No wonder Paul had chased after her. No wonder he'd risked his marriage for her. No wonder he'd saved all her letters.

"Well, we wouldn't want to do anything that would interrupt the goddess's flow," Todd muttered, nudging away his plate. "I guess we'll have to see her later."

"There's plenty for you to do while you wait," Claude told them. "Right here in the main building we've got a library packed with books, and backgammon, and a piano. You can take a stroll around the grounds, although it's kind of dark, so I wouldn't recommend that. Or you can go back to your cabin. There's a phone there. I'd be happy to give you a ring if Laura emerges."

"I think that's what we'll do," Todd decided for both of them. Sally almost balked. Maybe she'd prefer to play backgammon, or lounge around the piano singing old show tunes with Hawley and the twins. Or traipse about the grounds in the dark until she fell and broke her wrist so she could sue someone.

Going back to the cabin with Todd until Laura showed her goddess face was probably a better option. Smiling and thanking Claude for dinner, she excused herself and left the dining room with Todd.

"This place gives me the creeps," he grumbled as soon as they were outside, picking their way carefully along the poorly lit path to the cabins.

"I thought those people were interesting."

"They're pretentious dilettantes! I know more about writing than they do."

"You know more about writing news articles, maybe."

"Which is *real* writing, not the jerking off these folks do. I mean, what was that crap the bearded guy was talking about—how a writer must hearken to the muse's siren? Give me a break. A real writer hears a siren and follows the fire engine, because wherever it's going, there's bound to be a story."

"That was his point," Sally argued. "You obey the siren and find your inspiration."

"'Hearken'?" Todd snorted. "What normal person uses the word *hearken* in a regular conversation?"

"These people don't have to have regular conversations! They're artists."

"Yeah, and the world really needs artists like them." Sarcasm bathed each word. "I bet they've all heard of Vigo Hawkes, too."

Sally bristled. *She'd* heard of Vigo Hawkes. "Just because your own life is so limited—"

"My life isn't limited. I'm just not a bombastic *artiste* with a swollen ego, like those turkeys."

"You're a snob. You've got the biggest ego of all."

"No. I've just got the most sense." He yanked open the cabin door and stomped inside. "I swear, if the Battle of Mondaga Lake ever gets fought again, I hope someone lets me know. I want to enlist in the hunters' army."

Sally stomped in after him and slammed the door behind her. "You're a jackass, Todd. Those people were lovely, but all you can do is sit in judgment of them. You can't begin to open your mind to the possibility that the whole world isn't filled with jackasses like you!"

"Anyone who uses the word *hearken* is a jackass in my book. Especially if he uses it in reference to the muse."

"What word would *you* use in reference to the muse?"

He circled around on her. The lamp by the easy chair spilled golden light behind him, turning his face into shadow. "I don't believe in muses! When you run a newspaper, you have deadlines. None of this touchy-feely creativity shit."

"That's because you aren't a poet."

"Thank God I'm not!"

She wanted to argue, but when she slowed down long enough to think, she realized that she agreed with him. Thank God he wasn't a poet. Poets had affairs with other people's husbands and wrote sappy letters. Todd...

Todd was who he was. He wasn't introspective or elegant or sensitive, but he was honest and loyal. And he didn't use the word *hearken* in ordinary conversation, which—if she was going to be as honest as he was— she considered an asset.

She became aware of the silence in the cozy cabin, the warmth of the light emphasizing the dark forest beyond the windows. She became aware of Todd standing before her, just two strides away, staring at her. She became aware of the bed behind him, and the energy inside him, and the fact that she liked the sound of his voice, even when they were arguing, as much as she liked the sound of his laughter.

She wished she could get back to arguing with him. Arguing was safer than thinking about how tall he was, how broad his shoulders were, how long his legs. It was much safer than thinking about the remoteness of their cabin, the icy bite in the air outside, the thick quilt and plump pillows on that damn bed.

"Sally," he murmured, sounding hoarse.

She had to say something, or do something. "Maybe I ought to give Rosie a call and see how things are going."

"Things are going fine." He took a step, halving the distance between them.

"I'm sure they are, but—"

"Sally." One more step and he blocked the bed completely from her view. Which was good, she told herself. She didn't want to think about the bed, not when Todd was so close to her, when he was sliding his hand under her hair to her nape and bowing his head, when she felt the heat of his mouth an instant before it captured hers.

They'd kissed before. She knew what to expect. She could handle it.

No. No, she couldn't. Not when they were alone like this, far from home, not when she'd lived so many long, lonely months without sex, not when he stood before her so big and real and male, not when he'd said the most romantic words a man could ever say to a woman: *I'm sorry.*

She couldn't handle it at all. So she went ahead and kissed him back.

His hand fisted in her hair. His other hand swooped around her waist and hugged her tight. She slid her hands inside his jacket so she could cling to his shoulders, and she let herself go. She remembered how powerfully she'd reacted the last time he'd kissed her, but this was different. This was hot and deep and less than three feet from a bed.

Without breaking the kiss, he shoved her cardigan down her arms. She shoved his jacket down his. Still kissing, he tugged at her jumper. She fumbled with his shirt. He stroked her cheeks, her ears, her throat, dug his fingers into her hair and pulled out the barrettes. She nuzzled his chin and felt the scratch of his day-old beard against her lips.

Together they staggered to the bed and tumbled onto it. She kicked off her sandals; he kicked off his loafers. He stopped kissing her and reached down to stroke her bare legs. They'd been cold, but his hands warmed them. Big, blunt, manly hands, tracing the contours of her calves, the creases behind her knees, shoving the jumper up and out of his way so he could caress her thighs.

She made another futile attempt to unbutton his shirt.

If only he'd stop moving, if only *she'd* stop moving. But she couldn't, not when he was running his palms along the fronts of her thighs that way, creating heat and friction that made her want to burst out of her skin. He stopped long enough to tear off the shirt himself, then hauled her jumper over her head. She pulled off her own shirt and he shucked his pants. The faster they finished undressing, the sooner he would put his magical hands back on her, so she scrambled out of her underwear and watched him dispense with his boxers.

Oh, God, he was beautiful. Todd Sloane. She'd glimpsed his bare chest that one time, but she never would have guessed the rest of him would be so divine. Rounded shoulders, taut biceps, an athlete's legs, a navel so deep and narrow she wanted to lick inside it, an erection so full she got other ideas about what to do with her tongue. He turned from her to open his suitcase, and she admired his streamlined back and the knotted muscles of his buttocks.

Why had she never noticed how handsome he was? Probably because she'd been married to his best friend, and he'd despised her for not being the wife he would have liked his best friend to have. And she'd despised him for despising her, and for knowing her husband better than she knew him, being closer to her husband than she could ever hope to be.

But she and Todd didn't despise each other now. She could never despise someone who kissed her the way he did, who touched her the way he did, who knew better than to use the word *hearken* in casual conversation.

Turning from the suitcase, he tossed a condom on the nightstand next to the bed. The sight of that premeditated foil square snapped her out of her sensuous fog. "You planned this," she accused him.

He sprawled out on the bed next to her, brushed a heavy lock of hair out of her face and then let his hand trail down to her shoulder. "No."

"Yes you did. You brought that. You planned this."

"I brought Band-Aids, even though I'm not planning to get cut."

She tried to find a chink in his logic, but his hand drifted farther down and rational thought became difficult. He fondled her breasts, kissed them, squeezed and kneaded and sucked them, and she realized that whether or not he'd planned to get laid, she was very glad he had come prepared.

And then she stopped thinking altogether, let her hands and mouth and body do the thinking, let her senses guide her. She learned what kind of touch made him gasp, what kind made him moan. She learned what made him arch his back, what made him close his eyes and shudder. She learned that if she shifted her hip he would slide his hand across her belly, if she rolled her head back he would brush his lips feather soft against her throat.

She learned that her imagination wasn't all that great, because she'd never even begun to imagine that Todd Sloane could make her feel so overheated, so restless, so greedy. She'd always enjoyed sex, but she'd never imagined she could be teased into such a state of frustration and need, a yearning so desperate it hurt. When at last he entered her, she'd never imagined she would whisper, "Thank you."

"The pleasure's all mine," he whispered back, and then he moved inside her, at first in slow, controlled thrusts but then faster, harder, until she was certain the pleasure was all hers. Her body convulsed, but he kept going, his eyes closed as he propped himself above her, his hips pumping, his back damp with sweat until another climax beckoned, lured her to the edge and sent her over.

He pressed deep, threw back his head and groaned. It was a sound even more lovely than his laughter. After a moment, he sighed and lowered himself into her arms. He was heavy, his large bones digging into her soft flesh in an uncomfortable way, but she didn't care. She just held on to him, his hair tickling her cheek, his ragged breath sighing into the hollow of her neck.

She just held on and smiled.

Seventeen

For the first time in his life, Todd understood what it meant to fuck your brains out. He felt as if he had come in his mind as powerfully as he'd come the usual way.

His head felt as heavy and limp as the rest of him. It would take more energy than he possessed at the moment to roll off her—and more willpower, too, because God, her body felt good under his. Had he actually thought she was chubby? Round, yes—in all the right places. Her breasts were pillows designed to give a man wet dreams, and her bottom filled his hands perfectly. She didn't have a fashionably sleek look, but it appealed to him just fine.

Despite his exhaustion, he forced himself off her, afraid he'd suffocate her if he didn't move. She inched back, giving him enough room so he wouldn't fall off the bed, and he settled on his side facing her.

Her hair. That was another wet-dream feature. Sally was spectacular.

"How many times do you not plan to get cut?" she asked.

The words resembled English, but they made no sense. "Huh?"

"Well..." She traced the veins and bones on the back of his hand. "You said you brought Band-Aids along even though you didn't plan to get cut. I was wondering how many times you didn't plan to get cut. How many Band-Aids you brought.''

Understanding, he laughed. ''I think it was a six-pack.''

''A six-pack. Hmm.'' She moved her hand up his arm. He watched her fingers as they traveled over his skin. Her unmanicured nails were short, giving her hand an almost childish appearance. It didn't feel like a child's hand on him, though. It felt magnificently womanly as it reached his shoulder and then wandered down onto his chest. ''So you aren't planning to do this five more times?''

He laughed again. Even in the aftermath of glorious sex, Sally could drive him crazy. Not just with her words, either. Her hand, exploring his nipple, was also driving him crazy.

At last he understood how Paul could have wound up in an affair with her, despite the fact that they were all wrong for each other. He'd probably slept with her once and become hopelessly addicted, a risk Todd was facing right now. She stroked up and down his sternum and a circuit closed between the skin beneath her fingertips and the nerves in his groin, which began to stir from its lethargy. What he couldn't understand was how Paul could have had an affair with anyone else when he'd had Sally waiting in his bed at home.

Her hand ventured lower, stroking the fine hairs below his stomach, and his penis twitched. He really didn't have the strength to make love again so soon. But she let her hand scoot lower and all the blood in his body flowed south like a tidal wave.

''Sally,'' he sighed, then gave up and covered her hand with his, guiding her onto him, knowing this playful skirting-the-issue stimulation wasn't going to get them where she obviously wanted to go. He leaned forward to kiss her, and her mouth opened for him. He brought his other hand down and her legs opened for him, too, those warm, smooth thighs spreading to welcome him. He recalled how tightly they'd sandwiched his hips, how they'd flexed when she climaxed, and the memory turned him on so much he began to wonder whether they'd use up the damn six-pack before midnight.

The phone rang. It sat on the nightstand right next to his head, and its bell was so shrill he flinched. Sally's eyes flew open and she bolted upright.

It rang again. Todd ran through a few expletives, then reached for the receiver. "Yeah?"

"Hello! It's Claude!" The guy's voice vibrated with exclamation points.

"Yeah." Todd cleared his throat. "Hi."

"I thought you'd want to know—Laura has emerged."

"Oh. Okay." He pushed himself up to sit and rubbed his forehead between his eyebrows. The blurriest part of his brain seemed to be located somewhere around there.

"I didn't tell her you were here. I didn't want to spoil the surprise."

"Okay, well, great. Thanks. So, she's in that big building?"

"She's in the kitchen right now. Once she's done there, she'll probably go to the game room to watch the twins play backgammon. She doesn't play it herself, but she loves to watch the twins."

Todd bet she did. Now that Paul wasn't around, maybe she liked to make a threesome with Tweedledum and Tweedledee. Watching them play backgammon might be her idea of foreplay. "We'll find her," he assured Claude. "Thanks."

He set the receiver back in its cradle and gazed at Sally. Her hair looked too inviting spilling down her back. Her breasts looked larger when she was sitting up. Her thighs... He'd never been a thigh man before he'd met her. But hers were amazing.

Sally Driver. Hard to believe she could have such an effect on him, but she did. His groin clenched when he remembered the feel of her hand on him just moments ago, as he remembered the feel of her all snug and wet around him a few minutes before that. Hard to believe— but the truth was in his body, in his nerves, in the blood pumping through his veins. He wanted her again. And again. He couldn't imagine ever having enough of her.

If they confronted Laura now, they probably wouldn't get to spend the rest of the night in this little love nest tucked in among the trees. They'd meet the woman, say their piece, get Sally's pocketknife, and then take off before Laura and her colleagues could engage them in a new Battle of Mondaga Lake.

Maybe he and Sally could spend the night in that motel an hour away, the infested place. Not a big fan of rats and roaches, he nixed that idea. They'd drive to Lake George—which was a tourist mecca, which meant all the hotel rooms would probably be booked. So they'd continue to Albany...and then Sally would say, *We're only a couple of hours from home. Let's just go.* And they'd drive through the night back to Winfield, and they'd never get to use the other five condoms he'd brought with him.

Shit.

Sighing, he turned from her and swung his legs over

the side of the bed. "Time to have it out with Laura," he said.

Heading back to the main building, Todd forced himself to expel from his mind all thoughts of making love with Sally. He refused to acknowledge how much different her shapeless denim jumper looked now that he knew what was underneath it, how resplendent her hair was. She hadn't been able to find her barrette, which he'd dropped on the floor, so her long auburn mane hung loose around her face and down her back, and seeing it reminded him of its herbal smell and its crinkly texture. He refused to remember how heavenly her arms, now swinging at her sides, had felt circled around him, holding him to her. He erased it all from his gray matter so he could concentrate on the task at hand.

Whoever Laura Ryershank was, he thought, she'd have to have been pretty damn spectacular for Paul to have risked what he had with Sally.

Of course, no matter how great Sally was in bed, she could be a pain in the ass. Paul had always been cerebral; maybe Sally's lack of college degree had turned him off, and he'd needed an erudite poetess to turn him back on. Maybe that cloying claptrap Laura had written him had flicked his switch in a way lusty kisses and silky skin and exuberant passion couldn't.

Maybe Todd would never understand what Paul had been up to. Maybe he had never really understood Paul at all. His best friend had kept so many secrets from him. He'd never even hinted at how sensual Sally could be. All he'd ever done was complain about her.

Todd felt cheated. He'd wasted his best-friendship on a deceitful prick.

He tried to remember his part in this mission: not to

avenge Sally's betrayal but to find out why Paul had been a deceitful prick, why he'd denied his alleged best friend access to the truth about himself. When Todd had started the search for Laura, he'd hoped that meeting her would exonerate Paul, that she would assure him Paul had loved him and never intended to shut him out from this part of his life.

Everything was different now, though. Todd had made love to Paul's wife. Maybe *he* was the deceitful prick. Paul had been deceitful first, but still...Todd couldn't shake the twinge of guilt nipping at his conscience.

They fled into the main building, escaping the cold mountain air, and Sally started toward the dining room. Todd let her lead; he figured that as a woman she would have special radar directing her to the kitchen. She halted at the dining room doorway, tilted her head and then shook it. "There's no one there," she guessed, just from listening. "Where do you think they'd be playing backgammon?"

From the far wing of the building came faint laughter. "That sounds promising," he said.

Nodding, Sally swiveled on a sandaled foot—she'd donned blue-and-white striped socks, which looked strange with her sandals—and marched across the great room in the direction the laughter had come from. Her back was straight, her chin high, her gait purposeful. She'd walked the same way the morning she'd stormed into his office with the letters and demanded an explanation from him. It was her angry-woman-on-a-mission strut. She seemed to be suffering no aftereffects from their little romp at the cabin. That she could put that interlude out of her mind more easily than he unsettled him.

The laughter grew louder as they entered a hall, and

louder yet as they neared a doorway. On the threshold Sally froze. Unable to stop so quickly, Todd bumped into her.

The doorway opened into a cozy lounge. The twins hunched over a table with a backgammon board inlaid in its surface. Each was armed with a leather dice cup. Nose to nose, their posture and attire identical, they reminded him of a Rorschach test.

But they weren't the reason Sally had screeched to such an abrupt halt. She'd obviously reacted to the woman with them. She was slim and petite, clad in a purple tunic, black trousers and tooled white cowboy boots. Her hair dropped down her back in a long silver braid. When one of the twins glanced toward the door, so did she.

She had to be seventy years old at least, maybe older. Her face was a mesh of deep creases and fine lines. The skin beneath her chin pulled taut over the tendons on either side of her neck and her hands were as gnarled as some of the roots he'd driven over coming up the driveway to this building. Her pale gray eyes glinted with curiosity as she took them in. "Can I help you?" she asked.

"Surprise!" Claude hollered, launching himself out of a chair at the far end of the room and clapping his hands. "They're from Winfield, Laura!"

"Yes," Sally managed to say. "We're from Winfield. We came to see you."

"How lovely," the woman said, her wizened face breaking into a smile.

This was the goddess? The beautiful, charismatic poet? She was old enough to be Paul's grandmother!

"Can we go somewhere and talk?" Sally asked.

"If you'd like. Perhaps we could have some tea." She

patted one of the twins on the shoulder and crossed to the doorway.

In the hall, he sized up the woman. Could Paul have possibly—? No way. Even though she had a pretty decent figure for a senior citizen...and maybe she'd qualify as charismatic. Beautiful, even, in a septuagenarian kind of way. Sexy enough to be elected prom queen at the Senior Center ball.

But Paul and her together? Merely picturing his young, healthy buddy with Granny Yokum made his eggplant lasagna do gymnastics in his digestive tract.

They returned to the dining room, strolled through it and entered a kitchen equipped with professional appliances—six-burner stove, aluminum-doored refrigerator, stainless-steel counters and large cast-iron pots hanging from racks along the walls. It seemed like much too elaborate a room to boil water in, but the slender silver-haired woman filled a kettle with water, set it on the oversize range and turned on the gas. Then she plucked some tea bags from a canister and dropped them into three mugs pulled from a cabinet.

Todd hated tea, but he was too stunned to say so.

None of them spoke while they waited for the water to boil. The old saying about watched pots floated through Todd's mind as the minutes ticked by. He sneaked furtive glimpses at Laura Ryershank, taking in the slight droop of her eyelids and the pleats of skin around her eyes, the fine frizz of hair framing her heart-shaped face, the sagging flesh beneath her chin. No matter how deceitful a prick Paul was, Todd just couldn't see it. Nope. Laura Hawkes he would have believed, but not this one.

As she steeped the tea in the mugs, he contemplated a way to get out of this, to say there must be a mistake, thank the woman for her time and leave. He wanted to go back to the cabin, to that big, solid bed, and resume what he and Sally had been doing before Claude had to spoil everything by phoning them. But he wasn't even in the mood for that. He was pretty sure he could get back into the mood with a little help from Sally, but right now...

He realized he wasn't even all that eager to return to the bed in the cabin. He just wanted to grab their bags, toss them in the car and get the hell out of here.

Sally clearly had other ideas. As soon as the three of them had carried their cups to the dining room and taken seats at one end of the long table, she started talking. Just like when they'd visited Laura Hawkes, Sally decided to turn this error into an interesting adventure. "You have such a splendid reputation at Winfield College," she began. "We just had to come and meet you in person."

"It's a long way to come just to meet me," Laura said with a crinkly smile. "I'll be back in Winfield in a couple of weeks for my final visiting artist reading. You could have waited until then."

"But we wanted to meet you here. My husband—my late husband, Paul Driver—always spoke so highly of you."

Todd shot Sally a glance. Why was she hinting around? Did she actually think her late husband, Paul Driver, had slept with this woman? Did she actually think he *could?*

Evidently, she did. She observed Laura's face as closely as a botanist observing a budding orchid while she waited for a response. Did she see a rival in the woman? A femme fatale? A superannuated nymphet?

"Paul—what did you say? Driver? I don't recall ever meeting him. I'm so sorry for your loss, though, dear."

Okay? Todd wanted to say. *Are you satisfied? Can we go now?*

But Sally didn't want to go. "So how does that all work out, your teaching in Winfield and coming here to write?"

Much to his dismay, Laura Ryershank decided to tell them how it all worked out—the unabridged version, starting with her graduation from Winfield College with the Class of '48. After college, she'd traveled to Europe and engaged in dalliances with assorted postwar types. She'd returned home, married three times, had her early works published in the Yale Younger Poets series, taught graduate students, taught second-grade students, hosted a salon in Greenwich Village, founded a small press, sold her small press to a major publishing house and retired on the profit she'd netted in that transaction. She'd spent most of her summers at Mondaga Colony, writing and savoring nature, as she put it, and ultimately she'd wound up on the board of directors. She'd been giving poetry readings and master classes at Winfield for years and was thrilled to have been named the visiting artist this year. She believed that artists needed to live in communities like Mondaga Colony, where they could nurture and support one another, because society truly didn't nurture and support its artists, even though without those artists life wouldn't be worth living.

At least she didn't hearken to the muse, Todd thought sullenly, trying not to gag on his tea while Sally sat forward in her chair, apparently enraptured by the small silver-haired woman. He hadn't noticed Sally's earrings before—he'd had other things on his mind—but when she moved her head and her hair fluttered back from her face, he noticed that the items hanging from her earlobes bore an uncanny resemblance to gold-toned squids.

No more than a half hour ago—he discreetly checked his watch, unsure whether he'd been listening to the elderly poet for minutes or hours—he'd been craving Sally the way a dead man craved entry to heaven. Had sex with her really been so breathtaking? Had he really felt, in that endless moment when he'd completely lost himself inside her, that Sally had been the woman he'd been waiting for all his life? Now all he could see were her most irritating qualities: her intense fascination with nonsense, her infatuation with artsy types, her shallow attempt at depth—and her silly earrings.

He wanted to go home. Now.

But she had to hear more. She had to interrogate Laura Ryershank about the Battle of Mondaga Lake— "Oh, yes, it's true about the tire getting shot out. But Hawley stopping a bullet with his shoe? Ha! Hawley is a novelist, don't forget. Fiction is his life" —and about the creative process— "Trees are the poet's greatest inspiration. Trees are God's stilts. So when you surround yourself with trees, you can almost feel God teetering overhead."

Maybe God ought to lose his balance and come tumbling down, crushing all the poets, Todd thought churlishly.

Eventually, his tea half consumed, he excused himself and left the two women jabbering. Laura Hawkes redux, he concluded. Sally obviously enjoyed making friends with Lauras who weren't her husband's mistress.

He hiked back to the cabin. A mean, selfish part of him sneered at the prospect of Sally getting lost trying to locate their cabin in the dark without him to guide her. Once inside, he saw the rumpled quilt on the bed, the head-shaped depressions in the pillows, and a low ache tugged at his gut.

Yes, she *had* been breathtaking.

But she was also Sally. Friendly to a fault. Intrigued by life. Hungry to learn, to see the world through other people's eyes. Eager to break the rules, ignore the rules, hearken to her own muse, whatever that muse might be.

Damn. All those irritating aspects of her, the traits that set him to grinding his teeth—*they* were what made her breathtaking. Her enthusiasm. Her intensity. Her pushiness. Her boldness. She was juicy, and Paul had been as dry as stale toast, and Todd...

Todd was dying of thirst.

He wanted Sally. Even though she'd rather spend an evening interviewing an old lady about what life had been like in postwar France or what exactly she'd meant when she said trees were God's stilts, or what it felt like to hold an actual book you had written in your hands— even though she'd prefer that to wrapping her legs around Todd and letting him bury himself inside her until they were both sweating and writhing in ecstasy, he wanted her.

So instead of tossing his things into his suitcase, he pulled out the box of condoms and left it handy on the night table. Then he took a shower—a quick one, because the hot water ran out while he was soaping his chest. He ran his razor over his cheeks and chin, brushed his teeth and climbed into bed, knowing she'd be worth the wait.

And when she returned to the cabin sometime later, awakening him with her exuberant chatter about how Laura had given her an autographed copy of her most recent book and Claude had given her the recipe for the vegetarian lasagna they'd had for dinner, and damn but she wished she could write because these people were just so amazingly talented and complex—babbling the whole time she was in the bathroom, even when she was brushing her teeth and her words came out unintelligible....

He didn't have to know what she was saying. It didn't matter. What mattered was that she was there, spiky with energy, vibrant with the sheer joy of having met new people with new ideas.

When she slipped under the quilt beside him and her joy filled the bed, he knew she was worth the wait.

Eighteen

"The brownies were great, Mommy!" Rosie announced, bouncing up and down on the porch as Sally and Todd climbed out of the Saab. "They were so good! We didn't save you any. I gave one to Trevor and we gave a couple to Helen's husband, and then we ate the rest. We made them, so they were ours. We had such a good time!"

So did I, Sally thought, racing up the front walk with her arms outstretched. She felt horribly guilty that she hadn't missed Rosie more, that she hadn't been counting the milliseconds until she could close her arms around her beloved daughter. Blame it on Todd. Blame it on the fact that her worst fears about taking an overnight trip alone with him had come true—and far from being appalled, she was bewildered and delighted and mildly in shock about the whole thing.

The trip had been a failure in one respect, of course. They hadn't found the right Laura. But somehow, that didn't matter quite so much. How could she be stewing about Paul's cheating heart when her own heart had moved on to better things?

She gathered Rosie in a crushing hug that lifted her off her feet. "So, you had fun?"

"Yup! Helen's husband came over and he mostly

watched golf on TV, which is really boring. And I taught Helen how to play DragonKeeper—''

''You did what?'' Todd asked, climbing the porch steps and setting Sally's bag down.

Rosie grinned up at Todd. ''I taught her Dragon-Keeper and some other computer games. She really liked them. This tooth is loose, Mommy,'' she added, using her tongue to wiggle one of her front teeth. ''I bet it falls out soon. Helen said the tooth fairy is supposed to bring me five dollars.''

''Five dollars? Try fifty cents.''

''No. Helen said five dollars.''

''You taught my mother DragonKeeper?'' Todd interrupted, scowling in disbelief. ''Where is she?''

''She's inside.'' Rosie shoved open the front door and charged into the house. ''I taught her Dark Thunder, too. She was really good at it. She beat me in one game, even.''

''She beat you at Dark Thunder?''

''Yup. I think she liked DragonKeeper better, but that's a harder game so she didn't win it. And I 'splained to her about the list...''

''What list?'' Sally asked, but Rosie was out of earshot, scampering down the hall in search of Helen. ''Helen? They're home!''

''I know that, sweetheart. I also know you bolted from the kitchen instead of helping me with the lunch dishes.'' Sally followed Rosie into the kitchen, where Helen was standing by the sink, wedging a glistening plate upright on the drying rack. She had on a dowdy, comfortable-looking beige knit outfit—slacks and a matching short-sleeve top. Her hair was mussed.

Sally fell back a step, astonished. She'd never seen Helen with a hair out of place. She'd assumed Helen cemented her coif into shape with lacquer—or perhaps crimson-tinted polyurethane.

But hairs were awry on Helen's head today. Strands curled in the wrong direction behind her ears, strayed daringly across the part, tufted and fluffed in a disarray that would have looked human if the color had been more natural.

She didn't look frazzled, though. She beamed a grin at Rosie, then directed her smile to Sally and Todd, who had entered the kitchen right behind Sally.

"You're playing DragonKeeper?" Todd asked.

"What list?" Sally asked at the same time.

Helen shrugged, folded the dishcloth neatly and draped it over the spout to dry. "I told Rosie I didn't understand how computers worked, so she taught me. I made it as far as level five in the Dragon game—"

"Level six," Rosie corrected her, the proud teacher gloating over her student's progress.

"And I've pretty much gotten the hang of the mouse and the arrow keys. Rosie taught me that just because it's called a cursor doesn't mean you're supposed to curse at it."

"For an old lady, Helen knows lots of cool curses," Rosie added.

"If you worked at a newspaper for forty years," Helen told her, "you'd know lots of cool curses, too."

"What list?" Sally persisted.

"That list on the computer disk," Rosie answered. "You know, Daddy's gamers."

"His what?"

"His gamers. That's what he called them. All those lawyers he used to play games with."

"What games?" Sally remembered the disk with the list of telephone numbers on it; Todd had found it in

Paul's office. She exchanged a quick look with him. He appeared as puzzled as she felt.

"Daddy told me they were these other lawyers, and they all used to play games with each other in chat rooms or something. Like computer games where they played against each other on their own computers. Daddy told me not to tell 'cuz he was playing when he was supposed to be working. He said he got bored at work, so he played."

Sally eyed Todd again. He shrugged.

At least they could forget about finding Laura on that list. But she was still unnerved—that her husband had had not just one secret life but two, as a cheating husband and as a cheating lawyer. He'd probably been billing his clients for all the hours he'd spent playing with his "gamers." Winfield's legal demands hadn't been enough to keep him entertained.

He'd been bored—with his job and with his wife.

And he'd discussed at least one of those boredoms with his daughter.

Had he discussed Laura with Rosie, too? Had he told her he'd played with another woman and then sworn her to secrecy?

The possibility sickened Sally. "Excuse me," she mumbled, darting out of the kitchen, heading straight for the stairs and up, not caring if everyone in the kitchen thought she was rude.

She hurled herself into her bedroom, slammed the door and let out a quiet sob. The son of a bitch! Living a double life—a *double* double life: playing games with his career and with his marriage. The career games were no big deal. For all she knew, he'd indulged in them during his lunch hour, a diversion while he ate—al-

though if he'd only played during his own time he
wouldn't have asked Rosie to keep the games a secret.

But what truly nauseated her was that he'd shared his
secret life with Rosie. His own five-year-old daughter,
dragged into the shadow world he inhabited and bur-
dened with the enormous responsibility of keeping her
mouth shut. Which she had, until now.

Everyone—at least, everyone in this house—had
known Sally's husband better than she had. Todd and
Paul had been best friends for fifteen years. Helen had
known Paul almost as long. And Rosie…Rosie was the
Driver he'd confided in.

Sally stormed to the closet, shoved open the door and
yanked his fancy suits off their hangers. She derived
cathartic satisfaction from flinging them to the floor,
rumpling his perfectly creased trousers, kicking the tailored sleeves of his jackets and listening to the buttons
click like chattering teeth. She gathered his belts and
hurled them across the room, watching them unfurl and
snake through the air. She grabbed one of his prissily
buffed loafers and flung it at a wall, then grimaced at
the black scuff it left on the paint as it fell.

The bedroom door swung open and Todd barreled into
the room. "What the hell are you doing?" he asked,
ducking to avoid getting beaned by another flying loafer.

"That bastard!"

"Hey, no news there, but come on." He batted down
the moose-skin slipper she'd lofted in his general direction, then closed in on her, grabbing her wrist before she
could tear the Black Watch plaid bathrobe from its
hanger. He leaned into her, pushing her halfway into the
closet, and she felt his warmth against her, his strength.

She wanted to cry but she was too angry—and she'd

be damned if she was going to fall apart in Todd's arms like a helpless ninny.

"He told Rosie," she wailed. "He told her about that list."

"Yeah, well, he loved her." Todd rubbed the back of her neck, which annoyed her because it was soothing enough to defuse her anger. She wasn't ready to stop being angry yet.

"He didn't tell *me* about the list," she snapped. "In other words, he didn't love me. Right?"

"Who the hell knows? It doesn't matter."

"It *does* matter. He told her about the games. What if he told her about Laura?"

"Is that what you think? That he'd tell her about that?"

"Maybe he told her what he did with my knife. Maybe he told her he had a hanky-panky pen pal. And I can't even ask her. How can I ask her if she knew her father was an adulterer? It's too revolting. And it would make her feel bad for not telling me sooner. I don't want her to feel bad."

"So don't ask her." He brushed a kiss against her forehead.

She almost wished he could be the creep she used to think he was—just so she could fume a little longer, throw a few more items around the room, maybe kick and stomp and break a couple of Paul's possessions.

But as long as Todd was holding her, raveling his fingers through her hair, brushing kisses against her forehead, it was impossible to stay mad. "I want his stuff out of my bedroom," she muttered.

"Fine. You'll get his stuff out of your bedroom. Could it wait a couple of minutes? My mother is downstairs wondering what's wrong."

She didn't want Helen thinking she'd gone insane. Or Rosie, for that matter. She had to pull herself together. And damn it, Todd was helping her, as if he cared. As if last night—and that morning—had been about more than just the chemistry between them, a chemistry so outrageously combustible they ought to write up their findings and submit a paper to the Nobel Prize committee.

Todd was treating her as if he honestly, truly, cared about her.

"All right," she murmured, releasing the last of her anger on a sigh. "I'm all right."

"You're going to come downstairs?"

"Yes." She took a deep breath, let it out, nodded and stepped out of the closet. "I'll come downstairs."

"Okay." Todd took her hand, led her across the room—en route, she gleefully ground her heel into the fine worsted of Paul's favorite pinstripe suit—and ushered her out of the bedroom. He released her hand when they were halfway down the stairs, and she was grateful. She wasn't ready to inform Helen or Rosie of her relationship with Todd yet. She didn't even know exactly what the relationship was, other than the Nobel Prize in chemistry aspect of it and Todd's ability to talk her out of a first-class snit.

Helen and Rosie were at the foot of the stairs, Helen's overnight bag on the floor beside them. "Mommy, can Helen baby-sit for me again?" Rosie asked.

"Of course." Sally felt Todd touch the small of her back, and she had to exert herself not to lean into him. It was a tiny, meaningless touch—just enough to communicate that he'd like her to leave Rosie with Helen and spend another night with him.

Or maybe the touch was accidental. Maybe Sally's

mind was talking to itself; maybe she was the one long-
ing to spend a night with him. A fresh surge of guilt
overtook her when she acknowledged how willingly she
would hand her daughter over to Helen for the chance
to make love with Todd again.

She was overloaded. Overwhelmed. The trip, the sex
and the discovery that Rosie knew at least some of her
father's secrets congealed into a quivering wad of anx-
iety that pressed down on her, causing her knees to ache.

Still, she had to act normal. "Helen, I really appreciate—"

"No speeches," Helen insisted as Todd lifted her
overnight bag. "It was my pleasure. And yes, Rosie—"
she didn't have to bend down too far to reach her arms
around the child "—I'd love to baby-sit for you again.
I'm going to beat you in DragonKeeper one of these
days."

"Prob'ly not," Rosie said matter-of-factly.

"Well." Helen straightened up and smiled at Sally,
"I'll see you at the café."

With that, she waltzed out of the house, leaving Todd
and her suitcase behind.

He glanced at the bag, then lifted his gaze to Sally.
"I guess I'd better be going, too."

Sally nodded. She wished he would stay, which made
it more imperative that he leave. Given how vulnerable
she felt, she didn't want him around, offering a convenient shoulder to lean on. She needed to find her way
back to life as she knew it.

"I'll call you," he said. Then, his mother's suitcase
in hand, followed her out the front door. Sally closed it
behind him.

"Wanna play DragonKeeper?" Rosie asked.

That was the last thing Sally wanted to do. "Sure,"

she said, extending her hand to Rosie and letting the girl drag her down the hall to the den, where the computer and Paul's game disks were waiting.

Only seven phone messages, none of dire importance. A few bills, a few flyers, a new catalog from his favorite model-car-kit company and an invitation to the fifteenth reunion of his graduating class at Winfield High School—but he'd known about that already because he'd published information on it in the Community Listings section of the *Valley News*.

Everything seemed so normal back at his town house after a day and a night away. So why didn't he *feel* normal?

He tossed his suitcase onto his bed, zipped it open and pulled out his dirty socks and underwear. He carried them to the hamper in the bathroom—a habit for which he had Paul to thank, since Paul had once threatened to shove him through the window of their dorm room because he'd left dirty laundry on the floor. It had been an empty threat, given that Todd had stood four inches taller than Paul and outweighed him by a good thirty pounds, but for the sake of peace and amity, Todd had gotten better at putting things—especially fetid gym socks—where they belonged.

"Paul," he muttered, staring at the pile of wrinkled clothing in the hamper and remembering the pile of Paul's wrinkled suits on the floor of Sally's bedroom. "Paul, what did you do? Who the hell did you turn into?"

A man who'd cheated his partners out of a few hours of work, that was who. No big deal, Todd told himself. He knew Paul's partners at Wittig, Mott. Paul had probably accomplished twice as much as they did, in half the time. So he'd developed a network of game players and mooched time from the firm.

But why discuss it with Rosie? And why tell her not to tell a soul?

Paul had gotten weird.

Maybe it was Todd's fault. He'd been the one to lure Paul to Winfield. Paul might have been happier at some high-power eighty-hour-a-week law firm in New York or Boston, where he could have been earning six figures before he made partner, even though he'd have had no time to enjoy all that money and he'd have had to spend an outrageous chunk of it on living expenses. He might have preferred that life, the adrenaline rush of scoring in the big time, the competition, the hustle. The crowds, the noise, the pollution—maybe that was what Paul had wanted.

Instead, he'd agreed to give Winfield a try. And then he'd met a counter girl at a coffee bar, and he'd knocked her up, and he'd felt trapped in this sleepy, cozy Berkshire valley town where the major news stories revolved around sewer bonds and zoning ordinances—and the occasional traffic fatality. Paul's death had been one of the biggest headlines of the winter.

If Todd hadn't lured Paul to Winfield, Paul might not have gotten bored with his job and his wife. He might not have resorted to getting his kicks with little-boy indulgences: computer games and a mistress.

Jesus Christ. It was all Todd's fault.

His phone rang. Sally, he hoped. He could explain to her that he was responsible for Paul's having given away her knife, and—if he was lucky—she'd offer absolution. Or at least an invitation to spend the night. He didn't want to think about her with her face mottled in rage and her eyes shimmering with suppressed tears, the way she'd looked when he'd found her rampaging through Paul's suits. He wanted to think about her soft and breathless, coming in his arms.

And sure, she'd really forgive him for having been the reason her husband fucked up his life and broke her heart. She'd really be happy to get naked and celebrate Todd's wonderful insight with him.

Swearing under his breath, he dived across the bed to reach the phone on his night table before the third ring. "Hello?"

"Todd." His mother.

He should have let the machine answer it, but now he was stuck. He rolled onto his back and stared at the ceiling. It had the texture of cottage cheese. "What?" he said none too graciously.

"We didn't have a chance to talk after we left Sally's. I wanted to know how your trip went."

"It went fine."

"You took care of that business for Paul?"

"Yeah." He knew better than to offer an answer that would give his mother any openings. Like him, she was a well-trained journalist and a formidable interviewer. He didn't want to be interviewed about the thirty or so hours he and Sally had been out of town.

"It all went smoothly?"

"Yeah."

"For Sally, too?"

"Yeah."

"I've got to tell you, spending that time with Rosie was very special to me, Todd. I feel like I'm being re-born."

"From baby-sitting with Rosie?" He knew the girl. She was okay. Borderline-obnoxious, but generally okay for a kindergartener. Not what he'd consider an inspirer of rebirths.

"She showed me that necklace you gave her. Todd, that rice kernel—I never saw anything like it before. A true marvel."

"Uh-huh." *Can we end this conversation now? I'm not in the mood.*

"Rosie's a precious child, I'll tell you. There's a lot of Paul in her."

Great. Maybe I can ruin her life, too. "I'm glad you had fun."

"Even your father didn't mind. He came over with pizza last night. We all ate pizza, and then he watched TV while Rosie and I played DragonKeeper. I'm getting the hang of it, Todd. You'll see—I'm going to be a whiz on the computer at the newspaper."

"Come on, Mom. You're working at the café now. You don't have to keep coming into the newspaper every day. You're emeritus, remember?"

"I'm just saying. There's a whole wide world out there, Todd. Computers, a new job—which is part-time, so of course I'll still be coming into the newspaper, just to keep my finger in it. I wish I could get your father to try something new."

"He did. Golfing every day is new for him."

"He's not as sharp as he used to be. We had a debate over dinner about Canada. He insisted that Cape Breton Island was a part of Nova Scotia. The man gets an idea in his head and he just won't let it go. That's a symptom of Alzheimer's, you know, that stubbornness—"

"Mom. Cape Breton Island *is* a part of Nova Scotia."

"It is?"

"There's nothing wrong with Dad's mind. He's worked hard all his life, and now he wants to play. He really wants you to go to Hilton Head with him. A nice relaxing getaway, just the two of you. That seems like a reasonable wish."

"You think so?"

"More than reasonable, it's romantic. You ought to be flattered."

"You think?"

"If you're being reborn, why not be reborn as his playmate? I'm not saying you've got to golf all the time with him. You're both figuring out different things to do with your lives. But just because you're not working together on the *Valley News* doesn't mean you should forget about doing other things together."

"Romantic?" She sighed. "Maybe you're right. I never thought I'd hear you of all people sing the virtues of romance."

"I wasn't thinking of virtue," he joked.

"All right, so maybe I'll go with him. Not for a whole month, but maybe a couple of weeks. If Sally can spare me from the café."

"She can spare you." Todd would make sure of it. "Look, I've got to go."

"Okay. Romantic, huh? Maybe you ought to listen to yourself, Todd. You're a smart boy. A little romance wouldn't kill you, either."

"Right." He said goodbye, hung up and returned his gaze to the textured ceiling. Romance wasn't his strong suit—at least not the kind of romance that involved flowers and Kenny G, candlelit dinners and surprise trinkets from the Jewelry Box. Denise had often complained that he was missing the R gene.

To him, romance meant arguing and laughing and worrying if the woman you were thinking of was sad or suffering. Romance meant wanting to make her feel better.

He reached for the phone, punched in Sally's number and waited for her to answer. "Hi," he said once she did. "I want to make you feel better."

Todd fixed dinner. On the phone, he'd told Sally he had a craving for real meat, and when he arrived at her house, he brought with him a flank steak, some marinade and a bottle of red wine that, he assured her, the guy at the liquor store had insisted was good. Given what it cost, Todd predicted that it wouldn't taste like rotgut.

In the time between his dropping Sally off and his returning with gifts of food and drink, she had played a game of Dark Thunder with Rosie, then gone back to her bedroom to remove the evidence of her tantrum. She'd folded all of Paul's suits neatly and placed them in a carton. Next week she would take them to Goodwill.

She'd get to his bureau later. She hadn't forgotten her last attempt to go through his drawers. She doubted any more land mines lurked within the folds of his clothing, waiting for her to shake out a garment and detonate them, but she didn't care to test her luck.

If she hadn't gone through his drawers, though, she and Todd would have never made love. That was an unnerving thought.

She was feeling fragile, and fragile wasn't a condition Sally was used to. She'd always been strong and tough. Her mother used to say she was like one of those weighted punching bags with a smiley clown face on it—no matter if she got knocked down, she always bounced back up again, wearing a dopey grin.

Sally didn't think that was true. She could lose her temper, mope, feel wounded and put upon and testy just like anyone else. But she did tend to bounce back. She saw no point in letting a punch flatten her.

Today, however, she felt raw, exposed and delicate. She kept wondering what else Paul might have told Rosie. What if he'd been entertaining Laura at the house in front of her? What if, while Sally had been at the café in the dawn hours, setting things up for opening, Todd and Laura and Rosie had been eating breakfast together at the table where Sally now sat watching Todd putter around in her kitchen? What if Rosie had grown so comfortable with Laura it hadn't been a hardship for her to obey Paul's command that she not mention the woman to her mother?

The possibility tormented Sally. She'd always believed she and Rosie shared an unbreakable bond, forged in love and trust. Sally was the one who did art projects with Rosie, who helped her plant pansies in the garden, who picked her up from school, conferred with her teachers and hung all her school projects on the refrigerator. She was the one who took Rosie to her doctor appointments and the playground behind the Francis Hopgood Elementary School. She was the one who pushed Rosie on the swing while Rosie screeched, "Higher! Higher!"

She'd bought Rosie her purple hat. Paul never would have bought it for her.

But Paul had done things with Rosie, too. He'd told her about his games and his "gamers." Just thinking about it brought tears to Sally's eyes.

"This is going to be the best meal you've had in days," Todd predicted, filling two glasses with wine and carrying one to the table for her.

"I liked the lasagna," she said.

Setting down the glass, he angled his head and peered

into her downcast face. "Hey," he murmured, "has any-one ever told you you look ugly when you pout?"

A laugh slipped out. "You sure know how to sweet-talk a woman."

"You bet I do." He slid his thumb under her chin, tilted her face up and zeroed in to kiss her.

"Is dinner ready yet?" Rosie bellowed, bursting into the room and scaring them apart. "I'm starving!"

Todd mouthed a curse, but he was grinning as he straightened up. "Five minutes. Think you can wait that long?"

"No," Rosie said, kneeling on her chair and distrib-uting napkins from the butterfly-shaped dispenser at the center of the table. "I think I'm gonna starve to death. Wanna hear something really weird? Helen's husband eats *anchovies*."

"He does?" Sally faked a shocked look.

"They're so gross, Mommy. He brought these pizzas, and his had little fish on it. Eeeuw."

"This, from the kid who wolfed down tempura at Quincy Market," Todd teased as he sliced the steak into strips.

"That's different. It's shrimp."

"You're a shrimp, too. Do me a favor, shrimp, and carry that bowl of salad over to the table."

Sally leaned back in her chair. She couldn't remember anyone ever making dinner for her in her own kitchen. Paul never had. All those casseroles her neighbors had sent her after he'd died hadn't been made in her kitchen, not with her sitting idly and being waited on.

It was enough to make her fall in love with Todd. Not only did he apologize, but he cooked dinner for her. Even if this was the only time he ever cooked dinner, and even if his primary reason for doing it was to ensure that it wasn't a vegetarian meal... If making love with him, and laughing with him, and arguing with him, and knowing he believed she'd been wronged in her marriage hadn't already caused her to fall in love with him, having him cook for her would have done the trick.

She was in love. With Todd Sloane, of all people. The very thought made her want to giggle.

While they ate, Todd grilled both Sally and Rosie about their opinions concerning a Sunday edition of the *Valley News*. Rosie was all for it, as long as it included color comics. "I can read, you know," she said. "Not the newspaper part, because they print everything too small. You should make bigger print. But the comics have big print, most of them."

Although a Sunday edition was the last subject Sally wanted to discuss, she lent her views, grateful that Todd had taken on the job of keeping the conversation alive. "We need more local news on Sunday," she said. "Local movie listings, local letters to the editor. The *Boston Globe* is full of letters from people who live in Boston, complaining about things that happen in Boston."

"It's got good comics, though," Rosie pointed out.

After dinner, Rosie asked if she could watch her video of the *Rugrats* movie. Sally not only said yes but suggested to Todd that they watch it with Rosie. She needed some hip-to-hip time with her daughter. She had to make sure the bonds between them were still tight, particularly after she'd spent a night away and not missed Rosie as much as she should have.

Todd was clearly less than fully engrossed in the movie. At one point, Sally glanced at him, seated on Rosie's other side, and noticed that his eyes were closed and his respiration was suspiciously even. Well, why shouldn't he be tired? He'd done a lot of driving yesterday and today, and very little sleeping in between.

It used to annoy her when Paul fell asleep while watching videos with Rosie. But Paul had been Rosie's father. He'd had an obligation to pay attention, to be fully in the moment with his daughter. He'd frequently come home from work late because he liked to meet Todd at Grover's for a drink after work. She hadn't begrudged Paul that, but she'd thought, if he was going to go out for a drink with his friend, he ought to stay conscious when he watched videos with Rosie.

Besides, he'd snored.

Todd shook himself awake as the final credits scrolled down the screen. "You can rest," Sally told him. "I've got to give Rosie a bath."

"Oh—I—" He sounded groggy and sweetly befuddled. "I'll just watch some grown-up TV." He picked up the remote control and began channel-surfing.

"Did Helen give you a bath last night?" Sally asked as she and Rosie trooped upstairs. If she hadn't freaked out that afternoon, she would have asked Helen more about how things had gone: what time she'd tucked Rosie into bed, what she'd fed Rosie for breakfast, whether she'd given Rosie a bath. All those essential questions mothers were supposed to want answers to had gone unasked. It occurred to Sally that maybe they weren't so essential, after all. If Helen had fed Rosie caramel corn and mashed potatoes for breakfast, what was Sally going to do about it? If Rosie hadn't taken a bath last night, so what?

As it turned out, Rosie had taken a bath. "Helen brought this bubble-bath stuff. She said it was very fancy and it had rose oil in it or something, and since I was Rosie she was letting me have some. It didn't make bubbles, though. She said it wasn't supposed to, but I thought it was called bubble bath.''

"Bath oil?" Sally guessed.

"Maybe that was it." Without a shred of modesty, Rosie wriggled out of her shirt as soon as she reached the top of the stairs. By the time Sally had the water running into the tub, Rosie was naked, sitting casually on the lowered lid of the toilet and interrogating her mother on what the point of bath oil might be if it didn't make bubbles, because bubbles were the best part. Taking a hint, Sally squirted a hefty spray of Rosie's favorite bubble bath into the tub.

She puttered around in the bathroom while Rosie soaked and played with the bubbles. Rosie believed she was old enough to take baths by herself, but Sally didn't want to leave her alone, on the chance that she might bang her head against the porcelain edge of the tub, slip beneath the water's surface and drown. So she pretended to be busy doing other things that just coincidentally required her to remain in the bathroom: straightening out the towels, rinsing the sink, taking inventory of the toiletries in the medicine cabinet.

"So, you had fun teaching Helen Daddy's computer games," she said casually, unsure whether she wanted to probe Rosie's relationship with Paul.

"She played pretty good for an old lady." Rosie filled her cupped hands with bubbles and blew on them. "You know what's kind of silly? I think she had more fun with me than I had with her."

"She's got grandchildren," Sally explained. "I think she thinks children are special."

"Well, *I'm* special." Rosie blew on another mound of suds, sending small puffs of scented foam into the air. "She said it's very important for children to have good baby-sitters. If you have a good baby-sitter, you can have fun and be safe at the same time. And you don't miss your mommy.''

''That's right.''

''But she's an old lady. Most baby-sitters are teen-agers.''

Sally and Paul hadn't gone out together very often, but the few times they had, they'd hired Candice Latimer's daughter from across the street. ''Like Kate Latimer?''

''Yeah, only Kate wasn't as nice as Helen. She just did homework and watched MTV.'' Rosie half heartedly wiped her face with her washcloth. ''Daddy had a baby-sitter.''

Sally dropped the tube of toothpaste, which she'd been moving a fraction of an inch along the edge of the sink. ''When he was a child, you mean?'' she asked, trying not to sound as astounded by the revelation as she felt. ''Did he tell you about this?''

''No, Helen did. She said Daddy told her he had a wonderful baby-sitter. This was before I was born,'' she clarified.

''I should think so. If he was young enough to need a baby-sitter he was too young to be a daddy.''

''No, I mean he told Helen before I was born. Helen said he used to visit her and her husband when he moved here. She said Daddy was like an extra son or something, and she thought he was so nice. And I look just like him.''

''You do look a lot like him,'' Sally agreed. ''Did he keep visiting Helen after you were born?''

''No, 'cuz then Daddy had me. And you.''

Sally bet he was happier about the former than the latter. He *had* loved Rosie. And God knew, Sally had tried to be a good wife for him. She'd tried to make him happy.

Another wave of guilt washed over her. She was weary of worrying about what had gone wrong in her marriage, where she'd failed, where Paul had failed, how unfairly the happiness had been distributed between them. The hell with Laura. The hell with the knife. Life went on.

"You're turning into a prune," she warned Rosie as she lifted the drain plug. In less than a half hour, Rosie would be in her pajamas, under her blanket, protected by her dream catcher as she sank into sleep. And then Sally could join Todd, and cuddle up to him on the couch, and fight with him over the remote control for a while. And then they could tiptoe upstairs and close themselves up inside her bedroom and make love.

That was more important than missing knives and mystery girlfriends. Life went on, and Sally was ready to go on with it. She was ready to forget about what had gone wrong and focus on what was going right.

She didn't feel fragile anymore. She didn't feel like pouting and looking ugly. A few important things were going very right in her life. What had gone wrong was history, over and done with. Maybe it just didn't matter anymore.

Nineteen

"I have to show you something," Tina said.

A week ago, Sally might have greeted this statement with heart-thumping dread. But she wasn't who she'd been a week ago. She'd shed her bitterness and anger like a cicada molting its shell and had emerged...well, a happier cicada.

Maybe sex in and of itself was therapeutic, but she happened to think love might also have something to do with her transformation. She ought to have been petrified about falling in love—with Todd Sloane, of all people— but she wasn't. She was careful enough not to use the l word around him, but she was willing to use it around herself.

God, he was incredible. Whether he was on top or underneath, kneeling on the floor with her pulled to the edge of the bed so he could make her come with his mouth or standing while she was perched on her dresser, her legs tight around his waist... If Sally were the type of woman given to blushing, she'd be as red as a stop sign just thinking about the hours she and Todd had spent alone together.

But it wasn't just sex. She was in love, and life was good. Behind the rain clouds drooping low in the sky and leaking onto Main Street, the sun was shining. She had enough joy in her life to forget about her pocket-knife.

She also had enough joy in her life to smile at Tina and say, "What do you have to show me?"

Tina scanned the tables. They were occupied by the usual assortment of customers: Officer Bronowski gnawing uncharacteristically on a bagel, the writer in black drugging himself with espresso, a couple of kaffee-klatschers perking up their morning with date-nut bread and cappuccino. No one seemed in drastic need of attention, so when Tina motioned with her head toward the kitchen, Sally nodded and followed her down the counter.

Tina's expression was eerily radiant. Sally should have taken that as an omen, but she was in such a buoyant mood she didn't want to brace herself for the worst, not even when Tina hoisted up her Winfield College T-shirt, stretched down the cup of her bra and displayed her tattooed breast.

It said EDWARD.

Sally grimaced. "What did you do?"

"It was easy," Tina bragged. "I used some foundation to cover the line in the H, and then I added the other lines with a pen. It was real easy to turn the O into a D."

"But...*EDWARD?*"

"Well, everybody calls him Eddie, but you can't change Howard into Eddie so easily."

Eddie? Pawing through her muddled memory of the past weekend, she recalled Tina babbling to her about some cute staff guy from the *Valley News.* "Is Eddie that newspaper person?"

Tina issued an infatuated sigh. "We went to this club Saturday night..."

"You didn't drink, did you?"

"Sally." Tina rolled her eyes.

"You're underage. And when you go out drinking you could wind up pregnant." It had happened to her, even though she hadn't been drunk the night she'd conceived Rosie. Or any other night she'd gone out with Paul. But the underlying lesson was important. She'd imbibed wine with him when she was only twenty, and she'd gotten knocked up.

"Well, I'm not pregnant. I didn't even take off my shirt. I wouldn't until I was sure I could get rid of the *HO*. It looks good, doesn't it?" She modeled her breast, turning from side to side in the overhead light. "I've got to be sure the foundation won't come off if he kisses me. Or the ink. I mean, it would be really gross if he wound up with black lips and my breast smudged back into Howard."

"It would indeed."

"But we're not up to that yet. I was just trying this out to see. I mean, my life isn't over, Sally. Even if Howard goes to Dartmouth, my life isn't over."

Not as long as she had a supply of Edwards she could date. Getting rid of the *HO* might be easier than finding more Edwards.

"Hello?" A familiar voice rolled toward them with the force of a sonic boom.

Sally hurried out of the kitchen to discover Helen hovering at the counter. Unlike the last time Sally had seen her—at her house Saturday afternoon—today she was groomed down to the last precise strand of hair, her outfit stodgy but impeccable and her jewelry tasteful to the point of banality. She looked like a model in a Gould's Department Store circular.

Had Todd told his mother that he and Sally were involved? She doubted it. The whole thing was too new, too embryonic. Surely that wasn't the reason Helen had come to the café.

"Hey, Helen," Tina said, grinning sheepishly and turning to Sally. "Helen brought Rosie here Saturday morning. Greta had made blueberry scones, so your daughter made a pig of herself."

"Blueberry scones are her favorite," Sally said, then smiled at Helen. "Don't tell me you love this place so much you can't stay away on your days off."

"I'm not here to work," Helen said. "I'm here for coffee. Actually, a bunch of coffees. See what they've turned me into at the newspaper? I'm an errand girl."

Sally laughed. "How many coffees?"

"Let me see…" She pulled a square of paper out of the pocket of her blazer and held it at arm's length, squinting to read what it said. "Todd wants a jumbo of 'normal coffee.' I think that means nothing flavored. Gloria wants a small decaf, light, with sugar. Eddie wants—"

"Eddie?" Tina's eyes flickered to brightness like a fluorescent lamp.

"Eddie Lesher. I understand he stopped by here on my recommendation—and now he's hooked."

"He's hooked?" Tina's eyes flickered again. "How come he didn't come in to get his own coffee?"

"He's on assignment this morning. Covering a long-range planning committee meeting on traffic tie-ups at Main and East. All right, he'd like—"

"On assignment." Tina gave another swooning sigh. "That sounds so cool. I'll get his coffee."

"I didn't tell you what he wanted yet."

"That's okay. I know." Tina plucked a large to-go cup from the stack and carried it to the coffee urns, eager to fulfill the order for her new, conveniently named darling.

"She's in love," Helen clucked softly. "I can always tell. I pick up vibrations. Madame Constanza has nothing on me." She stared directly into Sally's eyes, but apparently she wasn't picking up any vibrations from her, because all she said was, "Stuart wants a flavored with skim milk and Nutrasweet. I think that's everybody—oh, except for me. I'll take a jumbo cup of mocha java."

Sally unfolded a cardboard tray. "That's quite an order."

"I never should have opened my mouth. Now that I've told everyone at the paper about this place, nobody wants to drink the in-house stuff."

"I should give you a finder's fee," Sally joked.

"No need. My payment is your daughter teaching me how to use a computer. Did you know I'm surfing the Net now?"

"Really?"

"Well, not exactly surfing. Dog-paddling. But there's a Web site where you can buy discount airline tickets. I found some wonderful, inexpensive flights to Hilton Head. Walter and I are going to go down there in June. Todd thinks it'll be romantic."

"I'm sure it will." Sally held her breath, waiting to see if Helen was going to pick up vibrations now that she'd introduced the subject of romance.

If Helen sensed anything, she chose not to comment on it. "I had a good time with that daughter of yours," she said as Sally busied herself filling cups with various coffees.

"She had a good time with you, too." Sally snapped a lid on a cup, penned Decaf on it and wedged it into the tray. Thinking about how good a time Rosie had had with Helen awakened a memory in Sally's mind. She tried to ignore it. It related to the past, and she had resolved to put the past away and remain focused on the present.

But that relic of the past clung like a burr to her brain, refusing to let go of her. She fixed Todd's coffee, picturing his face, recalling the warmth of his hands on her, the heat of his body, the snide remark he'd made about her earrings—she'd been wearing her lightning-bolt ones, which she thought were pretty tame. He'd said they were sharp enough to skewer him, and only a man hater would wear earrings like that, to which she'd responded that she happened to be quite selective in her misanthropy, so the correct phrase should be a particular man hater, or an individual hater, or maybe just a Todd hater—and he'd declared that for his own physical well-being he was simply going to have to keep his head away from her ears, which was when he dragged her to the edge of the mattress and knelt on the floor...

Her cheeks started burning again.

"What?" Helen asked. If she was ever going to get any vibrations about Sally, now would be the time. But she seemed totally oblivious.

"I was just thinking," Sally said, knowing she had to say something. "Rosie told me the two of you talked about Paul."

Helen looked concerned. "Is that a problem? I wouldn't have mentioned him if it depressed Rosie. But she seemed so upbeat, and I thought she might want to hear about him, since I knew him from his days as Todd's roommate at Columbia and all."

"No, that's okay. She does like to talk about him. I guess it keeps him alive for her."

"Good." Helen pressed her hand to her chest and bit her lip. "I'd hate to upset her."

"You didn't." Sally ran her thumbs gently around the lid on Todd's cup, snapping it secure. She ordered herself not to ask anything more—but the question slipped out, anyway. "Rosie said you talked about Todd's baby-sitter. He never mentioned a baby-sitter to me."

"Oh, that." Helen chuckled. "Rosie was all caught up in the subject of baby-sitters—perfectly reasonable under the circumstances—and I told her about Paul's. He'd mentioned her once at a party, years ago—a bunch of newspaper people, some of our political friends, Todd and his wife, and Paul. We were all fairly lubricated, and we got to talking about first love and puppy love. As I recall, Denise—that was Todd's wife—got very snippy because Todd remembered so much about the first girl he'd ever fallen in love with. Someone from high school, I don't remember who. Denise stormed off and Todd had to go find her and make up with her. It was a ridiculous spat. He socialized with an awful lot of girls in high school. I never asked for details. His father explained birth control to him, and we left it at that."

Sally smiled. This was interesting. Someday she'd have to ask Todd about all his high-school sweethearts.

But right now the subject was Paul. "What does that have to do with Paul's baby-sitter?"

"Paul confessed that she was his first love. I guess he must have been about seven, and she was in her early teens—thirteen or fourteen. Anyway, he was passionately in love with her, he said. She used to give him chocolate chip cookies and run her fingers through his hair, and he was smitten. Laura. Oh, he went on and on about Laura."

Laura.

Pure coincidence, Sally told herself. There were millions of Lauras in the world. She and Todd had hunted down two candidates for Paul's Laura, and neither of them had been the right one. Surely a teenager who'd baby-sat for Paul when he'd been a bratty little kid wouldn't be the right one, either.

That was all it was—a coincidence. Some deeply implanted association, so that when he'd met the Laura who had become his mistress, the name had resonated inside him on a subconscious level. Who knew—if he'd met a woman named Bertha, he might not have embarked with her on an affair so torrid it included discussions on existentialism and the gift of Sally's knife.

Nothing but a coincidence.

And now she was going to put the entire matter out of her mind, because living in the past, nursing grudges and regrets, didn't suit her. She wanted to move forward, to live the rest of her life, to stop seething over past betrayals and deceptions, to chirp like a happy cicada.

She wasn't going to think about Paul's Laura, ever again.

Todd slid the ham and Swiss omelette onto a plate and carried it to the table. Others might not think beer went well with omelettes, but Todd believed the combination was perfect.

Besides, he'd started the evening with beer, and he didn't like to change beverages in midstream.

He'd gone down to the Chelsea after work today and played a couple of racks of pool with an old buddy of his from his high-school days. Emery was the best auto mechanic in Winfield, and one of the two best pool players from their graduating class, Todd being the other. So they'd split two games of eight ball, drunk a few beers and discussed their fifteenth high-school reunion. Betting on pool was boring, but betting on which of their classmates would show up bald, which would show up fat and which would show up rich and slick kept them amused. They'd both agreed that if prizes were handed out at the reunion, Patty Pleckart would win the prize for class curmudgeon.

He found it necessary to spend time away from Sally. As it was, he thought about her far too much. He saw her two or three nights a week plus weekends, and those nights he stayed away from her he wound up dreaming about her. She had him under a spell.

Granted, it was a terrific spell, one he was in no rush to break. He'd never before met a woman he had so much fun arguing with. When he'd been the editor of his high-school newspaper, he used to run a column called "Pro & Con," in which two writers—usually one other writer and himself—would consider an issue from opposite sides. "Pro & Con: Should the President be Impeached?" "Pro & Con: Is Bill Gates a Handmaiden of Satan?" "Pro & Con: Should Winfield Have a Leash Law?"

He'd loved arguing, as long as his opponent was worthy. A good sword-clashing debate pumped him up and turned him on. And Sally was the worthiest opponent he'd ever had—or at least, the worthiest opponent who looked better naked than dressed.

He could get attached to her. Deeply committed. And maybe in time…well, maybe. But he was too old to lose his head over a woman. He'd done that once and he'd survived, but divorce wasn't one of those activities that got better with practice, and he had no intention of rushing into something that might not work.

Besides, she was Paul's widow. She'd married his best friend—that lying bastard.

Determined not to think about her tonight, he thumbed through his most recent model-kit catalog while he ate. It was time to order a new kit, something to keep him occupied on those evenings he wasn't at Sally's house, waiting with forced patience until Rosie went to sleep so he and Sally could move their arguments to the bedroom. On page seventeen he discovered a kit for a classic Dusenberry. Not his usual kind of model, but all those details—the running boards, the elaborate grille, the movable windshield wipers—would offer a reasonable distraction.

He wondered if Rosie would enjoy building a model car. He wouldn't trust her with a tube of epoxy, but he could buy her a beginner kit, with simple pieces that snapped together without glue. He and Rosie could work side by side, right here in the kitchen. They'd put on some Jimi Hendrix, crank up the volume and build cars together. She might enjoy it.

And there he was, indirectly thinking about Sally again. Thinking about himself as some kind of surrogate father for Rosie, for Christ's sake. He didn't want to be Rosie's father, although God knew she deserved a more honest father than the one she'd started out with.

The phone rang. He scooped a forkful of omelette into his mouth, then tilted back on the rear legs of his chair until he could reach the phone on the wall behind him. He lifted the hand unit, swallowed, straightened his chair and said, "Yeah?"

"Todd? It's Sally."

A burst of warmth flowered open in his chest at the sound of her voice. When he'd been married to Denise, hearing her voice hadn't given him that strange sensation, a combination of joy and panic, protectiveness and susceptibility.

He tried to keep his voice free of complicated emotions. "Hey, Sally. What's up?"

She didn't say anything for a minute. His smile waned and he reached for his beer. The sweaty brown glass felt too cold against his palm, but he took a quick slug of the stuff—which tasted too cold. The spot in his chest that had been burning cooled off, too.

"Sally?"

"I have to tell you something," she said.

Oh, God. She couldn't be pregnant. He'd been really careful about that. Even if she hadn't learned from her past mistake—which wasn't to imply Rosie was a mistake, but she sure hadn't been part of anyone's life plan—Todd had learned from it.

If Sally wasn't pregnant, she was calling to tell him something else. Something worse. "What?"

"I know who Laura is."

He took another slug of beer, buying time to consider his response. He and Sally hadn't talked about Laura since their trip to Mondaga Lake. It was a tacit agreement between them, nothing they'd worked out, just something they both seemed to understand: that while Paul used to be the only link between them, they now had other things bringing them together, other bridges connecting them. They weren't joined by shared rage or indignation or pain.

Once he'd stopped beating himself up about what a shitty friend Paul had been, he'd started feeling a lot better. So he'd let it lie.

But now she was reintroducing the subject, and he had to adjust his perspective accordingly. "You know who she is?"

"Yes."

"When did you find out?"

"Three weeks ago."

Three weeks ago? Right after Mondaga Lake, right after they'd become lovers? Suddenly he felt a whole new version of rage and indignation and pain. "You knew and you didn't tell me? You've been keeping this a secret from me?" What was with the Drivers? Had they made a pact, before Paul died, that they'd both keep secrets from Todd?

Damn it, this hurt. His chest was burning again, this time with fury.

"I'm sorry, Todd—I can't be sure, actually, and I just sort of wanted to forget about it. I didn't even want to think about it anymore, you know?"

He knew. He hadn't wanted to think about it anymore, either.

"But… I just… You're right. I didn't want to keep it a secret from you. I just wanted to pretend it didn't matter."

"Okay." He'd forgive her. Unlike her may-he-rot-in-hell late husband, Sally came up with the truth eventually. Of course, Paul might have come up with the truth eventually, too, if his car hadn't skated into a tree at sixty miles per hour.

"Anyway, I was sitting here this evening, and Trevor's sleeping over, and he and Rosie—"

"Trevor? That kid next door?" Todd had heard Rosie mention her neighbor.

"Yes."

"He's a boy, Sally. You're letting a boy sleep over with Rosie?"

She laughed. "They made a tent out of a sheet and a

couple of chairs in the den. They're using sleeping bags.'' She paused. "They're five years old."

"Right." He shouldn't assume that just because he'd never be able to crawl under a sheet in the den with Sally and not tear her clothes off, Rosie and Trevor couldn't behave with decorum.

"Anyway, they were talking about baby-sitters, and I just…well, I had to call you."

"Baby-sitters."

"When Paul was a little boy, he had a baby-sitter named Laura."

"A baby-sitter." This was beginning to sound like a typical Sally story: amusing but irrational.

"He loved her."

"I loved my grandma. What's your point?"

"Your mother told me Paul once told her that this baby-sitter, Laura, was his first true love. He had a terminal crush on her. She was only a few years older than him. Well, seven years older. We're not talking Laura Ryershank."

"Okay." He forked another bite of omelette into his mouth and tucked it into his cheek so Sally wouldn't be able to tell he was chewing while he spoke. "He had this baby-sitter who was seven years older than him, and he thought she was the sun and the moon rolled into one. This would have happened a long time ago, Sally. More than twenty-five years ago."

"Yes, but… Well, it was niggling at me. So I called my in-laws."

Todd almost choked on his food. Paul's parents had been so aloof, so chilly and distant, that Paul had naturally gravitated to Todd's parents the instant he met them. The Drivers were very, very wealthy, with homes in Greenwich, Connecticut, Vail and Barbados. They'd sent Paul to boarding school. When would he have even needed a baby-sitter?

"You know, his parents and I were never close—"

Understatement of the decade, Todd thought.

"But I told his mother that while I was going through some of Paul's things, I found some old poems he must have written to a baby-sitter named Laura when he was a little boy, and I thought the baby-sitter might like to see them. And his mother told me his baby-sitter was named either Laura Rose or Laura D'Orsini—with an apostrophe in it. She married someone named D'Orsini, some minor prince or a cousin of a count or something, but they got a divorce a few years ago, so Paul's mother wasn't sure if she'd kept her married name or reverted to her maiden name. Either way, she lives in Southport, Connecticut."

"Okay." Todd sipped some beer, slowly this time, holding it on his tongue as if it were wine. It tasted better than wine, though. A little less complex, a little more bubbly, sour and satisfyingly gulpable.

"Laura *Rose*," Sally emphasized. "Did you know Paul was the one who came up with the name Rose for our daughter?"

"No, I hadn't known that." And it was, admittedly, a suspicious bit of evidence. "What had you wanted to name her?"

"Blossom."

"She's a lucky girl." He rotated the bottle slowly in his hand, trying to decide what he wanted to do about Laura Rose D'Orsini.

"He loved her, Todd. And then she got a divorce, and she's a couple of hours away by car, just the right distance—and, you know, with that royalty connection, she'd probably write all that flowery junk."

"Royalty and existentialism don't mix."

"Maybe that's why she got a divorce."

Todd took a deep breath. He'd been satisfied to stop looking for Laura. Maybe it would have been better if Sally had continued to keep this secret from him after all.

As if she could read his mind, she said, "I just couldn't keep it in anymore. I kept waiting for the thought to leave me alone, but it didn't. So I'm telling you. What do you think we should do?"

He ruminated.

"Should we track her down?" Sally pressed. "Or should we just forget about the whole thing?"

"I guess it depends on whether you want your pocketknife back," he said.

Twenty

"Are you sure you want to do this?" Todd asked for at least the seventeenth time.

"I want my knife." Sally leaned back in the contoured leather seat of his Saab, her sunglasses shielding her eyes from the glare of a brilliant Saturday afternoon on Connecticut's Gold Coast. She knew her roots were buried in rocky soil miles from Beacon Hill, a culture away from the rarefied air of the Mondaga Colony, far enough from the world of Winfield College that during her two years as a student she'd sometimes felt she ought to be carrying a passport. But Gold Coast Connecticut was the worst, probably because Gold Coast Connecticut was where Paul's parents lived, and Paul's parents had never bothered to disguise their belief that she was a bottom-of-the-barrel slut who'd seduced their son and tricked him into marrying her.

She and Todd weren't going to be visiting the Drivers. Todd had indicated quite clearly that he didn't think much of Paul's parents, either, which only made her love him more.

Southport clung with proprietary arrogance to the coastline of Long Island Sound. From the charming village center, roads radiated out into mansion territory. The closer to the water they drove, the grander the houses.

According to the directions they'd received at the gas station on Route 1, Laura Rose D'Orsini's address put her home right on the water.

The Saab's windows and sunroof were open, letting in the balmy May sunshine. Sally had worn a flowered cotton dress that tied at the waist in back. She focused on the comfort of the dress, the sweet, grassy scent of the breeze and the calm demeanor of the man beside her. She and Todd had gotten through Laura encounters before, and they'd survived. Now, when they were likely to face the real Laura, they were lovers, a united front. They'd get the knife and move on with their lives, just the way Sally had intended for them to move on with their lives before Helen had mentioned that Paul's childhood baby-sitter had been the object of his undying love.

"I think you're supposed to turn here," she said, glancing at the directions she'd jotted on a scrap of paper as the gas station attendant had dictated them.

Nodding, Todd steered around the corner. The road was narrow, bordered by emerald lawns and canopied with maples and sycamores. Sally caught a faint whiff of salt water.

Laura Rose D'Orsini is going to be rich, she reminded herself. *She's going to be charismatic. She's going to be sophisticated, elegant, glamorous. But she writes gushy letters. And she's got my knife.*

"That's it," she said, pointing to a pair of white gates that stood open on either side of a blacktop driveway.

"What would we have done if the gates were closed?" Todd asked wryly.

"Battered them down with the car."

"Not my car."

"Do you mean to say you care more about your Snob than about finding Laura?"

"You bet I do."

The driveway wasn't too long, and the house at its end wasn't too big. White clapboard surrounded by slate patios, it sat on a promontory overlooking the sound. The land alone must have cost a king's ransom—which, if Laura's former husband was royalty, shouldn't have put too much of a dent in her bank account.

"Who would have thought," she muttered, "that a girl who grew up in a trailer could end up consorting with the ex-wives of princes?"

"Yeah, and cruising around in my cool car," Todd teased.

Ignoring him, she shoved open the door and filled her lungs with the dense, sour fragrance of the sea.

"I wonder if they've got Swan Boats here," Todd said as he climbed out of the car and met her by the front bumper. "The water looks a little choppy for paddleboats."

"Let's just hope she's home so we don't need to pass the time on a boat." Sally hoisted the straps of her tote bag onto her shoulder and started toward the broad veranda that faced the water.

Todd touched the small of her back. "You sure you're okay?"

She *had* to love him. How could she not, when he showed such concern for her?

"Of course I'm okay." She spoke with enough resolve to convince herself. Why shouldn't she be okay? She'd faced two other Lauras, both times assuming she'd found the right one. It was always possible that this Laura would turn out to be a wrong one, too. Just because there were a whole bunch of clues pointing to the prince's American ex didn't mean Sally and Todd might once again discover that this wasn't the Laura they were searching for.

Together they climbed the porch steps and approached the door, an artist's fantasy of carved and polished wood and beveled glass. For the first time in all their Laura travels, the doorbell was easy to find. That could be a sign, although Sally wasn't sure what it was a sign of.

She pressed the button, waited, and then saw motion through the glass, a shadow sweeping across the door before it opened.

She swallowed. *Of course I'm okay,* she repeated to herself, but the conviction was no longer there. Not when she stood toe to toe with a woman whose very appearance seemed to define the concepts of charisma, sophistication, elegance and glamour. She was tall and slender, with a neck so long it reminded Sally a little of an illustration in Rosie's copy of *Alice in Wonderland,* on the page where Alice had taken a bite of the cake that said "Eat me." This woman's neck was much more graceful than Alice's, of course. Her hair was ebony, her complexion alabaster, her eyes onyx. Her head belonged in a sculpture garden.

The woman had on an outfit of white silk, the slim-fitting slacks flattering her fat-free legs and the top a swirl of fluttering sleeves and sleek draping. Pearls the size of small onions adorned her ears, and an even larger pearl framed in diamonds dangled on a chain around her neck.

"You're not the piano tuner, are you?" she asked, gazing at Todd and Sally.

Sally swallowed again. She was not going to let this splendid woman intimidate her. She was not.

"I'm Sally Driver," she said.

The woman paused for a long time. She didn't say, *Sally who?* She didn't look confused.

This was their Laura. They'd found her.

Far from feeling victorious, Sally suffered a throb of dread so profound her entire body trembled from it.

This Laura was magnetic, majestic, magnificent. She was sleek and fashionable, poised and polished, a woman who would never walk around with a box of animal crackers in her tote bag. Sally's gaze drifted to the pearl earrings again. She imagined South Sea oysters competing to see who could make the prettiest pearls for Laura Rose.

She wished Todd would touch the small of her back again. That was his signal to her, a light infusion of strength combined with an assurance that he had faith in her. He didn't touch her now, however. He was too busy scrutinizing the woman standing in the foyer of the stately waterfront house.

"Sally Driver," she said evenly, her eyes flashing, her manicured red nails fluttering as she wavered between offering her hand to her guest and reaching for the door to close it. "Ah." Another long pause, and she turned to Todd. "And you're...?"

"Todd Sloane."

"Oh, yes! Todd Sloane. The newspaperman."

Todd seemed to stand a little taller at that remark. Clearly, Paul had mentioned him to Laura, and he seemed rather pleased about it. Paul must have mentioned Sally, too—in her letters she'd bemoaned the existence of his wife—but Sally didn't feel pleased at all.

"Well," Laura said, studying them as if trying to guess their heights. "Why don't you come in."

She was going to be *civilized,* Sally thought ruefully. If Laura was civilized, Sally would have to be civilized, too, and she wasn't sure she wanted to be. She might want to scream or throw things, but she wouldn't be able to if they were all acting mature and diplomatic.

Reluctantly, she removed her sunglasses, hooked them over the neckline of her dress and stepped into the Palazzo D'Orsini.

Laura Hawkes's Beacon Hill town house was a hovel compared with the ex-princess's seaside abode, which turned out to be a lot larger than it had appeared from the driveway. Vast, airy rooms opened in all directions, one of them containing nothing but a concert grand— the instrument in need of tuning, Sally presumed. Did Laura play? Musical talent would only be gilding the lily. She didn't need to *do* anything. She didn't need skills or gifts. Her appearance alone was enough to justify her existence.

"Lyman?" she murmured into the air. If her voice were a fabric, it would be burgundy velvet.

A man materialized in one of the doorways. Silver-haired and tidily paunchy, he wore tailored trousers, a white shirt and a white apron similar in style to the aprons Sally and the staff wore at the New Day Café. He waited attentively until more burgundy velvet emerged from Laura: "Would you please fix us some lemonade? I believe we'll retire to the back patio." With a silent nod, Lyman departed.

A butler. The woman had a butler. Not a young, sexy one, either, although she could certainly afford any kind of butler she wanted. But then, she hadn't needed a young, sexy butler when she'd had Paul.

They reached the back patio through a maze of rooms the functions of which Sally couldn't begin to guess. Laura led the way, her gait so smooth it was almost as if she were gliding along on roller skates. Her shoulders didn't rise and fall; her enviably slender hips didn't sway.

Sally glanced at Todd as they followed Laura through a French door and outside to an expanse of slate on the opposite side of the house. Todd didn't return her look. He seemed transfixed by his surroundings. Sally couldn't blame him.

The back patio overlooked the water, which indicated that the house was set on a spit of land protruding into the sound. A flight of stairs led down from the patio to an Olympic-size pool surrounded by more slate, with a cabana and a bathhouse positioned conveniently on either side of the pool. From that level, another flight of stairs descended to a private beach.

Sally had to exert herself not to hyperventilate.

Had Paul felt at home in such surroundings? Had the opulence appealed to him? Or had he not even noticed it? In the presence of a deity like Laura D'Orsini, he might have found the pool and the beach superfluous.

They sat on comfortable white sling chairs on the top patio. The rear wall of the house was white, the sand on the beach below was white and Laura's ensemble was white. Sally felt crude in her colorful dress.

She focused on her breathing: in, out, in, out. Laura D'Orsini breathed, too. Inside all that white silk, she had a pair of lungs no healthier than Sally's. She was flesh and blood and bone—although Sally wouldn't be surprised to learn that, as refined as she was, she never had to go to the bathroom.

Lyman emerged from the house carrying a silver tray on which was balanced a large crystal pitcher of lemonade and three crystal glasses. He filled the glasses, distributed them and receded into the house.

"I'm sorry about your loss," Laura said to Sally.

Sally tried not to choke on her lemonade. Was she supposed to say she was sorry about Laura's loss, too?

The afternoon light lent Laura a shimmer she didn't need. "Paul was a special man."

"I guess you'd know," Sally muttered none too graciously. She was more than willing to concede first place in the graciousness competition to Laura.

Laura sipped daintily from her glass, then lowered it to a table at her elbow. "Sally, I want to assure you that if I'd known Paul was married, I wouldn't have become involved with him."

"Yeah, right."

"I'm not that kind of woman. I would never knowingly get involved with a married man." Laura's lips were exactly the same color as her fingernails. "I would have insisted that he get a divorce first."

Wonderful. Either way, she qualified as a home wrecker.

Evidently detecting the thunderbolts of animosity firing from Sally's eyes, she turned to Todd. "How did you find out about me?"

"Short answer?" Todd smiled. "He saved your letters."

"Oh, he did? How romantic." She shot Sally an apologetic look, then turned back to Todd. "He told me so much about you, Todd. You were an anchor in his life." She swiveled again to Sally, her exquisite face arranged in a pose of sympathy. "I want you to understand, Sally, that none of this was your fault."

"That's a relief," Sally grumbled sarcastically. "I was feeling really guilty that my husband was having an affair with you."

"What I mean is, it wasn't just some *thing*."

"Oh," Sally snapped. "I'd been sure it was a *thing*."

Todd sent her a quelling look, a warning that she wasn't acting civilized enough. She didn't care.

"Paul and I had a history," Laura explained. "Quite a complicated history. He'd been in love with me long before he met you."

"Right. When he was seven, I heard. Some kind of pedophile thing, was it? Oops—I'm sorry. I forgot. It wasn't a *thing*."

Laura looked even more sympathetic, as if she felt just terrible about how painful this all must be for poor Sally. "I never knew he loved me until my marriage. He was a senior in high school then. His family and mine had been neighbors and friends, so of course he attended my wedding. He asked to dance with me, and as he spun me around the floor—it was a waltz, as I recall—he told me he loved me. Needless to say, I was stunned. He was just a child—well, a teenager—and I was a new bride. He had tears in his eyes. Of course there was nothing I could do. He was so young and adorable."

"Oh, yes. Paul was so adorable," Sally muttered.

Laura overlooked her surly tone. "I'd heard from my parents that he went to college and law school. I was happy for him. Alas, my own marriage was not particularly happy."

It was damn profitable, though, Sally almost said.

"When I got divorced, my husband retained the vineyard in Tuscany and I took this house. Todd must have heard about the divorce from his parents, and he contacted me. I swear to you that I didn't know he was married."

"So he lied to you. Welcome to the club."

"He did tell me eventually, Sally. He told me about your lovely daughter—"

"Keep my daughter out of it." It pained Sally to think

Rosie might have been named after this gorgeous, privileged, extraordinarily blessed woman. Why couldn't her little girl have been named after a grotesque loser?

Laura sighed, a whisper of breath that seemed to say, *Well, I've tried to be pleasant. I've given it my best effort.* Then she shifted in her chair and crossed her legs in Todd's direction, cutting Sally out of the conversation. "Paul's death was a terrible loss. I grieved as much as anyone."

Todd nodded. He was obviously willing to be civil enough for himself and Sally both. "It was a nasty accident," he said. "Black ice. You don't see it until you're on top of it, and then it's too late. He shouldn't have been driving his Alfa Romeo, of course."

"Not an appropriate vehicle to drive in that weather."

"He probably thought he was indestructible."

"I suppose we all do, to some extent," Laura agreed, lifting her glass and holding it before her, almost as if she wanted to clink glasses with Todd.

How nice, Sally thought. They were making friends, bonding in their shared belief that Paul had thought he was indestructible. Todd stared into Laura's face as though it was physically impossible for him to look away. Maybe it was. She was that spectacular.

Sally watched the two of them talk, paying less attention to the words than to the movements of their mouths, the alternation of their voices. Todd was telling Laura about rooming with Paul at Columbia, how Paul's meticulousness had forced him to become a neater person. Laura said she thought Todd appeared to be a remarkably neat fellow. Todd told her about the time he and Paul took the IRT downtown to a punk club in SoHo and Paul freaked out at the sight of all those rockers with spiked hair and pit bull collars. Laura commented that she couldn't believe Todd would have been freaked out. "Paul was provincial, in his own way. As a journalist, I'm sure you're much more open to adventure."

"I try to be," Todd admitted.

Sally's vision narrowed on Todd. He was basking in Laura's approval, savoring it. When Laura touched his arm he leaned toward her.

Why did she have to fall for the type of man who would fall for Laura? That probably included every type of man in the universe, but here she was, watching Todd, the man she loved, sucking up to the same rich, alluring woman who'd possessed Paul's heart.

Sally couldn't bear it. She was who she was—the Not-Laura, the Un-Laura, the antithesis of Laura—and she was losing Todd to Laura the way she'd lost Paul to her, the way she'd lose any man to her.

"Excuse me," she said, breaking into their charming chatter. "I need to find a bathroom."

Laura seemed dazed for a moment, as if she'd forgotten Sally was there. "Oh—well, there are several. If you don't find one, ask Lyman to direct you."

"Thanks." Sally pushed to her feet, walked to the French door with as much dignity as she could muster and entered the house.

She didn't want to find a bathroom. She just wanted to get the hell away from Laura's mansion, away from the woman who could so easily woo away the man Sally loved.

Todd. She wanted to weep. Todd was as smitten as a thirty-three-year-old man as Paul had been as a young boy. He was entranced. He was enchanted. One smile from Laura, one touch, and he was melting like ice cream in the sun.

She'd thought he was better. She'd thought he'd cared

for her, wanted her...even loved her. And maybe he had. Maybe it was easy enough to love Sally until someone like Laura came along.

The hell with him. She knew how to survive a heartbreak. She'd done it before, in the very recent past. She was getting the hang of it.

It took her less than a minute to retrace the route to the front door. She stepped outside, closed the door quietly behind her, slipped her sunglasses on and headed down the driveway to the road.

They were less than a mile from the pretty downtown village where they'd stopped for directions. Her sandals were comfortable, and the leaves of the arching trees lining the road provided shade—although she had a tube of sunblock with her, just in case. She could walk to town, find out where the nearest bus station was and take a cab there. She was pretty sure she had enough cash for a cab, and she could put the bus ticket on her credit card.

She'd go home, get Rosie from Trevor's house and swear off men. Not an impossible task. Not even an especially difficult one when she considered what assholes the men in her life were. Her father, her husband, her lover. One she'd never even met, one she'd never really had and one...

One she hated.

She'd fought with him. She'd let him see her anger and sorrow. She hadn't knocked herself out to make him happy, and it hadn't mattered. He'd been happy with her just the way she was.

Until now. Until he'd discovered that a princess was more desirable than a peasant.

Screw him.

A Jaguar convertible drove slowly past her, the driver

gaping at her as if he'd never seen a pedestrian before. She ignored him. She also ignored the woman driving the Mercedes SUV and the man driving the dark green Bentley. She just kept walking. The exertion simultaneously soothed and fueled her. By the time she reached town, she'd be over Todd. She promised herself she would.

The distance to town seemed to expand with each step she took. Her feet puffed in the heat, and sweat filmed her skin. Her hair felt heavy on her back, but when she paused to excavate in her tote bag for a barrette, she couldn't find one. The damn bag seemed to have gained five pounds during her walk, but for all the clutter inside it, she couldn't even find a ribbon to tie her hair back with.

It didn't matter. She wanted to feel lousy, and being hot, sticky, frizzy haired and puffy footed fit her mood perfectly.

Eventually she reached the village. An eatery beckoned—the Southport equivalent of the New Day, a small café with round tables and drinks for sale. She'd buy herself a *real* lemonade, not one served in priceless crystal but one served in a plastic tumbler, the way lemonade was meant to be. She'd drink it, catch her breath, then inquire about cab service to the bus station.

The café was cool and gloomy after the bright sun. Sally stood in the doorway until her eyes adjusted, then removed her sunglasses and peered at the prices posted on the wall above the counter. For the cost of a glass of lemonade in this joint, a person could enjoy a tall iced cappuccino and a bagel at the New Day.

But then, this place was probably patronized by the ex-wives of dukes, not college kids and seedy professors, cops and housewives, newspaper staffers and a man

writing the Great American Novel, which he would undoubtedly dedicate to Sally for having kept him in coffee
during its creation.

She greeted the middle-aged woman behind the
counter with a smile of sisterhood and ordered a lemonade. "Is there a bus station near here?" she asked.

"There's a train station just up the block," the woman
said helpfully as she filled a textured plastic cup with
lemonade for Sally, who gratefully wrapped her fingers
around its humdrum surface.

"Can I get a train going north from there?"

"The trains go west and east. Where do you want to
go?"

"North."

"Well," the woman said, collecting the dollar bills
Sally extended to her and handing her back a pathetically
small amount of change, "you can take the train east to
New Haven and then pick up the Amtrak there. That'll
get you north."

"Thanks." Sally stashed the pennies in her wallet,
plucked a napkin from the dispenser on the counter and
carried her glass to a marble-topped pedestal table away
from the window. She didn't want to look out on the
picturesque street. She wanted to sulk and fume. She
wanted to pout and be ugly.

The sweat began to dry on her, chilling her. A sip of
the lemonade chilled her even more. She lifted her hair
off her neck and fanned it up and down, then let it drop
against her back again.

She sorted her thoughts.

What surprised her the most was that she was more
upset about Todd's betrayal than about Paul's. Paul had
been her husband; he'd committed adultery; he'd had a

torrid love affair with that woman, that paragon, that golden goddess.

All Todd had done was embody a bunch of clichéd male reflexes, gazing at her with stars in his eyes and hanging on her every word. All he'd done was indicate to Sally that, given a choice, he'd pick Laura.

Why did it hurt so much she wanted to weep? Why did she suspect that at least some of the perspiration on her face was actually tears? Why did the thought of going back to Winfield alone and spending the rest of her life loathing that no-good son of a bitch leave her feeling desolate?

The door swung open, and a couple of teenage girls bounced in, skinny and giggly. Sally lowered her eyes to her glass and took a heady sip. Sweet and bitter, just the way lemonade was supposed to taste. Sweet for what love could be like, and bitter for what love too often was.

She loved Todd. She hurt because she loved him in a way she'd never really loved Paul. Oh, of course she'd *loved* Paul, because he was her husband and the father of her daughter, because circumstances had compelled them to make a life together and Sally's motto always was to make the best of the life you were living, and if the life you were living was that of a wife in a marriage, you might as well love your husband.

But with Todd... With Todd, circumstances hadn't compelled her. She'd known him long enough to experience a gamut of emotions with him, and all those emotions had come together to create love. Todd had exasperated her. He'd infuriated her. He'd challenged her. He'd actually taken the time to consider who she was and how she felt about it.

Paul never had. He'd married her because it had been

the decent thing to do, and then he'd never really given her much consideration at all—except to snicker about her behind her back when he'd met Todd for drinks after work.

Todd had never done anything with her because it was the decent thing to do. He'd done what he'd done with her because he'd wanted to. Chosen to. Needed to. Because he'd felt something for her, deep inside.

And now he was flirting with the belle of the Connecticut Gold Coast. What he'd felt for Sally deep inside wasn't strong enough to keep him from looking elsewhere, looking for someone wealthier, fancier, classier, lovelier.

The door opened again. She bowed over her drink, uninterested in viewing more giggling teenagers. The lemonade bathed her tongue and sent another chill down her spine. She prayed she wouldn't start blubbering in the back corner of this overpriced café.

A click on the table caused her to shift her eyes. There, lying on the veined-marble surface, was her pocketknife.

She lifted her gaze high enough to view Todd's midsection, then focused back on the knife. It looked okay, the plastic handle faded to a creamy beige, the hula girl's lei draped discreetly to conceal her breasts, her smile nearly rubbed off but still saucy.

"This is all I've got of your dad," her mother had told her. "This and you. You're the best thing he left me. So if you want, you can have the other thing."

Her knife. The knife she'd given Paul because she'd wanted to believe he meant that much to her.

Todd pulled out one of the wire-backed chairs and dropped onto it. Sally avoided looking at him.

"I've been driving around this fucking town for a half hour, trying to find you," he said.

"Well, you found me."

"Why did you disappear like that?"

Because I was jealous. Because I couldn't bear to see you gazing at Laura the way Paul must have gazed at her, the way a man gazes at a woman he adores. "You and Laura seemed to be getting along just fine without me," she said. "I wasn't really needed."

"You weren't *needed?* What's that supposed to mean?"

"It's supposed to mean that you and Laura were getting along just fine without me, reminiscing about what a swell guy Paul was. The two of you have so much in common. She's beautiful and you've got eyes. She's wealthy beyond words, and you drive a Saab. She loved Paul and so did you."

"Paul was a two-timing asshole. He cheated on Laura, too, don't forget. He didn't tell her he was married for quite a while."

"You're right. Gee, I feel so sorry for her." Sally silenced herself with a sip of lemonade. It definitely tasted more bitter than sweet.

"And meanwhile, you decided to disappear. One minute I'm talking with Laura, and the next minute I'm worrying that you took a wrong turn on your way to the bathroom and wound up in Long Island Sound."

"Big deal. I can swim."

"You know what?" He sounded seriously pissed off. "You're crazy."

"I am not."

"I can't believe you just vanished like that."

"It was what I wanted to do," she said, at last feeling

defiant enough to look at him. Her vision filled with him, his dark eyes, his gloriously thick hair, the sharp angle of his jaw, the sensuous line of his mouth even when he was scowling. "I wanted to walk away from the whole thing. Laura, my stupid marriage, my cheating husband, everything. I just wanted to walk away, and I did."

"You wanted to walk away from me?"

"As you said, you were talking to Laura—for more than one minute, if you want to get technical about it." He was too handsome. Too big and strong and angry, and sexy. She lowered her gaze back to the knife lying on the table.

"The lady needed to talk. She missed Paul. She's still in mourning for him. I didn't think you'd mind, since you don't seem to be in mourning for him anymore." He hesitated, and when he resumed, he sounded troubled and tense. "Maybe I'm wrong. Maybe you're still in mourning for him."

"No."

"Then what?"

"Then *you.* You were obviously turned on by her—"

"You're crazy." But he sounded less angry. "She was like something from another planet, Sally."

"The rich, gorgeous planet."

"The affected, pretentious planet. She was—God, I can't believe I'm saying this, but she was too thin. I've recently discovered that I'm a breast and thigh man."

"Wonderful. I'll order you a chicken."

"You're the chicken. You're the one who ran away."

"I didn't run," she snapped, although her anger was fading along with his. "I walked. I didn't feel like sitting on the sidelines watching yet another man make a fool of himself over Laura."

"Oh, so letting her talk about Paul makes me a fool? Maybe I'm just a nice guy."

Sally snorted. The hula girl looked as if she was winking at her. "Did she tell you why Paul gave her this?"

"She said he'd wanted to give her something she could never get anywhere else. With all her money and connections, she could have bought pretty much anything she wanted. But she couldn't have bought anything as tacky and cheap as that knife. That was why Paul gave it to her."

"And she didn't mind giving it back?"

"Not once she heard how much it meant to you."

"In other words, she thinks I'm tacky and cheap."

"Well you are, aren't you?"

She glanced up sharply to discover Todd grinning. Pursing her lips, she reached for the knife. He clamped his hand over hers, warming her skin, warming all the chill out of her.

"You're not going to stab me, are you?" he asked.

"Not today. If I stab you, I can't get a ride back to Winfield with you."

"Admit it—you love my car."

"I hate your car."

"I love you, Sally."

Her mouth softened. So did her heart. Her eyes filled with tears, tears she'd never wanted Todd to see, tears she'd never expected to shed. He'd said he loved her, the only thing she needed to hear, and she wanted to bawl her head off.

"Do you mean that?" she asked.

"No. I'm lying. I think we've both discovered how much lying can enrich a relationship." He shook his head. "Laura is the end of a story, that's all. I'm a newspaperman. I had to see the story through to the end, and maybe make a little sense out of it. How on earth could you think that meant I was turned on by her?"

"Given her attributes, it's hard to imagine you *wouldn't* be turned on by her."

"Well, I wasn't. You're the one who turns me on, Sally. You." Even as he pinned her hand to the table, he moved his thumb gently against her wrist. "I don't know how this happened. I sure wasn't planning to fall in love with you."

"But you brought Band-Aids?"

It took him a minute to understand what she was saying. Then he smiled. "You make me laugh. You make me feel. And then—the thought that my talking to Laura could make you jealous—"

"I wasn't jealous. Just because she's everything I'm not—"

"Which is exactly why I'm here, with you."

A few tears escaped and slid down her cheeks. "I love you, too," she whispered.

His fingers tightened on her, letting her know he'd heard her. Then he released her wrist and handed her her napkin, which she used to wipe her tears. "Let's go."

"I've still got half a glass of lemonade."

He lifted the glass to his lips and drained it in three gulps. "There. It's finished."

He set down the glass, rose from his chair and pulled her out of hers. When he wrapped his arms around her, she very nearly started crying all over again, and laughing, and demanding that he tell her one more time that he loved her, just so she could be sure. But she *was* sure. His hug told her he loved her. The kiss he planted on her lips told her. The passion and tenderness in his gaze told her.

"Let's go home," he said.

She dropped the knife into her tote bag, took his hand and walked out of the café with him, into the blazing sun, thinking there was nothing in the world she'd rather do than go home with Todd.